A sense of huge unfairness at her situation threatened to bring tears to her eyes. She pushed the thought aside. Things were as they were and crying about them wouldn't change that.

She clenched her fists and took a step forward. 'Now you listen to me, Jock Mur—'

A shadow fell between them.

Mattie turned and saw a powerfully built man, who she judged to be all of six feet tall and with the breadth to match. His black hair had been tightly cut to frame his broad forehead and strong cheekbones. He had a beard, like almost every other man but, whereas the fashion was for untrimmed and bushy, his was scraped clean on his cheeks and throat and then followed the blunt lines of his jaw. His wide, authoritative stance had the quality of a coiled spring.

His eyes flicked over her face and then looked at Jock.

Jean Fullerton was born in the East End within the sound of the Bow Bells. She is a trained nurse and has three daughters. Her first novel, *No Cure for Love*, won the Harry Bowling Prize, and her second novel, *A Glimpse at Happiness*, was shortlisted for the RNA Romantic Novel of the Year award.

By Jean Fullerton

No Cure for Love
A Glimpse at Happiness
Perhaps Tomorrow

Perhaps Tomorrow

JEAN FULLERTON

An Orion paperback

First published in Great Britain in 2011
by Orion
This paperback edition published in 2011
by Orion Books Ltd,
Orion House, 5 Upper St Martin's Lane,
London WC2H 9EA

An Hachette UK company

1 3 5 7 9 10 8 6 4 2

A CIP catalogue record for this book
is available from the British Library.

ISBN 978-1-4091-2081-0

Typeset by Input Data Services Ltd, Bridgwater, Somerset

Printed and bound in the UK by
CPI Group (UK) Ltd, Croydon, CRO 4YY

The Orion Publishing Group's policy is to use papers
that are natural, renewable and recyclable products and
made from wood grown in sustainable forests. The logging
and manufacturing processes are expected to conform to
the environmental regulations of the country of origin.

www.orionbooks.co.uk

To the Romantic Novelists' Association on their 50th year and in particular to their excellent New Writers' Scheme, which set me off on this wonderful journey.

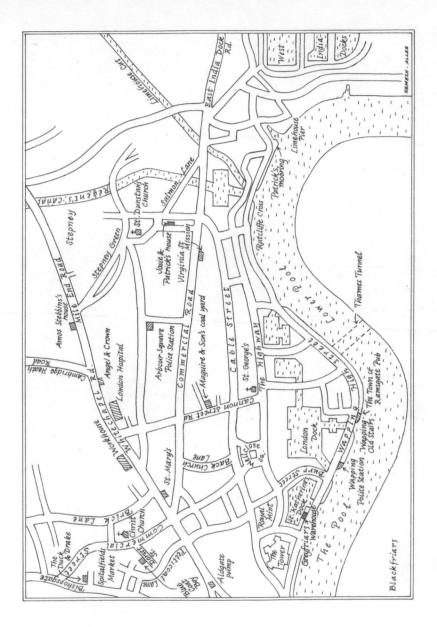

Chapter One

Mattie Maguire, owner of Maguire & Son's coal yard, woke to the light tap of the knocker-upper's cane on the window and Brian, her three-year-old son, chattering to his wooden soldiers in his cot at the foot of her bed. As her mind cleared of sleep, Mattie ran through the day's chores: see the deliveries out, order the fodder for the horses and visit Morris & Co, her wholesalers at the Limehouse Basin. Regardless of the coils of trepidation winding in her stomach, Mattie had no other choice but to negotiate the price of coal with steely-eyed Mr Morris. She would have to take her courage in both hands and go.

Brian stood up. 'Mammy!' he called, bouncing up and down on his straw mattress.

Mattie pushed all thoughts of coal and Mr Morris aside and raised herself onto her elbows. 'Good morning, young man. And seeing as how you're up with the lark I suppose I had better get myself going, too,' she said, smiling at her son as he stretched his arms out for her.

She swung her legs from under the covers, then lifted Brian up and sat him on the china pot taken from under the bed. Leaving him to his business, Mattie padded across the floorboards and collected water from outside the door.

Kate, her younger sister, always left the pitcher there before she went to work at Hoffman's bakery. Although they damped down the fire in the kitchen range at night, the water in the side boiler stayed hot enough for a warm wash in the morning. She poured half the water into the china basin on the stand to wash Brian before she dressed him.

'Fasten your buttons, sweetheart,' she told him, as she started her own wash.

Brian's bottom lips jutted out. 'Can't.'

Mattie went to help him as she always did, but then stopped short. Most three year-olds had at least one, if not two younger brothers or sisters competing for their mother's care, but Brian was her only child. She had to be careful not to turn him into a Mammy's Boy.

'Now, Brian, the delivery men will be here soon and I have business to see to before the market opens, so why don't you try for Mammy?'

Brian stood with his arms at his sides, staring up at her for a few moments, then grabbed the sides of his smock and started mangling the buttons thorough their corresponding holes.

'There's a good boy,' Mattie said, as she stripped off her nightdress and plunged her hands into the warm water. 'We have a delivery from the depot today, too,' she said, as she sponged her arms.

'Big cart?' Brian asked, looking very like his father as he concentrated on his task.

'Yes, the big cart,' she replied, drying herself off. 'And I'll need to keep a close eye on them. Last week they tried to charge me for best kitchen when they only delivered the standard grade. Have you finished?'

Brian dropped his hands by his sides again, this time to show off his efforts to dress himself.

Mattie smiled and beckoned him to her. 'There's a clever boy,' she said, kissing him on the cheek. 'But there's one in the wrong hole.' She adjusted his buttons and said, 'Now off you go. Your gran will have your breakfast ready for you downstairs. And don't run!' she called after him as he clattered down the stairs.

She watched him for a moment then wrapped her corset around her bodice and fastened the steel hooks and eyes. She then stepped into her petticoat, tied the front laces and shrugged on her dark blue day dress. Looking into the speckled mirror on the wall, Mattie made sure everything was in place, then, taking the brush from the dressing table, she slipped off the rag knot holding her long night plait and brushed her ebony locks into order. With an assured twist, she whirled them into a bun at the nape of her neck and secured it with pins that she kept in the pink-and-blue china bowl on the dressing table.

Dressed and ready, she went to the window and pulled back the curtains. Only the first traces of dawn were streaking the sky yet beyond the fence an army of men wearing flat caps and roughly hewn clothes were already trudging towards the river. Casual labourers had to be at the docks before the gates opened if they were to have any chance of catching the foreman's eye for a work ticket.

Mattie's thoughts turned to her appointment at Morris's. No matter which way she added up the bills and subtracted them from her earnings, it was clear that Maguire's Coal Yard was only just scraping by. If she wanted to ensure that her son would never have to wait in line for a mean-hearted foreman to pick him out, she had to persuade Mr Morris to give her the discount that other yards in the area enjoyed. If he wouldn't, she wondered how much longer she'd be able to stay in business.

Mattie pushed away the gnawing worry about the unpaid bills ruffling up the invoice spike in the office. Perhaps Mr Stebbins would see a way for her to turn her fortunes around.

Come on my girl, she thought, as she turned from the window. *Maguire's won't run itself.*

Queenie Maguire, Brian's granny, had already buckled her grandson into his chair and set a boiled egg before him by the time Mattie came into the kitchen.

Queenie barely reached Mattie's shoulder. Her face had a childlike quality that contrasted with her knotted, red knuckles, and in the early morning light her fine, almost white, hair showed a hint of the gold it used to be.

'I thought I would make a start on the smalls,' Queenie said, lifting her hands from the soapy water and letting the rivulets of suds meander down her wiry forearms. 'Get them out of the way before Brian gets up.'

From the moment Queenie had looked on her dead son, Brian, her mind had shot off on a wild journey. She'd been stupefied until the day of his funeral, after which she paced the house day and night searching for him. When she couldn't find him in her own home, Queenie would wander the streets until she was returned by either the City police, who'd find her in Cheapside, or by the Metropolitan who'd discover her under Bow Bridge. Queenie's wandering ceased when young Brian was born. She was right enough in the house, cooking and cleaning, and could be left safely to tend to the wee one, but in her mind her dead son was always in another room, on his way home, or still out working in the yard.

'Your sister came by, you know, the young one with blonde hair, but she went off,' Queenie told her. Mattie gave a weary smile as she cracked an egg into the frying pan for her own breakfast. She'd given up telling Queenie that Kate had lived with them for three years and went out early to her job. The confusion was just another symptom of her mother-in-law's jumbled brain. She tipped the frying pan up and the egg slid to one side. She plopped a slice of bread into the sizzling fat, and when it was brown on both sides she lifted it out with a fork and slid her egg on top.

The back door opened and Mattie's brother Patrick strolled in. 'Morning sis,' he said, grinning at her. 'Morning, Mrs M.'

Queenie smiled across at him by way of acknowledgement.

'Patrick?' Mattie replied, wondering why he was standing in her back door and not at the rudder of his barge, *The Smiling Girl*. 'Is Josie alright?' Although her sister-in-law's last pregnancy had been uneventful you couldn't be too careful.

'She was when I left her half-an-hour ago.'

Queenie dropped a wet towel into the tin pail beside her. 'Have you seen Brian, Patrick? He should be in the yard.'

Pain tightened around Patrick's eyes. 'No, Mrs M, I must have missed him.'

'Well, no matter.' Queenie gave him her boys-will-be-boys look. 'You'll catch him at the bar in the Town later, no doubt.' She turned back to the washboard.

'Can I get you a bite of breakfast?' Mattie asked.

Patrick rubbed his hands together. 'That would be grand.' He pulled out a chair and sat down at the table. 'And how's my favourite nephew?' he asked, ruffling Brian's hair.

'Me fine, Uncle Pat,' Brian replied, through a mouthful of bread soldiers.

'That's my boy,' Patrick tousled the child's hair again. 'Eat all your egg and you'll grow up to be as tall as your father, won't he, Mammy?' he said looking at Mattie.

Mattie nodded and cracked another egg in the pan. She poured them both a mug of tea then sat next to Brian with her own breakfast.

'I thought I'd drop by today as, well, you know true enough what this week is, Matt.'

Of course! What with worrying about seeing old man Morris in an hour, and having to get her books in order before Mr Stebbins came by, she'd forgotten that it was her wedding anniversary on Friday. Well, it would have been had her husband still been alive.

'That's good of you, Patrick,' she said, trying not to feel guilty that it hadn't been the foremost thing on her mind.

Patrick put down his knife and fork. 'I wish I could.'

'What?' Mattie asked, spooning sugar into her brother's mug.

'Catch Brian at the bar later,' he replied in a flat tone.

Patrick and Brian had been friends since they were bare-footed youngsters sitting on the kerb. They still would be if it weren't for Harry Tugman and his fellow thugs who rampaged through the town of Ramsgate just six weeks after Mattie and Brian were married. Brian had bled to death in Patrick's arms and even now, three years

4

later, whenever Patrick said his friend's name, pain and guilt still echoed in his voice.

He shook his head. 'I don't know. It seems like only yesterday me and Brian were strutting around in Moses Brothers buying our suits for the wedding. I still can't believe he's been gone almost three years.' He picked up his cutlery again. 'Forgive me, Mattie. I'm sorry. I know it's worse for you.'

It *had* been worse, but somewhere in the passing of time the pain had almost slipped away.

'Well, it's not as if I haven't had things to keep me occupied,' she said, sipping her tea. 'What with running Maguire's and raising Brian.' She glanced at her son licking the butter off his fingers. 'That's enough to keep me from fretting.'

Patrick squeezed her hand. 'You're so brave, Mattie, facing life alone.'

It was true. She was alone but, for the moment, content to be so. She was only twenty-eight, hardly an old woman, and she hoped Patrick didn't have the notion that she wouldn't marry again if the right man came by. But then she hadn't met anyone to take Brian's place so it wasn't worth arguing the point.

She swallowed the last of her tea. 'It's been grand of you to drop by but I have to go,' she said, squeezing her brother's hand. 'I have to see Mr Morris and then get back in time to log in the deliveries. After which I need to go over the accounts again before Mr Stebbins visits at the end of the week!'

Queenie turned from the sink. 'I don't know what my Brian will say when he hears you've let the Fatman look over the books.' She pulled a sour face. 'His eyes have a mean, tight-fisted look about them.'

'Oh, Queenie.' Mattie laughed. 'How can you say such a thing after he paid for the Sunday school's summer tea?'

Queenie tutted and, lifting one of Mattie's shifts from the tub, wrung it between her hands. 'I wouldn't trust Mr Fatman as far as I could throw him. And at his poundage that wouldn't be too far.'

Mattie stood up. 'You finish your breakfast, Pat, and tell Josie I'll pop around as usual on Tuesday,' she said, fetching her bonnet from the peg behind the door. 'And give your three a kiss from me.'

'Alright, Matt. I'll keep this fellow company for a bit.' He grinned at Brian, who grinned back.

'I'll be back in a while, Queenie, and we'll go to Watney Street to get a bit of something for tea,' Mattie said, setting her bonnet on squarely and tying the ribbon to one side.

'Perhaps we can find ourselves a nice bit of fish,' Queenie replied, throwing another piece of washing in the rinsing bucket. 'You know how Brian likes a bit of poached haddock.'

Pain flitted across Patrick's face again at the mention of his best friend and Mattie wondered if it wasn't time for her brother to let the grief of Brian's death slip away, too.

Mattie headed off towards the Highway, the main thoroughfare that ran parallel to the river. From before dawn until well into the night a constant stream of drays carried goods from the docks to the city, their iron-rimmed wheels churning the horse droppings and rotting vegetation into pungent slurry as they went.

Both sides of the road were lined with shops selling all kinds of wares from spades, rope and hard tack in Petersen & Sons, ship's chandlers, to African masks, strutting ostriches and roaring lions in Jamrach's Animal Emporium.

Mattie joined the throng of women with children clutching their skirts and baskets on their hips, making their way to the early markets. She squeezed past deep coils of rope and barrels of pitch outside shipwrights and only just avoided becoming tangled in clothes hanging from the awnings of the second-hand clothes merchant.

As she turned into Medland Street, she could see Morris's large front gate. Although her bonnet hadn't budged an inch during her fifteen minute walk, Mattie patted it in place, squared her shoulders and continued into the yard. The tarry smell of a thousand tonnes of coal tingled in her nose as she crunched her way over the grit on the path between the mountains of black heaped either side.

As she drew near to the yard office at the far end of the enclosure, she caught sight of Ginger Conner, Sam Wooten and Taffy Roberts, three of Morris's drivers, who were well known in the local pubs, mainly for being thrown out of them. They were dressed in baggy-kneed, coal-stained trousers and heavy canvas sleeveless jerkins, with half-opened jute sacks on their heads to protect their necks and shoulders from the razor-sharp coal they hauled all day. They had yet to start work but their faces were already black as minstrels.

She had hoped that by now the delivery men would be out on their rounds. As she approached, they turned and ran their eyes slowly over her. Resisting the urge to fiddle with her bonnet again, Mattie fixed her eyes on the office door and walked across the yard.

Ginger stood away from the wall he'd been lounging against and took the pipe from his mouth. 'You're a bit of an early bird ain't you, sweet'art?' he said, with a leer creeping across his face.

'And a very pretty one, too,' Taffy added, stepping closer so that he loomed over her and fixed his eyes on her breasts.

'I've come to see Mr Morris,' she told them, hoping none of them could hear the quiver in her voice or the pounding of her heart.

Sam Wooten placed a coal-blackened hand on his chest and glanced at his fellow drivers. 'Oh, Bejebus, and there I was thinking that the darling girly had come down because she'd been dreaming of me, lads,' he said, in an exaggerated Irish accent. Taffy and Ginger snorted. Sam lent forward, his breath floating across Mattie's cheek in the cold morning air. 'I'll tell you this, Mrs M, I've had one or two dreams about you meself.' He adjusted the front of his trousers.

Despite the queasy feeling in her stomach Mattie held Sam's gaze. 'Will you step aside, please?'

He blew a stream of smoke out of the corner of his mouth. 'You can squeeze by,' he winked. 'Give me something else to dream about.'

The door behind them opened and Mr Morris stepped out. The owner of the yard was a squat man with a cigar clenched in his teeth, a shiny bald head and a beard as thick as a hedge. He was dressed in a smart brown suit but, unfortunately, like his drivers and the rest of the yard it too was covered in a fine coating of dark dust.

He gave the men a sharp look and their leering expressions vanished. They stood up straight.

'There's today's rounds,' he said, thrusting several sheets of paper into their hands. 'Get a bloody shift on. I don't pay you to stand around yapping.'

The three men touched their foreheads and left.

Mr Morris snatched the cigar from his mouth. 'I hope they weren't annoying you, Mrs Maguire.'

'Not at all,' Mattie replied, knowing that any complaint would only result in her getting a late or wrong delivery.

'Come in,' Mr Morris stood back to let her pass. 'Take a seat.'

His office was a larger version of her own, with a desk at one end, shelves full of accounts books, empty sacks against the wall and, in the far corner, a set of weights and a large brass weighing-scale that was probably as tall she was.

She glanced down at the dirty cushion on the chair as she sat, knowing her gown would be ruined for the rest of the day. Her hand shook very slightly as she undid the drawstring bag on her wrist and took out Maguire's weekly order. She handed it to Mr Morris who'd returned to his leather chair on the other side of the desk.

'You didn't have to bring next week's order down so early,' he said, placing it in a brown folder.

'I thought I would bring it with me as I've come to talk to you about something else, Mr Morris.' Mattie drew a deep breath, 'I would like to ask you if I can have the same discount you give to the other yards you supply,' she said in a rush.

An irritated look replaced Mr Morris's jolly smile and he folded his arms across his barrel chest. 'I don't negotiate this early in the day.'

'I quite understand,' Mattie replied, trying to maintain a level tone. 'But I'm sure you'll see that it is impossible for me to meet you in the Admiral with the other coal merchants.'

'Mmm. I suppose it is.'

'And that's why I hoped, as Maguire's is such a long-standing customer, that you would make an exception and discuss the matter with me now.'

'Discount. Eh?'

Mattie nodded and gave him an encouraging smile.

The chair creaked as he shifted his position. 'It's not as easy as that ... there are things to be considered.'

'I always have my order in in good time and I settle my end-of-month account,' Mattie said as her pulse galloped on. 'You tell me, Mr Morris, when have you *ever* had to chase Maguire's for money?'

'I can't think of—'

'Never,' Mattie cut in as her need overrode her caution. 'Maguire's always pay promptly.'

Mr Morris nodded. 'I know but, as I say, there are other things to take into account. Complications, you might say.' The chair leg banged on the floor as he sat forward. 'Can I be frank with you, Mrs Maguire?'

Mattie nodded.

'It's you being a woman that's put the cat amongst the pigeons. Some of the other merchants are uneasy having a woman competing with them. To them it don't seem natural, somehow, to have a woman running a coal business.'

'I wouldn't have to if my husband were alive but, as I do, its only fair that I be given the same discount as my competitors.'

Mr Morris's jovial expression returned. 'Mrs Maguire, I *would* like to but I can't afford to upset my other customers.' He shrugged and gave her a helpless look. 'You understand, I'm sure. Now, if you'd excuse me, I am a busy man.' He looked down at the papers on his desk.

The column of figures from last week's balance sheet flashed into Mattie's mind. She could not afford for him to say no to giving her a discount.

'Mr Morris.' He looked up. 'If the Chamber of Commerce were to hear that one merchant was denied the same trading terms as their competitors, they ... they might consider it to be unfair practice.'

Mr Morris's cheeks mottled purple above his beard and Mattie wondered if she'd gone too far. She had come to negotiate with, not antagonise, her supplier, but what choice had she left? And it *was* only fair.

'I do understand your position, Mr Morris, but you must understand mine. I have a coal yard employing four men and I support myself, my mother-in-law and, most importantly, my son.'

Mr Morris chewed the inside of his mouth and studied her under his heavy eyebrows. The sound of blood rushing through her ears threatened to deafen her as she waited for him to reply.

'Your husband was a good man, Mrs Maguire, and a sad loss.' Mr Morris leant across his desk. 'I'll give you sixpence in the pound discount on all your bills *if* Maguire's continues to pay promptly and if,' he tapped the side of his nose, 'we keep the matter hush.'

A bubble of laughter rose up in Mattie. *Sixpence in the pound!* Just by a quick reckoning she knew that would give her at least an extra five shillings a week. The weight that she'd been carrying around for weeks suddenly lifted from her shoulders.

'Thank you. Thank you so very much, Mr Morris,' she said, standing up and offering him her hand.

Mr Morris regarded her for a few moments, then rose and took her hand. 'Well then,' he growled, with just a hint of a twinkle in his eyes. He walked her to the door and opened it for her. 'But Mrs Maguire. This arrangement is *strictly* between us. Do you understand? *Strictly!*'

'Thank you, Mr Morris, I do,' Mattie replied, resisting the urge to hug him.

Morris went back into his office and Mattie retraced her steps across the empty yard. The Highway would be packed by now so she turned into Butcher's Row to take a short cut home. In front of St James's Church she noticed that children had chalked out the squares of a hopscotch grid. She looked up and down the street and, seeing it deserted, grabbed her skirts in one hand and her bonnet in the other to hop and skip to the end of the game. Laughing, she smoothed her skirts back into place. Of course it was not the sort of behaviour a respectable widow should indulge in, but: *sixpence in the pound*!

Chapter Two

Nathaniel Tate clambered down from the *Colchester* 'Thunder' and put his hands in the small of his back. After a thirty-mile journey over unmade roads there wasn't a part of his six-foot frame that didn't ache. Outside the Golden Lion Inn at the east end of Romford High Street, two ostlers coaxed and cajoled the sweating horses out from between the shafts while another two brought a fresh team from the stables.

Through the low, dimpled windows of the coaching inn, local farmers in their smocks and battered hats sat eating their midday meal and enjoying a tankard or two. As he couldn't afford the first and thought it too early in the day for the second, Nathaniel turned and walked into Romford's wide, cobbled market square. The old shops were still as he remembered but every now and then a brash new stone building thrust up between them like a gold tooth amongst old molars.

As today was Wednesday, farmers from as far away as Orset and Brentwood had set up stall on either side of the central thoroughfare and leant on the temporary wooden pens which held the cattle offered for sale. A couple of dairy maids selling fresh milk from a brown-and-white cow looked Nathaniel's way. They nudged each other and glanced at him shyly as he passed by.

He stopped in front of St Edward's church, then ducked his head to pass under the porch and walked down the line of gravestones. Just before he reached the end he spotted the upright stone he was searching for. Removing his hat, he stared down at the finely chiselled lettering on the granite tombstone.

MARJORIE TATE

14th September 1817 to 9th January 1843

Beloved daughter and devoted mother
Asleep with her daughters
Lillian aged five and Rosina aged three
Until the final trumpet call

All he'd ever loved summed up in a few words on a cold stone.

He'd mourned them for nigh on two years but now, standing by the neat plot with the sun warming his face, he felt the wound afresh.

He raised his head and stared at the church's oak doors, remembering how he had strolled between them with Marjorie on his arm and both their families laughing behind them. Nathaniel's mind moved to the small cottage, not half a mile from where he stood, and how he'd scooped her into his arms and carried her over the threshold. He remembered how shy she had been on their wedding night and how careful he'd been not to hurt her. Then the image changed into Marjorie's heart-shaped face the last time he'd seen it: across the courtroom, drained of colour and screaming his name as her father dragged her from the public gallery. Nathaniel had gripped the iron edge of the dock until his knuckles cracked, resisting the rough hands that pulled him back to the filth and cloying stench of a prison cell.

The gravel on the path behind him crunched under a heavy foot. 'May I be of assistance, sir?'

Nathaniel turned. Behind him, curled up like a dry leaf in autumn and with a battered hat shading his eyes stood the sexton, Toby Atrill.

The aged attendant had been sexton for as long as most could remember. He would rest on his shovel as Nathaniel and his fellow pupils from St Edward's school marched past every Wednesday for the midweek service. Nathaniel had been one of the few scholarship boys but his father had still had to scrimp and save to equip him with his books and pencils for what he called Nathaniel's 'chance of betterment'. He had been right, too. He'd walked out of the school gates at fourteen and straight into the town's largest corn suppliers, Fairhead & Co, as a clerk, something almost unheard of for a farm-worker's son.

Nathaniel looked back at the headstone.

Toby's opaque eyes blinked in the bright spring sunlight. 'I see this memorial has caught your attention. Did 'e know the family?'

'Once,' he replied.

Toby shook his head. 'The saw bones said poor Miss Marjorie and her daughters died of the influenza but there be many around these parts that do say she died of shame.'

'Do they?'

The old graveyard attendant sized up Nathaniel's ill-fitting jacket. His second-hand clothes didn't sit at all well and strained the stitching across the shoulders to their limits.

Toby jabbed his pipe towards the stone. 'Yes, sir, they do. Miss Marjorie married where her father, God rest him, wouldn't have wanted her to, but she would have the lad and her father gave in.' Toby's face creased into a dozen crisscross lines. 'You know how fathers are with their girls.'

A lump formed itself in Nathaniel's throat.

'Anyhows, they were married in this very church. Happy they were, too, until greed reared its ugly head.'

'How so?'

The old man drew on the pipe again. 'Now, the particulars escape me just at the moment but the lad she married got mixed up in some money business. They caught him though. The case went right up to the county judge at Chelmsford. The lad argued it was the senior clerk, one Amos Stebbins, who took the money but no one who knew Amos believed it. Not with him being a gospel churchgoer. When they found the evidence against Miss Marjorie's young husband – black-and-white evidence at that – it were an open and shut case and he got himself a one way ticket to Botany Bay.' Toby tilted his head and looked him over again. 'Are you from the Old Church end of town, then?'

'A long while back.'

Old Toby studied his face. 'You do have a familiar look about you.'

'Do I?' Nathaniel replied, looking down steadily at the old man.

The sexton shrugged. 'Ah, well, I must be mistaken. My eyes aren't as good as they used to be,' he raised the shovel. 'I must get on. There was a young 'un fished out of the Rom three days ago. He's set to be buried before the day's end.' He started to pick his way towards the back of the graveyard.

'This Amos Stebbins,' Nathaniel called after him. The sexton turned. 'What happened to him?'

'He moved to London.'

'Do you happen to know where?'

Toby lifted his hat and scratched his head. 'Now let me think ... Let me ...' His rheumy old eyes lit up. 'Whitechapel! That's where 'e went. Whitechapel. Just this side of the city.'

Nathaniel fished in his pocket and gave the old man tuppence. 'I'm obliged to you. I shouldn't keep you from your task any longer.' He turned up his collar then retraced his steps back to the lintel gate.

'Hey there, fellow,' Toby's voice called after him. 'Wait a moment! Aren't you—'

Nathaniel didn't respond. He just pulled down the front of his hat and pressed himself into the thick of the market day crowd.

Nathaniel waited until the night coach to Chelmsford disappeared around the corner and then stood and dusted the grass from his trousers. Pulling his hat low over his face he slipped out from the shadows and glanced down the dusty lane.

He crossed the road, slipped behind the hedgerow then, keeping close to the bush, he made his way towards the small cottage at the far end of the field. Stepping quietly back into the lane, he went to a side door half hidden by a crab-apple tree.

He knocked lightly and heard the inside bolt slide back.

Nathaniel's vision clouded for a second as his sister, Emma, opened the door. She was just shy of forty now and had thickened around the middle. Grey streaks cut through her dark-chestnut hair but the kindness in her hazel eyes remained unchanged.

'I'm sorry we don't give at the door,' she said, starting to close it.

'Emmy!' he whispered.

The colour drained from her face. 'Nathaniel?'

He glanced up and down the empty lane again then stepped inside, closing the door behind him. 'Is Jacob here?'

She shook her head. 'Master's best cow's in calf and he's playing midwife 'til it's born. But ...' She looked him over again and tears welled up in her eyes.

They stared at each other for a moment then she threw herself in to his arms.

'Oh. Nat, thank God you're alive!' she sobbed.

Nathaniel rested his chin on the top of her head and closed his eyes.

He couldn't remember his mother; she'd died in childbirth when he was only three. Emma, seven years his senior and the eldest girl in the family, had brought him up. It was she who had sewn his shirts, kissed him better when he grazed his knees and tucked him in each night.

'Praise the Lord. I feared I'd never see you again in this life.' She dabbed the corner of her eyes with her apron. 'When were you pardoned? I knew them lawyer types would see senses and—'

'I wasn't.'

Emma clamped her hands over her mouth and her eyes widened with fear.

Nathaniel went to the small window and glanced out again

'I daren't stay more than a moment or two but I couldn't leave for London without seeing you.'

She grabbed his arm and dragged him towards the fireside chair. 'You'll stay until I've fed you, that's for sure. Before you goes up there to London or any other such fancy place.'

'I can't. It's not safe.'

Emma pushed him into the chair. 'Well, that ain't no mind to me, how you're here; you're still my sweet old Nat.'

Nathaniel smiled. He doubted that, after four years as a convict in Botany Bay, there was any of the sweet old Nat left.

'Now you rest your bones while I fetch you some vittels.'

He was about to argue, but suddenly his limbs seemed to lose their strength and he slumped into the wheel-back chair by the warm chimney breast.

A satisfied smile lit Emma's rounded face. 'That's better,' she said, getting a bowl from the wood dresser.

Nathaniel let the peace of his sister's cottage soothe his soul. The main room was no more than three spread arms' length in both directions and with a beaten-earth floor. The open hearth was similar to the one he'd played beside as a child. On one side sat a kettle with a wisp of steam escaping from its spout and, on the other, flames licked around a blackened belly-pot. The smell of fresh bread and something meaty made his stomach rumble.

'Look at you!' Emma poured a ladle of stew into the bowl. 'I'll tell you straight, I hardly recognise you, what with that beard. And your hair! I remember how it used to curl around your ears. What in the Lord's name happened to it?'

Nathaniel brushed his hand over his closely cropped head. 'I stopped shaving it about a month ago when I got to Hamburg. That's why I look like a yard brush.'

'But why did 'e shave your head?' she asked, handing him the bowl and a chunk of bread.

'To keep the lice from living in it.'

Emma gave him a bleak look. 'Do it be as terrible as them newspapers say?'

Nathaniel studied her round face. How could he explain to Emma, who would never have travelled more than ten miles from her place of birth, what Botany Bay was truly like?

'I can't describe it,' he replied, pressing his lips together firmly.

She ran her work-worn hand down the side of his face. 'My poor

Nat,' she said in her old loving tone. 'I suppose you skipped off when you got the parson's letter.'

'I did.'

She handed him a spoon. 'I didn't want you to learn about Marjorie and the girls like that but there was no other way. That's why I asked him to pen it for me.'

'I understand.' Nathaniel swallowed the lump in his throat as the image of Marjorie and the children's headstone flashed into his mind. 'What exactly happened?'

Emma drew up the stool and sat down. 'Marjorie managed to support herself and the girls for a year but then the rents went up. So they moved to one of the East House cottages, them along by Mowbray's Farm.'

Cottages! Cowsheds more like. His lovely wife and precious daughters forced to live in one of those ramshackle hovels!

'Why in God's name didn't her father offer her a home?'

'He did, but on the condition that Marjorie stopped calling herself Mrs Tate,' Emma's face softened. 'You know yourself what she would have said to that. He did pay for the headstone.'

Well, that explains the omission of 'much loved wife.'

'I heard he paid over eight pounds for the stone,' Emma continued. 'Eight pounds! More than the likes of us sees in a year but, as folks said at the time, it would take more than eight pounds to ease his guilt at letting his only daughter and grandchildren perish for 'is pride.'

Nathaniel used the bread to mop up the last of his stew and set his bowl down. 'How did they die?' Emma rested her hand on his arm. 'There 'ad been a wet autumn that year and the influenza started in the bottom end of the town. A body would feel chilly in the morning then burn with the fever by nightfall. There wasn't a day that passed without a man carrying a small coffin to the churchyard. Rosy caught it first, on the first Monday of the New Year, then Lilly came down with it four days later. I went up to help Marjorie. She was ill herself by then, coughing until she was red in the face and hot to the touch but she wouldn't rest. We nursed the children day and night. For two weeks we tried to get barley water between their lips and sponged their little bodies to keep them from burning. The doctor gave us some syrup to ease their breathing but it were no good. Rosy died on the twenty-fourth and Lilly left us two days later. We buried them together the following Monday. After that Marjorie took to her bed and never left it again.'

Nathaniel let out a roar of pain and buried his face in his hands. 'Oh, Marjorie, my darling. How can you be gone?' he sobbed.

'My poor, poor Nat,' Emma said, enveloping him in her strong arms. Nathaniel buried his head in the soft folds of her lap and cried until his ribs ached. He untangled himself from her embrace and looked up.

'And my girls. My darling girls. Do you remember Rosina's dimples as she smiled and how she'd called her sister Lele because she couldn't say her name?' Emma nodded. 'And the way Lillian used to stick her tongue out when she was concentrating and how proud she was when she finally managed to write her name without getting her 'a's facing the wrong way.' A bitter smile spread across his face. 'I remember the day she was born as if it were yesterday. It was midsummer and I sat up all night in the garden, gnawing my nails to the quick with worrying if Marjorie and the baby would survive. Then just before dawn I heard the cry. Do you know, Emmy, even now I can still smell the morning grass as I made my way across the garden back to the house. And when I held Lillian for the first time, all red and wrinkled, I thought I would die from the sheer joy of it.' The hollow ache that had started in the churchyard welled up again. 'And now that small baby I held on that summer morning is lying in a cold grave. And I should be alongside them.'

Emma stroked his hair. 'Hush, lad. It ain't your time yet,' she answered.

'And it shouldn't have been theirs,' he whispered. 'How can I live without them, Emma? How?' he wiped his face with the heel of his hand. 'I blame myself.'

'It weren't your fault. It were that daft judge who couldn't see the truth under his nose. But even if you'd been here, Nat, there was nothing you could have done to stop the influenza sweeping through.'

'Maybe not, but I could have done something to save them. They were my responsibility and I should have been with them.' An unbending expression hardened his face. 'I should have realised the sort of man Amos Stebbins, my trusted friend and my children's godfather, truly was. I blame myself but I also blame *him*.' He stood up. 'I have to go, Emma. I've things to do.'

Her mouth pulled tightly together. 'Is that why you're off to London? To get Amos for what he did to 'e?'

Nathaniel didn't answer. Emma grabbed his arm 'You're all in, Nat. Why don't you stay here the night? We're right off the beaten track and no one comes near or by. You'll be safe enough, and tomorrow ...' She looked at him, willing him to agree.

'Old Toby saw me in the graveyard.'

'Did he know you?'

'I'm not sure. Maybe. But if he told the police then this is the first place they'll look. I can't have you or Jacob arrested for harbouring a felon.'

He opened the door a crack and peered out. It was almost dark, and five miles to the White Horse on the Romford Road, but if he stretched his legs he could be there before ten. With a bit of luck he'd be able to bribe the driver of the night coach to let him on board and he'd be in London before dawn.

He gripped his sister's upper arms. 'I love you, Emmy, and, God willing, I'll see you again.' He hugged her to him and kissed her on the forehead before gently letting her go. 'But Amos Stebbins destroyed everything I held dear and I'll not rest until I've done the same to him.'

Chapter Three

Amos Stebbins stepped through the door of his warehouse on St Katherine's dock and took a long, deep breath. A smell reminiscent of rotten eggs told him that the tide was out. He struck a match on the wall to light his cigar then turned in the direction of river. It was a fine day so he decided to take a stroll by the Tower on his way to his solicitor in Aldgate.

The tide was indeed out and the banks of the Thames were alive with scavengers gleaning what they could from the malodorous silt before the water of the Thames flowed back again. The hollow-eyed children and scrawny women who foraged for metal and bone were barely kept alive by the work but at least it stopped them applying to the parish for relief. When the superintendent of the workhouse gave his annual report to St George's vestry a few months ago, a number of Amos's fellow church elders had almost been persuaded to slacken the rules for admittance. Even Mr Garrett, the vicar, had wavered. That was until Amos drew them back to St Paul's second epistle to the Thessalonians – *if any would not work, neither should he eat* – and that put an end to such philanthropic thoughts.

After a brisk walk in the summer sun Amos stopped outside the door of 49 Goulston Street, just off Whitechapel High Street and a hundred yards from the public baths and washhouse.

You could be forgiven for passing the front door of Glasson, Glasson & Webb, Solicitors at Law without giving it a second glance. The unobtrusive brass plate beside the front door was the only indication that behind the faded paint and upswept steps a successful law firm operated. The door opened before Amos could grasp the curved brass handle.

'Mr Stebbins,' greeted David Kimber, the office boy as he ushered Amos in. 'What a pleasure to see you.'

In keeping with his lowly status in the firm, David was dressed in an ill-fitting suit and a frayed, overwashed shirt. He was no more than thirteen and struck with the unfortunate combination of an unbroken voice and a face covered with angry pustules at various stages of gestation.

'Thank you. How are you settling in?'

'Very well, sir,' David replied, as he took Amos's coat and hat.

'I hope you are diligent about your work,' Amos said, puffing a stream of cigar smoke into the boy's face.

The boy coughed. 'I am, sir, and I hope to be a credit to you for recommending me.'

David's mother was a member of St George's congregation. Amos always made it clear to the ragged element of the fellowship that he would not give their petty troubles any attention but, as Mrs Kimber had curtsied so prettily, he had made an exception. She was known to be respectable so there was no danger to his reputation in showing her favour.

'Make sure you are.' He fixed the lad with a hard stare. 'I haven't seen you at church these past weeks.'

'No, Mr Stebbins,' the young clerk said, looking suitably shame-faced.

Amos's thick brows pulled together. 'The man who kneels in gratitude before the Lord will prosper,' he said, in the tone he used to address the parish council.

'I'll make s ... sure I'm there on Sunday, Mr Stebbins,' David said, touching his forehead deferentially.

Amos favoured him with a benevolent gaze. 'Very well. Now, young man, take me to Mr Glasson.'

David led him through to the office of Ebenezer Glasson, the first Glasson on the firm's brass plate. He opened the half-glazed door and Amos marched in. The office was no more than twelve feet by twelve and set at the back of the house. It was dominated by a dark oak desk that seemed to be as old as its owner. There was an inkwell to one side, next to a rhino horn pen holder that sprouted a dozen or so quills. Bookcases lined three walls and were filled with law books of all sizes and, by the look of their faded leather covers, dating back several decades. The sunlight from the large window cut across the space, capturing particles of dust in its beams.

Ebenezer Glasson pushed his spectacles up his nose and rose to his feet. 'Mr Stebbins.' He extended his hand.

Amos stepped forward, accidentally crushing a taper of sealing wax under his boot. He took the solicitor's bony hand. 'Sir.'

'Take a seat,' Glasson indicated the visitor's chair. 'How is business? Flourishing I hope.'

'Middling,' Amos replied, knocking the wax from his shoe onto the carpet. 'I'd be happier if the warehouse was a little fuller but the *Maisy Rose* docked with a full cargo of rubber last week and I sold that for a good profit.'

'So you do still prosper.'

A sombre expression settled on Amos' face. 'It pleases the Lord to show me favour.' His eyes narrowed. 'Have you got the deeds?'

'I have them here,' Glasson said, shuffling through the papers in front of him. He drew a sheet out from under several others and held it aloft. 'Here we are. The freehold to Kratz's pickled-herring factory signed and sealed.' He handed it across to Amos. 'And if I can just get our map,' the old man said, stretching up to retrieve a scroll from a high shelf behind him, 'we can see where we are.' He plopped the rolled-up sheet of paper on a small side table, sending up a puff of dust.

Amos unfurled it across the desk and a deep sense of satisfaction spread through him as he cast his eyes over the chart showing the area from the City boundary to the river Lea three miles away. The cartographer had done an excellent job, drawing the sweep of the Thames at the bottom and the Commercial and Mile End Roads running parallel above. Amos studied the line of blocked-out properties running from Wapping Basin across the map to Bow Bridge. A smile curled across his lips.

Mr Glasson resumed his seat and peered at the map. 'Now let me see ...' he picked up a pen and jabbed it in the ink. 'With Kratz's in your possession,' he said, scratching ink over the square that represented the pickle yard, 'you are almost ready to set up the Wapping to Stratford Railway Company. Once you have the deeds to Maguire's you will own every plot of land over which the railway will travel.' A rare smile creased his face. 'Except, of course, the two plots of land in Bow you were kind enough to put my way. But are you sure you can acquire the coal yard for the price you want?'

'Of course. I've been hearing whispers for months now that it's struggling. Frankly, I don't know how the Maguire woman has kept it going for this long – but she won't be able to for much longer.' He flicked a speck of dust from his sleeve. 'I plan to make her an offer soon, but I thought perhaps I'd call on Mr Tucker and his associates first. Nothing too dramatic,' he continued as alarm flashed across his solicitor's face. 'Just enough to drive the price down and encourage Mrs Maguire to sell sooner rather than later.'

Mr Glasson chewed the end of his quill. 'I hope you're right,

Stebbins, because if she gets wind that she owns the last property needed to build the railway she'll demand at least ten times the market price.'

Ten times! Twenty-fold more like, thought Amos. Kratz's had taken him deep into his credit at the City & County. If he were forced to pay more than a hundred and fifty for Maguire's he'd be bankrupt.

He'd sailed close to the wind before, especially at Fairhead's, the feed merchants where he had been senior clerk. The opportunity to his pockets with their quarterly taking had been too much to resist. But then he was young and impetuous and hadn't laid his plans properly. He'd learnt his lesson. Thankfully, his godly reputation had kept the local dullard of a constable from investigating, but Amos knew that he had to act fast once the county court officer was sent from the Chelmsford Assizes. Luckily, Amos had befriended Nathaniel Tate, the junior clerk, and had surreptitiously buried a couple of the money sacks in Tate's back garden. He put the authorities on to it to head them off his tail and it worked. Providentially. They believed that they had their man, as did the judge and jury.

But Amos was older and wiser now and nothing, certainly not a ha'penny coal yard like Maguire's, was going to stand between him and a large fortune.

He stubbed out his cigar in Glasson's crystal ashtray and stood up. 'Thank you for your time.'

The solicitor rose. 'Would you care to join me for lunch, Mr Stebbins?'

Amos shook his head. 'Perhaps another time. I'm dining at the Three Tons with a few of the Middlesex Deserving-Poor Committee.' His lips curled. 'They probably want a donation although I take the view that, since it's the Almighty who has ordered the estate of the poor, I am reluctant to oppose His will in the matter; but there is no harm in sharing a convivial meal with them.' He took out another cigar and bit off the end. 'And don't worry. I'll have the deeds to Maguire's sitting alongside the others within the month.'

Amos ground the cigar butt under his heel and burped loudly as the beef and onion pie settled. Tucking his cane under his arm he walked into Tucker's slaughterhouse at the back of St Mary's Church. Crammed into the pens in the cobbled yard stood a dozen or so muddy cows. Through the open door of the barn, the slaughter men could be seen poking and prodding a handful of unhappy beasts into position over the drainage channel. In the other storage shed pig's carcasses, some still twitching, hung upside down on hooks as the blood drained and slowly meandered toward the central grill. The metallic smell of fresh blood wafted over Amos as he picked his way between the piles of manure and rivulets of urine towards the office door.

Inside he found Ernie Tucker, a thick-set man who always seemed to be on the point of bursting out of his clothes, sitting behind his desk. Dicky Dutton, his foreman, stood behind him. They looked up as Amos entered.

'Mr Stebbins,' Tucker said, standing up and wiping his sweaty bald pate with a handkerchief. 'What brings you down to our neck of the woods? I 'ope you ain't asking for a donation towards the Fallen Women Society or some such, because we already gave.'

Dicky, whose angelic-looking white blond hair, freckled nose and blue eyes were quite at odds with his blood-splattered forearms, winked. 'Yer, every night to the dollies in Paddy's Goose.'

They laughed heartily.

Amos mustered a smile. 'No, I'm not here on church business but my own.'

Dicky flicked the chair on the other side of the desk with a bloody rag. 'Why don't you take the weight off your plates of meat?'

'I'll stand if it's all the same,' Amos replied, noting the damp patch on the seat. He pulled his leather cigar holder from his inside pocket. 'Smoke?'

'Ta, very much,' Tucker said, tucking it behind his ear. 'So, Mr Stebbins, what is it we can do for you?'

Amos struck a match and drew on his cigar. 'I was very pleased with the service you did me in regards to the pickle factory and wondered if you and your associates might be amenable to assisting me again.'

Dicky clenched the cigar in the side of his mouth and grinned. 'Who?'

Amos blew a series of rings upwards towards the dusty rafters. 'Maguire & Son's, the coal yard on Cannon Street Road.'

'That's run by a woman, ain't it?' Tucker said.

'Yes, Mattie Maguire. She's a widow, so there's no man to worry about. I want her business nobbled.'

'I knows her,' Dicky said, with a mischievous glint in his eye. 'She's a nice bit of how's-yer-father and no mistake.' He grabbed his crotch and the long blade hanging from his belt flashed. 'I shall have a bit of fun with her, I can tell you.'

Amos' eyes narrowed as he looked at the man behind the desk. 'I can't afford to raise suspicions. Do you understand? I don't think either of us wants the police poking their noses into our businesses now, do we?'

Tucker cuffed Dicky's head with the back of his hand. 'Don't you take no notice of him, Mr Stebbins. We'll be in and out without her noticing a thing, won't we?'

Dicky's jovial countenance fell. 'So you don't want me to rough her up a bit?' he asked in a disappointed tone.

'Not yet,' Amos replied. 'But if she doesn't get the hint . . .'

Dicky brightened instantly.

'Well, I must press on,' Amos said, stubbing out his cigar in the overflowing hoof ashtray on the desk. 'If I hurry I'll be in time for evening prayers in the Lady chapel.'

Tucker rose to his feet and offered a chubby, black-nailed hand. 'Always a pleasure to do business with you, Mr Stebbins. And don't worry, we can keep mum.'

Mattie yawned as she opened the back gate and walked into the coal yard from the house. Three of the four wagons were already loaded, with the drivers at various stages of harnessing the horses. The fourth wagon driven by Freddie Ellis, her deceased husband's cousin, still sat by the fence.

The horses stood patiently as their harnesses were secured, their breath billowing out from their nostrils in the early morning chill. Every now and then the crack of a large hoof on the yard cobbles would echo around. Flossy, Brian's old horse, nudged at the canvas nosebags with her muzzle as they stood ready to be secured over her whiskery lips.

Eli Watson, their longest serving delivery man, turned from his tasks as Mattie approached.

'Morning, Mrs Maguire,' he said, shrugging on his leather jerkin and buckling it securely above his paunch.

Mattie smiled at him. 'Morning yourself, Eli.'

He nodded at the fence. 'It looks as if kids have been pinching coal again,' he said, indicating the scattered pieces at the bottom of the coal heap.

'Perhaps I should get myself another yard dog,' Mattie replied, wondering where she'd get the money to feed another mouth if she did.

The two other deliverymen, Billy Ball and Pete Drummer, touched their caps to her.

'We'll be out in less than a half turn of the clock,' Billy told her as he backed their fourteen-hand bay mare, Poppy, between the shafts of number three wagon.

Mattie nodded towards number two wagon. 'Anyone know where Freddie is?'

Before they could answer the yard gates squeaked open and Freddie appeared.

He was the son of Queenie's eldest sister who'd died some years back and he'd been apprentice to a furniture maker in Hackney until he fell out with the man. After that, Freddie tried his hand in the wine trade but was sacked after being found unconscious and smelling heavily of the spirit he was supposed to be stock-taking. Queenie had a soft spot for him and at her request Brian had given him a job just after Mattie and Brian married.

Freddie spotted Mattie and a broad smile spread crossed his face.

'Sorry, Mrs M, I didn't hear the knocker-up,' he said, saluting his fellow delivery men with a tap of his cap.

'Again,' Mattie replied.

'Once me head hits the pillow I'm dead to the world.' He winked at her. 'How's that fine boy of yours today? I said to Pete only yesterday, "I swear he has the look of his father about him more each day." Didn't I, Pete?'

Mattie laughed. 'Munching bread soldiers when I left him an hour ago.'

Freddie sidled over to Mumble, the number two cart horse, who blew through her nose and shook her head at him. He collected her harness from the peg and threw the broad leather girth over the mare's back, untied her halter and led her into the centre of the yard.

'Don't you worry yourself none. I'll have this rig out in half a mo,' he said, casting his gaze around to include the other three men in the conversation.

Mattie bit her lower lip. It was the fourth time he'd been late in two weeks and she really ought to say something, but he was popular with the housewives – a little too popular for some of the husbands' liking, maybe. He pulled in custom and right now she needed that. Besides, he was family, and he always managed to put a smile on Queenie's face.

Mattie went over and stroked Mumble's soft muzzle. 'Can you get back for the hay delivery?'

'For you, anything,' he said, as he clipped Mumble's nose bag on.

'And pop in on Queenie before you leave. It will cheer her up,' Mattie said.

A boyish grin spread across Freddie's face. 'Consider it done, sweetheart.'

Sweetheart! Mattie gave him a questioning look. She tried to run a friendly yard but not even Eli called her anything but Mrs M.

'Right, Eli, open those gates,' shouted Pete, putting his foot on the running board of his wagon. 'And I'll get—'

But he was stopped by a loud, nerve-jarring grinding, then the sound of splitting timber as the cart lurched sideways. The front wheel sprang from the axle and rolled across the yard. The sacks loaded on the back tumbled off, sending chunks of coal bouncing across the yard. Samson, the horse between the shafts, squealed and kicked out wildly as the weight of the cart pulled him down.

Mattie sprang forward and caught the flaying reigns. Her nails dug into her palms but she held on and tried to steady the young horse.

'Get him out!' she screamed as the cart toppled towards her.

Billy and Eli dodged between the flaying hooves and tore frantically at the harness to set the terrified horse free, Billy bracing himself against the horse's flanks to try to keep him upright. Samson reared again and lifted Mattie off her feet.

'Help!' she screamed.

'Lend a hand, man,' Eli bellowed across the yard at Freddie.

After a moment's hesitation Freddie started forward then stumbled on the scattered coal.

'For the love of Blazes,' Eli spat out, as he let go of the harness and dashed around to catch the reigns. 'I've got the boy, Mrs M,' he said, winding them around his hands. 'You move away before you're hurt.'

Mattie let go and stepped back just as Billy released the girth buckle. Samson reared up dragging the traces through Eli's hands. He kicked out and one iron-clad hoof smashed into the old man's forehead. Eli plummeted to the floor. Samson jumped and kicked a couple of more times before trotting across the yard to his stable. Mattie dashed over to where Eli lay lifeless on the ground with Billy and Freddie on her heels.

She knelt beside Eli and untied his necktie to staunch the blood pouring from the gash in his forehead.

'Is he dead?' Freddie asked as he bent over her.

Eli groaned and his eyes flickered open for a second, then closed again.

'Praise be to the blessed Virgin,' Mattie whispered crossing herself three times. She looked up at Freddie. 'Quick. Run and fetch the doctor from Chapman Street.'

Chapter Four

Josie Nolan wrapped the tea cloth around her hand and pulled down the front oven door. She reached in, slid out the baking tray and put it on the table. The two children on the other side leant forward, their eyes fixed on the dozen fragrant tarts so hot that the jam was still bubbling. Mickey's hand shot out to take one but his sister Annie caught it before he could. Annie and Mickey were her husband Patrick's children by his first wife, but as neither child could remember their real mother she was their mother in all the ways it counted.

'Not yet, Mickey, or you'll burn your fingers, won't he, Mam?' Annie said, looking up at Josie.

'That he will. Your Aunt Mattie will soon be here so, Mickey, go and see if Gran needs a hand bringing in the washing. Annie, be a love and pop up and fetch your brother,' Josie said, thinking that her three-year-old son, Rob, should be waking from his afternoon nap.

Both children dashed out of the kitchen on their errands, and just as Josie popped the last tart on the plate, she heard a knock at the front door. She took off her apron, hung it on the kitchen door and hurried down the hall to answer it.

'Mattie!'

There wasn't a time when she didn't know Mattie. They had sat together as tots mothering their rag dolls, and though Josie was married to Mattie's brother, in truth they were more sisters than sisters-in-law. Josie remembered Mattie's wedding day, her eyes sparkling with love and happiness as she practically danced down the aisle. There couldn't have been a happier bride in the kingdom than Mattie Nolan on that fine June morning.

Mattie was holding Brian and shifted him on her hip. 'I swear this child puts on a pound a day.'

Josie tickled her nephew under the chin. 'If he eats like his Uncle Patrick I shouldn't wonder at it. Come in and put him down.'

Brian turned his head into his mother's shoulder but laughed at his aunt. Mattie lowered him to the floor and took off her bonnet. She removed her son's top coat, revealing his gingham smock and dark drawers underneath. Having gained his freedom, Brian toddled to the bottom of the stairs and sat down on the step. He started playing with the toy soldier he'd brought with him.

'Is Pat home?' Mattie asked, hanging up her hat and coat on the hall stand and laying Brian's over the top.

Josie shook her head. 'He took the *Laughing Girl* out early this morning but he knows you're coming. He should be here soon.'

Josie hugged her friend and kissed her on the cheek.

'It's good to see you, Josie,' Mattie said, the warm tone in her voice matching her words.

'I just wished we lived around the corner like we used to.'

'So do I,' Mattie replied, 'but only if we could live here in Stepney Green.'

'Auntie Mattie!' Annie called from the landing above.

The women looked up and Brian clambered to his feet as he saw his cousin Annie making her way down the stairs, carrying her brother Rob.

Josie opened the parlour door. 'In you go and make yourself comfortable while I get the tea.'

Josie went to the kitchen, where her mother-in-law, Sarah, was by the table folding up the sheets she'd just brought in from the garden.

'Mattie's here,' Josie said, taking the tea caddy down from the shelf above the range and spooning the dry leaves into the tea pot.

'How does she look?' Sarah asked, setting the last of the sheets on the top of the basket.

'Tired.'

Sarah took off her overall and hung it next to Josie's apron. 'With a lively child, poor Queenie to look out for and a business to run, I don't wonder at it. Perhaps, next week I'll go over on Friday as well as Tuesday to give her a hand.' She flexed her hands and the bones cracked.

Josie glanced at her mother-in-law's swollen knuckles and at her puffy ankles.

'She'd appreciate that but don't over-do it,' Josie replied.

Sarah slowly made her way to the dresser and started to collect the tea cups. Josie took them from her. 'You go and see that grandson of yours.'

A tender expression spread across the older woman's face. 'Ah, well – I will. But mind that tray's not too heavy, you know.' She glanced down at Josie's growing stomach.

'Go away with you, Ma,' Josie laughed.

By the time Josie nudged open the parlour door with her hip and carried the tea tray in, the children had already emptied half the toy box and were deeply involved in a made-up game while Mattie was busy chatting to her mother, who was sitting in her usual chair by the fire with her knitting already in her hands.

Josie noticed that although Mattie was smiling, her eyes didn't have their usual spark and there were dark shadows beneath. Her mouth, too, had a tight, anxious quality about it and her shoulders sagged as if they were carrying the weight of the world, or at least the burden of a struggling coal yard, upon them.

'There we are,' Josie said as she placed the tray on the table. She gave everyone a cup of tea, then picked up her own and took a sip of tea.

'Are things any better at the yard?' she asked Mattie.

'No.' She looked bleakly at Josie. 'In truth it's getting worse each day. And with Eli still off . . .' For a brief second Mattie's chin wobbled but she steadied it.

A twinge of guilt tugged at Josie. She asked Patrick only last week to drop by Mattie's yard to see if she were all right. He said he would but got caught upstream when the tide turned.

Patrick had helped his sister by looking over Maguire's books for a few months before Brian was born, while Eli ran the yard. At that time they'd turned a small profit and once she'd weaned Brian, Mattie took over running the business. She had to: Queenie and Brian depended on her and without the yard they would have been not only homeless but destitute.

It was hard, but when had Mattie ever been afraid of grafting? So, despite having a babe in arms and an addled mother-in-law, Mattie had learnt all about the coal trade from scratch. Josie doubted she could have done what her friend had to keep Maguire & Son's afloat for three years. And it was the devil's own luck that just as things were looking up the price of coal suddenly increased. Several of the smaller yards had already been bought out by Huggins down by Blackwall, who had also been trying to take trade from the other surviving yards like Mattie's. Her position wasn't helped by the fact that she was a woman trying to operate a very male-orientated business. She found out very early on that in business there was no such thing as chivalry.

'You know Patrick will come by anytime you need a bit of help.'

'I know, but when would he have the time? You told me a few weeks ago he'd had to hire another boat to keep pace with the demand. What with waiting for wind and tide to shift his cargos he barely has time to sleep, let alone ruin his eyes trying to understand my scribbling.'

'He would come by if you needed him,' Josie told her. 'At least you've got Flashy Freddie.'

Mattie's unhappy expression deepened. 'He's not much help.'

Josie's eyebrows rose. 'How's that? The way he was telling it to Patrick last week it sounded like he was all but running the yard.'

'Oh, I'm sure. He's jolly enough with customers, but since Eli's been off Freddie struts round the yard ordering Billy and Pete about. Twice I've asked him to be back in time to give a hand with Morris's delivery and each time he's trotted in just as all the work was done. He doesn't fill his order book in properly so it takes me double the time to tally it up. He's always very sorry, he says, and gives me his stock cheeky grin, but when I'm trying to make three wagons do the work of four it's not funny any more. And he's still turning up late. I was going to have a word with him but ...'

Josie saw the start of a tear in Mattie's eyes. She reached out and squeezed her friend's hand.

Mattie gave her a fearless smile. 'Don't you fret, Josie love. Things are looking up. I've got the discount from Morris that I've been after for months and Mr Stebbins himself is coming by to look over my books to see if there is anything to be done.' Her smile widened. 'So, who knows? I might be taking a house around the corner from you yet.'

Mattie brushed Flossy's dappled rump as the mare crunched her way through a bale of hay. The horse kicked her iron-shod hoof on the cobble and shook her head, happy to have a day free from pulling a coal wagon. Mattie, on the other hand, felt quite the opposite at having a cart standing idle.

She wiped her forehead with the back of her forearm and eyed the piles of coal at the end of the yard. It was already June but the weather had been as hot as August for two weeks. The trade always dipped this time of year but since Easter the demand for all grades of coal had nearly halved. So much so that she hadn't needed to restock the yard this week.

The gate creaked open and Kate walked in. She was dressed in her serviceable cotton work gown and had her hair tied back. She was as tall as Mattie at five-foot-three inches but her own generous curves were without the soft roundness of motherhood. Unlike Mattie, Kate had her mother's colouring, with hair as golden as ripe corn. Her eyes were like her mother's too, more green and gold rather than Mattie's deep shade of brown. She'd lived with Mattie since Brian Maguire had died. In recent weeks the ten shillings she gave Mattie for housekeeping was sometimes the only reason Mattie had food in the cupboard

'Have I missed Ma?' Kate said, setting the metal hoop on a chain that served as their yard bell spinning as she passed.

'Only just. She went back on Billy's cart about half an hour ago. She said she was sorry she couldn't stay until you came home but then she'll see us both at Mass,' Mattie replied.

Kate looked over to the empty cart. 'Any news of Eli?' she asked, patting Flossy's neck.

'He's better but still in bed. Doctor's orders.'

Kate gave her an anxious look. 'So there's been no number-one delivery again today.'

Mattie shook her head. In readiness for Mr Stebbins's visit she'd spent several hours last night going through the accounts. She didn't want him to have to untangle her scribbled notes so she'd rewritten the last two months' income and outgoings into two neat columns.

'I got them all to take out extra sacks this morning and Pete and Billy have done the same with the afternoon round,' Mattie told her. 'But Freddie's not back yet and it must be past three now, if you're home.'

Kate twirled a stray lock of hair around her finger distractedly. 'He's probably been held up.'

Again, thought Mattie.

'He's forever being stopped for a chat. You know what a lark he is,' Kate added, wistfully.

The gate creaked open again and Muffy clip-clopped into the yard, trailing the empty cart with Freddie walking alongside. He had taken his coat off, rolled up his sleeves and undone his collar. Kate's gaze ran over him and the colour rose in her cheeks.

'Good afternoon, Mrs M,' he called, taking his hat off and sweeping a bow. 'You're looking very natty this afternoon.' He ran his fingers through the hair on his chest slowly, with his eyes fixed on Mattie. 'And Miss Kate, too, of course,' he added, his gaze flickering over her briefly.

Kate giggled and blushed. Mattie looked at her sister uneasily. Kate was friendly with young Alfie Lennon, the son of one of their old neighbours in Walburch Street but Mattie would be the first to admit that Alfie could never in a dozen years be described as *dashing*.

'The hay delivery has been and gone,' Mattie said, wondering why he was staring at her with such a daft expression on his face.

'Sorry, Mrs M. I was held up in Turner Street.'

He slapped Muffy's rump and she ambled over to the water trough and stuck her nose in, taking the cart with her. Freddie followed and slackened her girth a notch. His eyes flickered over Mattie again.

'But don't you worry none,' he said. 'By the time the old girl's had her fill, I'll have this lot' – he kicked the sacks of coal waiting to be taken on the afternoon round – 'on board and ready to go.' He grasped hold of the first bag and heaved it on to his shoulders. Kate's eyes followed his every move.

Mattie looped her arm though her sister's. 'I think Queenie's just making a cuppa.'

'Tell 'er her favourite nephew will be in to see her before he knocks off,' Freddie called as Mattie marched Kate across the yard and into the kitchen.

Queenie was already peeling potatoes for tea. 'Oh, it's your sister,' she said, smiling at Kate. 'Are you staying for tea?'

Kate played along happily. 'If I may.'

Young Brian stretched his arms and Mattie picked him up. 'And did you enjoy seeing Granny Sarah?' she asked, kissing his soft cheek.

It felt hot under her lips and her heart lurched. There had been two children ill just around the corner in Somerset Street only last week. The summer fever would be upon them in a week or two, rampaging through the tightly packed neighbourhood.

She looked at Brian more closely and her racing heart slowed. The redness was only on one cheek. 'I think one of his back teeth is coming through,' she said setting him back on the floor.

Queenie nodded and slid the kettle back over the flames. 'You look like you need a cuppa.'

'I certainly do. What about you, Kate?'

Kate didn't answer.

'I saw Alfie Lennon's ma in the market,' Mattie added.

'Mmm,' Kate replied, staring through the coal-speckled glass into the yard.

Mattie raised her voice. 'She thinks you're a nice girl.'

'Oh! That's kind of her,' Kate said, continuing to study the coal heaps.

'I thought I might drop in on Patrick and Josie on Saturday, Kate, for a bit of tea. Do you want to—'

'I've dropped my handkerchief,' Kate said, spinning around. 'It must have fallen out in the yard.'

Mattie spotted a corner of white cotton poking out from between the buttons of her sister's bodice. 'It's—'

'I won't be a mo.' Kate tore open the back door and disappeared.

Queenie handed Mattie her mug of tea and, cradling it in her hands, Mattie made her way to the window. Kate was standing with her hands behind her back and swaying from side to side, setting her skirts flowing around her legs. Somewhere between the back door and the yard she'd whipped off her hair scarf to let her long blonde plait hang to her waist like a bell rope.

Freddie was sitting on the cart with one leg hanging over and the other bent up. He said something to Kate and she laughed, then stood back as he shook the reins. Muffy plodded through the gates. Kate watched after him then headed back towards the house. She burst back into the kitchen and flourished the small white square.

'I found it!' she cried, with a flush on her cheeks and a sparkle in her eyes that Alfie Lennon would never see. 'Thank goodness I got to it before it was ruined. I had better get changed.' She bounced towards the hall door. 'Oh, and Queenie, Freddie said he'd pop by later.'

Something in the way Kate said Freddie's name sent alarm bells ringing in Mattie's head. Should she mention to Kate that Freddie had been seen slipping in the back door of Bessie Buckle's house? She didn't know. But if Kate was setting her cap at Freddie, her handkerchief wouldn't be the only thing in danger of being ruined.

As Mumble plodded along the familiar road towards the first delivery at the back of Whitechapel High Street, Freddie hooked his feet up on the shafts and pulled his tobacco pouch from his trouser pocket.

He jerked his foot and nudged the reins looped around the brake handle. Mumble moved to the left in response and Freddie filled his pipe. He lit it then put his hands behind his head and leant back. A smug grin spread across his face as he thought about Kate's silly story about mislaying her handkerchief. He wasn't born yesterday, and he could see by the look in her eyes that she just couldn't keep away from him. He smoothed back his hair and chuckled to himself. He couldn't blame her, and the way she eyed him up and down, well . . . a look like that could get a girl into all sorts of trouble, which ordinarily he'd be happy to be but he had recently come around to thinking that he ought to look to his future. Although the job in his cousin's yard had got him out of a fix he didn't want to be a coalman all his life.

A man like him, with brains and charm, shouldn't have to grub a living plastered in coal dust each day. And now poor Brian had been at his rest for three years he felt it was time to get himself a more comfortable life with his cousin's widow. In truth, Mattie had finished her mourning a year ago so it wouldn't be seen as disrespectful as if he'd started courting her sooner but, at the time, he'd had other ... interests, let's call them, occupying his time.

But no matter. What was a year or two? And he couldn't rush her. Sweet Mattie might have eyes that sent a man's pulse racing and a body that you'd want to feel under you but she was no fool. No sir. She'd seen off half-a-dozen men since her husband died, with their tails tucked right between their legs for trying to get their feet under her cosy table. But now Old Eli wasn't able to run the yard it gave him the chance to move in. On the quiet like, nothing to make her bolt or run scared. Gentle, as you did with a horse getting used to a new driver. Just a 'sweetheart' here or a 'honey' to start, then perhaps a touch of the hand or a brush-up-close, seemingly innocent, but enough to set her lonely little heart fluttering. It shouldn't take too much lovey-doveying. After all she'd been without a man for three years. It must be taxing her nature to sleep alone.

'Afternoon, Freddie,' a woman's voice shouted.

Freddie grinned. 'Afternoon, me little darlings,' he said, calling to the two women sitting outside their open front doors.

They were dressed in plain nondescript gowns and grey aprons but had dispensed with their usual head shawls on account of the warm weather. On either side of them were a handful of grubby children playing in the dirt.

The older one nudged the woman beside her. 'You got a delivery for us then, Freddie?'

They hunched up their shoulders and giggled.

'Only if your old man's not around,' he called back, as Mumble plodded the wagon past them.

A girlish blush, quite at odds with her lined face, flushed the older woman's cheeks. 'Shame on you, Freddie Ellis.'

'You don't have to worry about my old man,' said the younger woman, who had a mane of unruly red hair. ''E scarpered a year back, so come round any time you like, 'andsome.'

Freddie winked. 'I'll remember that.'

He clicked his tongue to urge Mumble on then settled back again.

He wondered if the redhead was truly without a man but then he turned his mind back to Mattie.

As he delivered the afternoon orders Freddie resolved to ignore the likes of Bessie and Annie. He'd save himself for the woman who could keep him with a shilling in his pocket every day of the week – Mattie Maguire.

By the time he'd shouldered the last sack of coal and trudged it through to the back of the Moon and Stars, Freddie's imagination had already changed the sign on the yard's double gates from Maguire & Son's to Ellis & Co.

As he strolled out of the pub's side door, Mumble ambled on, pulling the cart unaided towards the last delivery, Latimer Dairy, at the end of the street. Freddie shoved his hands in his pockets and strolled along beside the cart, nodding a greeting to the women sitting outside their doors stuffing mattresses with straw.

The horse came to a halt in front of the arched side entrance of Latimer's. She pricked up her ears as she heard the lowing of the cows inside. Freddie grabbed a sack and swung it onto his shoulders. Jogging it a couple of times until it sat squarely, he started through the arch towards the coal shed at the far end.

The dairy was in fact a courtyard surrounded on three sides by six low-roofed makeshift cottages. Ted Latimer, the owner, had taken off the front doors and made the downstairs rooms and sculleries in each of the dwellings into a stall for his cows while letting out the room above.

As Freddie reached the shed, Ted's daughter Ginny appeared in the open door of the far cottage. A slow smile crept across her lips as she saw him. Scooping her curly light brown hair off her face, she sauntered towards him.

'Warm, ain't it?' she said, her eyes flickering down to his open shirt.

'Fit to melt yer,' he replied, kicking open the shed door.

Bending forward Freddie shrugged the sack up his back then emptied the coal. He shook out the last few chips then turned to find Ginny standing in his path.

'Yer right,' she said, running her hands slowly over her chest showing above her neckline. 'I do feel as if I could melt.'

Freddie's eyes followed her fingers as they traced a line across the swell of her breasts.

'Why don't you come into the shade of the byre and cool yourself while I fetch you a mug of ale,' she said, running her hand up his bare forearm and disturbing the soft hair. 'I thought I might join you seeing as Pa won't be back for an hour or so.'

He *should* say no. The hay delivery was arriving at five and Mattie had asked him to see it in. If he wanted to convince her that she should cast aside her widow's weeds and marry him he ought to do as he promised, at least until he owned the yard.

Ginny pressed herself against him and gave him a groin-tightening sideward look. 'What do you say?'

Freddie's gaze ran slowly over her bare flesh then back up to her face. ''Ow long 'til your Pa gets back?'

Chapter Five

Nathaniel leaned in the doorway of 33 Minories, his eyes fixed on the solid-oak door straight across from him, while he tried not to attract the attention of the policeman strolling by on the other side of the road. He glanced up at the grand four-storey office and then back to the brass plate that had *Mr A Stebbins* etched into its burnished surface.

After leaving Emma's cottage, he'd caught the night stagecoach at the White Horse and crossed over the Bow Bridge just before six yesterday morning. It would have been quicker by train, but more expensive than slipping the coach driver a sixpence instead of the proper fare. He was let off at Cambridge Heath Gate and after eating a penny breakfast in one of the chop shops he walked the mile or so to Whitechapel High Street – the very boundary of the city.

He had been to London about ten years ago when he'd accompanied Mr Fairhead on a business trip but this time he was astounded by the press of people. Rough-shod labourers jostled with smartly dressed city clerks at the coffee stands as they handed over three or four coppers for their early morning drink. Between them, old women shuffled home after their early morning jobs as cleaners and young girls, with dark circles under their eyes, weaved their way between the crowds on their way to twelve hours of toil in half-lit factories.

The prices, too, astounded Nathaniel. Everything seemed to be double, if not treble, the money it would have cost him in Essex. He'd thought he had enough money for a week or so but at these prices he'd be penniless in a few days. Luckily, it had taken him less than half-an-hour's work to locate Stebbins. All he'd had to do was to work his way alphabetically down the addresses in the postal directory in the Aldgate Post Office until he found him.

Nathaniel shifted position and the newly sharpened knife, which he'd tucked into the back of his belt, pressed into the small of his back. He would be caught and hanged, of course, but what did it matter? He'd already lost everything.

Eventually, the oak door opened and Nathaniel froze as his eyes fixed on the man who had haunted him for the past four years. Blood pumped loudly though his ears.

Amos Stebbins had fattened up and now had a sizeable paunch and side-whiskers that joined his moustache. His sharply pressed pinstriped trousers and long woollen overcoat with its plush astra-khan collar stood in stark contrast to Nathaniel's threadbare suit. Stebbins's light brown hair was just visible under the shiny silk top hat perched at a jaunty angle on his head, and a diamond tie-pin twinkled beneath the swirls of his cravat.

Unbidden, an image of Marjorie entered Nathaniel's mind: his wife, with her hair unbound, laughing as she pushed Lillian on the swing. In vivid detail, he recalled the golden fleck in her hazel eyes and her generous smile. Then, if that scene were not enough, his mind summoned up the small attic bedroom where Lillian and Rosina slept curled together. Knowing he would never hold his children again or feel their slender arms around his neck brought the sting of tears to his eyes. He blinked them away and slowly reached around and gripped the knife.

But suddenly a feeling he hadn't experienced since being dragged from Chelmsford Crown Court caused him to falter: indecision. He'd have been dead if he'd shown the slightest hesitation in Botany Bay but now, on a London Street crowded with respectable citizens, Nathaniel's deeply buried moral code resurrected itself. It *was* wrong to take a life, even Stebbins's. But how else could he make the bastard pay for what he'd done?

Stebbins pulled out a fat cigar, jammed it in the corner of his mouth and lit it. He sucked on it a couple of times then exhaled a long puff of smoke, then turned towards the river and set off.

Nathaniel shoved his conscience aside, fixed his eyes on his quarry and followed.

A pleasant sense of well-being coursed through Amos Stebbins as he strolled down the Highway towards Maguire & Son's. A number of the shopkeepers standing outside their shops touched their hats as he passed and Amos nodded benevolently in return.

A couple of young boys dashed past and almost knocked him over but even being jostled by a handful of grubby guttersnipes couldn't dispel the sense of gratification glowing within him. No, nothing could cloud his day, for George Hudson, that great champion of the railway, entrepreneur, and Member of Parliament for Sunderland, had invited him to lunch at the House. On the strength of this he had sent his clerk to the tobacconist to settle his overdue bill and to fetch half a dozen of his favourite Cuban cigars, one of which he was enjoying while he made his way to see Mattie Maguire.

However, one small fly hovered over the day's ointment. Cecily was adamant that she wanted gas installed throughout the house, plus the parlour and dining room redecorated, which was putting a considerable strain on his pocket. Added to which there was the terse letter from Mr Fallon, the chief banker at the City & County.

Maguire & Son's double-fronted door came into view and a satisfied smile lifted the corners of his moustache. Tucker's men had done a better job than he could ever have hoped for by knocking one cart and a man out of service in a single blow. Now all he had to do was twist the figures to show that Mattie was teetering on the edge of bankruptcy and the deeds to number six Cannon Street Road would soon be sitting alongside the others.

He stopped on the kerb and waited for a cart piled high with jute bales to trundle past. Suddenly, a prickling sensation sent shivers between his shoulder blades.

Amos glanced behind. The knife grinder was still pumping away on his treadle and the sailors in their knitted smocks and canvas trousers were still lounging against the wall outside the Hope and Anchor.

He shook his head and, putting aside the odd notion, crossed the road. Inside the yard Maguire's three drivers were loading their wagons for the afternoon round. One wagon sat idle and empty against the back fence.

Mattie's three employees grunted and strained under the sacks of coal.

'Afternoon, Mr Stebbins,' Pete and Billy said, as they swung a hundredweight brown sack on the back of a cart. The horse shifted in the harness and the wheels squeaked.

Amos acknowledged them with a tight-lipped nod.

Billy climbed on the wagon and took up the reins while Pete went to his rig and did the same. The two wagons rolled out of the gate.

Amos caught sight of Freddie Ellis on the remaining cart. His eyes narrowed and his lips tightened further. *Fornicator*, he thought as he watched Freddie heave a sack of coal effortlessly onto the back of his wagon. With all the back doors Freddie slipped in and out of Amos was surprised he could lift his head, let alone a half hundredweight of coal.

'Afternoon, there Mr Stebbins,' Freddie said, giving him what

Amos considered too familiar a greeting. He jumped down from the wagon, sauntered over and pulled a small tin from his trouser pocket. He took out his pipe. 'Got a light?'

Amos hesitated then offered him a box of matches.

'Ta.'

'I see Eli's not back.'

Freddie drew in another couple of puffs then curled the bulb end into his palm the way that working men did. 'Poor old bugger's still off.'

Amos heaved a sigh. 'I'll have to have a word with the vicar. I'm sure the parish could do something to help. It can't be easy for Mrs Maguire to have lost him from the rounds.' He shook his head. 'What that poor woman's been through these last years.'

'Don't you worry about Mrs M. Even when Eli was here I was the one who took charge of things.' He winked. 'Of course, I let the old boy think it was him. Although I don't like to brag, I run the yard.'

Amos suppressed a smirk. If Freddie had truly been in charge the yard would have gone under years ago. 'Mrs Maguire is blessed to have you to rely on.'

'That's what I keep telling 'er.' Freddie bounded onto the cart. 'I had best be on me way. I've got to see a man about a dog.'

Freddie picked up the reins and sent the horse on. As the cart disappeared around the corner, Mattie walked into the yard holding her son's hand. She was dressed in her usual dark navy work dress, complete with its ghastly stained apron and her headscarf.

'Mr Stebbins,' she said hurrying over. 'Whatever must you be thinking of me not being in the yard to welcome you?'

Amos waved away her agitation. 'Think nothing of it, Mrs Maguire.' He patted Brian on the head. 'And young Master Maguire.'

Relief swept over Mattie's face. 'That's kind of you. Let me offer you a dish of tea before I show you the accounts – if you're not in too much of a hurry.'

'Thank you. It would be my pleasure,' Amos replied, all the while hoping that after a morning's housework Queenie would be snoring softly in the corner chair for the duration of his visit.

Mattie turned towards the house and as she did Brian pulled away and dashed for the stables. Mattie tore after him so quickly her scarf slipped off and her hair tumbled out. She caught her son and brought him back to her side.

'You pickle,' she laughed, putting her foot on her scarf to stop it flying away.

Amos watched, then his eyes moved to the crowded street, where he momentarily spotted a man he thought he'd never lay eyes on again.

Nathaniel Tate!

A cold hand clutched at his heart. He blinked and the man was gone. Amos swallowed hard to get the moisture back in his mouth. *It's the light playing tricks, nothing more. Do you hear? Nothing more.*

'I'm sorry about that,' Mattie said, trying to keep her hair in order with one hand. She tilted her head. 'Are you unwell, Mr Stebbins? You look pale.'

Gripping her skirts in one hand and balancing the tea tray in the other, Mattie climbed the wooden stair to her office. Resting the tray on the handrail, she opened the door and found Mr Stebbins just where she'd left him twenty minutes ago, sitting at her desk. Thankfully, he seemed fully recovered from his earlier turn, which he'd insisted was nothing. Mattie had been alarmed but now the colour had returned to his face. He glanced up and smiled as she entered.

'Just in time,' he said, setting the pen back into the inkwell. 'I've just finished.'

'Already! I mean . . . It takes me two days to do the end-of-month accounts.'

Mr Stebbins leant back and laced his fingers together across his colourful waistcoat. 'I'm sure it does but you must remember' – he indicated the book in front of him – 'this is a simple matter for me.'

'Of course it must be,' she laughed. 'After totting up the warehouse books mine must seem like a grocer's bill.'

'Mrs Maguire, it is a refreshing change.'

'Well, if you've finished, would you rather take your tea downstairs in the kitchen? Queenie's almost finished tidying up.'

He waved the suggestion away. 'No, no. I don't want to trample over dear Queenie's fine efforts.' His nose wrinkled up in a sort of boyish way. 'I am quite happy here.'

Mattie put the tray on the end of the desk and glanced at the open ledger.

'So, what do you think, Mr Stebbins?' she asked, almost not wanting to know what a truly dreadful state Maguire's finances were in.

Mr Stebbins shook his head mournfully. 'I'm sorry to have to tell you this, Mrs Maguire, but I can't see how you can keep going for more than a week or two,' he said, taking one of the delicate pink-and-blue cups and saucers from her. She'd brought out her rarely-used best china from the back of the dresser in honour of Mr Stebbins's visit.

'I didn't think it was that bad!'

'I'm afraid it is,' he said, helping himself to three lumps of sugar. 'According to the figures you are paying out more than you've got coming in.'

Mattie could hardly believe it. In fact she certainly couldn't! She might have missed the odd bill or put a credit in the wrong column but ...

'With all due respect, Mr Stebbins, I'm not sure how that can be. For instance, last month our income was twenty-five pounds, seven shillings and ninepence and our outgoings were twenty-four pounds and sixpence. I know I'm cutting extra turnips into the stew instead of giving my brother money to deposit in the bank, but Maguire's is still keeping its head above water.'

His doleful expression deepened. 'But that's because you are using the adding up and subtracting method of accounting, Mrs Maguire.' He traced his finger down the right hand column. 'Whereas I have applied the modern system.'

Mattie came around the desk and stood beside him. She studied the scribbled rows of numbers.

'But you've added the fodder, farriers and wheelwright bills in twice,' she said, running her finger along the page.

'Because feed, horse shoes and cart repairs are variable expenses,' he replied, patiently as if explaining the matter to a child.

Mattie totted up the totals across the bottom of the page. 'But this isn't the true figure,' she tapped the page. 'It can't be because if it was I'd have no money in the safe.'

He chuckled. 'Mrs Maguire, that's just your cash flow, not the overall value of your yard.' He scanned down the page again, 'But the truth of the matter is you were practically bankrupt before the incident with number one wagon and Eli but now ...' he shook his head. 'I tell you, unless you act soon, Queenie and that little lad of yours might very well end up in the poor house. Of course, I could arrange for you to have credit at the City & County Bank, just to tide you over.'

Mattie straightened up and folded her arms. 'Thank you, Mr Stebbins, but new accounting ways or not, I don't hold with owing anyone anything, not even a bank.'

An odd emotion flitted across Amos Stebbins's face, then his usual ebullience returned. 'Well, that's very commendable.' He picked up the cup and saucer and, cradling it in his palm, gripped the fragile handle between his finger and thumb. 'But if you don't want credit then the only course open to you is to sell the business.

'Sell?'

He took a noisy sip of tea. 'I don't see you have any choice. Property prices aren't as high as they were last year but I'm sure you could get eighty pounds for the business, lock, stock and barrel. I might even know someone who might be interested.'

Sell Maguire's for eighty pounds! The land alone was worth double that, not to mention the carts, horses and stock.

'It's kind of you, again, but my father-in-law built up this firm from a handcart and passed it on to his son. While there's breath in my body I'll fight to do the same for mine.'

The inexplicable look shot across Stebbins's face again, then he took her hand and patted it. 'My dear, dear, Mrs Maguire. May the good Lord hear your prayers.'

Mattie glanced back at the accounts book. This might be the new way of book-keeping but it didn't alter the fact that if there wasn't enough money in the safe at the end of the week to pay her creditors she would go out of business. None of what Mr Stebbins had told her made any sense and she would have to spend another three nights to get the figures to tally. But he had given her a whole afternoon of his time and she knew a recommendation from him could secure a place for Brian in St Katherine's school.

She smiled artlessly up at him. 'This new way of bookkeeping is all a mystery to me but I know you wouldn't tell me wrong, Mr Stebbins. So if you say Maguire's is running into difficulties then I'm not going to argue with you.'

Chapter Six

A church clock struck eleven as Nathaniel left the gas-lit thoroughfare of Whitechapel High Street and made his way towards 56 Thrawl Street, one of the many common lodging houses on the edge of Spitalfields. Once a smart family house, its dozen or so rooms now served as a night shelter for those whose only other option was to sleep wedged in a doorway.

The door had opened an hour ago but there were a dozen or so people milling around outside. A couple of local prostitutes dressed in little more than rags and rouge gave Nathaniel the once over. They beckoned to him but turned away when he didn't respond.

He stepped into the dingy kitchen where the smell of over-boiled cabbage hit him. The overseer sat in the corner with a beer in his hand and his bulging, piggy eyes flickering over everyone. He was completely bald except for a wiry clump of hair over each ear. His thick brows met in an angry knot and little thickets of dark hair sprouted from his nose and ears.

His wan and colourless wife slopped greasy soup into bowls, which she handed to lodgers sitting at the central table. Thankful that he'd at least had enough money for a supper of pie and mash, Nathaniel threw his thruppence in front of the overseer who spat a brown stream of tobacco-stained spittle onto the fire.

'Room four.'

Nathaniel made his way up the bare-board stairs to the second floor. Several men, tucking their shirts into their trousers, passed him as they came down from the women's rooms in the attic. Beds weren't the only thing available for a few coppers in Number 56.

He found room four to be no more than twelve feet by fourteen, with six box-beds placed side by side as if in the stockroom of a funeral parlour. Nathaniel went to the unoccupied wooden crate by the window, which meant he'd only have one neighbour snoring and farting next to him. He shrugged off his coat and folded it to use as a pillow; despite the deprivation he'd suffered in the past seven years he still couldn't bear to sleep underneath stained bedclothes. As he tried to get comfortable one of the fleas infesting the filthy bed linen

45

and damp straw mattress bit him. The two-foot, six-inch width was barely enough to accommodate his shoulders so he turned slightly onto his side. He wished he could have saved his money and taken his chance on the streets but the police patrols made it too risky.

The pale glow from a streetlamp filtered through the filthy glass beside him. Above, the boards squeaked rhythmically as one of the women upstairs earned her night's board. However, his present nauseating discomfort couldn't match the gut-wrenching stench of the battened-down hold he'd spent the best part of six months in. On board, the captain's regime dictated that men were only allowed on deck for an hour's exercise each day, during which they were marched in single file while the sailors jeered and spat at them. For the remaining twenty-three hours, they were shackled together by a chain that was bolted to the central beam. He'd performed all his bodily functions in a bucket, crouched between a small time pickpocket and a simple-minded lad known only as Boy. But even as men fought and died around him and he gagged on maggot-ridden dry tack and gruel, the thought of one day seeing Marjorie and his girls had kept him alive.

Again and again he turned over the image of Amos Stebbins staring out of the open coal yard gates. He cursed himself under his breath. Why had he been so damned careless?

For eighteen long months he'd spent almost every waking hour imagining that exquisite moment when he would see the lifeblood drain from Amos's face. But now he'd jeopardised his plans because he'd hesitated.

Tomorrow, he thought, and braced his shoulders against the side of the box. The noise above stopped and heavy feet clomped down the stairs. Cramp shot through Nathaniel's right calf so he flexed his foot inside his boot. He stared at the wall. The plaster under the window had cracked some time before and small lumps had fallen off to expose the brickwork beneath. Someone had pasted the front sheet of a newspaper entitled the *Working Man's Defender* over it to stop it flaking further. Nathaniel tried to decipher what remained.

Mr A——s St——ns, Benefactor or Exploiter?

Nathaniel lifted himself onto one elbow, carefully peeled the sheet from the wall and held it at an angle to read by the faint light coming in.

It has been reported that Mr St——ns, the owner of a Grey Friars warehouse and a local businessman has donated £70 to replace the lead stolen from the roof. When asked what prompted his generous gift Mr St——ns quoted Matthew chapter six, verse nineteen.

St George's-in-the-East's Parochial Parish council have wasted no time in ordering the replacement materials from Cashman & Sons.

But did they, dear reader, pause to consider how Mr St——ns acquired his money? If these solid citizens were to dig a little deeper into Mr A——s St——ns's business methods, they might discover that he has more in common with a Roman tax collector than the Good Samaritan. The further I investigate into his many, and often covert, business practices the more I would liken Mr A St——ns, businessman, parish councillor and, if rumours are to be believed, prospective Alderman, to a stone lying in a summer meadow – warm and benign on top but dank and corrupt beneath.

Mr St——ns would have us believe that he has taken the Lord's Word to heart, but I would remind him that the Almighty sees all and he cannot bamboozle the Lord as he does the Vestry Elders.

The editorial concluded by assuring the reader that the *Working Man's Defender* would not rest until it had brought Mr S to justice.

Nathaniel re-read the article.

Despite the draught from the missing windowpane a warm glow spread through him. He *wasn't* the only person who saw Stebbins for what he really was. Smyth-Hilton, the editor of the *Defender* seemed to be wise to Stebbins too. More importantly, he wasn't just some gullible fool who'd been taken in by Amos but someone with influence and connections. Perhaps he would be interested to hear his story.

Nathaniel carefully folded the sheet of newspaper and tucked it in his breast pocket.

He had thought that killing Stebbins would settle the score. He was mistaken. Death would be far too generous a way of dealing with the bastard. And if it was time to take a lesson from the Good Book, how about Exodus twenty-one, verse twenty-four? *An eye for an eye and a tooth for a tooth?*

'Coogan!' Amos shouted at the half-glazed door to his office.

The handle rattled and Walter Coogan, the warehouse's chief clerk, stepped in. 'Yes, Mr Stebbins?'

'I have some important matters to attend to and I don't want to be disturbed.' He tidied the bills and receipts on the desk in front of him.

'Very good, sir.'

The door closed. Amos shuffled the papers a couple of times then leant back in his chair and put his feet up on the desk. He wove his fingers together across his stomach and settled his chin on his chest. His eyelids drooped as he gazed out of the window over the brown-brick warehouses of St Katherine's dock.

A mass of masts and rigging swayed back and forth as the ships anchored off shore waited for a berth and rolled with the tide. It was said that in the Pool a man could walk from Wapping to Rotherhithe without getting his feet wet and Amos could believe it.

It had been bad form of Galvin and Ross, the partnership who had sold him Grey Friars warehouse, not to mention that the entrance to St Katherine's was too narrow for the heavily laden merchantmen to enter. By the time he'd taken ownership the docks were already losing custom to the Blackwall Railway that ran from the Minories to Brunswick Docks up river. No matter though. It would be of no consequence in a few months when he floated the Wapping to Stratford Railway Company and all his financial worries would be over.

He let his eyes close and reassured himself yet again that he couldn't possibly have seen Nathaniel Tate outside Maguire's. He'd heard that Tate's wife and children had died some while back and, as he drifted off to sleep, he let himself contemplate all the unspeakable foreign diseases that might have sent Tate to an early grave in Botany Bay.

Suddenly the door burst open. Amos started awake and only just avoided falling backwards out of the chair. He slammed his hands on the papers strewn across his desk and glared at Walter.

'What's the meaning of this?' he growled. 'I—'

'It's the police,' the clerk cut in as three officers in their frock coats and top hats marched into the office, their heavy boots stamping on the polished floor.

With a mighty effort he stood up and greeted them. 'Good afternoon, Sergeant,' he said, catching sight of the insignia on the high collar of one of the officers. 'What can I do for you?'

'I am Sergeant Lockwood and these are constables Mills and Hanson.'

The two bewhiskered police officers touched their hats respectfully. 'I hope you'll forgive our intrusion, sir,' the sergeant said from underneath his full moustache. 'But it is a matter of some urgency we need to discuss with you.'

'Sit, sit,' he said, indicating the chair. 'What is it?'

Sergeant Lockwood removed his hat and smoothed his sparse fair hair before taking a seat. Mills and Hanson remained standing.

'We have received information from the Essex constabulary that a certain Nathaniel Tate has been sighted in Romford and has been making enquires as to your whereabouts.'

Perspiration burst out on Amos's forehead and a sudden tightening of his windpipe choked off his breath. His hand went to his collar and he loosened his necktie.

'I thought Tate was in Botany Bay.'

'He escaped.' The sergeant's voice seemed to come from far away.

'Escaped! How?'

'I'm not acquainted with the particulars, sir,' Sergeant Lockwood replied, 'but I understand the news of the death of his wife and children prompted his return.'

A memory of Marjorie flashed into Amos's mind. He always thought her a timid creature, so he'd been shocked when she slapped his face outside Chelmsford Crown Court.

'I've come to warn you to be on your guard, Sir. It's just a precaution and I'm sure we'll have him back under lock and key in a day or two.'

Amos unbuttoned his jacket. 'What sort of lax regime allows a dangerous criminal like Tate to jump on board a ship and return to England? I shall write to the Home Secretary ... no, ... no ... to the Prime Minister. Yes, the Prime Minister no less, and demand to know what we pay taxes for if not to have the corrupt and immoral elements of our society removed!'

The sergeant stood up. 'I can't answer to that, Mr Stebbins, but if you should see him—'

'I have!' The officers exchanged surprised glances. Amos clasped his hands together. They were hot and moist. 'I thought I was imagining it but ...'

'Where was this?'

'Outside Maguire's coal yard in Cannon Street Road.'

'Hmm ... If you saw Tate he must have seen you. I would advise you not to visit there again and to be extra diligent about your personal safety until we apprehend him.'

Amos nodded rapidly because suddenly he couldn't speak.

'I bid you good day then, Mr Stebbins,' the sergeant said as he and the two constable left.

Amos stared blindly ahead for a moment then jumped to his feet. He collected his hat, coat and cane from the stand then flung open the office door. Walter Coogan stared at him from behind a pile of tanned hides. Amos marched past him wrenching his arms into the sleeves of his coat as he went.

'Where are you going, sir?' Coogan called after him.

'To the gunsmiths in Artillery Row.'

Nathaniel waited for the dun carthorse pulling the brewer's dray to plod past and then he started to cross Bishopsgate. He stepped over a drunk lying in the gutter and made his way down a narrow set of rickety stairs to the Duck and Drake.

The public house, which in truth was little more than a cellar below street level, was clearly named in an earlier time when the area was pasture and the odd water fowl or two might have been seen waddling around. That rural landscape had long given way to the crumbling houses that now made up the north end of the Shoreditch rookery.

Nathaniel opened the door and stepped in. The stench of unwashed bodies mingled with tobacco, while underfoot a slippery mixture of beer, spit and sawdust coated the stone floor. The walls had once been painted white but were now a sickly yellow and speckled with beer stains as well as darker flecks that could easily have been dried blood. A couple of the men at the bar turned in his direction and gave him the once-over before returning to their drinks.

''Ello, there 'andsome,' whispered a young woman as she slipped her arm in his. She could have been no more than twenty, with a once pretty face framed by light brown hair that was fixed like an untidy bird's nest on one side of her head. There were dark smudges around her eyes and the mauve and yellow of a faint bruise on her right cheek but, compared to some in the bar, she was a beauty. She grinned, revealing a chipped front tooth. 'I'll make you feel like a king for sixpence.'

'No thanks.' He made his way past her to the bar, where he handed over a tuppence in return for a large tot of rum. The gin was cheaper, but was usually laced with sulphuric acid to give it some bite so Nathaniel thought it wiser to pay the difference. He turned to face the room, leant back and looked around.

In the far corner, just to the right of a curtain and half hidden from view, three men sat at a table. Two of them wore tight checked jackets and short crown hats set back on their heads. One chewed on a cigar while the other scraped the dirt from under his fingernails with a narrow blade. Both of them had been cheated of a neck, but by way of compensation had been given fists like shovels. Between them sat a stocky man, munching his way through a plate of boiled beef and potatoes.

Nathaniel strolled towards them.

The two bruisers stood and blocked his way.

'Wot's yer game?' asked one, shoving his face close to Nathaniel's.

'Getting 'is face cut, that's wot,' the other replied, flecks of spit escaping from his mouth.

'A word,' Nathaniel replied.

'I'll give you a word. Feck off.'

'That's two,' Nathaniel replied conversationally.

The first brute snatched at his knife. Nathaniel's hand shot out and grabbed the dirty scarf hanging around the man's neck and yanked his bullet-shaped head down. He whipped his own knife from the back of his belt and jabbed it upwards, nicking the surface of the thug's throat. The man struggled but Nathaniel held him firm. He glared at the other heavy, and said, 'One move and your chum's finished.'

The other man looked at the man still eating his dinner. 'Guv?'

The man wiped the grease from his mouth and threw down his napkin. 'Get out of the way you fecking pair of apes and let me old mate Nat through.'

Nathaniel let go of the scarf and the bully boy collided with his fellow. There were a few sniggers as the two danced backwards as they regained their footing. They shot Nathaniel another furious look and then made themselves scarce.

Nathaniel slid his knife back under his jacket. 'Hello, Boyce.'

Two bluebottles settled on the greasy smears left on the surface of Boyce's empty plate. 'You ain't forgot what I taught you, then?'

'How could I?' Nathaniel grinned.

'Did I ever tell you what a lily-livered sight you were when the lobster-backs marched you up the gangplank?

'Once or twice,' Nathaniel replied, as his first few brutal days in the penal colony flashed through his mind.

'You were lucky you were sent to number six hut. If it had been another con on the bunk above you they would have left you to take your chances, but being the soft 'arted sod I am I took pity on you.'

'And thank God you did or I doubt I'd be standing here now.'

Boyce looked him up and down. 'I did wonder 'ow you'd fair after I was shipped back, but you look well enough.'

Nathaniel glanced around. 'Are you back at your old game?'

'Among other things, but I do like to keep my hand in by picking the odd lock or two. Just for old times' sake,' Boyce replied, as he worked something out from between his front teeth with his knife.

Nathaniel's grin widened. 'So you're still an old cracksman, then?'

'The same as you're still a fecking ploughboy.'

Nathaniel took the seat opposite.

'Sally! Get us a drink,' bellowed Boyce.

The dusky barmaid lolling at the end of the bar collected a bottle and two glasses then sauntered over. As she stopped at the table her full lips spread into a broad smile showing a set of spectacularly white teeth.

'Watch yer, cock,' she said, with a London twang quite at odds with her African ancestry.

Boyce smacked her rear. 'Be a good girl and 'op it.'

She gave Nathaniel another luscious look before swaying back to the bar.

Boyce poured two generous measures of brandy. He shoved one glass across the table towards Nathaniel and raised the other. 'To us! The ploughboy and the cracksman.'

Nathaniel raised his smudgy glass. 'The ploughboy and the cracksman.' He threw his drink back, enjoying the burn of the spirit as it washed down his throat.

'You skipped off then?' Boyce asked as he poured them another.

'Aye, after I got a letter from my old parson telling me that my family were dead.'

Boyce raised his eyebrows. 'Now I am right sad to be told that, mate.' He leant across the table. 'You're going to snuff the bastard, then.' It was a statement, not a question.

'Not as such. He destroyed everything I had so I thought I'd return the compliment. He's quite the gentleman now. He owns a controlling share in the Grey Friars warehouse in St Katherine's dock. He lives in a quality house on Mile End Road and he's married with a stepdaughter. He's also a member of St George's in the East's Parish Council, governor of the St Katherine's School, and is tipped to become a city alderman. But not everyone is fooled.' Nathaniel reached into his inside pocket and pulled out the sheet of newspaper he'd peeled off the doss house wall.

'This reporter for one seems to understand Stebbins's true nature,' he said, and read the editorial to Boyce.

Boyce whistled through his teeth. 'Sharp stuff. You're not thinking of blowing your cover and talking to this Smyth wotnot are you? Just 'cos he spouts on a bit about Stebbins don't mean he won't shop you to the peelers if you turn up on his doorstep.'

'I know, I know,' Nathaniel replied, carefully refolding the sheet of paper. 'But he *could* be an ally. I'll check him out – and his newspaper – before I decide if it's worth the risk. In the meantime I need to find out everything I can about Stebbins, especially anything he doesn't tell his wife or the vicar about.'

Boyce rubbed his none-too-clean hands together. 'Just leave it to me, Nat, me boy. I'll find out what you want to know right down to how often he wipes his arse!'

Amos rolled his head sideward and studied the profile of his sleeping wife. She lay on her back with her mouth open and the frothy lace of her nightcap encircling her face. With each breath her expansive bosom rose and fell under the crocheted coverlet, while a faint whistle cut through the silence of the bedroom. Her leg had sprawled against his and he pushed it away with his foot. He shuffled sideways to increase the space between them. She muttered at his touch but didn't wake.

He sighed and stared up at the canopy. The clock in the hallway below struck two and Amos wondered if he would still be wide awake when it struck four. The image of Nathaniel Tate outside Maguire's yard floated into his mind and a cold hand clutched at his innards. Even a full bottle of brandy hadn't settled his churning stomach, nor had his favourite dish of roast pork with bubbled crackling, which remained untouched on his plate. How could he eat, think or sleep when his very life was in peril?

It wasn't his fault that Tate's family had died. It happened all the time – it was the way of things. As the prayer book so rightly said, 'in the midst of life we are in death'.

Of course, Marjorie could have stayed in her little home had Tate not been transported to the other side of the world, but then why didn't her father take her in? If Tate wanted to reckon with anyone he ought to be seeking out her father for his unchristian neglect.

He simply *had* to fabricate the evidence that convicted Nathaniel. *If I'd been caught with the quarterly takings I wouldn't be the successful business man I am now. And where would St George's church be without my generous donations?*

When it was announced from the pulpit that the lead from the church roof had been stolen did he count the cost? No. He had risen to his feet and, before the whole congregation, and selflessly pledged to replace it. And there wouldn't be a Sunday school tea each year without his munificent provision. There had been a whisper that the parish council were considering putting up a plaque of appreciation. Not that he was concerned with the praise of men, of course. Goodness was it's own reward.

Amos took a deep breath and tried to calm the almost paralysing fear that had gripped him since the police had visited his office that afternoon.

Cecily turned away from him and farted; the clock in the hall chimed out the half hour. Amos threw off the covers and swung his legs out of bed. He put on his slippers and padded across the room to use the commode behind the screen in the corner. As he stood relieving his aching bladder he glanced through the window at the shadowy doorways and murky passageways. What if Tate already knew where he lived and was just biding his time before striking? Even with his new percussion pistol Amos knew he'd be dead before he could cock it. The claw grasping his gut tightened and panic rose up in his chest again. He slammed the commode lid down.

Before he climbed back into bed he sank on his knees and looked up at the Cross above the headboard. He put his elbows on the coverlet and clasped his hands together. God knew he wasn't a bad man. And of course he should have kept the eight and ninth commandments, but everyone knew that those whom God had chosen for a special purpose were tested the most. The Bible was full of such examples. Abraham who lied to secure land; Jacob who deceived his father and cheated his brother Esau out of his inheritance; Gideon, who'd strayed off the path with his love of gold. And what about King David? He was forever falling off the straight and narrow.

It was unfortunate that he'd been forced to frame Tate, but he was convinced that the harshness of the penal colonies was much exaggerated. Besides, Tate was of yeoman stock and used to a more basic existence.

Cecily rolled over onto one elbow. 'Husband, are you unwell?'

'No, my dear, just the spirit of God stirring me from my slumber.'

'Would you like me to pray with you?'

'I think I must commune with God in solitude. You go back to sleep.'

Cecily lay down again and within a few moments her regular breathing told Amos she had nodded off.

Amos repositioned his elbows and fixed his eyes on the Cross.

It was clear that God was testing his resolve by sending Nathaniel Tate just as he was grappling with the problem of the Maguire woman. But he, Amos Stebbins, was one chosen for greater things. As the old hymn said, 'God moves in a mysterious way, his wonders to perform,' and who was he to question the Almighty's plan ...

Chapter Seven

Mattie held the inventory in one hand and shoved a pencil behind her ear as she opened the door to the office. A large wagon from Morris & Co was undertaking the tricky manoeuvre of backing into the yard. Bill stood behind the rig and signalled to the driver, whose mate, Bert, held the reins of the lead horse to coax it backwards, all the while blocking the street. The pedestrians waited impatiently, occasionally shouting at the driver to get a move on. Freddie was nowhere to be seen, as usual, and Mattie's heart sank when she saw that Jock was today's driver. The bull-headed Scotsman was one of Morris's top men and, to give him his due, he could turn a team of horses and a five-tonne coal wagon on a sixpence but he was better known for his capacity to start a fight in an empty field.

Mattie already had a fuzzy headache and thirty minutes with Jock Murray would be guaranteed to double it. Brian had fidgeted most of the night and kept her awake, and when she'd finally managed to drift off, Katie got up and dropped her enamel chamber pot, which clattered loudly down the stairs. On top of all this, Queenie was having one of her musical days – singing off key and non-stop all morning.

Squaring her shoulders, Mattie rested her free hand on the banister and made her way downstairs. As she reached the bottom step, Jock spotted her from his platform on the top of the rig. 'Oi, oi! Here comes my little darling. Would you mind telling your men to get a fecking move on, ducks. I ain't got all day.'

Mattie fixed him with an steady stare. 'If you want it done faster, why don't you get down and give them a hand.'

Jock hawked and spat on the ground, just missing her feet. 'Got to keep the horses in check,' he said, showing her the limp reins. 'Where's that old windbag who works here?'

'Watch your mouth, Jock. Eli's not well.'

She'd visited Eli the day before and taken him some soup. He looked well enough sitting by the fireside in his daughter's kitchen but, although all his other functions had returned, his left arm still hung lifeless by his side. She was relieved to see Eli on the road to recovery and silently wished him back at work. Number one cart had been idle for two weeks now and she was losing customers to Huggins.

Jock rolled his eyes. 'Ach, pity, 'cause he seems to be the only one around here who knows what 'e's fecking doing.'

He jumped down from the rig and ambled over. He couldn't have been more than a few inches taller than Mattie, but he was brawny so he looked shorter and gave the impression of being as wide as he was tall. He stopped much too close to her, as he always did, but Mattie forced herself to stay put. He grinned, showing a set of even, but heavily tobacco-stained teeth. Like all the men who worked with coal Jock had a fine dusting all over his face, clothes and hair. An indolent look crept into his eyes as they ran slowly over her breasts before coming to rest on the bare flesh above her neckline.

'Where do you want me to put *it*?' he asked, shoving his hands in his pockets.

Ignoring her heart crashing in her chest, Mattie gave him her iciest look. 'As close to the old stock as possible. As you always do.'

Jock smirked. 'You don't mind me asking, like, because, as many a pretty girl hereabouts will tell you, I'm eager to please.' He flapped the front of his corduroy trousers, sending coal dust fluttered down.

Mattie suppressed a shudder. 'Why don't you just unload?' she said wearily.

His eyes ran boldly over her again. 'I'd love to.' He looked down at her chest again. 'Any time.'

Mattie turned her back on Jock, who gave a low laugh. Trying to ignore the fact that his eyes were probably glued to her rear, Mattie walked around to the back of the rig where Billy was helping offload the coal.

She tilted her head to one side and studied the delivery. Lifting her skirt clear of the sooty dust beneath her feet she stepped onto the newly formed mountain. It skidded a little. She got her balance and then picked up a lump. She turned it over in her hand, scratched the surface and then sniffed it.

'Stop!' she shouted. The two men ceased shovelling. 'This is sub-bit and I ordered black-bit.'

Bert took the nugget of coal and scratched and sniffed it as she had. 'You're right, Missis,' he said. 'Hey, Jock!'

Jock had climbed back on the rig and was lounging across his seat with his feet up on the side. He glanced around. 'I'm having a smoke,' he shouted holding up a tatty roll of paper.

Bert waved the piece of coal. 'It's the wrong sort.'

Jock drew theatrically on the twisted butt then flicked it in a large arc away from him. He jumped down and snatched the coal from his mate's hand. 'What's the poxy problem?'

'This is sub-bit,' Mattie said. 'I ordered black.'

Jock tossed the chunk in his hand back on the pile. 'Well, I've unloaded it now.'

Mattie set her mouth into a firm line. 'Well now, so you have. But I ordered black-bit and that's what I expect to be delivered.'

Jock's eyes narrowed and any trace of congeniality vanished. 'Listen, dearie. I ain't fecking shovelling it up again 'cause you fecking say so.' He waved at the hillock of shiny rocks. 'Just mix it with the black you've got left and no one will be any the wiser.'

'I'm not going to ruin my reputation because of your mistake. Start loading it back on.'

Jock stepped in front of her. 'Leave it be,' he growled at the men behind her without taking his eyes from her face.

They did.

He loomed over her and despite her resolve, Mattie took a step back.

'Now you listen to me, sweet'art,' he said in a low voice. 'You ordered fecking coal and coal is what you've got. If you want the same next week and the week after you had better get out of my way, sign my chit and fecking shut up.'

Rage and impotency twisted together in Mattie's stomach as she stared up into Jock's hard-bitten expression. She didn't have to look at the order sheet to know that she would be billed for the higher-grade coal. With one wagon idle and the seasonal demand for the sub-bit heating coal dropping away, the yard was barely making enough to pay the wages and put food on the table. If she was bullied into paying for coal she couldn't sell, the business wouldn't last the month.

A sense of huge unfairness at her situation threatened to bring tears to her eyes. She pushed the thought aside. Things were as they were and crying about them wouldn't change that.

She clenched her fists and took a step forward. 'Now you listen to me, Jock Mur—'

A shadow fell between them.

Mattie turned and saw a powerfully built man, who she judged to be all of six feet tall and with the breadth to match. His black hair had been tightly cut to frame his broad forehead and strong cheekbones. He had a beard, like almost every other man but, whereas the fashion was for untrimmed and bushy, his was scraped clean on his cheeks and throat and then followed the blunt lines of his jaw. His wide, authoritative stance had the quality of a coiled spring.

His eyes flicked over her face and then looked at Jock.

'I don't like hearing a woman spoken to in that fashion,' he said, in a mellow voice with a hint of a country accent. 'I'd advise you to apologise.'

A belligerent expression screwed up Jock's unshaven face. 'Who the feck are you?'

'Someone you don't want to cross,' replied the newcomer.

Bert threw down the sack he was holding and rolling up his sleeves, started towards them. Billy turned the peak of his cap to the back and did the same.

'See 'im here?' Jock said to his mate as he came to stand alongside. ''E thinks he can order me around.'

Bert laughed nervously as he eyed the man challenging his mate. Billy stopped next to Mattie and stood with his feet apart and his arms folded across his chest.

Jock stepped forward. 'It appears this fella has a problem with me. So what are you going to do about it?'

Nathaniel Tate's eyes narrowed and he stepped forward also. 'Knock you all around this yard so even your mother wouldn't recognise you. Now, apologise,' he barked, as the men in the yard crowded around.

'You can try,' bellowed the driver.

He shifted his weight then punched out with his left. Nathaniel sidestepped and caught his fist mid-air, forcing it back. The tension in Jock's arm turned to pain as Nathaniel threatened to snap his wrist. Nathaniel twisted his grip, side-stepped and shoved the man's arm up his back then wedged his free arm under his stubbly chin.

'I said, apologise,' he repeated, as the driver struggled against his grip.

The stale odour of sweat and beer wafted up as Jock Murray fought Nathaniel's headlock.

'I'm fe—' Nathaniel tightened his hold. 'I'm ... sorry ... missus,' he forced out.

Nathaniel released him and the driver staggered away with his hands at his throat.

'Now, unless you want me to go around to your master and tell him you're after cheating a customer, I suggest you pick up that shovel,' Nathaniel nodded at the discarded spade. 'And start using it.'

The driver flexed his twisted arm for a second then snatched up the shovel. 'You 'eard,' he growled at Bert, kicking a jagged lump of coal and sending it bouncing across the cobbles. 'Get this lot back on the fecking wagon.'

Nathaniel picked up his hat, which had fallen off in the tussle and turned to look at Mattie.

Today her ebony hair was hidden under a red-and-blue scarf but several tendrils had escaped, curling around her oval face and drawing attention to her high cheekbones and small square chin. The soft blush on her cheeks heightened her beauty.

'Thank you for your help. You've performed a miracle in making Jock apologise but I don't think the Virgin herself could stop him swearing. But thank you Mr ...?'

'Archer. Jack Archer,' he said, combining his middle and his mother's maiden name.

'I'm Mrs Maguire of Maguire & Son's.' She nodded towards the open gates with the red and gold lettering painted across them.

'Well, I'm pleased to have been of service to you, Mrs Maguire.'

'You're not from around here, are you, Mr Archer?'

'How can you tell?'

'The way you talk. Country-like.'

'You must have an ear for such things, Mrs Maguire,' he said. He dusted the coal specks from his hat. 'I should be on my way.'

'Of course,' she said. 'And thank you once again for stepping in as you did.'

'I'm glad I was passing. I'm sure the brute wouldn't have taken such liberties if your husband had been in the yard,' he added, strangely annoyed that a man should leave his wife to face such a foul-mouthed rogue alone.

'I'm sure he wouldn't have, but my husband died three years ago,' she said softly.

'I am sorry,' Nathaniel replied, knowing such words were no more use than a solitary raindrop to quench a fire.

'Ah, well. Sure, I'm not the only one, ' she told him, then put on a bright smile. 'I'm grand.'

'Except when you have to deal with the likes of him.'

'And having a driver off sick.' She nodded at the idle cart. 'And a child who never sits still. And,' she turned her face to the sky and her headscarf slipped back to reveal the rich lustre of her hair. 'Having the sun blazing in the sky fit to melt yer so no one has need of coal.'

She laughed a low throaty laugh that stirred something in Nathaniel that he'd almost forgotten was there. When she'd first turned and looked at him, he'd thought that she really was pretty but now, with the sun bathing her face in a warm glow, he saw he was mistaken. She wasn't pretty at all, she was beautiful.

Stebbins! He reminded himself.

'And doing all the orders and accounts,' he added, in what he hoped was a conversational tone.

She laughed again. 'I certainly wish I'd taken more notice of arithmetic at school, that's for sure.'

'I really must be on my way,' he said, making no move to do so. 'I heard there was a job going at Crane Wharf.'

'You're too late for a morning ticket, so you'll only earn half a day's money – even if you can get something this afternoon.' A thoughtful expression settled on her face. 'I hope you'll forgive me being bold, Mr Archer, but you're obviously new to such things. The gate callers, who allocate work tickets, give it to their regulars who stand them a pint or two in the hiring pubs. It might be days before you get the nod. You've done me a service and I'd be obliged if you'd allow me the chance to do the same for you.' She glanced towards the empty cart. 'My driver Eli is sick, and if you're not afraid of hard graft you could take his round, just for a week or two. The first delivery has to be out by seven and in the afternoon by two, but you'd be finished as soon as that's done and you've sorted your rig for the morning. It's heavy work but I pay fifteen shillings a week and a hot midday meal.'

Nathaniel was taken aback. He'd been looking for money in hand, not permanent work, but taking Mrs Maguire up on her offer would help him find out about Stebbins. But what if he were a regular visitor? If Amos spotted him he'd find himself sailing back to Botany Bay with an additional seven years on top of the original sentence. Still, if he kept his wits about him, it would be worth the risk.

'Fifteen shillings and home cooking,' he said. 'How could I refuse?'

Cecily Stebbins shifted in her seat to ease the pinch of her corset as her husband Amos took his place at the brass spread-eagle lectern. He opened the large, gilt-edged church Bible and Cecily smiled at him encouragingly. Naturally, as he was about to read the words of God himself, Amos didn't respond. He cleared his throat. 'The Lesson for today is taken from the second book of Kings, chapter nine, starting at verse thirty.' His eyes narrowed and his gaze ran slowly over the congregation. 'The Lord's judgment on Jezebel.'

A little thrill of anticipation ran through Cecily. Amos always made the back of her neck tingle when he read from the Old Testament. When his measured tones told of how God's wrath slaughtered unbelievers and cast them down the fiery pit, you could almost smell the burning.

Her eight-year old daughter, Ruth, shifted beside her and Cecily looked at her sharply. Ruth was the daughter of her brief first marriage to Mr Oliver, who had unwisely stepped out in front of an omnibus travelling at full speed. He left the bulk of his estate to his daughter in trust. Cecily could have lived comfortably enough on her two-hundred pounds-a-year widow's portion but had decided to return to her father's house.

Ruth lowered her head, setting her ringlets jigging against her bonnet rim and studied her gloved hands. With her mid-brown hair, broad forehead and deep-set brown eyes, Ruth was so very like her late father. She was a pretty child with a sweet nature, but it was a pity she hadn't inherited Cecily's own honey-coloured locks and blue eyes to give her the 'English Rose' look, as the *World of Fashion* called it, because it was considered a mark of fine breeding.

It was through her dearest departed papa, Jonathan Delahay, that Cecily had met Amos. He had just come to town from Essex and had rented a small office next door to her father's clockmaking shop. As a widow just the wrong side of thirty, and with a figure that a kind soul would describe as Rubenesque, Cecily had resigned herself to a life alone, but, Amos had declared his admiration for her within a few weeks and she became his wife three months to the day after first setting eyes on him.

As Amos's forbidding tones described the wantonness of the 'harlot queen of Israel', Cecily's eyes fixed on her husband's thickset hands. Under the expensive Chinese-blue silk of her new gown, her shoulders slumped. How long had it been since they'd had relations? During their spring visit to Brighton four months ago ... and before that? Just after twelfth night, if she recalled the occasion correctly. A twist of unhappiness caught in Cecily's throat. How she longed for him to reach for her, hold her and cherish her instead of merely extinguishing the lamp and rolling over to sleep.

She sat bolt upright and concentrated on the ornate crucifix on the altar. *Shame on you, Cecily Ruth Stebbins, for allowing such physical thoughts to creep into your mind. And in church of all places!*

Amos was the most considerate of husbands and she should be grateful that, with deference to her sensibilities, he subdued his base urges to spare her. What wife could ask for more? *But is it so wrong to crave a little bit of loving now and then*, a small voice in the back of her head replied.

'Here endeth the lesson,' Amos boomed out.

Only the sound of his feet marching across the stone floor broke the silence. He took his seat on the other side of Ruth and the service continued. A hymn, the briefest of sermons, and then the congregation rose to their feet. With the promise of Sunday dinner awaiting them, they sang the final chorus.

Cecily picked up her gloves and beaded bag. 'Your reading of the passage was masterful as always, Mr Stebbins.'

'Thank you.' He looked beyond her.

Cecily turned to see what had caught her husband's attention and saw Mattie Maguire in the pew across the way from them.

As a good Anglican she should disapprove of Mattie, who was not only a Roman Catholic but Irish to boot. But she couldn't help but admire her, running the coal yard, raising her son, and caring for her afflicted mother-in-law patiently – even bringing her to church every Sunday so that the poor woman could draw comfort from God's word. Added to which there had never been a whiff of scandal attached to her, which is more than could be said for some of the widows she met as a pastoral visitor for the League of Hallowed Homes.

Today, like every other Sunday, Mattie was dressed in her best twill gown and matching jacket edged with worn braid trim. It had seen better days but it had a few more years in it before it was ready to be sold on to the rag trader. Her bonnet sat squarely on ebony hair but, unlike Cecily's own couture creation, it had a modest brim, allowing her face to be clearly visible. Cecily gave her husband a questioning look.

'I was just pondering what an example of forbearance Mrs Maguire is in her care of poor Queenie,' he told her, as they watched Mattie persuading old Mrs Maguire to put her bonnet on the correct way. 'Perhaps we should give her a word of encouragement.' He offered Cecily his arm.

Cecily curled her hand around her husband's arm. 'You are, as ever, so mindful of others,' she said, inclining her head and setting her hat feathers bobbing.

Amos didn't contradict her. With Ruth following, they strolled over.

'Good morning, Mrs Maguire,' Cecily said.

'And to yourselves, Mrs Stebbins. Mr Stebbins. And Miss Oliver.' She smiled at Ruth who smiled back. 'The vicar was in fine form this morning, wasn't he?'

'Indeed,' Cecily replied. She turned to Queenie. 'And did you enjoy the service, Mrs Maguire?'

Queenie's work-worn face creased into a rapturous grin. 'I liked the singing. My son's in the choir. Did you see him?'

'Of course we did,' Cecily replied. 'Standing at the back, wasn't he?'

Queenie nodded. 'That's right. You can't miss him.'

'And how are you today, Mrs Maguire?' Amos asked the old woman, articulating his words slowly as one would to a small child. 'When I saw your daughter-in-law on Wednesday at the yard she said you were a little unwell. Are you any better?'

From the other side of the church the choirboys burst from the vestry. They had changed from their long blue gowns back into their tatty trousers and grubby shirts.

'I'll go and fetch Brian,' Queenie said, as she scurried over to the boys on the chancery steps.

'I am so sorry,' Mattie said apologetically. 'If you'll excuse me I ought to follow her ... just in case.'

Amos waved her apology aside. 'Please, don't give it another thought.'

'Thank you,' said Mattie. 'And thank you again for taking the time to call at the yard this week.'

She hurried after her mother-in-law.

Cecily stared at her husband. 'You didn't mention that you visited Mrs Maguire this week, my dear.'

Amos looked surprised. 'I'm sure I did, my love.'

'I don't think you did, husband.'

Amos took her hand and wrapped it around his arm. 'Well, if I didn't it was because as soon as I'm home the heavy burdens of business fade from my mind.'

'So, you had business with Mrs Maguire?'

'Of course. Why else would I call?' His eyes flickered past her. 'Oh, I've just spotted Mr Dunn. Will you excuse me for a moment, my dear, while I have a quick word with him. I'll meet you and Ruth outside.'

Cecily watched him go, then looked back at Mattie, who was walking out of the church with her arm looped in Queenie's. As she watched them head for the door a feeling of uneasiness crept up Cecily's spine. Even her second-hand clothes didn't disguise the fact that Mattie Maguire was a handsome woman, with generous curves and a surprisingly slender waist. She herself had to grip the bed post each morning while her maid laced her corset. Perhaps she should cancel her weekly order of chocolates from Hewett's in Regent Street. But what if it was too late and Amos had already . . .?

Cecily laughed.

'What is it Mama?' asked Ruth as she took her mother's hand.

'Oh, just something very amusing crossed my mind. Let's go out into the sun to wait for Mr Stebbins.'

Still smiling Cecily walked her daughter out of the church. Yes, how funny. It was unimaginable that her husband, Amos Stebbins, churchwarden, guardian of the Wapping Workhouse and St Katherine's School and pillar of the local community would ever transgress any of God's laws, especially with the act of adultery.

Chapter Eight

Boyce placed his hands on the polished surface of the table and stared blankly across at the man opposite. 'What'd you say then?'

Aaron Ishovich, or Russian Harry, as he was know hereabouts, stared back, the ringlets on either side of his face trembling ever so slightly.

'A five shillings a dozen?' he replied stroking his long beard.

Boyce's eyes narrowed. 'Seven and a tanner or I'll offer them to Esther.' A small tic started in the corner of the pawnbroker's left eye. 'It's my last offer,' Boyce added, stroking the pair of kid gloves on the table between them.

The two men stared eyeball to eyeball for a moment or two then Aaron's shoulders relaxed. 'Done.'

Boyce jumped up and spat on his hand. 'Put it there.'

Aaron Ishovich rose to his feet and they shook on the deal.

The pawnbroker picked up his felt hat. 'You're a thief you know.' He said it without rancour.

Boyce grinned. 'My boys'll deliver them on Friday,' he said wiping the damp off on his palm down his trousers. 'Show Mr Ishovich out.'

One of his men held back the threadbare curtain to the passage leading to the back door.

Boyce smacked his lips together. 'All that haggling's dried me out.'

He went to the back of the pub and into the Duck's main bar. It was only half full but then Spitalfields market wouldn't have closed yet. The barmaid slid a drink across the bar to him and he spotted Nathaniel sitting in a quiet corner.

Nathaniel had changed so much from the young man whom he'd been chained to for six weeks in the bilge of the ship, that Boyce reckoned his own mother would have had trouble recognizing him. When he'd first met Nathaniel the law had just plucked him from the comfortable life of a country clerk and thrown him into a world he never dreamed existed and hadn't been raised to deal with. But by Christ he'd learnt. And fast. He'd learnt to eat his dry ship tack as soon as he had it in his hand or have it filched off him. He learnt to see everything and tell nothing, to look for an angle in any situation, stand by a mate and take the lash without a murmur.

Boyce had been drawn to him from the moment they were chained together in that stinking hold. He'd worried about it at first – was he going a bit Nancy? – but then one day as they were trudging around on deck on their hour's exercise, Nathaniel laughed at something and in an instant Boyce understood.

Jem! That's why he'd taken to Nathaniel – because he reminded him of his elder brother. Jem had sheltered him and fed him when he was just a snotty-nosed kid and taught him how to survive. It was Jem who schooled him to slip a purse out of a pocket or a watch from a chain with a feather-light touch. He'd taught him the way to raise an unlocked window without a squeak and what to take from a jewellery box and what to leave behind.

He'd been dead almost twenty years now. Boyce had nursed him as best he could on the bare floor of the attic in Golden Lane. He'd rubbed his brother's icy hands to get some blood in them and forced brandy between his chattering teeth to ease his pain. But Boyce had been but a lad, less than a dozen years old, and could do nothing except watch helplessly as Jem coughed up his lungs and died.

But for all his thievery Jem was honest, straight. If he gave his word he'd never go back on it, and if he was your pal then he'd stand by you in the face of the Devil. Nathaniel was just the same. On more than a handful of occasions Nathaniel's quick wits and courage had saved Boyce's life. And for that and for Jem, Boyce was going to see him right as far as the bastard who'd sent him sailing to Australia was concerned.

Nathaniel looked up as Boyce approached.

'Sally! Bring us another bottle,' he shouted as he took the chair opposite Nathaniel. 'Wot you see and wot you know?'

'Quite a bit since I left this morning. And,' Nathaniel leant forward. 'I've got a bit of a problem.'

The bar placed the new bottle on the table and blew Nathaniel his customary kiss.

'What sort of problem?' Boyce asked.

'I've taken a job.'

'What! Are you out of your mind?'

'Ha! Probably. I went back to the coal yard where I saw Stebbins last week and the owner, Mrs Maguire, was having trouble with a delivery driver. I stepped in and she offered me a job.'

'And you took it.'

'Well, yes. She knows Stebbins and I thought—'

'She's a looker, then.' Boyce grinned.

'That's *not* why I took the job.'

'Sure, you never,' Boyce replied, taking a mouthful of drink. 'Look mate. See Susy over there.' He indicated a slim young woman whose red hair was piled incredibly high in contrast to her indecently low neckline. 'She's clean – only been on the hook for a month – and she's a country girl, too. Why don't you take her upstairs and when you're done you can have a chat about sheep or fields or whatever the feck yokels talk about. It'll help you get some right thinking about this job.'

Nathaniel laughed. 'You're a daft old bugger, Boyce. But I'm serious about working at Maguire's.'

Boyce topped up their drinks. 'Have you lost all your marbles? How can you drive a cart around the streets all day when there's a fecking wanted poster outside every nick from Houndsditch to Bow with your name and description plastered all over it? Someone's bound to recognise you. If you're brainless enough to take that job you might as well march into one of Old Robert's shops and turn yourself in.'

Nathaniel shook his head. 'The description on that poster could fit half a dozen men in this bar. And if Maguire's were a bakers or grocers I'd agree with you but it's a *coal yard*. Get it? All the deliverymen wear split sack over their heads and they're so black from the dust I doubt I'd recognise myself in a mirror. I'm only standing in for Mrs Maguire's man, who's injured, so I won't be there more than a week or two at the most.'

Boyce sucked his gums. 'I don't know. I suppose if you trim your hair short so it don't curl and keep the beard you might get away with it for a bit. But it's still chancey. What are you going to say when people ask you who you are?'

'That's where you come in, Boyce, my old mate.' A conspiratorial smile spread across Nathaniel's face. 'I need you to find me some kith and kin.'

Reverend Garrett looked around at the members of St George's parish council and cleared his throat. 'All those in favour of Mr Stebbins's proposal that we send a letter to Superintendent Jackson urging him to take action—'

'Urging him in the *strongest* terms,' interjected Amos.

'Urging him in the *strongest* terms,' the clergyman corrected himself, irritation flitting across his face. 'To take action against the increasing numbers of women soliciting along the Highway, say aye.'

'Aye,' replied the dozen men around the table.

Amos was pleased that yet again his eloquence had carried the day. 'Thank you, gentlemen. I'll write to Superintendent Jackson first thing in the morning.'

'No, thank *you*, Mr Stebbins, for taking it upon yourself to remind the police of their duty in this matter,' said Mr Harris the verger. Several heads nodded in agreement and Amos basked in their approval. 'Having such women loitering on every street corner is a disgrace. It attracts the lowest sorts into the area and now respectable women are being accosted – and in broad daylight, too! Why, only last week my wife was importuned by three sailors.'

'Disgraceful!' exclaimed Dunn the choirmaster.

'They must have been very drunk to accost *your* wife,' Amos said, imagining Letty Harris, whose face could scare a gargoyle, fighting off a pack of marauding sailors.

'Sir, my wife is a jewel among women.'

Amos placed his hand over his heart. 'Mr Harris, you mistake my meaning. I mean, that these ruffians must have been very drunk indeed not to see what a paragon of respectability your wife is.'

'Just so, Mr Stebbins.'

'Well, gentlemen.' Mr Garrett straightened the set of papers in front of him. 'If there is not any other business?' The men of St George's parish council shook their heads. 'Then I have nothing further other than to thank Mr Stebbins for taking this matter up on our behalf, and again to thank him for his generous pledge of seventy pounds for our new altar frontal and church linens ...' a dozen pairs of eyes looked at Amos with approval. 'And I declare this meeting closed. If we could just bow our heads. Almighty and everlasting ...'

With the committee's attention elsewhere and his hands concealed from view, Amos slipped his fob watch from his pocket and flipped it open.

Nine-thirty! And he knew that Mr Dunn would want to speak to him before they left.

Then he remembered. It was the first Wednesday and Cecily was hosting the League of Hallowed Homes monthly Bible study and prayer meeting. If the parish council could argue the back leg off a donkey for endless hours, their wives could trump them, so a later finish wouldn't interfere with his plans. Even if he returned home at midnight Cecily wouldn't be concerned as he often remained into the small hours discussing pressing church matters with the vicar, or so she believed.

Of course, he shouldn't have offered to pay for the new church fabrics. The deeds to Maguire's yard still eluded him and Fallon at the City & County was squeezing his credit again. But a man in his position had to set the example of selfless giving. More importantly, if there was even a hint that his finances weren't as sound as he professed them to be he could lose the investors he'd been cultivating to set up Wapping & Stratford.

Why hadn't Maguire's gone under? Had it not been for the possibility of Nathaniel Tate lurking in shadows waiting for his chance to jump him, he would have gone to the yard and pressed Mattie harder to sell but, even so, she surely couldn't possibly go on for much longer ...

'Amen,' concluded Mr Garrett.

'Amen,' replied Amos, as he stood up from the table. The committee broke into small groups as they collected themselves together before heading home. Mr Dunn caught his attention and skirted around the table towards him.

'Thank you for your support about the letter, Dunn,' Amos said, as the choirmaster reached him.

'Think nothing of it. Now about the Wapping and St—'

'Shh!' Amos took his arm and pulled him to the side. 'Not here.'

'Well, let's stroll to the Hoop, we can talk there without fear of being overheard,' Dunn replied.

Amos pulled out his watch again. 'Not tonight.' He snapped it shut and slid it back in his pocket. 'Meet me in the church on Friday. Three o'clock. We'll talk then.' He tapped the side of his nose. 'Discretion, Dunn. Discretion.'

Collecting his hat, coat and walking stick from the stand, Amos took his leave of his fellow vestrymen, wished the vicar a restful night and left the church as the clock struck the three-quarters of the hour. He sent up a prayer of thanks when an empty cab rolled up to the church gates just as he walked out of them, and within minutes he was heading north.

He sat back, lit a cigar, and lost himself in his thoughts as the cab rolled through the City and on to the leafy suburb of Islington. After half an hour or so the driver turned into a quiet street.

Amos knocked his cane on the roof. 'This will do,' he called.

The cab pulled to a halt. Amos stepped out, tilted his tall silk hat over his eyes, and handed the half-crown coin to the driver without glancing up. London cabbies knew better than to look too closely at a gentleman stopping off at certain establishments but Amos couldn't be too careful.

'What time, guv?' he asked from the back of his rig.

'Just after midnight,' Amos replied, tucking up his collar. 'And wait here.'

The whip cracked and the cab moved off. Amos stepped back into the shadows and looked both ways. Satisfied that he was indeed alone, he turned and walked briskly to the white steps of the last house in the road, but before he could use the lion's head knocker the door opened.

Amos stepped in, unhooked his cloak and removed his hat. He handed them to a dark suited servant who bowed respectfully and kept her eyes averted. She indicated a side room and said, 'If you would come this way, sir, I will inform the mistress you have arrived.'

He followed the servant into Madame La Verne's sumptuously furnished parlour. French style chairs and sofas were dotted around the room, and a large gilt mirror hung above the fireplace. Amos stood in front of the fire with his back to the empty hearth, his eyes resting on the large picture opposite, which depicted the rape of the Sabine women. The door opened and Madame La Verne swept in. Her pale blonde hair was secured with a spray of red ostrich feathers and her breasts were tightly laced and squeezed into two creamy mounds above the top of her evening gown. She gave him the widest of smiles.

'My dear Monsieur S,' she said, with only the faintest trace of London twang, and crossed the floor to greet him, her peacock-coloured silk skirt rustling as she glided across the floor. She held out her hands and he took them.

'Madame,' he said pressing his lips on her gloved fingers.

She gave him a coy smile. 'I 'ave such a delight for you tonight, Monsieur.'

A tingle of excitement ran down Amos's spine, and he adjusted the front of his trousers. Madame's eyes followed his hand. 'I can see you are eager,' she said, 'and I know you will not be disappointed when you see the little *bonbon*.' She crooked her finger. 'Shall we go to the green room?'

She beckoned him into the hall and up the stairs to a bedroom. Like all the other rooms in the house it was lavishly furnished, with an old fashioned four-poster bed covered in a shiny satin bedspread. The walls were painted in soothing pastel stripes and there was a large floor-to-ceiling mirror fixed to the wall on the right side of the bed.

Madame La Verne clapped her hands lightly and a little girl sitting at the dressing table stood up obediently.

Amos' mouth dropped open. Her wide blue eyes were set in a heart-shaped face and there was a pretty flush on her soft cheeks, which highlighted the deeper tone of her rosy mouth. Most of her fair hair had been tied with a ribbon on the top of her head, but several strands curled over her shoulders. The sleeveless muslin garment she wore was almost transparent and allowed Amos to see the shape of her slender body, budding with the first hint of maturity.

Madame La Verne pushed the girl forward. 'Say hello, Daisy.'

A smile crossed Amos's lips. They were always named after flowers.

The young girl's eyes darted up to the woman beside her. Madame gave her a tight-lipped look and Daisy took two steps forward.

''Ello, Mister,' she whispered, with a warble in her voice.

Now that she stood within an arm's length of him, he could see the rapid pulse at the base of her neck. He reached out and ran his finger around her jaw and chin, enjoying the softness of her tender skin. Daisy started to tremble. He loved it when they did that.

'Is she not adorable?' Madame asked. 'And quite untouched.'

Amos trailed his finger down the child's neck and across her bare shoulders.

'She looks very young.'

A simpering expression spread across Madame's face. 'She's slow in maturing.'

Girls like Daisy, born and bred in the rookeries, lived a feral, half-starved existence and learnt the ways of men very early in their lives. Daisy was fortunate to have been taken up by Madame – well, her mother was, at least. The price of her virginity would probably feed the rest of the family for a month or two.

'The usual compensation?' he asked, studying Daisy's young lips.

'I thought two guineas extra, perhaps,' Madame answered, her face a picture of professionalism. 'Slow maturing and untouched. A rare combination, don't you think, Mr S?'

Amos's gaze ran over Daisy's fresh young face. The child raised her eyes and gazed back up at him. Her lips parted. Amos shifted his position.

'Very well,' he said, taking the little girl's hand and drawing her to him.

Madame bowed and silently left the room.

'Why don't you sit here?' Amos patted the top of his thighs.

She climbed on to his lap. Her small frame started to quiver and Amos petted her shoulder, enjoying the contrast of the delicate bones of her arm with his large hand.

'There there, sweetheart, you like that, don't you?'

She nodded. Amos pulled her closer and kissed her cheek. She gave him a little smile.

'That's better,' he said, kissing her again but on the lips this time. 'Now, why don't you call me, Papa?'

Chapter Nine

'Thank you,' Mattie said, taking the plate with a wedge of ginger cake on it from Josie and setting it beside her tea cup.

Now that Brian had given up his afternoon sleep, Mattie had resumed visiting Josie every Tuesday as she used to. Sarah was in the kitchen finishing the weekly washing and keeping an eye on the children, who were playing in the back garden. This was the only hour the two friends could chat without having to wipe noses and break up squabbles. Freddie had dropped Mattie off as usual, and it was the fact that he'd spent the whole journey telling her how the colour of her gown suited her, how much he enjoyed having a 'pretty gal' beside him, and generally sitting far too close for Mattie's comfort, that she'd finally decided to mention his peculiar behaviour to her best friend.

'So what exactly is Freddie doing?' Josie asked, cutting herself a slice.

'It's a bit difficult to say.' Mattie wondered just how best to explain. 'Thinking back, it started just after Eli became ill. I have to say at first I thought I was just imagining it. But when he'd called me darling for the third time in a week I—'

'He called you darling!'

'And sweetheart and love.'

'That's a bit of a liberty, isn't it? I know he's family, but even so. I hope you told him.'

She hadn't. What could she say? Stop being nice? And if she accused him of flirting with her and he denied it she would blush to the roots of her hair.

'You know what he's like, Josie. You're the one who called him Flash Freddie. It's what he is. Half the time I don't think he knows he's doing it, giving women the eye, I mean. And really I can't complain too much about his cheeky chatter because it's brought me at least a dozen customers, so I just ignore it. But then I noticed that he kept . . .' the corners of her lips twitched.

Josie eyes twinkled. 'What?'

Mattie laughed. 'He sort of keeps looking at me like this.' She half-closed her eyes, raised one eyebrow and gave her friend a flirtatious look.

'No!' Josie chuckled.

'And this.' Mattie tucked her chin in and looked at Josie sideways from under her brow while a teasing smile played across her lips.

Josie covered her mouth with her hand. 'Oh, my.' She coughed. 'How *do* you keep a straight face?'

Mattie shook her head. 'I don't know,' she replied, struggling to get her words out between giggles.

'How odd,' Josie said, as she got control of herself. 'Not that he shouldn't flirt with you – I'm sure you have that all the time – but I wonder what's got into him.'

'Oh that's easy,' Mattie laughed. 'It's not me he's after but a raise.'

'Are you sure?' Josie asked. 'I mean, it could be that he's admired you all this time and now that a respectable amount of time has passed since Brian died he thinks it's time to declare himself.'

The laughter she'd only just contained bubbled up in Mattie again. 'Oh, Josie, you'll really have to stop reading those penny romances. This is Freddie we are talking about. Flash Freddie, the housewife's bit of relish.'

Josie rolled her eyes. 'What am I thinking?' she patted her stomach. 'It's the baby. It's giving me all sorts of strange notions.'

'It can't be much stranger than Freddie's notion to sweet-talk a raise out of me. And even if that were the case, you must know that Freddie Ellis is the last man on earth I'd marry. He might be able to charm the birds from the trees but can you imagine what Maguire's balance sheet would look like after a week with him in charge? No, it's clear that now the yard is picking up Flash Freddie is trying all his tricks on me so that when he asks for more money I'll give it without a murmur.'

'The yard's picking up? I'm so pleased to hear that.'

'Yes, thanks to the recent damp weather.' Mattie drained the last of her tea. 'And I've taken on a man, temporarily,' she said, as an image of Jack Archer – his sleeves rolled up and collar undone – effortlessly shouldering a hundredweight coal floated into her head.

'Anyone I know?'

'No. He's not from around here.'

'Where's he from then?'

'Sussex somewhere.'

'Who were his references?'

'He didn't have any.'

Josie stared at Mattie in astonishment. 'Mattie—'

'I was having an argument with one of Morris's drivers and he intervened. He said he was looking for work and I offered him a job. It's only until Eli gets better'

'But even so. Without references!' Josie eyes grew even wider. 'I mean, he could be anyone. There was a poster outside Wapping police station offering a reward for an escaped felon who has been seen in the area.'

'Josie, will you listen to yourself?'

'Alright, alright. I grant you I'm running on a bit but still, you should have asked for references.'

Of course Josie was right. She should have, and in the normal way of things she would have, but somehow, deep down, Mattie knew she could trust him.

'Look, Josie. He arrives each day on the dot, is loaded and away in half the time it takes the other drivers. He's always respectful and in only one week he's added three households to his rounds and the customers like him.'

A smile tugged at Josie's lips. 'He's handsome then?'

'I suppose so, in a dark sort of way,' she said, thinking about the way his closely trimmed beard followed the strong line of his chin. 'Actually, I'm hoping Kate might look in his direction. I'm sorry to say, Josie, but I have a suspicion that she's fixed her sights on our Flash Freddie.'

'I thought she was walking out with Alfie what's-his-name.'

'So did I. Alfie's a nice enough lad. Hard working, good to his mother but ... well, dull.'

'Have you said anything to her?'

Mattie shook her head. 'What can I say? She's a grown woman after all. And now with Freddie paying me compliments and acting like a lovesick idiot, if I mention it she might think I'm after him.'

'I see what you mean.'

'I had a word with Ma about it when she was at the yard on Friday and she tried to talk to Kate but she just ducked the issue and then breezed out of the kitchen,' Mattie replied.

'What about if I had a word with her after Mass?'

Mattie shook her head. 'She knows you're my friend and likely to jump to the same conclusion. Then there'll really be trouble.'

She had already seen Kate's unhappy face when she heard Freddie call Mattie sweetheart over the dinner table two days ago. Hopefully Freddie would ask her to increase his salary and when she refused he'd revert back to his old self. Then she could tackle the problem of Kate.

Josie picked up the tea pot and poured them both another cup of tea. 'What a muddle,' she said, adding milk to both cups. She beamed across at Mattie. 'Still. Perhaps this good looking coalman of yours *will* turn Kate's head.'

Mattie spooned a chunk of sugar into her cup. 'Yes, let's hope so . . .'

'Ho there, girlie! You waiting for me?' one of the dockers outside the Bell and Compass called across. Kate looked the other way.

'I've got a thruppence hereabouts,' another one shouted, fumbling in the front of his trousers. 'It's the going rate for an up the wall!'

Kate had been waiting on the corner of Ensign Street for almost half an hour, knowing Freddie usually came by at about this time. St George's clock struck four mellow notes and tears rose at the back of Kate's eyes as she thought about the way he'd looked at Mattie yesterday. Of course, Mattie hadn't seemed to notice. Kate picked up the basket beside her feet and, with a last look up the street, started home.

Perhaps it was a good thing she'd missed her ride home with him. If he was too blind to notice her there were plenty of others who did. Obviously, when one of the handsome naval officers who came to Wapping from Deptford, or a red-coated captain from the Tower garrison swept her off her feet he would realise he'd missed his chance.

A horse clip-clopped behind her, rolling the iron-rimmed wheels across the cobbles.

Kate's heart did a double beat. *Freddie!*

Her head snapped around and she found herself looking up at Mattie's new driver. He was sitting on the side of the empty cart while Flossy plodded the familiar route home. She shaded her eyes from the sun.

'Miss Nolan,' he said, pulling the old horse to a stop. 'I know we're almost home but why don't I give you a lift?'

She should say no. Freddie had taken against Jack and didn't like her talking to him. To Freddie's way of thinking there were a hundred local men who knew the coal trade better than Jack Archer and her sister shouldn't have taken him on, but Kate liked Jack's relaxed easy manner and confidence. It also occurred to her that if Freddie saw her riding with Jack, it might give him pause to think.

She handed Jack the basket and jumped on board. He snapped the reins and Flossy started off again. When Kate waved to a couple of her friends as they rolled along she saw their open-mouthed envy when they caught sight of her driver. As the wagon turned into the yard, Mattie appeared through the side gate of the house. Kate stared at her sister for a moment, then realised she was without her headscarf and apron. Added to which she was wearing her dark green gown with its pin-tucked bodice and not her usual navy one. Jack offered Kate his hand and she climbed down.

Mattie's gaze flickered between them. 'Good day?' she asked.

'I'm done in,' Kate replied. After six hours of kneading dough and sliding tins in and out of the hatch, the cotton shift under her corset was plastered to her skin. She'd already promised herself a good hot wash in the tin basin after supper.

'The fires of hell couldn't have been hotter than the ovens today, but I've brought us a couple of loaves that won't last to the morning. I thought I'd make a bread pudding with the raisins and sugar Pat brought last week.'

'That sounds delicious,' Jack said, jumping down from the rig.

Mattie's gaze followed him. 'Kate's a very good cook. I don't know what the Hoffmans would do without her. She has the lightest touch with pastry and her bread's like a feather it's so airy. She'll make some lucky man a good wife one day.'

Jack smiled mildly at Kate but then the intensity returned to his eyes as they settled back on Mattie. 'I'm sure.'

'You're back earlier than I thought you would be.'

He slapped the horse affectionately on the rump. 'This old girl knows the route so well I just let her plod on while I deliver the coal. If I slept in one morning I daresay she could unload the sacks and take the money as well.'

Mattie laughed a light, carefree laugh that Kate hadn't heard for a long time. Jack started to unhitch Flossy and Mattie stroked the horse's neck. 'She's a grafter is our Flossy,' she said, rubbing the soft muzzle. The horse raised her head in recognition.

'She's not the only one,' Jack said, nodding at the stack of sacks folded neatly by the stable. 'And I suppose you've been to the market, too.'

'We wouldn't be eating tomorrow if I hadn't been,' she said. 'It does my mother-in-law good to get out if she's having a ... troubled day.'

'She is very fortunate to have you to care for her.'

They stood and looked at each other as Kate observed their exchange. There hadn't been a dry eye in Knockfergus, the area north of the Highway, the day Brian died. Mattie had sworn she'd never marry again but then, as their mam often said, never is a quick word to say but a long time to live.

'Kate works hard, too. Up at four every morning without fail. I don't know what I would have done without her these last few years. But I'm sure she'd like to have a home of her own one day. Wouldn't you, Kate?'

'Yes, I would,' she replied, just as Freddie's wagon turned in. A curl of pleasure settled in Kate's stomach but she gave him a cool look.

Jack removed Flossy's halter causing her to shake her head and start towards her stable. 'I'd better settle her in before the hay delivery arrives.'

Mattie watched him for a moment or two then turned to Kate. 'Do you think he's handsome?' she asked, the flush on her cheek slightly more noticeable.

'Well yes, I suppose he is,' Kate replied. 'In a big brotherly sort of way.'

'He never shirks and he's the sort of man who would turn his hand to anything to make sure his family didn't go short.'

'Oh, Mattie,' Kate laughed. 'How can you know anything of the sort? He's only been here a week.'

'He's thirty-three and was born in Hastings. His mother died when he was six and he went to live with his gran, he went to the parson's school and was top of the class for arithmetic. I believe that, too, as he can tally up the money from the round.' Mattie tilted her head. 'He's an educated man.'

Kate raised an eyebrow. 'Is he married?'

'For goodness' sake, Kate! I can't go prying into the man's life.'

Kate started giggling.

'What's so funny?'

'I was just wondering how he ever managed to get out of the yard with you quizzing him all day.'

Mattie looked across at Jack rubbing down the carthorse with a handful of straw.

'Jack Archer is a man to trust. More than some around here.' Her eyes darted over to Freddie. 'And,' she squeezed Kate's arm, 'I think he likes you.'

'Do you?' Kate looked at her sister in astonishment. Didn't Mattie see the warmth in Jack's eyes when he looked at *her*? Couldn't she hear the admiration in his voice?

'Well, aren't you the prettiest girl in the street?'

'I think he'd be calling *you* that, not me,' Kate replied, hardly able to keep the amusement from her voice.

Mattie's cheeks flamed. 'What nonsense!' She patted the bun at the nape of her neck with her free hand and lowered her eyes. 'He's just friendly, that's all. He's the same with Pete and Billy.'

'Well, then, I hope to goodness he doesn't look at them the way he looks at you or there'll be trouble.'

Mattie rolled her eyes. 'You've got some odd notions and no mistake.' She glanced back to where Jack was shovelling coal into the hundredweight sacks for the next morning's delivery. 'Take it from me, Kate, men the likes of Jack Archer don't come by too often.'

Whoever named this place Hope Alley had a cruel sense of humour, thought Nathaniel as he followed Boyce down the narrow passageway between the tightly packed two-up two-down houses on either side. He'd seen their like before huddled around Romford Church. But whereas the squat homes in his native town had small patches of land at the rear where the farm workers could raise a few cabbages or carrots, what had once been gardens here was now hard packed earth cluttered with traders' handcarts, ladders and barrels. Although there was still a country feel to the place, it was mainly due to the smell of the pigs being fattened in makeshift pens and the cluck of scrawny hens scratching alongside them in the dirt. At the top end of the alley was a decrepit pump from which the households drew their daily water.

'Almost there,' Boyce told him with a reassuring grin. 'And don't worry,' he said, indicating Nathaniel's hat that he'd pulled down over his eyes. 'The Old Roberts don't patrol around here. And,' he winked, 'if people see you with me they'll know better than to gab about it.'

Nathaniel cast dubious eyes around what would soon be his home.

'What did you say their names were again?' he asked, as they stopped in front of the house at the end of the row.

'Tubby Roscoe and his wife Dolly,' Boyce replied, as he bashed on the door with the side of his fist. Something akin to a pack of wolves snarling and yapping crashed against the other side of the door making it judder on its hinges. 'They breed dogs.'

Nathaniel had been working at Maguire's for five days and as he would probably be there for a few weeks yet he needed to have some plausible explanation for his sudden arrival in the area. As he stared at the peeling paint on the front door, and the cracked windowpanes, Nathaniel wondered who exactly Boyce had selected amongst his many acquaintances to be his new 'family'.

'Get back you beggars!' screamed a woman's voice from inside the house. 'Mister R!'

The door rattled as the unseen woman struggled to master the pack of hounds. A man's voice ground out a string of expletives and the barking grew fainter. The door opened and a woman's face appeared. She was probably a year or two older than Nathaniel, at thirty-five or so. But with her dirty grey hair and spindly frame she looked much older.

Nathaniel wondered if there was anything about Dolly Roscoe that might convince anyone that they were born of the same parents. She barely reached four-foot-ten-inches, while he had to duck to avoid lintels. Her chin was round and receded instead of square and blunt. Her skin was peppered with freckles and her hair still showed the odd strand of red. In short, the other end of the scale from his dark colouring.

She looked at Nathaniel suspiciously before she spotted Boyce. 'Oh, Mr Boyce. Wot an unexpected pleasure,' she said, opening the door to let them in and then swiftly closed it behind them.

'Hello, Dolly,' Boyce said stepping in and giving her a wink. 'How's me best gal.'

'All the better for seeing you,' she replied coyly, and quite at odds with her haggard demeanour.

'Me and Dolly go way back, don't we?'

'That we do,' she agreed. 'Of course that was when I was known as China Rose.'

'Is that where you come from?' Nathaniel asked, trying not to think about what may have squelched under his foot.

Dolly doubled over and slapped her thigh. 'Bless me, no. I just had some regulars amongst the Orientals in Limehouse. Of course that was before I met Mr R. I don't turn tricks no more,' she said, with a broad grin that displayed her missing front teeth.

The door at the far end of the hall opened and a man wearing a stained, long-sleeved, three-button vest, grubby trousers and unlaced boots shuffled into the passageway. He looked Nathaniel up and down.

'I've thrown 'em in the yard,' he said, closing the door to the scullery at the far end of the passageway. 'This who you need a bit of 'elp with, Boyce?' The pipe in his mouth bounced as he spoke.

'That's right, Tubby.'

Nathaniel heard the faint click of the front handle behind him. He grasped the knife stuck in his belt and spun round.

Standing in the doorway was a blue-eyed blonde, a swarthy brunette and a bleary-eyed sailor. The girls' gowns were unbuttoned, allowing their breasts to spill out. Nathaniel let go of the blade.

'Oh, Boyce,' they shrieked in unison.

Leaving the sailor propped up against the door frame, they dashed past Nathaniel and hugged Boyce.

''Ello, girls.' Slipping his arm around their waists he looked at Nathaniel. 'This here is Nancy.' He tickled the blond who giggled. 'And this is Bella.' He squeezed the other girl.

Ducking under Boyce's arm, Bella swayed, hands on hips, over to Nathaniel.

'And who's this?' she asked, walking her fingers up his chest.

Nathaniel closed his hand over hers to stop its progress. 'Jack Archer,' he replied trying to ignore the fact that she'd wedged her crotch against his thigh.

She stretched up and gave him a lavish kiss. 'Well, Jack, I do a special rate for big, handsome fellas.'

'Put him down, Bella,' Boyce said. 'He ain't here for a bit of jiggy.'

Bella ran her finger around Nathaniel's jaw. 'Pity. Maybe another time.'

The sailor stumbled into the hallway and knocked into Nathaniel. 'Sorry mate,' he said, through his rum-soaked breath. His unfocused eyes swam for a few seconds before he spotted the two tarts.

'There you are, you little minxes,' he said, wagging a playful finger at them.

Nancy hooked her arm under the sailor to hold him up. 'Up we go,' she said, looking at Bella and jerking her head towards the stairs.

'You had better come in here,' said Tubby pushing open the door to the front room.

The furniture in the couple's main living area consisted of one old wooden bed covered with grey bedclothes, a table with their half-eaten supper on it and a couple of old upholstered chairs with more stuffing protruding out than padding within. A mantel shelf, with a couple of tallow candles stuck in to pools of wax at each end, sat over an empty fire grate, while faded curtains hung from a rope strung across the window and kept out what little sunlight there was.

'So what's the fiddly?' Tubby asked, scratching his rear.

'This is me old pal, Jack Archer,' Boyce said, thumbing towards Nathaniel, who was trying not to stand within flea-jumping distance of the bed. 'And Dolly's long lost little bruvver.'

'What's he done?' Dolly Roscoe's asked, her eyes darted over Nathaniel. ''E ain't no killer, is he? I wouldn't get a wink of sleep if I 'ad a murderer in—'

'I've killed no one,' Nathaniel told her firmly.

'Well, what you done then?'

Nathaniel turned to Boyce and raised an eyebrow. Boyce's eyes narrowed as he studied the dog breeder and his wife.

'Now, now, Doll,' Tubby said, perspiration beading his bald head. 'What you don't know you can't tell and Mr Boyce's business ain't none of ours.'

Alarm flashed across Dolly's face. 'Oh ... oh, pardon me, Mr Boyce.' She laughed nervously. 'You know what I'm like.'

Boyce's eyes fixed on the couple as they stood uncomfortably before him. 'I do. But Jack's like my own flesh and if any—'

'Don't you worry,' Tubby cut in. 'Jack'll be as safe as houses with us. Won't he Doll?'

She nodded her head like a rag doll being shaken.

'I thought he could lodge in your empty room at the back.'

Tubby rubbed his chin. 'I suppose. Although now we've got the blood out of the floorboard we were going to let it again. You know times are hard and—'

'I need a cover not charity,' Nathaniel cut in. 'What did your last lodger pay?'

'Two shilling a week.'

Nathaniel pulled out the coins from his pocket. 'Here's a crown. That's two weeks' rent and enough for me to have a bucket of hot water when I get in each night.' He handed it to Dolly.

'Right you are, Jack. Do you want a evening meal, too. It's no trouble.'

Nathaniel glanced at the half-a-dozen cockroaches darting around the base of the cooking pot. 'No. I'll make my own arrangements.'

Boyce walked to the door then turned. 'You won't let me down will you, Tubby?'

'Of course not, Mr Boyce. You can count on us.'

Boyce touched his temple in a salute and went back into the hall, Nathaniel following.

'Boyce, do you really think people will believe that Dolly Roscoe and I are related?'

'Why not?'

Nathaniel ran his fingers through his hair. 'Well, for a start you look more like my sister than she does. And what about—'

A door on the first floor opened and Nancy, Bella and the sailor appeared at the top of the stairs. The sailor staggered, buttoning up his flies, with the girls close behind. Nathaniel and Boyce stood back to let them pass. Bella winked at Nathaniel as she and Nancy left the house looking for their next client.

'And what about them two?' Nathaniel asked, as the door closed. 'What if Mrs Maguire finds out there're two trollops living in the room next to me?'

'Just tell her they're your nieces.' Boyce laughed and jabbed him lightly in the chest. 'You're the fecking idiot who took the job and made me the fecking idiot who had to find you some kith and kin. Now I grant you, Tubby and Dolly ain't the Duke and Duchess of Westminster but they'll keep mum.'

Nathaniel looked doubtful, but said, 'I suppose you're right.'

'Course I am, and it's only for a week or so.'

Mrs Maguire's cheery morning smile and happy greeting sprang unbidden into Nathaniel's mind. 'Well, perhaps a little longer,' he replied, in what he hoped was a matter of fact tone.

Boyce's sharp eyes searched his face. 'I hope as 'ow you ain't getting fond of that Irish woman who runs the yard.'

'Her name is Mrs Maguire.'

'Oh, is it now.'

'Yes it is, and I'm *not* getting fond of her. It's just that it might take me a little longer to find out how Stebbins is connected to the yard.'

'Well, that's all right then.' Boyce clapped his hands and rubbed them together. 'You and your sister must have a lot to talk about after all this time so I'll leave you to it.'

Nathaniel opened the door for him to leave. As he passed him Boyce paused. 'A word in your shell like, old son. Why don't you take advantage of Bella's special rate to save your naggers leading you off in the direction of Mrs Maguire?'

Amos sat chewing the corner of his moustache and tried to ignore the gurgling in his stomach as the cab negotiated its way west along Leadenhall Street. The dyspepsia that had started as soon as he swallowed the first mouthful of kipper at breakfast now had an unyielding grip on his vitals. He punched his chest but the hard knot at the back of his breastbone didn't budge. It was hardly surprising that his digestive system was out of sorts. His wine merchant's bill had arrived with the morning post, along with a curt letter threatening to stop further supplies unless it was paid. There was even a hint that the rogue would have recourse to the law should payment not be forthcoming.

Damned impertinence!

And if that wasn't enough to sour a man's appetite the morning post had brought another rude letter from Fallon at the bank.

It was too much to bear that a man such as he, a respectable businessman, a prospective alderman no less, should be harassed by tradesmen and jumped-up money changers. A tremor of apprehension passed over him. If he didn't secure the deeds to Maguire's yard soon Fallon would call in all of his credit and that would be the end of him.

If anyone had told him three months ago that Maguire's would still be in business he would have laughed in their face. He'd thought that with old Eli injured, not to mention an unusually warm summer, the yard would have gone under weeks ago, but it seemed that September's unseasonal cold snap and a week's worth of heavy rain had come to Mrs Maguire's aid – which is why he was having to go cap in hand to meet the City & County's chief banker.

The cabbie brought the horse to a halt. Amos stepped out and handed the driver a shilling. 'Keep the change.'

'And good health to you, guv,' he said, touching the peak of his cap.

The bank sat on the corner of Lombard Street and Nicolas Lane, just around the corner from the Bank of England.

It had been founded in the last century and had a reputation for solid investment and discretion. It had been Cecily's father's bank, which is why Amos had opened an account there. Of course, that was in old Mr Wilburton's time. He had been an old-fashioned gentleman banker and had a proper understanding of an entrepreneur's needs. He hadn't allowed himself to be shackled with all this regulation nonsense that was creeping into too many of the City's financial institutions.

The tall doorman jumped forward. 'Good morning, sir,' he said, pulling open one of the heavy doors by its gleaming brass handle.

Stowing his cane under his arm, Amos fished out a penny tip. As the door closed behind him the hubbub from the street outside grew faint and the calm of the entrance hall took over. The scratch of pens coupled with whispered voices joined together in an odd mix of industry and worship, giving Amos a feeling of financial well-being.

Fallon's young clerk, Deacon, looked up from his scribbling. He was a small, wiry fellow who looked only just old enough to shave. His well-oiled fair hair shone in the light from the gas lamps and his pale eyes were somewhat bloodshot from hours studying the heavy account books on his desk. He walked briskly towards Amos.

'Good morning, Mr Stebbins,' he said, curling forward and rubbing his hands together. 'What a pleasure it is to see you again.'

'Deacon,' Amos replied, 'Would you tell Mr Fallon I'm here to see him?'

'Is he expecting you, sir?' The clerk asked glanced nervously at the half-glazed door that led the banker's office.

'No.' Amos replied, fixing him with a bellicose stare.

A tic started in the corner of Deacon's right eye. 'If you care to take a seat,' he said, indicating the winged-back chairs in the corner of the lobby area, 'I'll inform him of your arrival.'

The clerk scurried off and Amos paced back and forth for a full five minutes until the clerk returned.

'If you would follow me, sir,' he said.

Amos marched towards the chief officer's door. Deacon grasped the brass knob and paused. He cleared his throat. 'May I be so bold as to congratulate you on your fine letter in *The Times* last Monday, calling for tighter controls in our prison.'

Amos puffed out his chest. 'Too kind,' he said, the clerk's reverential tones going some way towards soothing his colicky temper.

Deacon opened the door and Amos walked in, scrutinising the man behind the desk. Only a year or two older than himself, Amos guessed that as a child Wilfred Fallon would have been described as delicate. He was barely five foot five tall and had a frame like a schoolboy, which made him look slightly incongruous in his expensive Savile Row suit.

He rose to his feet. 'Mr Stebbins, ' he said, coming around his desk to offer Amos his hand.

'Mr Fallon.'

'Please take a seat.'

Amos paused for a second then threw his tails back to perch himself on the edge of the chair.

Fallon sat down and looked over his half-rimmed glasses. 'I trust you are well?' He paused. 'And that you have received my letter.'

Amos glared across the desk at the banker. 'I did, and frankly, I object to the tone.' He leant forward and jabbed at the desk top with his index finger. 'And I'll tell you this, Fallon, I shall move my account if I see another arrive at my breakfast table couched in the same objectionable language.'

He sat back and waited for concern, if not outright fear, to show on the banker's face. He was disappointed.

'That of course would be your prerogative,' Fallon replied, 'but at this present time . . .' he glanced down and traced his finger along a column of figures. 'You might find another institution reluctant to accommodate you. I wrote so that we could talk discreetly before the directors instruct me to take matters further.'

A trickle of cold sweat broke out between Amos's shoulder blades. 'Directors? Take things further? Good grief, man. What's all this nonsense about?' he asked, changing tack to a come-on-old-chap tone.

'I'm afraid I cannot regard an overdraft of a thousand pounds as nonsense, Mr Stebbins.'

A thousand pounds! I thought it just seven hundred.

He forced a laugh. 'Is that all?'

Fallon set his lips in two thin lines. 'I do not think this is a matter for merriment.'

The chair creaked under Amos's weight. 'Look here. I own the Grey Friars wharf and a portfolio of shares in other city companies. Frankly, Fallon, your clerks can't have any understanding of a balance sheet versus capital holdings if they are shoving such trivia under your nose.' Amos drew out a cigar, making a play of lighting it, and continued. 'I take it as a personal slight being sent rude letters over a measly thousand pounds. My assets are worth six times that amount.' He blew circles of smoke upwards and re-crossed his legs. 'Not to mention my reputation, which is solid as the gold in your vaults.'

Fallon pushed his spectacles back in place. 'Your assets may be worth that – but not to you. The City & County hold the mortgage to Grey Friars of . . .' he lifted a sheet of paper with a wax seal attached, 'two thousand pounds, which you required eighteen months ago to ease your liquidity problems and, as far as I can see, the wharf is still barely in profit.'

Amos felt the blood rise to his head. The damned impertinence of the man! But he shouldn't be surprised by Fallon's disrespectful, nay, anarchical attitude to his social superiors. After all, he was a Methodist.

'I still have my other business interests and investments.'

'True, but some of them are not performing as well as they should.' He scanned the ledger again. 'The Anglo-Bolivian Mining Company, for example. You invested heavily in it a few months ago but have seen no return.'

'It's early days.'

'When you requested a banker's draft for the purchase of the shares I distinctly remember you telling me that the mineral deposits were near to the coast, whereas in fact the deposits are almost three hundred miles into the interior through an almost impenetrable jungle. And I have it on good authority that the company's own engineer stated quite clearly that the initial cost of getting minerals out would be three times what the directors who proposed the venture indicated in the share prospectus.'

'How could you know about the engineer's report?'

'This is a bank, Mr Stebbins, it is our business to know. Other than eight hundred pounds, which is held in trust for your step-daughter, almost all of your assets are mortgaged to us, and the majority of your other investments are worth less now than when you bought them. I have a duty to protect the City & County's shareholders and depositors from bankruptcy.'

'Bankruptcy?'

'Yes. Caused by your unsecured debt dragging the bank into insolvency, which is why I will not sanction any further credit on your account.'

The moisture evaporated from Amos's mouth but he jumped to his feet. 'Damn it! How am I supposed to do business without credit to draw on?'

Fallon didn't answer.

Perspiration sprang out on Amos's brow as his mind went to the drawer full of unpaid bills in his desk. He rested his hands on the desk. 'Listen to me, Fallon, I have an investment opportunity on the horizon that is guaranteed to make us both a fortune.'

Fallon raised an almost invisible eyebrow. 'A rubber plantation in Canada perhaps? An ice mine in Arabia? Really, Mr Stebbins, there isn't anything you could say that—'

'George Hudson.'

'George Hudson? *The* George Hudson?'

'The very same.'

The banker's pale complexion flushed.

A warmth spread through Amos's belly. He wasn't surprised at Fallon's sudden change of tune on hearing the Railway King's name.

George Hudson had gone from living above a provincial draper's shop in York to owning a country estate, a townhouse on the north side of Hyde Park and sixty per cent of the trains that puffed up and down the country.

'You have a project involving Mr Hudson?' Fallon asked, rising from his desk and moving to the sideboard with the drinks tray on it.

'I can't tell you all the details as yet,' Amos replied, 'but I *can* tell you I am meeting him in the House in a week to discuss a new railway line. Just a small one,' he added as Fallon raised the decanter.

'Well, this shines a different light on the matter,' Fallon replied.

Amos laughed – a little too uproariously – as relief swept through him.

Fallon handed him a large brandy. 'I hope you will ask the City & County to handle any company monies.'

Amos took a slow sip as some of his anxiety ebbed away. 'Could you handle such a large investment?'

It was Fallon's turn to look offended. 'I can assure you we are able to provide any service a joint stock company might need. *Any* service at all.'

Amos finished his drink. 'There is just the little matter of my credit, of course. I must have working capital if I am to progress the matter.'

The banker's buttoned-up expression returned. 'I will need further securities.'

'My two clippers, the *Tempest* and the *Dolphin*,' Amos replied.

What were two old buckets against the chance of partnership with George Hudson, who practically shat money? There wasn't an investor in the land who wouldn't give their right hand to be linked to a company of his.

The banker hesitated. 'And I have your word that the City & County will be offered first option of a share issue?'

'Without question.'

'And that you have all the necessary title deeds to the land over which your railway is to travel.'

'Of course,' Amos told him smoothly. There was now no conceivable way the Maguire yard could stay in business for much longer.

Fallon extended his hand. 'Well, then. I shall prepare the papers and extend your credit once you've signed them. Please feel free to draw on your account at the City & County as you require.'

A satisfied smile spread across Amos Stebbins's lips. 'Thank you. I will.'

page and remembered how he'd smiled down at her as he handed it to her that afternoon. Before she could prevent it, her stomach leapt excitedly.

She picked up the pen again and ran down the list of her creditors, carefully re-checking the amount against the delivery notes she'd taken from the spike in the desk. There was a knock on the door.

She looked up and there stood Jack.

Breathe, she reminded herself.

Unlike the other drivers, Jack liked to wash the worst of the day's grit off before he left and Mattie had willingly supplied him with a bucket of water and a bar of soap. He'd clearly just completed his evening's ablutions as his hair was still damp and curled around his forehead and cheekbones. The oil lamp hanging above threw blocks of shadow across the strong planes of his face.

Goodness, that man's easy on the eye, she thought before she could stop herself.

'Mrs Maguire said you were here,' he said, dipping his head to avoid the doorframe and stepping into the office. 'She seems better today.'

'It was the third anniversary of Brian's death last week, you see, and well ...'

'Pete told me,' he said quietly.

The warm tone of understanding in his voice washed over her. They stared at each other for a moment. 'Kebble's man finished unloading the fodder, and the wagons are ready for tomorrow.'

'Thank you,' Mattie replied. 'I'll see you in the morning then.'

A dart of pain shot across her forehead and she rubbed her temples for relief.

'You look tired. Are you almost finished?

Mattie shook her head. 'No, not by a long chalk. I've only just started to enter the bills and sales, let alone balance them, and the longer I look at these numbers the less sense they seem to make.'

He came around behind her and leant over her shoulder.

'Perhaps I can help,' he said, placing his hand beside her own.

Mattie's eyes fixed on the well-formed hand resting beside the ledger. Like the rest of him, there was a casual power in the strong fingers with their neatly clipped nails. She noted the fine line of hair tracking up from his wrist to his little finger and the ridge of tendons under the tanned skin. As her eyes took in all the details, Mattie wondered what his hand would feel like running over her bare skin.

'I know,' he said. 'If you read out the bills, I'll enter them on the page.'

'That would be helpful, but surely after a day's work you want to be getting along.'

He pulled a chair over and took the quill from her. 'I'm ready when you are.'

She picked up the first docket from the pile. 'Alright then ... Kebble's. Four carts of hay, two pounds, five shillings and sixpence.'

Jack wrote the charges under the fodder merchants, and then all the others waiting to be entered, until the last of them was impaled on the collection spike.

Mattie reached for the four order books but Jack's hand rested on them first.

'Let me.'

She shouldn't take advantage of his good nature by asking him to spend another hour or so itemising the customer's orders, but suddenly the luxury of having him share her burden for even just a moment or two was too much to resist.

'If you're sure you don't mind,' she repeated, secretly thrilled at the thought of having his company for a little longer.

He opened the first one and placed his finger on the top line and then he looked at her sideways. 'I wouldn't want your eyes to lose their sparkle because you've been squinting at numbers.'

Mattie's heart thumped in her chest and then raced off at a gallop. She studied the area just below his cheekbone where his beard gave way to smooth skin and she imagined what it might feel like to place her lips there. The wedge of unruly hair he had combed back with his finger fell forward and Mattie had to almost sit on her hands to stop herself from reaching forward to repositioning it.

Mattie Maguire, what to goodness, are you thinking?

She looked at Jack's bare forearm, and saw how the corded muscles moved as he wrote.

It took some while but, at last, he was finished. 'There we are, done.' He closed the last book and stretched his arms behind his head.

Mattie studied the result. A frown ruffled her brow.

'Oh dear,' she said, as her eyes reached the bottom line of the page. 'Perhaps I ought to think about Mr Stebbins's offer,' she muttered.

'Mr Stebbins?' He repeated looking at her intently. 'Is he a friend of yours?'

She shook her head. 'I only know him because I take my mother-in-law to the Sunday service at St George's. He's a member of the vestry committee and owns Grey Friars warehouse. He's very important but very kind.'

'Is that so?'

'Truly.' She glanced at the figures again. 'He even came and looked over Maguire's books a while back but I can't say it helped much.' She shot Jack a shy look. 'To be sure, he's probably so used to dealing with vast sums of money that he's forgotten how a small company like Maguire's works. He tried to tell me that the business was about to go under but I can add and subtract, and anyone with half an eye could see that although we don't make a fortune, we are breaking even. But I don't think he understood because he kept telling me I had no option but to sell the yard. He even said he'd help me find a buyer and sent a note yesterday urging me to act before it's too late.'

Jack raised an eyebrow. 'You own the yard?'

'Yes. My late father-in-law bought the title about twenty years ago. I know if I sold it I would have some cash to see me through, but I just can't. My husband's father built this yard up from nothing and passed it on to my husband, who wanted to do the same for our lad Brian. Unfortunately he ... he didn't live long enough to see that happen. So I have to do it for him now.'

He glanced down at the open book, catching his lower lip with his teeth, showing Mattie a faint image of the boy he must have once been.

'Mrs Maguire,' he said, formally. 'If you're intent on keeping the business for your son, I have a suggestion or two to help.'

Mattie closed the garden gate to the house and cast her eyes around the yard, which was bathed in the late afternoon sunlight.

'Afternoon, Mrs M,' Billy called.

'Afternoon, Billy. How have you fared today?'

'I did all right around Prescott Street,' he replied as he set the broom against the fence. 'But there were only a handful of deliveries down Samuel, James and William Street and none in the alleys.'

Mattie struggled to maintain her smile as she thought of the unpaid delivery bill from Morris sitting on top of Kebble's invoice.

The day after Jack had helped her with her accounts he'd spent the next evening sketching out a crude map of the area on a large sheet of paper so she could mark out Maguire's customers. The next evening they re-organised the delivery route so that the older horses,

Samson and Flossy were given three local deliveries each day and the younger two were allocated customers further afield.

It had taken the horses a week to learn the new route and after only two weeks of the new system Mattie was able to do something she hadn't done for over a year: give Patrick money to deposit in Maguire & Son's account.

Something darted across the yard and Mattie turned just in time to see a large grey rat scrabbling towards the stable. It was a hazard of living so close to the river.

Pete whistled between his teeth. 'Did you see the size of that one? Blimey, if they get any bigger we'll be able to put them between the shafts and drive them.'

'That's the third I've seen this week,' Mattie said, as she watched the rat slither through a broken plank in the stable wall. 'I'll go take a look.'

'Be careful, Mrs M,' Billy called after her as she marched across the yard.

The three horses raised their heads in mild interest as she entered the stable and edged her way between the stalls towards the hay store. She cocked an ear to listen for the tell-tale scurrying. Thankfully, the only sound was that of the horses crunching their suppers. She leant the broom against the end of the stall and wiped her brow with her forearm.

Someone walked into the stable behind her.

'Freddie,' she said, surprised that he was still in the yard even though it was past five.

He stood with his hands in his pockets and his cap at its usual angle – with the peak over his right eye. He'd unbuttoned his shirt and had artfully retied his kingsman.

'Afternoon, Mrs M,' he said, swaggering towards her.

'Yes, afternoon, Freddie,' she said, as he stopped an arm's reach from her.

'You're looking very fine to day, Mrs Maguire. I've always liked you in that gown.'

Here we go again Mattie thought as she suppressed a smile. *He's certainly laying on the old sweet talk with a trowel.*

She was amused by Freddie's attempts to soften her up but she wished he would just come out and ask her for a raise. In fairness, she hadn't increased her drivers' wages for almost two years and she'd already thought to give them all a raise of two shillings a week in November if the yards still prospered.

'Thank you, Freddie. Now about—'

'In fact,' he took a step nearer and glanced swiftly around . 'There's someone nearby who thinks you look dandy each and every day. I think you know who I mean.' He winked.

Jack! Mattie's heart did a little double step.

Her eyes opened wide. 'Surely not . . .' Freddie gave her a roguish grin. 'Really?'

He nodded. 'And why not? You're a good-looking woman.'

An image of Jack strolling across the yard, harnessing the cart and sitting at her table eating his dinner flashed into Mattie's mind.

'Oh, Freddie, I never thought . . .' Mattie looked away so he couldn't sense her excitement.

'And it's about time someone took part of the burden of the yard off those delicate shoulders of yours.'

He was right. What with the work they'd done over the past week and his quiet overseeing of the yard, Jack had certainly eased her load. A feeling like warm honey spread through her.

She gave Freddie a friendly smile. 'Well, I can't say it's been easy these last few years.'

'Now haven't I seen you struggling on since poor Brian died.'

'What choice did I have?'

'None. Though a grand job you've made of it all. And I might say, you've shown Brian proper respect by keeping yourself to yourself these three years, if you get my drift.' Mattie's cheeks burned. 'But, perhaps, it's time you started thinking about putting away your widow's weeds.' A playful expression spread across his face.

Mattie grabbed hold of her dancing imagination before it took flight and cleared her throat. 'I think it's a little too soon for that.'

Freddie looked puzzled. 'Well, if you say so.' He straightened up and became serious. 'But perhaps, while we're here alone, like, Mrs M – Mattie, if I can be so bold – if I could just ask you . . .' he swallowed.

'I know what you're going to ask but if you could just wait a little longer,' she said, annoyed with herself for being so easily drawn in by his flattery. 'Perhaps we can talk about it just before Christmas.'

Freddie's happy expression slipped a little but then it rallied. 'I was 'oping for a bit sooner but' – his eyes twinkled – 'as long as we understand each other what's a few months.'

'Let's see how it goes and ask me in November. Well,' she said in a tone she hoped would put an end to their conversation. 'I'd better go and see to Brian.'

Leaving Freddie staring after her Mattie retraced her steps. As she stood in the doorway, number one wagon trotted into the yard. Jack had removed his protective sack and the autumn breeze ruffled his hair. The warmth of desire gathered behind her breastbone turned to ice as she watched him smile down at her sister, Kate, who sat proudly beside him.

The clouds that kept the temperature down for most of the day finally moved aside and let the late afternoon sun warm Nathaniel's back as he crossed Whitechapel High Street. The last few stalls of the market were just closing and the costermongers called back and forth to each other as they cleared the rotten stock from their barrows before wheeling them into the storage yard.

Nathaniel went into Jack and Jill's pie shop, and after exchanging a bit of light-hearted banter with Jack Peirce he bought himself a penny mutton pasty. Placing the carefully wrapped still-hot pie, in his pocket, he continued past the bare-footed children picking over the vegetables in the gutter. He noticed a young woman balancing a child on her hip and his mind drifted back to Mattie Maguire.

Nathaniel had asked himself many times in the last week how he could forget his wife so quickly. In truth, he hadn't. He would never forget Marjorie, their young family and the love they had shared. But the Nathaniel who courted the squire's daughter in the fields and orchards around Romford wasn't the same Nathaniel who fought like an animal for his existence in Botany Bay.

In any case, it didn't matter about the whys and the wherefores. After all, a person wasn't allocated a set quantity of love that once given was gone forever. It multiplied and changed, and having loved once he knew he needed to love again. And now he loved Mattie Maguire with her dark, sparkling eyes. But what could he offer her?

A rat-catcher strolled past with three white-and-brown terriers at his heels and his day's work strung up on a pole over his shoulder. Nathaniel turned his focus back to the present and sauntered the last fifty yards down Hope Alley.

Two shillings a week was nothing less than daylight robbery for the damp and dirty room he rented from the Roscoes. Sure, he was grateful to Boyce for his cover story, but after being eaten alive by bed bugs on the first night, he'd scrubbed the iron bedstead with caustic soda to clear the insects and their eggs, burnt the old mattress and replaced it with a new one stuffed with fresh straw. He'd then dragged the bed from the wall and placed each leg in metal pie dishes filled with vinegar to prevent more insects from climbing up into the bed.

As he entered the passageway there was an explosion of barking behind the door leading to the scullery at the back. The door opened and Dolly poked her head out. 'I fought it was you, Jack,' she said, struggling to keep the half dozen snarling and snapping dogs behind her.

The bow-legged, barrel-chested scrappers that she and Tubby bred seemed to be much favoured by the inhabitants of the area. Each Sunday morning Dolly and Tubby would pile the pups into their handcart and trot themselves off to the livestock market in Club Row two miles away. They lived in the grubby front room but the dogs pretty much had the run of the scullery and the handkerchief-sized back yard. A black snout poked out around the side of her skirt and Dolly blocked it with her leg.

'Get back yer bugger!' she shouted over her shoulder, the lank-grey rats' tails of her hair sliding over her face as she turned her head. She glanced back at Nathaniel. 'I've just taken yer water up. It should still be hot.'

'Thank you,' he said, putting his foot on the first step.

His diminutive landlady started to close the door and the dogs, as if sensing they had missed their opportunity to escape, launched themselves at it, yapping and barking with added gusto. A small dog wriggled through the gap and ran towards Nathaniel wagging its tail and hindquarters excitedly.

Nathaniel bent down and scratched behind the dog's ear and was rewarded with a lavish hand washing by a lolling tongue. It was only a young dog, a pup really but with enormous paws. It wriggled around Nathaniel's leg pleased with the unusual personal attention.

'Come back you bugger!' Dolly yelled again, kicking backwards into the pack of dogs behind her to keep them from following the escapee. 'Mr R!'

The front door opened and Tubby stepped out. 'Wot?'

'One of the young'uns got out.'

Tubby heaved a sigh then lumbered over and caught the pup by the scruff of its neck. It yelped and tried to get away but Tubby held on and dragged it towards his wife. The dog twisted its head and looked beseechingly back at Nathaniel. A memory of being dragged from the dock at Chelmsford Crown Court in a similar fashion flashed into Nathaniel's mind.

'How much do you want for him?' he asked, as the smell and the sheer terror of the court holding-cell flooded back to him.

Tubby's eyes widened at the unexpected offer. 'I don't know 'ow as I want to sell 'im,' he said, giving the dog what Nathaniel took to be an affectionate shake. 'He's shaping up to be one of my—'

'How much?'

'A shilling and sixpence.'

Nathaniel reached into his pocket and pulled out a couple of coins. 'I'll give you nine pence.'

Tubby shook his head. 'I couldn't take less than one and three-pence.'

Nathaniel put the pennies back in his pocket and turned back to the stairs.

The breeder dragged the dog back to the bottom of the stairs. 'I'm robbing meself, so I am, but a shilling and not a penny less.'

Tubby spat on the palm of his hand and released the dog.

'Done,' said Nathaniel, handing over his hard-earned shilling and grasping Tubby's hand, thankful for the bucket of hot water waiting for him. He clicked his fingers and the dog shot to his side.

'Come on then, boy,' he said softly.

The dog hesitated for a moment then scampered up the flight of stairs, his feet barely touching the wooden boards. Nathaniel followed and opened the door to his room. He pulled out his pie and put it on his one plate. The dog made to jump for it.

'No!' Nathaniel told it firmly.

The dog's ears dropped and his tail curled under again. Nathaniel stroked his head. 'Good boy.'

The dog's tail and ears perked up. Nathaniel set a quarter of the pie on a scrap of newspaper on the floor. The pup snatched at it.

'No!' Nathaniel repeated.

The dog's body grew tense as its hunger fought with a deeper instinct not to challenge the dominate male.

'You can have it,' he told the pup in a softer tone and on command the dog snuffled up his share of the supper. He poured himself a beer and ate the rest of the pie, while the dog sat at his feet licking the paper. Nathaniel studied his new friend. Unlike Tubby's usual mutts, this dog had a long-haired pelt of black and tan with splashes of white on his enormous paws and long snout. With a last lick of the paper, the pup sat back on his haunches and cocked his head. His ears flopped forward, making him look somewhat comical. His thumping tail disturbed the dust on the floor.

'Here boy,' Nathaniel patted his leg and the dog stood on its hind quarters to rest its big paws on his thigh.

A lump formed in his throat as he remembered Lily rolling around in the middle of the half a dozen black and white puppies born to their neighbour's dog in Como Street. He had promised her a puppy for her next birthday, but he couldn't live up to his word because when she turned five he was half a world away.

Nathaniel scratched behind the pup's ear again. 'I know a little lad who'll enjoy playing with you.'

Chapter Eleven

'Mama.' Cecily looked up from the embroidery hoop at her daughter sitting beside her on the sofa. 'Did my real papa tuck me in each night?'

'Of course he did,' Cecily answered. 'Although you were very young so I don't suppose you remember.'

'No I don't,' Ruth replied, tugging at one of her ringlets.

Cecily reached out and stilled her hand. 'Remember what we agreed, sweetheart.'

Ruth smiled apologetically and released her hair. 'Sorry, Mama.'

'Your father, God rest him, would tuck you in so you wouldn't get a chill, then kiss you and tell you to sleep tight,' Cecily said, selecting a skein of bright green wool.

She was making a new cover for Amos's church kneeler as a birthday present. This one had St George on it, and she was just about to start on the fiery dragon twisting in agony at the point of the holy soldier's lance.

'Just like Mr Stebbins does,' Ruth said, looking up at Cecily with a baffled expression.

'Yes, just like Mr Stebbins,' Cecily replied. 'And, Ruth, you know how upset he becomes when you forget to call him Papa.'

'But he isn't my papa.'

'Ruth!'

Ruth's chin jutted out. 'Well, he isn't, is he?'

'No. Not in the natural way but there can't be many men who would take such an interest in their stepdaughter as Mr Stebbins does with you. Why – isn't he always buying you pretty things and sitting you on his knee?'

'Yes, but ...' Ruth pressed her lips together and looked at her mother.

'But what?'

'When he comes in at night to tuck me I ... I don't like it.'

'Now, now, Ruth. That's not very charitable of you is it? And as I've told you on a number of occasions, we have a lot to thank Mr Stebbins for.'

'But ...'

'You don't remember living over your grandfather's shop, do you?'

'No,' replied Ruth, looking down at the crumpled sampler in her hand.

'Well, it was cramped and smelly, and if it wasn't for Mr Stebbins we'd still be living there, and you wouldn't have a pretty room and a garden to play in like you have now.' Cecily gave her daughter a stern look. 'Mr Stebbins works very hard to give us all the nice things we have now. I tell you, young lady, there are hundreds of orphans in the workhouse who would love to have a papa like Mr Stebbins to kiss them goodnight. He has tried very hard to be the very best of fathers, so is it too much to ask that you call him papa?'

Ruth's lower lip trembled and she started fiddling with her hair again. 'But Mama, I asked Maisy Latimer if her father had to check her nightdress when she was in bed and she said he never did and—'

'Ruth!' Cecily snapped, looking furiously at her daughter.

Cecily noticed that, despite smearing her daughter's finger tips in mustard, Ruth had managed to bite her nails down to the quick again. Cecily's heart quickened with anxiety. Her own mother had been a martyr to female hysteria and the vapours and she just prayed that her daughter wouldn't take after her. She slid over and put her arm around Ruth's slender shoulders.

'Mr Stebbins is only doing what all fathers of pretty daughters do, so let's not have any more silly nonsense about nightdresses.'

Cecily released her daughter and held out the rectangular piece of linen she was embroidering. 'What do you think?' she asked Ruth, who had tucked herself into the corner of the sofa.

Ruth forced a smile. 'It's nice.'

Cecily picked up her needle and cut off a length of wool. 'Well, I hope it lasts longer than the last one. I tell you, Ruth, I believe the holy saints in heaven couldn't spend more time on their knees praying to God than your dear papa.'

Mattie untied her apron and glanced in the mottled mirror to the side of the sink. She smoothed her hair back and tucked a few stray wisps into place, then peered out of the window. There was no trace of Freddie even though it must be almost two. This was the third week in a row that he'd been late picking her up to go to Josie's. She cast her eyes around the yard and watched Jack heaving coal onto number one cart in readiness for the afternoon delivery.

She often found herself in the yard just as Jack was ready to set out on his afternoon calls, and often again when he came back in the evening. Kate had teased her, saying she did it on purpose just to see him, which was ridiculous. She was in and out all day with people ringing the yard bell for a bucket of coal. Anyhow, she had a perfectly good reason for going into the yard this afternoon while he was there. She checked herself in the mirror again and headed out.

In the small back garden Queenie was pegging up the last few pieces of washing and Brian was playing with his ball.

As Maguire's had the main delivery to the yard on Mondays, Queenie always did the washing on a Tuesday. Otherwise, the dust thrown up from four new cartloads of coal would be disastrous for any washing drying on the line. And it wasn't just the washing that had to be protected: it was Queenie's habit to stuff newspaper into the windows of the house before she went out on a Sunday, yet the fine black dust always managed to creep in and settle on the surfaces.

Mattie tilted her face to the warm late afternoon sun and drew in a deep breath; she just caught the sickly sweet whiff of the local sugar refinery over the tarry smell from the coal.

'Come on, Brian,' she said holding out her free hand, 'Let's go and wait for Uncle Freddie to take us to Auntie Josie's.'

'We see Annie and Mickey?' Brian asked as he jumped up.

'And Rob and Granny N, *if* we ever get there' she said, as Queenie straightened his clothes and kissed him on the cheek.

'I'll be done by the time you get back,' Queenie said, taking the wooden peg from her mouth and pinning it over one end of Mattie's best petticoat. 'And I'll have all this dried and folded before Brian gets home. A man has the right to find his house in order at the end of the day.'

Mattie gave her a wan smile and went into the yard. She looked at the open gate, almost willing Freddie to trot in. Brian spotted Jack and tried to break free but Mattie held on to him. Flossy was a steady horse but it was still dangerous for Brian to get too close to her iron-shod hooves. Jack's new pup, Buster, leapt down from the back of the wagon to dash over and greet Brian in his usual way, nuzzling the boy's hand and barking enthusiastically.

Jack turned and smiled at Mattie. A sensation she'd almost forgotten ran through her and took her breath away. Even in his rough working clothes and with dirt on his face he was one of the most handsome men she'd ever seen. *Shame on you*, she thought, but could not tear her eyes away from him. He looped the reins over the cart break and strolled over.

'I see Freddie's delayed again.'

'Yes.'

'I know I'm on the Bethnal Green round, but why don't you let me take you to your brother's house.'

'Well, I *would* like to get there before the sun sets so I think I'll do just that,' she replied, thankful that he couldn't hear her joyfully pounding heart.

'Come here, young man,' he said, lifting Brian on to the front seat.

Brian immediately took up the reins and urged Flossy on. The horse looked around with mild interest but continued to munch her way through the oats in her nosebag.

'Hold on there,' Jack said with a rumbling laugh. 'Let's get your ma on board.' He took her basket and set that behind the seat then held out his hand to help her up. Mattie took it and a dart of excitement shot up her arm as his fingers closed around hers. She looked up and found herself staring into his dark eyes, which ran slowly over her face as if taking in all the details. She leant towards him, knowing she shouldn't. His free hand took hold of her elbow.

'Mind your step Mrs Maguire.'

Gathering up her skirts, she climbed in beside her son. Jack checked the horse's traces again and then leapt on the wagon in one fluid bound. Buster followed and took up his place behind the driver's seat sticking his nose underneath to sniff at Brian's chubby leg.

Jack settled himself beside Mattie and took the reins from Brian, then clicked his tongue to urge Flossy forward. While he watched the road ahead, Mattie took the opportunity to run her eyes slowly over his well-balanced shoulders and down to the corded muscles of his bare forearms.

'It was good of you to offer Kate a lift the other day,' she said.'

'It was on my way,' he turned and looked down at her, 'and she was lively company.'

A twinge of jealousy tugged at Mattie but she pushed it aside. Wasn't that what she had planned all along? For Kate to fall for Jack and he for her? Of course she had; it was working out just as she hoped. And she was pleased. Truly she was.

Jack's deep voice cut through her thoughts.

'Who delivers here?' he asked, looking over the new houses lining both sides of the streets.

Mattie shrugged. 'Tyler's I think, but with so many new houses being built I don't think any one yard has all the business.'

'I think I might take a stroll up here tomorrow after the morning round and see if I can drum up a bit of business.'

Mattie glanced up at him only to find his gaze resting on her in the most unsettling way.

'I've had a thought about a way we might increase our customers,' Mattie said. 'What about if I gave you, Billy, Pete and Freddie an extra shilling for every new customer you signed up?'

'What, a commission?'

'Yes. Not immediately, of course, but say after they'd ordered for six weeks. If they order a hundredweight of ordinary kitchen a week then we'd make five shillings extra, even after I've paid the driver his bonus.'

Jack stared at her for a moment, then laughed. 'That's a grand idea. I wish I'd thought of it.'

'Well, you drew the map.'

'But you spent hours filling it in and had every customer's order in your head. If I'd had to reconfigure the delivery rounds from the paperwork I'd still be there now,' he said, an expression of frank admiration on his face. 'And it was you who thought of selling a half hundredweight from the yard for two shillings less if the buyer collects it.'

Mattie basked in his approval.

His eyes flickered uncertainly over her face. 'I hope you don't think me rude when I ask why you never thought to re-order the rounds before.'

Mattie shrugged. 'I just took up and ran the business as Brian and his father did, and I had Eli. He knew the ropes, so I left him to it until I'd recovered from having Brian.'

'I can't imagine how hard it must have been for you.'

'I walked about in a daze for months, what with getting up to feed Brian in the night and running the yard by day,' Mattie said, remembering the dark months after her husband died. 'And then there's Queenie. My husband was her only child and she's never been the same since they carried his corpse into the parlour. It's as if her grief is knotted up inside her and can't get out.'

'The loss of a child can do that to a person.' There was something in his voice that caught her attention. Although he laughed and joked with the other drivers, Jack said very little about himself that really mattered. Maybe he'd been married and lost a child. Although the question was on the tip of her tongue, Mattie held it back.

'When I look on those days now, I wonder how I survived,' she continued.

'You either find the steel in your bones and survive or you perish. And from what I've seen, Mrs Maguire, you have a will that won't ever surrender.'

They stared at each other and Jack's eyes changed subtly in a way that sent delight tingling up her spine. The sound of his voice saying her name echoed in her head as the bustle around them faded. For a moment or two they were the only two people in the world until he suddenly broke from her gaze and ruffled Brian's hair.

'And you have this handsome lad to keep you busy.'

Something tugged on her skirt. Mattie looked down to see Buster, crawling under the seat to get to Brian. He leapt between them and wedged himself next to the boy.

'They seem to understand each other,' Mattie said, thankful for something to call her mind back to the present.

Jack nodded. 'He's a scamp.'

'Who, Brian or Buster?'

'Both.'

They reached Oxford Street and Jack turned Flossy towards Stepney High Street and the old church of St Dunstan's.

'Come here, lad,' he said, lifting Brian to sit on his knee. 'Here now. You'll have to drive number one cart one day for your ma, so you'd better start learning.' He looped the reins loosely over Brian's hands and held them firmly in his own. 'Take hold.' Brian's small hand grasped the strips of leather.

'Walk on, Flossy,' Brian shouted at the horse.

They laughed as Brian shook the reins and urged the horse on. Several of the stall holders along the road smiled up at them and a couple of the passersby took their hats off to the boy as the wagon rolled past them. Every now and then Jack's hand would shoot out and stop Brian from toppling forward in his enthusiasm. Mattie sat back and enjoyed her son's innocent enjoyment and the strong presence of Jack beside her. As they reached the bustle of the High Street, Jack moved to take back the reins but Brian's lower lip stuck out and held on to them.

'Come on, lad, let me have them back,' Jack said gently, 'or your ma will give me my marching orders.' Brian looked up at Mattie for a second before giving the reins to Jack.

'You drive number one cart, Jack,' he said with the solemnity only a three year old could muster.

Jack steered Flossy carefully through the afternoon shoppers and turned into Belgravia Road. He pulled the cart to a halt outside number nine, where the door instantly opened and Josie stepped out. She smiled at Mattie, then her gaze moved to Jack and her eyes widened.

'Auntie Josie, Auntie Josie,' Brian shouted as he scrambled across Mattie's lap towards his aunt. 'I drove the cart.'

'Did you now?' Josie replied still looking pointedly at Mattie.

Annie came out and reached up. Brian shuffled to the edge of the seat and she hoisted him down. 'Come and see Rob,' she said, guiding him into the house.

Jack jumped down from the front and held out his hand for Mattie.

'You must be Jack Archer,' Josie said.

Jack touched his forehead. 'Good afternoon, Mrs Nolan.'

Mattie was puzzled. 'I thought you met when Kate visited last week.'

'I dropped Miss Nolan at the end of the road,' he explained. He took a step nearer and handed her basket to her. 'If it's all right with you, Mrs Maguire, I'll write up the daily takings in the morning. I have a bit of business to attend to this evening.'

'Of course,' Mattie said, suddenly aware that Josie was staring at her.

Jack picked up the split sack to place on his head. He nodded at Josie, then leapt onto the wagon in one self-assured movement. He turned and looked down at Mattie. 'Good afternoon, Mrs Maguire, Mrs Nolan.'

He urged Flossy forward and the wagon rolled on. Mattie stared after him for a moment then tore her eyes away.

Josie raised one eyebrow. 'So *that's* Jack Archer.'

Freddie slid off the side of the wagon as Mumble pulled it into Maguire's yard and brought it to a halt by the water trough. She lowered her head and took great gulps as Freddie slackened her girth. He looked around expecting to see Mattie come out of the back gate ready to go to her brother's house for her Tuesday afternoon visit.

A little niggle of rarely felt guilt jabbed at him. Actually, he was surprised Mattie wasn't waiting in the yard spitting feathers; he should have returned a full hour ago after the early afternoon delivery. It was hard graft humping sacks all day so he'd just popped in to wet his whistle and lost track of the time.

Of course, he couldn't tell her he had been propping up the Sword and Sun's bar. He'd have to say he was delayed or something. In any case he knew he could sweet talk her around, or at least he thought he could. If truth were told, Mattie had been a little more resistant to his efforts to win her than he'd expected. And it wasn't that he was losing his touch, far from it, it was just that she wasn't like most women he came across. Just as well, too. He didn't want a wife of his behaving like some others he could mention. However, he was none too pleased at having to wait to slip the ring on her finger.

If that bastard Jack Archer didn't always jump in and do whatever it was that he hadn't quite got around to, he would have proved to her by now how much she needed him, especially with old Eli still Tom and Dick. It was right and proper that as the new man Archer should do the hard graft; before too long Freddie would be his guv'nor. Unfortunately, it allowed Archer too many reasons to seek Mattie out.

Mumble raised her head and snorted, spraying fine droplets of water onto the dry yard floor. Freddie glanced at the closed garden gate again and then circled Mumble alongside the lumpy sacks stacked up and ready for the final afternoon delivery. Perhaps if he were loaded and ready to go when Mattie did appear it would take some of the sting out of her mood. He grabbed the first sack and heaved it on to the wagon. The rig rolled forward and Mumble pricked up her ears. Freddie had just grabbed the next load when Flossy trotted through the gates with Jack Archer standing on the front board. He jumped down as the horse made for the water trough.

'You're a bit late,' he shouted over as he took Flossy's blinkers and bridle off.

'I was held up,' Freddie replied, annoyed that he'd so readily given an explanation. 'You finished?'

'Yup. I'll be off in a while.'

'Don't forget you've got the daily taking to tally before you go,' Freddie said, pleased at the command in his voice. He glanced at the garden gate. 'Mrs Maguire won't be happy if you—'

'I've squared it with her.'

'When?'

'About an hour ago,' Archer replied, guiding Flossy back as he manoeuvred number one wagon into its place by the fence, 'when I dropped her off at Mrs Nolan's.'

'But it's my job to take her.'

'It's a pity you didn't do it then.'

He strolled past Freddie, and Flossy plodding across the yard after him on her way to the stable. Freddie's eyes followed him while he imagined Mattie talking and laughing with Archer as she sat alongside him.

He marched after him. 'I told you I was held up.'

Archer shook the last of the oats into Flossy trough. 'As you were when the Morris delivery arrived yesterday and the fodder the day before. Was it Molly, Betty or the barmaid of the Sword today?'

'It ain't none of your fecking business.'

'No, it isn't and I couldn't give a damn where you are or who you're with, but I don't like to see Mrs Maguire let down at every turn. She deserves better than that.'

'Oh, yeah, like you I suppose.'

Several emotions that Freddie couldn't quite interpret flashed across Archer's face.

'You want to take some water with it, Freddie, because the drink's addled your brain,' he replied in a flat tone.

Freddie jabbed his finger at him. 'Don't think I ain't seen the way you look at Mattie, Archer. And I know what your little game is.'

Archer laughed. 'Game! You're the one playing games. Trying to sweet-talk her so you can get your feet under her table.'

'And when you're totting up her books I bet you'll just let it slip about me and Molly.'

'Mrs Maguire's sharp enough to see for herself the sort of man you are, Ellis.' He stepped forward and loomed over Freddie. 'Now, unless there's something else . . .'

They stood eyeball to eyeball for a moment, then Freddie looked away. 'I've said my piece.' He poked his finger close to Archer's face. 'But I'm warning you – don't get any ideas about Mattie Maguire.' He stomped away before Archer could answer. Anger and humiliation twisted together in Freddie's chest, and as he returned to his task he distracted himself by telling Archer a few home truths in his head. By the time he'd finished Freddie vowed that the first thing he would do when he took over Maguire's was to give Jack Archer his marching orders.

Seeing the Whitechapel to Holborn omnibus about to leave from outside the London Hospital, Nathaniel dashed after it and jumped on the back plate. He swung up the narrow stairs at the back and squeezed onto a seat on the left side.

The omnibus passed along Cornhill and then swerved into the main shopping area of Cheapside. City gentlemen in their shiny top hats and sharply tailored jackets dodged between the multitude of vendors – from Armenian coffee merchants to stalls heaped with spices imported from Zanzibar. When the bus reached St Paul's, Nathaniel pushed his way off and headed towards its dome. It was the tallest building in London but Nathaniel was hard pressed to see its grandeur, hedged in as it was on all sides by tenements and warehouses.

A pungent aroma of raw sewage filled Nathaniel's nostrils. Pete was right – he'd told him the quickest way to find Fleet Street was to get off at St Paul's and follow your nose as the Fleet ditch would guide you to Ludgate. Keeping a tight grip on his leather wallet to save it from the light-fingered urchins who lurked in side alleys, Nathaniel fought his way through the crowds and down the hill. The last rays of the autumn sun were just fading when he spotted the sign for Norfolk Street high on the wall. He turned left, and then left again into Norfolk Court, to find the *Working Man's Defender* office and print works. He paused and stepped into the shadows.

In the impoverished and overcrowded streets of Wapping and Shadwell he was as safe as a man pursued by the law could be. Even the police only ventured off the main thoroughfares in threes and fours and never at night. Few people could read, so there was no need to furnish a reference to take a room or find work, and the whole economy was cash in hand and no questions asked.

Even when weaving number one cart amongst the tightly packed streets and offloading coal, he was known simply as the coalman or Jack. He had become comfortable in such surroundings. He might even find a way to convince Mattie to marry him. But if he walked into the newspaper offices his slim chance of future happiness could be lost forever.

Perhaps he should just turn away and hold on to what he had, but how would he ever look at himself in the mirror again if he did? He owed it to Marjorie and his girls.

Tucking up his collar, Nathaniel crossed the road. He walked around the back of a cart and looked through the dirty window in the half-glazed door. Inside, a couple of young men were bundling newspapers into stacks ready for distribution. The *Defender* was a weekly periodical and tomorrow, Wednesday, was publication day. He pushed open the door and was blasted with the sharp metallic smell of ink mingled with machine oil. One of the printers, muscular and with ink-stained fingers, turned from the machine whipping paper under the press and looked him over.

'Mr Smyth-Hilton?' Nathaniel asked

'Upstairs,' the printer replied, nodding towards a set of wooden stairs at the back of the print shop.

Nathaniel started up the stairs, which were so creaky he wondered if they could bear his weight. At the top he headed for the open door at the end of the landing. Inside, sitting at a desk was a man with his head down, and busily scratching his quill across a sheet of paper. Nathaniel knocked on the door frame. The man held up the palm of a surprisingly delicate hand, continued to write for a few moments then threw the pen down and let out a sigh. 'One cannot cut into the prose when it is in full flow, sir,' he said, looking up.

The young man had bright blue eyes and a rounded, almost feminine face. The fine moustache on his top lip set his age at twenty-five or thereabouts. His unfashionably long blond wavy hair was swept back from a high brow. The mulberry-coloured velvet jacket sitting on his narrow shoulders was high quality but worn almost through at the elbows. His shirt, too, showed signs of wear, with splodges of ink on the frilly cuffs and on the faded red cravat, which was tied loosely around his winged collar.

'Mr Smyth-Hilton?'

The young man stood up. 'At your service. What can I do for you?'

Nathaniel pulled out the sheet he'd peeled off the wall at 56 Thrawl Street. 'I found this plastered on a dosshouse wall.'

Smyth-Hilton's eyes flickered over it and his lips twitched. 'Dosshouse, you say? My, my, we must be going up in the world. It's usually found torn into squares and hanging from a nail in the privy.'

'It was the subject matter that caught my attention.'

'It is the right, nay the duty, of every Englishman to speak his mind and I warn you, you may smash my presses into scrap iron and beat my poor frail body to a pulp but I will never, never be silenced.' He placed a finely boned hand on his chest. 'It is my quest to expose the corruption and self-interest that keeps the working men of this country chained in poverty and ignorance. I shall not be intimidated by you, or anyone else Amos Stebbins sends to silence me.'

'If that's true then I was right to bring you these.' Nathaniel pulled the file from beneath his jacket and held it out.

The journalist took the file and flipped it open. He sat down and scanned the top sheet.

'Please, sit,' Smyth-Hilton said, waving his hand towards the chair in the corner, then returned to reading the file.

Nathaniel crossed the room to the window. Across the square a police officer checked the warehouse doors of the buildings opposite, shining his bulls-eye lamp up and down. He turned and shone the lamp to the upper windows. Nathaniel stood back from the window as a shaft of light cut briefly across the room.

Smyth-Hilton looked up from scanning the documents. 'Where did you get this?'

'I can't say.'

'I'm not surprised. It's clear these,' he held the papers aloft, 'were obtained by, shall we say, unconventional means.'

'Everything written there is genuine,' Nathaniel said, jabbing his finger onto the top sheet. 'These are copies of deeds of properties recently bought. Not one or two but dozens of them, all acquired at rock-bottom prices and then quietly transferred into Stebbins' name. There are the balance sheets of the accounts he has submitted to his Grey Friars warehouse shareholders, along with the much less buoyant ones kept under lock and key at his solicitors.' Nathaniel moved the first sheet away and pointed to the line of figures on the one below. 'There are also odd outgoings to unspecified recipients which might yield some interesting answers.'

'Yes, yes,' Smyth-Hilton said, 'but I would need to see the original documents for myself before I could print a word.'

'I understand but I thought, given your study of Mr Stebbins's activities, that you might be interested in them nonetheless.'

'What is it to you, Mr whoever you are?'

'That's my business at present.'

'Do I detect a country accent? Essex, isn't it?'

'Perhaps.'

Smyth-Hilton nodded slowly. 'I believe Mr Stebbins hails from that part of the world.'

'Essex is a big county.'

'During my investigations I have already unearthed a number of very interesting facts. One stands out in particular: prior to his moving to our fair city he was involved in some very nasty business whereby a great deal of money was stolen from his employer.'

Nathaniel's expression didn't change.

He would have been surprised if Smyth-Hilton hadn't found out where Amos came from and the scandal of the Romford money, but with a police officer nosing around in the yard below, the tiny office suddenly seemed to shrink even smaller.

'Is that so?'

'Yes. But his junior clerk, a local man named Nathaniel Tate, accused Amos Stebbins himself of taking the money. However, as a proportion of the money was found hidden in a box at the bottom of the clerk's garden, it seemed that Tate was the guilty party, not Stebbins.'

'Damning evidence indeed,' Nathaniel replied, remembering the look of horror on Marjorie's face when the small steel casket was unearthed beneath the children's vegetable patch. 'I don't suppose anyone considered the possibility that Stebbins might have put it there.'

'I read the court transcript. The possibility was mentioned at the trial but no one put much store by it.'

'Why should a jury believe the word of a lowly clerk with a stash of money in his garden against that of a respectable gentleman of the town?' Nathaniel asked with just a trace of bitterness in his voice. The memory of Amos's contorted expressions of sorrow about the hurt and betrayal he had suffered at the hands of one whom he had 'nurtured like a son', had completely hoodwinked the twelve jury men at Chelmsford Assizes.

'Why, indeed. I also know, through a few friends on H division, that Stebbins was warned a while ago that a certain Nathaniel Tate had escaped from Her Majesty's penal colony and had been seen in Amos's home town of Romford asking questions as to his whereabouts.'

The blood now pounded in Nathaniel's ears but he didn't move. 'I have no notion of what you're talking about. I came to you because I thought you were interested in uncovering the truth about Amos Stebbins but ...' he leaned forward, shut the file and went to take it back, 'if you're not ...'

Smyth-Hilton hand shot out and anchored the wallet to the desk. 'I didn't say that.'

Nathaniel held the other man's gaze for a few moments, then the reporter looked down at the collection of papers. 'I'll put a few feelers out.' He opened the file and started to flick through it again.

Nathaniel straightened up and strolled to the door.

'Where can I contact you, Mr ...?' Smyth-Hilton asked.

Nathaniel glanced over his shoulder. 'You can't. I'll drop by again sometime.'

Chapter Twelve

Amos Stebbins stood in the clockmaker's doorway opposite the Old Rose public house and pretended to admire the various timepieces. Inside, the old watchmaker, with a horn spy-glass wedged in his eye, regarded him curiously through the dimpled glass of the window.

Amos bent down as if he were inspecting the gold hunter watch in the centre of the display and surreptitiously looked across the road.

It must be nigh on eleven by now, so where on earth was she?

The shopkeeper had just taken off his buff apron as a prelude to coming out to offer assistance when Amos spotted Mattie heading off to buy her Friday supper. He waited until she was out of sight, then stepped out of his hiding place and marched briskly across the road. As he strode past the open gates of Maguire's he glanced in.

Good. Number one and two carts were back from their morning rounds. He continued on to the end of the road then turned and strolled back. Swinging his cane and with a jolly expression on his face Amos sauntered into the yard.

Number three cart was standing in the middle of the space with the bay horse between the shafts while Pete heaved sacks of coal on board. Number one cart was parked against the far wall which meant Flossy must be in her stable. Perfect.

'Good morning. Is Mrs Maguire in?' Amos asked, looking around the yard.

Pete put his hands in the small of his back and straightened.

'You've just missed her, she's gone to Shadwell fish market,' he replied, wiping the sweat from his forehead.

Amos snapped his fingers in the air. 'Oh, I forgot it's Friday. Do you think she'll be long?'

'Half an hour I expect,' Pete replied, swinging a sack over his shoulder and throwing it on the wagon.

Amos drew his watch from his waistcoat pocket. 'Mmm. I'm a bit pushed for time but perhaps I'll wait for a while. Number one cart not going out then?' he said nodding at the empty cart.

'No. Flossy threw a shoe this morning. Jack's just gone around to the farrier's to see if he can walk her around later.'

Amos laughed. 'So the old girl's got the afternoon off.'

Pete hoisted another sack onto number three wagon and grinned. 'I wish I had. Do you want to wait in the house? I'm sure Queenie would be happy to make you a cuppa.'

Amos waved the suggestion away. 'No, I wouldn't trouble her. You carry on. I'll just stretch my legs around the yard.'

Pete touched his brow and turned back to his task. Amos glanced over his shoulder to ensure Pete wasn't watching him and then he slipped into the stable.

Flossy, the yard's sixteen-hand piebald, who had pulled number one cart for as long as Amos could remember, stood munching her lunch in the end stall. She looked around at him, her large eyes showing even darker in contrast to her white face in the subdued light. Judging by her feather grey muzzle she was probably close to twenty years old, a good age for a draft horse. Amos walked across the straw covered floor towards her.

'There's a good girl,' he crooned, as he squeezed himself between her and the wooden partition.

Flossy shook her head. Amos fumbled in his pocket and pulled out an apple wrapped in greaseproof paper. A faint whiff of something drifted up and Amos rubbed his thumb over the sealing wax at the base. Thankfully, it was still intact. Tucker had warned him at least a dozen times that if the wax melted or fell out he was to discard the apple immediately. He placed it in the palm of his hand.

'Look what I've got for you,' he said, holding it near to the horse's mouth.

Flossy nuzzled it, snorted and turned her head away. Amos tried again, forcing the fruit between her loose lips. Flossy shook her head and backed away, her hooves clopping on the stone floor.

Amos grabbed the leather strap fastened over her nose. The whites of the old horse's eyes showed as she tried to pull herself free. Amos pulled her head down. 'Come on you piece of dogs' dinner, take it,' he snarled.

Flossy whinnied and flicked her head away again. Amos let go of the bridle and closed his hand over her velvety nose, pinching her wide nostril shut. The horse flattened her ears and opened her mouth. Amos forced the apple between her teeth, over her tongue. As Flossy's ground-down molars closed over his arm, Amos whipped his hand away. The horse coughed a couple of time then buried her nose in the bucket of water beside her. Amos watched for a couple of moment then, satisfied that the old horse had swallowed the apple, he walked smartly out of the stable with a glow of satisfaction at a job well done.

Pete had finished loading and was on the top of his wagon kicking the sacks firmly into place before setting out on the afternoon round.

'I'll have to go,' Amos called across without breaking his stride. 'Will you tell Mrs Maguire I called and I'll pop back tomorrow?'

Pete nodded. Amos's shoulders relaxed. According to the slaughter man the poison would start to take effect as soon as it reached the horse's stomach but he would be halfway down Cable Street by then. Tucking his cane under his arm and suppressing a smile Amos turned out of the gate and collided with Mattie.

'Mr Stebbins,' she said, straightening her bonnet. 'Are you waiting for me?'

'Mrs Maguire ... Yes, I am. Or at least I was. I've an urgent appointment elsewhere now. I'll call tomorrow.' He tipped his hat to her. 'Good day.'

'Good day, Mr Stebbins,' she replied, as he walked past her.

Amos picked up his pace and marched to the end of the street. As he turned the corner he stopped, took a deep breath and let his shoulders relax. He repositioned his top hat and tucked his cane more securely under his arm, then strolled on. As he made his way westward towards lunch at the Hoop and Grapes, a discreet smile settled across his lips. *Let's see how long Maguire's can keep afloat with only three horses.*

When Nathaniel spotted Stebbins turn out of Maguire's yard and march down the road towards him, he only just managed to step back around the corner. He pulled his cap down and leant against the wall, keeping his eyes on Stebbins's portly figure until he was certain he wasn't coming back and then walked around the corner to the yard. Mattie was talking to Pete beside number three wagon with her basket over her arm. She turned and smiled at him as he strolled over.

'You're back early,' he said, enjoying the sight of her.

She laughed. 'I could say the same to you. Can the farrier fit Flossy in later?'

Nathaniel nodded. 'I'll walk her around last thing.'

'Good,' Mattie replied. 'I can't afford to have her idle another—'

An ear-piercing scream from the stable, followed by wild banging and crashing echoed across the yard. Mattie dropped her basket and dashed towards the open doors with Nathaniel and Pete hot on her heels. They skidded to a halt just inside and stared in horror at Flossy.

Somehow she had wrenched herself free from where Nathaniel had tied her a few hours before and now stood in the middle of the stable with her eyes rolling and sweat glistening on her flanks. Her front legs were splayed apart as she drew in painfully rasping breaths. Her ears were flat and she trembled convulsively.

'Sweet Mary, what's happened to her?' Mattie asked. 'Has she rolled and twisted her gut?'

'I don't know,' Nathaniel replied. 'Pete, run and fetch the vet.'

Pete dashed out, and Mattie looked up at Nathaniel. 'Maybe she hurt herself on a nail or something. If we can get her back into her stall it will settle her until Mr Harris arrives. The old girl knows me.' She spread her arms and inched towards the horse. 'I'll see if I can catch her halter and coax her back. Aroon, me darling,' she soothed.

The horse tottered to the left but somehow kept herself upright. She snorted and drew her lips back in an agonising grimace. Nathaniel stepped forward and hooked his arm around Mattie's waist. He pulled her back just seconds before Flossy reared up and lashed out with an iron-shod hoof.

'I'm sorry, Mrs Maguire,' he said releasing her. 'But Flossy's in too much pain to know anyone or anything.'

Suddenly the horse threw her head back and shrieked, then crumpled on her front knees. Her head crashed to the floor as her nostrils flared unnaturally. A quiver ran over her sweaty flanks then her back legs gave way. She lurched sideways and crashed to the ground sending dust and hay flying into the air.

'No!' Mattie cried, pushing past him and throwing herself down beside the dying horse. She gently picked up Flossy's head and cradled it on her lap. Nathaniel hunkered down quietly beside her. The horse's hooves twitched and scraped on the ground. Nathaniel could see that the horse's eyes were beyond pain now. A thick lump lodged in his throat and the corners of his eyes tightened. Silent tears streamed down Mattie's cheek as she stroked the soft muzzle of the old horse. The only sound in the stable was Flossie's laboured breath. Then it ceased.

Mattie bent forward, laid her head on Flossy's cheek and wept.

'I'm so sorry,' Nathaniel whispered.

After a moment Mattie sat up. 'Thank you.' She wiped her face. 'Flossy was my late husband's horse ever since he was a lad of fifteen. She was the young horse of the stable then and I remember how she used to fling her head and whinny at him each morning. Just like she does . . .' She gave him a brave smile, ' . . . *did*, when you walk in each day.' She looked down at the horse again and a tear escaped and fell onto the whiskery muzzle lying in her lap. Nathaniel, feeling utterly helpless, watched her shaking shoulders.

After a few moments, Mattie slid Flossy's head onto the floor and started to rise. Nathaniel held out his hand to help her. She took it and stood up, then dusted down her skirt.

'Will you go around to the knacker's yard and—'

Pete crashed through the door. 'The vet said he'd—' He stopped as he saw the dead horse.

'I'll see to things,' Nathaniel cut in. 'You go in and make yourself a cup of tea.'

Mattie gave him a tight-lipped nod. Standing so close and feeling her palpable grief, Nathaniel struggled not to reach for her. Mattie bent down and patted Flossy's neck then stood up, blew her nose again and left the stable.

'Shall I call in at Wren's on my rounds to tell them to collect her?' Pete asked.

Nathaniel nodded. 'But tell them to come as late as possible to save Mrs Maguire having to see her go.'

Pete left. Nathaniel turned and looked into Flossy's empty stall. The rope-tether hung in shreds from the metal ring at the far end of the stall and the water bucket had been kicked over.

God, the poor old girl must have been in agony, he thought, looking at the deep gouges in the flagstones. *And I'd put a pound to a farthing that it wasn't by chance that Stebbins called just an hour before she took ill. But how?*

Nathaniel kicked over the straw bedding and spotted something. It was a square of greaseproof paper. He sniffed then pulled away sharply. It smelt of something he couldn't identify, but it certainly wasn't cox's pippin.

Stebbins! Nathaniel's fist clenched together. It was clear that Amos would stop at nothing to acquire Mattie's yard. But if he could stroll in and poison a dumb beast in broad daylight, what else was he capable of?

Josie slid the china pot under the bed and climbed back under the covers. Patrick stirred, wrapped around her, and she snuggled against him. There was just the faintest hint of light under the curtains and she guessed it was probably a little after four. She rolled her head and looked at the profile of her sleeping husband and thought again of Mattie's last visit.

When Kate, who was a hopeless romantic, had told her last week about the handsome new coalman who couldn't take his eyes off Mattie, Josie hadn't given it much mind, had dismissed the notion – until she opened the door and saw them sitting together on number one wagon. They looked just right together, a couple, and she herself would have put such a fanciful idea down to her condition had she not seen for herself the way Mattie looked up at Archer – with such palpable emotion that Josie had to look away.

'Patrick, are you awake?' she whispered.

'Mmm.'

'I can't sleep.'

'Pity.' He smoothed his hand over her swollen stomach. 'Is the baby keeping you awake?'

'It's Mattie,' she said.

Patrick groaned.

'Well … it's her new coalman.'

Patrick rolled on his back and placed his palm on his forehead. 'Josie, sweetheart, I have to be at the mooring at five,' he said, wearily. 'What is this about?'

'It's Mattie's new coalman, Jack Archer.'

'What about him?'

'Well, he's very handsome,' Josie replied. 'And I think he might be interested in her.'

'Well, he wouldn't be the first to cast his eyes in her direction these last three years but Mattie told me he was sweet on Kate.'

After seeing the look in Jack's eyes as they rested on Mattie Josie didn't believe that for one moment.

'Perhaps, but that's not what's unsettled me.' She sat up and turned towards her husband. 'I know this sounds silly but …'

'But?'

Josie took a deep breath. 'There's a wanted poster outside every police station in the area offering a reward for an escaped convict from Botany Bay. He was seen in the area.'

'And you … you … think Mattie's new coalman is the man?' he said, barely able to get his words out for chuckling.

'But what if he is?'

'Oh Josie,' he said, trying to keep a straight face.

'Yes, I know it sounds ridiculous, but he's new in the area and we don't know anything about him. He could be anyone. Shouldn't you make sure he's ok for Mattie's sake?'

'You're right. I'll pop down if I have time this week'

'Go tomorrow,' Josie answered looking up at him in the half light from the window.

He sighed. 'If I can, Josie. I've got—'

'Patrick!'

'All right, all right. I'll let Iggy see to the afternoon shipment.'

Josie stretched up and kissed him. 'Thank you.'

Patrick rolled his eyes. 'Women!' he snuggled her into him. 'Now will you go back to sleep and leave me to worry about Mattie's new coalman?'

'Yes, Patrick,' Josie replied, smiling to herself in the dark.

Chapter Thirteen

Patrick strolled along the narrow pavement of Wapping High Street towards the police station. He wasn't alone. The tide was in and there were sailors and dockers spilling out of every public house where they were taking their first mouthful of beer after a back-breaking day's work. Parched though his throat was after hauling a full barge of coal to Vauxhall, his end-of-day pint would have to wait an hour or two yet.

The notice board outside the red brick police station was full but in the middle of the wooden panel was the poster that had caused Josie's imagination to gallop away with her. Patrick scanned the placard.

The Receiver of the Metropolitan Police. July 1847

£20 REWARD

will be paid for the apprehension of

Nathaniel Tate.

Twenty pounds might be tempting but Patrick doubted anyone would try to collect it. The unwritten street law demanded that you avoided the police if you could or acknowledged them respectfully if you couldn't. If you didn't want to find yourself sinking to the bottom of the river with a ship's weight tied around your ankles, you told them nothing.

**A convicted thief and fugitive from
Her Majesty's penal colony in New South Wales.**

A thief! Well as far as that goes it depended on your understanding of the word.

The tradition of spillage dockers putting a bit of the cargo in their pocket was called theft by the ship owners, but sometimes the bob or two the docker got for selling his scrap of illicit goods saved their family from starvation. No one called the dock owners thieves for cutting their labourers wages to preserve profits.

Patrick moved on to the description of the wanted man:

**Tate is approximately six foot tall and square shouldered;
powerfully built. Hair dark & curly; eyes brown; complexion
tanned. Usually clean shaven. Cheek bones rather prominent;
chin blunt; forehead broad. Lips firm set. Quick and active
nature. Distinguishing mark; heart shaped tattoo on right
upper arm with the letters M, L & R within it.**

**Last seen in his home town of Romford wearing rough clothing.
Believed to be in the Wapping and Shadwell area.**

Enquires to Superintendent Jackson,
Arbour Square police station.

The description of this Nathaniel Tate could fit any number of men
in the street where he stood, including himself. Even the lettering of
the tattoo wouldn't necessarily single Tate out. Most men had at least
one crudely inked mark on their arms and often many more. If this
Tate had visited one of the local trollops they might see the mark
but, again, they wouldn't be trotting off to tell the police, not even
for twenty pounds.

Patrick re-read the poster. Then, adjusting his knapsack on his
back, he continued on his journey. If he were honest, he reckoned he
had more chance of being crowned king of Ireland than Mattie's
coalman turning out to be this Tate fellow, but he had promised Josie
to find out about Jack Archer and that was exactly what he was
going to do.

Nathaniel leant back on the chair and turned slightly so he could
study Mattie as she bent over the ledger.

Mattie scratched the pen across the bottom of the page and smiled
up at him. 'That's four weeks in a row that our profit's topped five
pounds. At this rate the bank manager will be inviting me in for a
cup of tea!'

The wind had tugged a few wisps free from under her scarf and
Nathaniel envied them their ability to caress her cheeks.

'It's your idea of the bonus that's increased the yard's takings.'

'And you signed up almost all the new houses in Beaumont Square,'
she replied. 'By the way I've been thinking about bringing Eli back.'

A chasm opened at his feet. 'That's for you to say, Mrs Maguire,'
he said, in an even tone. 'I knew the job was only temp—'

'No, no!' Mattie said quickly. 'Not to drive number one cart – he couldn't manage it. It's just that he's been with Maguire's for twenty years and I want to ask him to do a bit of light work around the yard.' She gave him a shy look from under her lashes. 'I know I only offered you the job on a temporary basis but I would like you to stay on permanently. If you want to.'

He had stayed too long already and should really say no, but with her beautiful face looking earnestly up at him, all sense and caution evaporated.

'Thank you, Mrs Maguire. With Eli in the yard it might save you from forever dashing in and out of the house. You might even have a chance to put your feet up in the afternoon.'

'What, with Brian around?' she laughed.

Buster, who'd been snoozing in the corner, lifted his head. Nathaniel turned to find Mattie's brother, Patrick, standing in the doorway. Nathaniel rose slowly to his feet. He'd heard the tales about Patrick's fight with Ma Tugman: how he'd laid out Charlie, her youngest, and wrestled a gun from Harry, the older brother. Patrick Nolan might be a respectable barge owner but he was considered to be a hard man in the streets of Knockfergus and beyond.

Patrick's eyes narrowed.

'Oh, Patrick,' Mattie said, standing up and patting her hair back into place. 'We ... I was doing the accounts,' she said, in a light, too breezy voice. 'I don't think you've met Jack Archer.'

Nathaniel extended his hand. 'Mr Nolan.'

Patrick's expression remained stony for a brief moment then he took Nathaniel's hand and an open smile creased his face. 'So you're my sister's new driver. My wife mentioned that she'd met you and I hear you've already found a horse to replace Flossy.'

'I have, which reminds me I should be getting on with the afternoon deliveries, if that's all right with you, Mrs Maguire.'

Patrick reached down and stroked Buster, blocking Nathaniel's route to the door. 'So where're you from?'

'The south coast.'

'Whereabouts?' Patrick asked, as he made a fuss of the dog. 'I only ask because when I sail the *Smiling Girl* up to Folkestone I always bring a fresh Dover sole for my wife. She loves them, doesn't she, Mattie?'

Mattie didn't answer.

Nathaniel picked up his cap, hooked on the back of the chair. 'I'm from Hastings.'

A jolly smile creased Patrick face but didn't quite reach his eyes. 'I know the place. Whereabouts?'

'In the old town in All Saint's Road, across from the church. If you know the net huts it's the road running up from there.'

The fisherman turned smuggler who had occupied the bunk beneath Nathaniel in Botany Bay had come from the old cinque port. After two years of listening to him talking about his home town day and night, Nathaniel felt he knew it as well as he did Romford.

'So what brought you to London?' Buster rolled on his back to have his belly tickled.

'Work.'

Patrick stood up and Buster scrambled to his feet and shook himself. 'And you're lodging locally.'

'With my sister and her husband in Hope Alley.'

'You've been working abroad I hear? India? Or perhaps—'

'If you'll excuse me, Mr Nolan.' Nathaniel clicked his fingers to bring the dog to heel. 'It's good meeting you, but I have the afternoon delivery to take out.'

Patrick straightened up and for one moment, Nathaniel thought he was going to block his way again but then he stood aside.

Nathaniel turned to Mattie. 'Good afternoon, Mrs Maguire.'

Ruth lay with the bed covers up around her chin and stared at the brass handle of her bedroom door. The heavy drapes were closed and the only light in the room came from the oil lamp on her bedside table. She'd been in bed for an hour, but although her eyelids were heavy she dared not allow herself to drift off to sleep just yet. A floorboard creaked outside her room. Ruth drew in a sharp breath and squeezed her eyes tight closed.

Please let it be one of those nights when he don't come,' she prayed silently, as she pressed herself into the soft mattress.

The footsteps drew nearer then stopped outside her door. Ruth's eyes flew open and fixed again on the polished knob as it slowly turned.

'You go to bed, my love,' her stepfather called down the hallway. 'I'll make sure Ruth is tucked in for the night.'

'Give her a kiss from me.'

Ice replaced the blood in Ruth's veins as Amos Stebbins stepped into the room.

*

Nathaniel turned into Hope Alley where he was greeted by the sight of Buttony Cox, the local cats-meat man, weighing out pounds of bloody flesh. The trader had set up his hand cart in the usual position and on the walls and windowsill cats paced and meowed as they waited for their suppers. The flesh was ground horse meat from old, winded nags sold by their owners to the knackers yard for a couple of shillings. Often families could barely afford to feed themselves but needed at least one cat to keep the mice at bay.

'Ca' me-e-et-me-yet-me-e-yet!' Buttony shouted, the mother-of-pearl buttons sewn around the edge of his collar twinkling in the faint gaslight. He spotted Nathaniel. 'Oi, Archer. You better tell your skin 'an blister to get out 'ere before it's all gone,' he called, handing a chunk of meat wrapped in newspaper to a customer.

Nathaniel was surprised that Dolly Roscoe hadn't already bought her two days' supply. With a dozen dogs to feed she was usually first in the queue.

'Sure,' he shouted back, treading carefully over the meandering trickle of slurry that ran down the central channel.

Whistling Buster to heel, Nathaniel walked the last few yards to the door of his lodgings and pushed it open. He had just set his foot on the bottom stair when the door to the parlour flew open and Dolly stepped out.

'Oh, Jack, sweetheart, you're home,' she said, her eyes wide and glaring at him. 'I was just telling *Mr Nolan here* 'ow much we did miss you and how grand it is to have you back after your wandering.' She leant back to reveal Mattie's brother standing uncomfortably in the middle of her shabby front room.

Nathaniel calmly turned and walked passed Dolly into the room.

'Mr Nolan.' He offered his hand. After just a second's hesitation Patrick took it. 'This is unexpected,' Nathaniel said, locking it in a fierce grip.

'I was just passing.'

'Have you offered Mr Nolan a cuppa?' Nathaniel asked Dolly, who was standing nervously beside him.

Patrick's eyes darted onto the collection of dirty cups and plate on the table with the flies buzzing around them. 'No, it's quite alright. I don't want to put you to any trouble.'

'It's no trouble,' Dolly replied shuffling over to the fire and moving kettle over the flames. 'I was just telling Mr Dolan—'

'Nolan,' Patrick cut in.

'Pardon me,' Dolly said, '—about our little cottage in Hastings and how I came to London while you stayed with Gran.'

Nathaniel smiled fondly down at his landlady giving a silent prayer of thanks that he'd made the Roscoes repeat his story about Hastings over and over until they got it right. 'I hope you told him how you saved me from the seagull that was after my crust?'

'No, I didn't.' She nudged Nathaniel in the ribs. 'I'm surprised you even remember. You were nought but a nipper.'

'Dirty great thing swooping down on me like that, how could I forget?'

Dolly had lived in Lowestoft as a child and the seagull story was hers. Nathaniel reasoned that if anyone did question her about her long lost younger brother, the nearer to the truth they kept their story the more believable it would sound. Of course he hadn't reckoned on Patrick Nolan dropping by but so far she seemed to have remembered the details.

She beamed at Patrick, who said, 'She also said that you lived in the shadow of the East Hill.'

'Bless me, no. The West Hill,' Dolly corrected. 'There ain't nothing but rocks under the East hill, Mr Bolan.'

'Nolan,' Patrick repeated. 'You know, I wouldn't have taken you for brother and sister.'

Nathaniel looked down at Dolly then back at Patrick. 'Wouldn't you?'

'No. Not at all.'

Dolly slid her arm around Nathaniel waist and he forced himself not to recoil. 'I guess I favour Ma and you have more of Pa's features.'

'Ahh,' said Patrick nodding slowly. 'That would account for it, but what still puzzles me is that you don't sound alike either.'

Nathaniel's face lost its congenial expression. 'Dolly, luv, Buttony's outside,' Nathaniel said, not taking his eyes from Patrick. 'You had better fetch the dog's vittles.'

'Oh my, so I had,' Dolly said, wiping her hands down her apron, 'Nice to have met you Mr Dolan, and I'll call you when supper's ready, Jack,' she said, giving Nathaniel a look of utter relief as she bolted through the door.

Nathaniel stepped in front of Patrick. 'You were just passing were you? Or perhaps the truth is you've come by when you thought I would be out so you could have a nose around.'

'I'm just looking after *my* sister's interests.'

'And what makes you think I might damage them?'

'Nothing, so far.' Patrick's expression hardened. 'But no one knows you, Archer, and no one's even heard of you before you pitched up at the yard six weeks ago so you're right – I've dropped by to check your story out.'

'And are you satisfied?'

The two men stared at each other 'Aye. I am.'

'Then I won't keep you from your supper, Mr Nolan.' Nathaniel opened the door. 'And feel free to drop by anytime. Perhaps next time you'll take that cup of tea.'

Patrick stepped forward until he was almost nose to nose with Nathaniel. 'Good day to you, Archer, but just so you know, God help you if I find out anything about you that could harm my sister.'

Chapter Fourteen

Dolly Roscoe's ear-splitting scream woke Nathaniel from a deep sleep and set his heart pounding. Below him, fists hammered on the front door and the dozen or so dogs at the back of the house added to the pandemonium by howling and barking.

Nathaniel sprang from the bed and splashed the ewer of water left for his morning shave over his face to bring himself fully awake. He shook the droplets from his hair and strode across the floor. Tearing back ragged curtains from the window, horror and panic cut off his breath as he gazed down at two stout constables.

Who had betrayed him? Smyth-Hilton? Maybe the reporter had summoned the police as soon as he'd left the office. Or perhaps Patrick Nolan wasn't satisfied with Dolly's story and called them. How else could they have found him? The picture of Stebbins, fat and prosperous, sprang into Nathaniel's mind and bile rose up in his throat.

He snatched his trousers from the end of the bed, yanked them on and managed to shrug on his shirt just as the front parlour door burst open and he heard the sound of heavy boots marching in the hall below.

Nathaniel's heart crashed in his chest and stopped his thoughts. He flattened himself against the wall, his ears strained to hear the click of the handle. Taking a deep breath, he tried to steady his chaotic mind. His eyes darted around the room and then fixed on the small skylight on the other side of the room. It would be a squeeze, but with a bit of wriggling he should be able to get through.

He shoved his feet into his boots, climbed onto the rickety dresser and peered out of the small window to the back of the house. Relief flooded over him. The alley at the back was empty. Then he noticed the steep incline and missing tiles of the lean-to roof below. He doubted it would take his weight but, even if by some miracle it did, he'd be very lucky to make it to the end without sliding off and breaking his neck. But what choice did he have? He had to get away. Images of the brutal regime in the penal colony flashed into his mind.

He couldn't go back. Not again.

Boots clumped on the floor below as he swung the small window open and gripped the frame to heave himself up. Then he paused. If the police knew where to find him, why were they searching below?

Climbing down from the chest of drawers he went back to the front window. The two police officers were still standing in the road but now, beside them, there was a pile of tatty furniture and Dolly in her nightcap and gown. The early morning ruckus brought out the whole street and a couple of women hurried over and threw their arms around her.

Keeping half an eye on the policemen, Nathaniel laced his boots and slipped on his coat. He opened the door quietly, tip-toed onto the landing and looked out of the window to the back of the house. There was no sign of the police. If he climbed out and down into the back yard he might be able to get away.

'Fecking put them down!' Tubby bellowed.

Nathaniel held his breath and peeped around the corner of the banisters. At the bottom of the stairs a squat man wearing a check jacket and with a shaved head marched towards the open front door.

'If yer paid yer rent each week instead of hiding under the table, you and your old lady wouldn't be out on the street,' he shouted, pushing past Tubby and throwing the cane chair out the door.

With his heart still pounding Nathaniel ventured down the stairs.

'Bailiffs?' he asked another man with oiled hair who stepped out of the Roscoe's front room carrying a three-legged table.

The man nodded. 'If you're lodging here, you'd better pack up and clear out.'

Nathaniel only just stopped himself from laughing with relief and returned to his room. He gathered up the copies of land deeds and accounts he'd given to Smyth-Hilton and slipped them into a slim satchel, which he concealed inside his shirt. He removed his belt and wound it around the dozen or so books he'd managed to collect and fastened the buckle securely. Finally, he tied his spare shirt, trousers and smalls together with his best tie, then heaved the mattress from the iron bedstead. He rolled it up and slung it over his shoulder and walked as casually as his racing pulse would allow him, down the stairs and out the front door. The two police officers eyed him.

They were taller by half a head than most men, with bushy moustaches and matching side whiskers. The brass buttons on their dark navy frock coats twinkled in the early morning sunlight and their top hats sat authoritatively atop their heads.

Shrugging the mattress more comfortably on his shoulder,

Nathaniel started down the street. The taller of the two officers pointed at him. 'Oi! You! Come 'ere.'

'Morning, officers,' he said, trying to remain calm.

The older one, probably ex-military by the look of the powder burn on the side of his face, looked him up and down.

'That yours?' he indicated the mattress over Nathaniel's shoulder.

'Aye. Bought and paid for,' he replied.

The younger officer studied him more closely. 'Where you from?'

'Hastings.' Nathaniel replied, as Mrs Roscoe's china was deposited none too gently on the pavement by the front door.

'My wife comes from St Leonards.'

Nathaniel forced himself not to react. The officers were only there to keep the peace but if he raised their suspicions in the slightest way they might decide to investigate him further.

'No more than a country mile away,' he said praying that it was.

The officer looked at him more closely. 'What's your name?'

There was an explosion of noise as Tubby's dogs bolted through the front door, yelping and barking as they tore up the street to scatter children and cats alike. Dolly let out a loud wail and slumped on the chair in the middle of her tatty possessions and sobbed. The two bailiffs emerged from the house and piled the last of the household linen on the wet cobbles. Tubby followed them with a guilt-ridden look on his fleshy face. As she caught sight of him Dolly sprang to her feet and rushed at her husband.

The officer beside Nathaniel turned and chuckled.

'You bastard,' she shouted snatching up a cooking pot to swing at him. 'I suppose you've spent all the rent in the Bell.'

Tubby dodged the iron pot. 'Now, Doll, I—'

'Don't you *Doll* me,' she replied, adjusting her grip on the handle and swiping at him again. He dodged back and a cheer went up from the crowd. Two of the dogs grasped the bottom of Tubby's trousers and snarled at him as Dolly went for it. There was a metallic-sounding bong as she landed a well aimed blow on the side of her husband's head.

The older constable knocked out his pipe. 'We had better break it up, Knight, before she kills the poor sod.'

Nathaniel adjusted the mattress again. 'I'll leave you to it then, officer,' he said, as he stepped away. 'I have to get to work before I'm docked an hour's pay.'

The younger police constable glanced back at him. 'All right, on your way then, chum. Although I don't know what your governor will say when you arrive for work with all your worldly goods on your shoulders.'

Male laughter greeted Mattie as she closed the garden gate and walked into the yard to start the day. Her jaw dropped as she saw Jack standing below her with a mattress across his shoulder and an awkward grin on his face. Staring at his tall frame and angular face in the crystal clear light of the early morning, Mattie knew she loved him. Well, actually she'd been in love with him for weeks and had to fight the urge to throw herself into his arms there and there.

'Ho, Mrs M, what do you think of this, then?' Pete said, as she reached the bottom step. 'Jack here's been turfed out by the bailiffs.'

Jack raised an eyebrow. 'My sister's husband spent the rent and I lost my bed.'

Jack's eyes captured hers and happiness bubbled up inside Mattie.

Billy's voice cut between them. 'I said that I didn't take old Jack to be a Bible studying man, Mrs M, but he seems to have taken up his bed and walked,' he said, slapping his thigh and guffawing at his own joke.

'You had better store your things in the office,' she said, as he fell into step behind her. He shrugged the mattress into the corner.

'Look, I'm sorry to ask, Mrs Maguire, but there's an advertisement in Swanson's window for a room going in Fenton Street, so would you mind if I nipped around there before taking the wagon out?' One corner of his mouth lifted. 'There's hardly a room to be had anywhere for less than three shillings a week and if I don't get around there smart it'll be gone. I'll not be more than half an hour'

'Of course,' she replied. 'But what about your sister?'

'Oh, she and Tubby have been talking about moving to Cambridge Heath so I was thinking of looking for a room anyhow.'

The unused room at the front of the house, thought Mattie. If she got an iron bedstead from the Webster's auction rooms ... She shook herself. What in the name of God was she thinking of?

Jack drained the last of his coffee. 'Well, I had better—'

'You could lodge in the front room,' she blurted out.

'I couldn't possibly impose,' he replied, a little too quickly.

'You wouldn't be. The room's been unused for years,' Mattie replied, willing him to agree but afraid for her peace of mind that he would.

Several emotions crossed Jack's face that she couldn't interpret, then one eyebrow rose. 'Won't people talk?'

Talk! It'll be around the streets before the sun goes down.

Mattie shrugged. 'Don't they always? And it's not as if I'm alone in the house. Kate is here, so is Queenie and you'll be downstairs.'

His expression changed subtly. Mattie caught an escaped tendril of hair and curled it back in place. She hesitated. 'If you would rather not, then I—'

'It's most kind of you, Mrs Maguire,' he replied, the deep tone of his voice sending delicious shivers though her. 'Perhaps if only for a night or two.'

Freddie pressed his back into the hundredweight sack of coal, reached above his head and grasped the raw edge of the sack to heave it onto his shoulders. His body ached with the weight and sharp edges of coal dug into the bones of his spine but he barely noticed the pain.

He trudged the few steps to the coal hole of the Artichoke and bent forward, and the chunks of coal tumbled through the round opening into the cellar below. One large lump bounced off the rim and landed at Freddie's feet, but in his mind's eye, instead of a fist-size piece coal, he saw Jack Archer's face.

'Ger in you fecking bugger,' he yelled, as he kicked the nugget of coal against the pub wall. It exploded into dozens of shards and splattered across the pavement. It was a pity he couldn't destroy the cocky bastard Archer as easily.

'Oh, Freddie, you're in a right mood today,' said Mrs Conner, the landlord's wife, who was watching him from the doorway.

Freddie scowled at her. 'You would be too if you'd had the day I've had, Missus. Same again Friday?'

'If you please. And I 'ope whatever's tightened your nuts has gone and you're back to your usual cheery self.'

Freddie jumped on the rig and took up the reins. Mumble started forward as the landlord's wife disappeared back into the pub.

Fecking cheery self, thought Freddie, as the wagon rolled down the road. Was it any wonder he was out of sorts?

When he came back for dinner and realised that Archer had already moved his gear in, Freddie had almost gone berserk and given into the urge to punch his face in but he held back. He might land a couple of blows but Archer would pummel him black and blue.

Lodge in! Huh! Offered him a bit of 'ow's your father more like. *And after she'd all but agreed to get spliced in the stable. And wasn't I the perfect gentleman? Fecking women don't know their own minds.*

The cart turned into Commercial Road and Freddie caught a

reflection of himself in the grocer's window. He adjusted the knot of his kingsman.

Well, she had her chance, he thought. *Plenty more fish in the sea.*

But fury surged up in him again as he saw the easy life he'd planned for himself disappearing over the horizon.

'Yoo-hoo, Freddie!' called a woman's voice to the side of him.

Freddie turned and a smile spread across his face. 'Hello, Kate.'

From his vantage point above he could see the pleasing swell of her breasts quite clearly. But what pleased him more than her face – and her pretty person – was the look of utter adoration on her face. Freddie ground his teeth. *That's* how Mattie should be looking at him.

'Can I have a ride back to the yard,' she asked.

'Of course you can, my little darling.'

He offered her his hand and he felt her tremble as she took it. Stepping onto the wheel she climbed up and a faint smell of flour and yeast drifted over to him. Gathering her skirt together, Kate sat down beside him.

Freddie studied her face. What was she? Sixteen, almost seventeen? And although she'd been walking out with that mummy's boy Alfie Lennon for months, Freddie doubted he'd have the gumption to push his luck. So sweet Kate was still an untouched flower.

'You're looking very pretty today, darling,' he said, and was rewarded with a flutter of eyelashes. 'If I were to tell the truth, Kate, you always do.' He gave her his sincerest look. 'I've wanted to tell you that for such a long time but I didn't want you to think I was being too forward.'

'Oh, Freddie, I'd never think that of you,' she replied, giving him another look of pure adoration.

'You don't know how happy I am to hear that, Kate,' he said in a soft voice. 'Especially as . . .' he bit his lip and turned away.

'Especially as what?'

He turned and gave her a mournful look. 'I thought you were sweet on Jack.'

'Jack? I'm not sweet on Jack! How could I be when I'm. . . .' she blushed prettily and looked away.

Freddie slid along the seat pressing his hips and thigh firmly against hers. Her eyes opened wide but she didn't move away.

'Are you saying you're sweet on me?' he asked, closing his hand over hers.

'I . . . I . . .' Kate turned, but not before he saw her flustered expression.

Freddie's wounded pride rallied. He was used to women giving him sly glances and allowing him a bit of slap and tickle but the yearning in Kate's eyes was enough to stir any man.

'Are you?' He pressed himself closer. 'Oh, Kate, say you are and I'll be the happiest fella in the street.'

She looked sideways at him from under her eyelashes. 'I didn't think you'd even noticed me. '

He looked astonished. 'Not notice you! How could I not notice you? In fact, I've nearly driven the cart into the gate before now because I can't take my eyes off you.'

Kate laughed. 'Oh Freddie, you are a lark. I just thought you saw me as a little girl.'

His expression changed to one of smouldering desire. 'See you as a little girl? Nothing could be further from the truth. When I look at you, my darling,' he ran his eyes over her slowly and brought the colour back to her cheeks. 'I see a woman. A woman that I'd be eager to hurry home to each day.'

Kate's eyes opened even wider. 'Freddie, are you ...' She put her hand on his bare arm.

Freddie screwed his face up into a forlornly expression. 'Forgive me, Kate, I shouldn't try to rush you. I respect you too much. Could I walk you out one night? I mean to somewhere respectable like Lusby's. There's an acrobat from Arabia and a clown with a little dog doing a turn on Friday.'

Kate turned on the seat. 'Freddie, you're such a gentleman and I'd love to. I'll tell Mat—'

'Can we keep things a bit quiet, for now, Sweetheart,' he said, sliding his arm around her waist and drawing her closer. 'Just until we've got to know each other better. Then, after a couple of months, I can speak to your brother, Patrick.' He gave her his most charming smile. 'I want to do things the right way with you, Kate, my love.'

Happiness lit up Kate's face. 'Alright, Freddie. We'll keep it quiet, if you say so.'

Mumble plodded around the corner into Little Turner Street, the narrow shortcut to the yard. As the street was practically empty Freddie tucked his finger under her chin and raised it, then pressed his lips onto hers. He felt her hesitate then she melted into him.

Freddie was triumphant. Mattie might not recognise his worth but her sweet little sister did. And wouldn't that be one in the eye for Mattie? He'd like to see the look on her face when she found out that he, Freddie Ellis, the man she'd turned her back on for Jack

Archer, was the same Freddie Ellis who'd ruined her precious little sister.

He pulled back and Kate opened her eyes. 'Oh Freddie, I'm so happy,' she said quivering in his embrace.

'Oh, Kate, so am I.' He kissed her again 'I'll meet you at the end of the street at seven o'clock tomorrow. What a night we shall have!'

Chapter Fifteen

Patrick wrenched open the saloon door and strolled into the Town of Ramsgate. A couple of the men at the bar looked over and acknowledged him with a nod before turning back to their conversation and beer.

The Town, a narrow public house wedged in between high wharfs, had been perched on the waterfront for over two hundred years. Nelson was reputed to have stopped there, and he and his lady love Emma Hamilton were thought to have rented a small house nearby. The low rumble of male voices mingled with the smoke and drifted up towards the rafters. It was in this same pub that he'd held Brian Maguire as he bled to death, lying in the spit and sawdust. Arthur, the landlord, a rotund, jovial fellow with a receding hairline, greeted him at the bar.

'Evening, Pat. The usual?' he asked, wiping his hands down the front of his long canvas apron.

Patrick nodded and Arthur filled a pewter tankard with cool, frothy beer. Patrick swallowed it in one go.

'Same again, I'm gasping. My throat's like the sands of Arabia with all the coal in it,' he said. 'But I shouldn't complain.'

'You busy then?' Arthur asked, sliding another pint Patrick's way.

'Double loads each day.' He took a mouthful. 'I'm thinking of asking old Wainwright if he'd lease me one of his boats.'

'I thought you took on another boat a month ago,' the landlord said, shaking the water off a pewter tankard and hanging it up on the bar's iron work

'I did, but with gas companies springing up on every scrap of marsh land from here to Putney I can barely keep up with demand.'

'I'm pleased to hear it,' Arthur replied, as Jock Murray staggered in with a couple of his mates. They had clearly just finished work at Morris's and still wore their jerkins. Rivulets of sweat meandered down from their foreheads leaving a white tracing through the coal dust on their faces.

Jock thumped his hand on the bar. 'Four pints, sweet'art.'

'You wait your turn, Jock,' she told him flirtatiously.

'Do I have to wait my turn to have a bit with you, Maisie.'

He then spotted Patrick. 'Afternoon, Nolan.'

'Jock.'

'Fecking hard day,' Jock said, as his pint arrived. 'Four deliveries and the lads have been unloading since noon. Four!' he raised the appropriate number of stubby fingers. 'And one of them was to your sister.'

'I thought Monday was Maguire's day.'

'It is, but now it's Thursday too.'

'Mattie did say the business was on the up,' Patrick replied.

A leer spread across Jock's fleshy face. 'The business ain't the only thing on the *up* since that fecking new driver of hers arrived.'

Patrick turned sharply and faced him. Jock held his fierce stare for a moment then looked away and slipped the barmaid a couple of coins. 'I'm saying no more than the truth. Since fecking Archer arrived he's practically taken over the place. He does the books, the delivery routes, and he's throwing his weight around.' Jock took a noisy swallow of beer. 'Course, I put 'im in his place right away but,' he shrugged, 'women get lonely.'

Patrick put down his tankard. 'Watch your mouth, Jock. My sister's a respectable widow still mourning her husband.'

Jock laughed. 'Is that a fact? That explains why she's got Archer lodging in her front room then? To dry her tears?'

The door to Mattie's office burst open and she looked up at her brother filling the frame.

She smiled at him. 'Hello Patrick, I wasn't ex—'

'Is Archer lodging with you?'

'Is that why you're here and not at home—'

'Is he?' he bellowed, striding into the room and planting his hands on the open ledger she was writing in.

Mattie carefully placed the quill in the inkwell. 'What if he is?' she asked, looking up at her brother.

Patrick raked his hands through his hair. 'For the love of Mary, Mattie. Have you no regard to what people might say? '

Mattie closed the book and stood up. 'People are always putting two and two together and making five.' She crossed the room to put the account book alongside the others on the shelf. She turned. 'Jack Archer has the front room downstairs and Kate's in the room next to me. He only comes into the house after hours for hot water. It's two shillings a week in my pocket for a room that's stood empty for three years. I just wish I'd thought of it sooner.'

Patrick's eyes narrowed. 'I don't like him, Mattie. There's something about him that I can't put my finger on but it's gnawing at my guts.'

'You don't have to like him,' Mattie replied.

'Have you met his family?'

'No, but—'

'I have. And I tell you this,' he said, pointing at her. 'Old Eli looks more like his sister than the scruffy baggage who opened the door to me then wittered on about her "dear brother Jack" and their "ma and pa". Even their bloody accents are different.'

Mattie's jaw dropped. 'You went around to Jack's lodgings?'

'I did. And I tell you something else—'

'How *dare* you go snooping around after one of my employees.' Mattie put her hands on her hips and glared at her brother. 'I don't come down the moorings and quiz your crew, do I?'

Patrick's gaze shifted slightly. 'I went to check him out, that's all. I am your brother.'

'So I suppose that gives you the right to go behind my back, does it?' Mattie shouted. 'You've got a bloody nerve, so you have.' She shoved him in the chest. 'This is my business and I've run it without your interference for three years, so I don't see why you're suddenly taking such a keen interest.'

'It's not Maguire's I'm worried about, it's this new coalman of yours. Even Josie's concerned that he might try to take advantage of you.'

'Did she say that?'

Patrick shifted his weight onto his other foot. 'Not in so many words but I'm sure she thinks he's the sort who'd wheedle his way into a woman's affections and I don't want you to be the talk of every street corner.'

'I'm sure Josie thinks no such thing,' Mattie replied. 'And when did you ever care about what people said? I'll tell you something for nothing. I'm not six years old anymore, Patrick, and I certainly don't need your yea or nay to let out my front room to anyone. So I'd thank you to keep your nose out of my business.'

'Well, I . . .' Patrick's face went red as they stood glaring angrily at each other, then he straightened up and pulled the front of his waistcoat down sharply.

'Fine.'

'Good.'

'I'll be off then.'

Patrick stomped across the office. 'I just hope for your sake that having Jack Archer in your front room doesn't lead you to forget that Brian's only just cold in his grave,' he said, then set the glass rattling in the frame as he slammed the door behind him.

As Kate turned the corner of Cannon Street Road, Freddie caught her hand and drew her into the shadows. He slipped his arms around her.

'So you enjoyed yourself then?' he asked, pressing her back against the wall.

'Yes, I did,' Kate replied, enjoying the feel of his arms around her. 'Oh Freddie, I've been so happy these past three weeks. And I wish I didn't have to but I must,' she said, untangling herself reluctantly from his arms.

He pulled her back. 'Not yet.'

He captured her lips in another passionate kiss. Kate melted into his embrace as shivers of excitement ran up and down her spine.

'What say we slip into the stable to say our goodnight?' he whispered.

'But what if Mattie sees us?'

'She'll have gone to bed hours ago.' His arm tightened as his gaze ran slowly over her face. 'I tell you, Kate, every fella in the Garret was green with envy when they saw me walk in with you on my arm.' He gave her a squeeze. 'Come on. Just for a coupla minutes.'

Kate gave him a peck on the cheek. 'Well, alright, but we'll have to keep very quiet.'

Freddie guided her towards the small door in the right gate. 'Don't worry. I won't give the game away.' He winked at her. 'After all, I don't want to get into trouble with my future in-laws.'

Kate looked up at the darkened house. It was probably almost ten o'clock so Mattie, who was up at five each day, would be sound asleep. Freddie caught her hand and hurried her across the yard into the stable.

'Over here,' he said, nodding at the hop of hay that had been delivered that afternoon. Holding her hand firmly he led her between the stalls and they sat down.

'Phew, it's hot in here, isn't it?' he said, shrugging off his jacket and rolling up his sleeves.

Kate's gaze ran over his sinewy forearms with their light dusting of dark hair and had to stop herself from reaching out to run her hands up them.

'It's the hay,' he explained. 'It makes its own heat. You look a bit flushed. Why don't you take your top coat off?'

He was right. It was warm, and the three ports she'd drunk at the variety theatre didn't help either.

'I think I will.' She unbuttoned her jacket and slipped it off.

Freddie turned and wound his arms around her, kissing her harder and deeper than he'd done before. Suddenly, she felt breathless and lightheaded. She pulled back and looked at Freddie. He had an unsettling but strangely thrilling look in his eye.

He rested back in the hay, pulling Kate with him. It flitted through her mind that lying in a byre with a jacketless man who had his sleeves rolled up wasn't quite proper, but when he snuggled her into the warmth of his body the thought evaporated. After all it was Freddie and they were going to be married.

He sat up and looked down at her. 'Do you mind if I take off my tie too,' Freddie asked, pulling at the knot.

'No,' Kate replied, her eyes fixed on his hands as they unthreaded his necktie and undid the first two button of his shirt.

'That's better,' he said, lying beside her on one elbow.

Kate reached up and stroked his face with her finger tips. 'I love you,' she said softly. 'Do you love me?'

'Do you have to ask?' He bent over and pressed his lips on hers. Kate put her palms against his chest and felt the hardness of his body. Her stomach fluttered and she kissed him back. His hand closed over her breast.

Kate sat bolt upright. 'Freddie!'

He looked surprised. 'I thought you said you love me.'

'I do, but we should wait until we're married.'

Freddie ran his hand inside his shirt and another button popped open. 'You're right, we should. And I don't want you to think I don't respect you, 'cause I do, it's just that' – he gathered her to him again and rolled her back into the fragrant hay – 'It's just that I can't help meself. See, I've never felt like this before.' He smiled sheepishly. 'I thought perhaps it might be time to drop by to see your brother.'

Kate caught her breath as she struggled to contain the bubble of happiness inside her.

'Oh Freddie. Why didn't you say?'

His hand returned to her breast. 'I wanted it to be a surprise.' He kissed her lightly across her cheek and around her ear. Kate's eyelids slowly closed. She felt Freddie's fingers unbutton the front of her clothing. She should stop him of course, but when his hand moved the thin fabric of her chemise aside, she lost her train of thought. She felt the tingle of cool air on her skin and realised that her blouse was fully open.

She struggled up onto her elbows. 'Freddie, I—'

His mouth closed over hers again and he rolled on top of her. Kate's mind swirled with exciting new sensations. Her skirt and petticoats were pulled up and she felt Freddie's hand on her thigh.

'Oh Kate,' he said, looking down at her with an expression of utter devotion on his face. 'Let's not wait. There's no harm in it, is there?'

'No, but what if I . . .' she blushed. 'You know.'

He laughed. 'I'll be careful, I promise,' he said, as his fingers slid under the edge of her drawers. His hand ventured higher and he kissed her across the top of her breasts. He shifted and his hand went to the front of his trousers.

'That's my lovely girly,' he said gruffly, as he tugged her under-clothes down.

As he heaved himself between her legs, Kate closed her eyes. He was right, there was no harm, and anyhow, they could be married before the end of the month.

Chapter Sixteen

Queenie rubbed her cloth in the tin of beeswax and slid it along the altar rail. Although it was only Tuesday – two days before the women of St George's did their weekly cleaning – the verger, Mr Harris, always left a polishing rag in the vestry for Queenie should God call on her to give the church that little bit of extra shine.

She rubbed the soft cloth back and forth in a large sweep, then her eyes drifted to the place where she'd stood as a young bride. She giggled and the sound echoed up into the vaulted ceiling of the empty church.

That had been a ruckus and a half. An illiterate Paddy and a grubby tinker were some of the kinder names her pa had called Tommy. Pa had locked her in her room and refused to give his consent until she told him she was in the family way, but she'd lost that one and the three after. There had been a little boy, named after his father, who'd stayed for a few months before his lips went blue. A boy and a girl followed on, but before their first birthdays they had joined their older brother in the graveyard. Queenie's fair brows pulled together and she buffed the wood some more. Her arm hurt but she carried on until the ache in her chest faded.

Then she had Brian. From the moment Ma handed him to her all wrapped in a towel and screaming, she knew he was her darling boy, her precious one who wouldn't leave her like the others. No early grave for him.

Grave! Grave!

Queenie's breath caught in her throat as the black, screaming horror that lived deep within her threatened to wake up.

'La, la la tra la la larrr!' she sang as she summoned up an image of Brian, driving the wagon, eating his dinner and sitting in front of the fire with his boots off.

The darkness slowly vanished and Queenie let out a breath. Some days she had to sing all day just to keep it at bay, but not today. She was safe.

Perhaps I'll get him a pot of whelks on the way home. He likes them with a bit of vinegar splashed over.

She picked up the tin of wax and the cloth and hobbled to the pulpit on the left side of the church. It was a grand affair, with deep moulded columns all around and rising some four feet from the floor. Queenie ran her fingers over one of the cherubs and thought of her grandson with his bright curls and dimpled cheeks.

Grasping the narrow iron rail she climbed the half a dozen stairs to the enclosed space within. She had a clear view of the pews between the carved pillars. She noticed there were some scuff marks on the floor of the pulpit where Mr Garrett stood, so she knelt down, intent on bringing the shine back to the dull woodwork. She was just about to start her work when the vestry door opened and two pairs of heavy feet marched across the flagstones. They stopped just in front of the pulpit. Queenie looked between the wooden posts and her mouth pulled into a tight line.

What's Mr Fatman doing here? she thought, leaning back to keep herself out of sight.

He was with Mr Dunn, the squat choirmaster whose wife often had the faint smell of gin about her.

Amos Stebbins extended his hand. 'So we are agreed, then,' he said, his voice booming around the empty church.

Mr Dunn held back for a moment then took it. 'We are, but are you sure you'll be able to get the deeds?'

'Fear not. I'll have Mrs Maguire's signature on the bill of sale for Maguire's yard within the month. Less probably.'

Queenie couldn't breathe. *Brian's yard!*

Mr Dunn ran his hand over his bald head. 'Mattie Maguire's no fool, Stebbins. If she hears the slightest whisper about the railway she'll work out that her yard is on the route and have us over a barrel.'

Railway!

'That's why I asked you to meet me here and not at my office,' Amos said, lowering his voice.

Shifty bugger.

He patted Mr Dunn's arm. 'I understand your qualms, Dunn. You're a man of good conscience, as am I, but may I remind you of Proverbs twenty-eight verse twenty-five: "... but he that putteth his trust in the Lord shall be made fat" – and I'm sure a yearly dividend of twelve per cent will help settle your mind. But if you'd rather I looked for other investors ...'

The choirmaster shook his head. 'No, no. I am content to leave the matter in your hands.'

I have to tell Brian, thought Queenie. The blackness in her mind swirled a little.

'Good, good. As soon as I hear that you have deposited the sum we agreed into my account I'll set the date for flotation, probably in a few weeks.' He held out his hand again and Mr Dunn shook it vigorously.

'It's a pleasure doing business with you, Stebbins.'

'The pleasure's all mine.'

Mr Dunn gave a small bow then turned and marched down the nave towards the main door. Stebbins slipped into the front pew and knelt with his head bowed for a short while before following him out.

Queenie held her breath. Once the Fatman was gone she would run home and tell Brian. He would know what to do. He would stop him from taking their yard.

As Amos reached the church doors, Queenie tried to stand but found she was kneeling on her skirt. She tugged it out but the tin of wax slipped from her hand and clattered down the pulpit steps. The metallic ring as it bounced off the stone echoed around the church.

Amos turned and retraced his steps. His eyes darted back and forth then alighted on the tin of polish. His eyes narrowed as they cast upwards and fixed upon her. Queenie's legs felt suddenly weak and she grabbed the handrail to steady herself.

Amos drew in a deep breath and the button of his waistcoat took the strain. He pointed at Queenie. 'How dare you lurk in the shadows and spy on your betters, old woman.'

Queenie started to tremble. 'I he ... he ... heard ...'

'What did you hear?'

'That you're after my Brian's yard because of your railway,' she shouted at him, her high voice screeching upwards into the rafters. 'And I'm going to tell everyone.'

Amos gave a hollow laugh but the sharpness in his eyes sent a chill through her. 'And who would believe you, the parish mad woman? You ought to be locked up. In fact, I'll call for the workhouse superintendent myself and have you taken away.'

Queenie shook her fist at him. 'I'm not mad and when I tell my Brian he'll stop you.'

'And how are you going to "tell your Brian", you mad old woman? He's *dead*.'

Queenie shoved his words away. 'Don't be daft, he's out on his rounds.'

'Is he?'

She nodded. The black horror flared up. *La la la*, Queenie sang in her head.

Amos put his face close to hers. 'I know that somewhere in that addled brain of yours you remember the night they carried your son, your only son, home from the Town of Ramsgate with his throat cut. Remember how white he looked, dressed in his best suit, his new wedding suit, lying in his coffin.'

The hellish blackness roared up, pushing against her thoughts as it yelled ugly, lying things at her. An image of her son's neck with the deep gash – all the way from his ear to his collarbone – burst into her mind. She saw the bloodless lips and unseeing eyes; the white collar turned red and his shock of auburn hair flopped back and forth as his head rolled. She crumpled like a rag doll onto the flagstones. A sob rent through her chest and tore her heart open, allowing all the pain and hopelessness locked away deep inside to pour out.

'He's dead! My Brian's dead!'

Sweat sprang out on Amos' forehead and he glanced over his shoulder at the vestry door.

'Shut up!' he ordered, gripping her thin upper arms and dragging her to her feet.

Queenie let out a piercing scream as her hand flopped forward at an unnatural angle. Amos felt rather than heard the bone snap. He threw her from him. Queenie sobbed as her injured arm thumped on the floor.

Amos grabbed a handful of hair and yanked her head towards him. 'I told you to shut up, you old crone.' Then he pulled out his neckerchief, screwed it in a ball and jammed it in her mouth. Twisting her hair in his hand, Amos dragged her across the tiles and behind the back row of pews.

Queenie's eyes bulged and her face went a motley red as she struggled against his grip. 'You're not going to tell anyone anything where you're going,' he snarled.

Without loosening his grip, he smashed her to the floor. The back of her head cracked onto the flagstones as he rammed the gag further down her throat.

Queenie's eyes rolled up and her hands began to lose their strength. The police would investigate her death of course, but at her age they'd probably conclude that she'd slipped, broken arm her and then suffered some sort of seizure. And there was no one to say otherwise.

The door to the vestry clicked opened suddenly.

'Who's there?' Mr Garrett's cultured voice asked.

Amos tucked himself behind the high back of the pew, dragged his handkerchief out of Queenie's mouth and let go of her. She crumpled to the floor and her booted foot kicked the wood.

'Who's there I say!' demanded the vicar.

Amos straightened up. 'It's only me,' he answered, slipping his handkerchief back in his pocket.

Mr Garrett screwed up his eyes and peered down the length of the church. 'Is that you, Mr Stebbins?'

'Yes, I was just having a few moments of quiet prayer.' Amos glanced around. 'I find the solitude of an empty church very conducive to commune with the Almighty.'

The vicar's face brightened. 'Indeed, and I'm glad you're still here as there is a small matter I need to discuss with you. It's about the Sunday school outing.'

He came down the chancery steps and started down the aisle towards Amos.

Amos walked down the centre of the church to meet the vicar. 'Let's go into the vestry,' he said catching the other man's upper arm and guiding him back towards the altar.

Suddenly one of the main doors at the far end crashed back. Amos spun around and to his utter astonishment, saw Queenie, hunched over and holding her broken arm across her, stumbling out of the door.

'Who now?' Mr Garrett asked, craning his neck and screwing up his eyes. 'Tell me, Stebbins. I can't see a thing without my infernal glasses.'

'It's probably one of the scruffy kids I saw hanging about in the church yard earlier,' Amos replied. 'I'll send them on their way. I'll join you in the vestry.'

He sprinted down the church and out into the graveyard just in time to see Queenie disappear through the gates and into the street.

Damn! Damn!

His first instinct was to dash after her but he held back. She was half mad and certainly delusional; everyone knew that, so if the batty old woman did start blabbering about him breaking her arm and trying to murder her, a flat denial on his part should quash such a ridiculous suggestion. But what if she started on about Maguire's yard and the railway? That might not be so easily brushed aside.

The sexton, climbing out from the grave he'd just dug, tipped his hat as Amos stood pondering in the church door. Amos nodded a greeting then went back into the church, which he found empty once again. He started down the centre of the church but stopped beside his pew and sat down. Clasping his hands tightly together Amos prayed that poor Queenie Maguire would find eternal rest, and soon.

With her breath burning her lungs, Mattie dashed the last fifty yards towards Maguire's double gates praying with every step that Queenie would be home. As she stopped in the centre of the yard to catch her breath, Jack came out of the stable.

'What's happened?' he asked, taking his jacket from the peg and shrugging it on.

'Queenie went to the church three hours ago and hasn't come back,' Mattie said, putting her hand on her chest to slow her breathing. 'I left Brian with Kate then went to the church but she wasn't there, so I ran along to Watney Street. She's not been there either.'

'That's not like her.'

'I know. I've asked a couple of the stall holders to keep an eye out for her but I'm hoping that she's come back. Have you been in the house?'

Jack shook his head. 'I've only just finished up.'

They walked across the yard and through the small garden, setting the chicken clucking as they made their way to the back door. Mattie kept praying they'd find Queenie but her chair by the hearth was empty. *Where on earth is she?*

Kate was there instead. 'Thank goodness you're back, Mattie,' she said, as she stood up. 'Did Freddie tell you?'

'Tell me what?'

'The butcher's boy from around the corner saw Queenie down by Trinidad Wharf an hour ago. I thought he'd let you know?'

'He sloped out when I arrived,' Nathaniel replied coldly. 'He's probably sinking his second pint by now.'

Mattie pressed her lips together and retied her bonnet ribbon. 'Wapping High Street is no more than fifteen minutes away. I'll have to find her.'

'You can't go there alone, it's too dangerous. I'll come with you,' said Jack.

Mattie didn't argue. In fact, knowing that he would say just that was the one thing holding her together. They left the yard with Buster trotting at their heels and made their way down Cannon Street Road towards the Highway. The working day had only just finished but already the local prostitutes and gamblers spilled out into the pavements. Nathaniel guided her through the crowds with a gentle pressure on her elbow and shielded her with his body. A hansom cab rolled towards her and Nathaniel caught her arm and brought her close to him as it splashed through a pungent puddle of stale water. They crossed into the relative quiet of Gravel Lane.

'I shouldn't have let her go,' she said, running over the afternoon's events yet again.

'Why wouldn't you?' he said calmly. 'Mrs Maguire goes to the church and back at least three times a week without any trouble. How could you know that today would be different?'

'You're right,' Mattie said, trying to ease her conscience. 'That's why I wasn't too worried when she wasn't there when I got back. Even when I found the church empty I thought she might have wandered down to Watney Street. She does that sometimes.' She looked up at Nathaniel. 'She's been so good of late that I'd started to hope her mind was sorting itself out but now I can't help thinking something awful must have happened to set her off like this again.'

'We'll find her.'

When they reached the cobbled road that ran alongside the river, the evening crowd of trollops were already milling around trying to attract the attention of newly discharged sailors.

'How far to where she was spotted?' Jack asked, as he sidestepped a broken bottle.

'No more than a half a mile down there.' Mattie imagined Queenie wandering along the riverside. 'Perhaps we should go to the police.'

'Maybe we should check down where the butcher's boy saw her,' Nathaniel said, trying not to show his alarm and ease his guilt at not agreeing with her.

She gave a little nod and a brave smile, which made him feel twice as bad. 'We're passing the Town pub and if Patrick's there, he can help.' She covered her eyes with her hand. 'Sweet Mary, there's miles of waterfront, Jack. We'll never be able to search all of it. She could be lying injured somewhere, in pain and not able to move. And the tide will be turning in an hour or two. What if . . .'

Nathaniel took hold of her upper arm. 'I promise we'll find her.'

'Please, let it be so,' Mattie whispered crossing herself.

They hurried on and within a few moments they were outside the public house.

'I'll see if your brother's inside,' Nathaniel said shoving the door open.

Mattie nodded. 'I'll go to the end and look along the quay side.'

Nathaniel sent Buster with her then had a quick look around the bar and left a message with the barman before dashing out again. He ran down to the river and caught sight of Mattie talking to a ferryman tying up his craft on the quayside. She had pulled her bonnet back from her face and the pale straw arc now sat like a halo around her head. As she heard his footsteps she turned.

'He said he saw something lying at the end of the jetty as he brought his boat in,' she said leaning over the flimsy railing and peering at the mud below. The barrier creaked as it took her weight.

She cupped her hand around her mouth. 'Queenie! Queenie!' she yelled, her voice echoing back from the space below the dock. She looked up at Nathaniel with near panic in her eyes. 'Sweet Mother. What if she's unconscious and can't hear?' Nathaniel glanced at the water swirling around the round oak uprights. If Queenie had thrown herself into the river her body would be halfway to Barking Creek by now.

'Let's search further along,' he said.

The wooden causeway creaked and dipped under foot as they rushed along. Buster scampered back and forth sniffing intently for a moment, then shot off along the narrow jetty barking furiously. Mattie gathered up her skirts and half ran, half stumbled after him. She gripped the rope strung between the mooring posts and looked over.

'Jack, there,' she sobbed, jabbing her finger at the river below.

Nathaniel scanned the muddy gloom. In the pale light he caught sight of a small figure crumpled in the mud.

'Queenie!' Mattie screamed. 'Don't worry, darling, we'll come and get you. Don't you fret none.'

The figure lying in the mud didn't move.

Mattie turned. 'Do you think she could have survived the fall?'

'It's possible,' Nathaniel replied, in a tone that said otherwise.

The river bed lay at least thirty feet below and even if she'd landed in the mud, the impact would break the bones of a woman half Queenie's age so he wasn't hopeful.

'You stay here.' He swung onto the ladder leading down to the river.

He jumped the last few feet, the stinking mud sucking at his boots, and slopped his way towards where Queenie lay on the stone foundations of the jetty. Her eyes were closed and her fine white hair feathered around her face like a lacy nightcap. There was a fresh bruise on her cheek and throat along with streaks of blood along her forearms. One leg was twisted under her at an awkwardly and the angle of her right arm told him at a glance that the bones had been snapped through.

He bent over her. 'Mrs Maguire,' he said softly, praying that she was still breathing.

She didn't move. Nathaniel stretched out his hand and gently moved a damp strand of hair away from her face.

Her eyelids flickered opened and her pale blue eyes looked up at him. 'Is that you, Brian?'

The light had almost gone by the time they turned into Cannon Street Road. Queenie's head had rested lightly on his chest as Nathaniel carried her the mile or so home. Once in the warm kitchen he set her down gently in her chair and lifted her feet onto the stool. Mattie placed a shawl over Queenie's legs while Buster rested his muzzle on her lap, looking up at her with sorrowful eyes. Nathaniel moved a step aside but the old woman clutched at his hand. He hunkered down next to her and Mattie did the same. She moved a strand of hair from her mother-in-law's eyes. 'Poor lamb.' A tear slowly rolled down her cheek.

Queenie's pulse in her neck was thumping at twice the natural rate and as she took each rasping breath there was a faint but distinct sound of fluid bubbling in her chest. She was leaning to her left with her arms curled around her ribs as if guarding them from further injury.

Kate knelt beside her. 'Where did you find her?'

'Below Trinidad jetty,' Mattie replied, another tear joining the first on her cheek.

'Poor Queenie.'

Mattie stood up. 'I'll have to get Doctor Corbett.'

Nathaniel rose to his feet. 'I'll fetch him,' he said, letting go of Queenie's hand.

'No! No!,' she screamed, gripping his sleeve, her nails almost tearing through the fabric. 'Don't leave me, Brian!'

He and Mattie exchanged a worried glance and then he tried to uncurl her fingers.

'There, Ma,' he said a trifle awkwardly, 'I'll not be a minute. Mattie's here.'

Queenie clung on tighter and started to sob. Mattie patted Queenie's free hand then tucked her shawl closer around her face.

'I'll go,' she said. 'Kate can come with me. It's only five minutes' walk to Chapmen Street.'

'Be careful,' he said. 'I don't like the thought of you wandering around alone.'

'It's better that you're here,' she said, then hooked her arm in Kate's. They left hurriedly together.

Without letting go of Queenie's hand, Nathaniel pulled a chair from the table and sat down. 'You're a good boy, Brian.' She reached up and stroked his hair. 'I used to brush those golden curls just to see them spring back.' Her cold, bony fingers twirled a lock of his hair. 'Do you remember how you used to come home with scuffs on your knees and I used to dab them clean?'

A lump formed in Nathaniel's throat. He could barely remember his own mother but Queenie's palpable pain had summoned up vague memories of a secure embrace and the faint smell of rose water.

'And you used to mend the rips in my trousers and scold me for fighting,' he said, sure that she had.

Queenie laughed softly then winced. 'But it never stopped you.' She kissed his hand then held it to her cheek. 'I told you not to go with Patrick Nolan. He was always scrapping with someone but you hung around with him anyhow. I know boys fight but I was scared I'd lose you like the others.' Her watery eyes ran over his face. 'You're my only joy, Brian.' The lump in Nathaniel's throat thickened. Queenie's blue eyes searched his face. 'Promise me you won't let the Fatman take our yard for his railway.'

Unease crept up Nathaniel's spine. 'Who's the Fatman, Ma,' he asked, gently.

'Him who's always at the church and came around here poking his nose into the books,' Queenie replied, wrinkling her nose as if she smelt something foul. 'Said he was trying to help but I know better 'cos I heard him and the singing man talking by the pulpit.'

'What did they say?'

'Such horrible things! And when I told him you'd stop him taking our yard he hurt my arm,' she held out her arm with the improvised splint Mattie had secure the break with. She caught his hand again and pressed it to her face. 'He said you were dead but look, here you are my own dear boy, right in front of me!'

Before he could ask her any more her eyes closed. Nathaniel sat for the next ten minutes holding Queenie's hand while her breath grew ever more shallow. When the kitchen door opened and Mattie, Kate and Doctor Corbett walked in, Queenie started awake.

The doctor took off his top hat and put it and his black bag on the table. Nathaniel moved away so the doctor could have the chair. 'Now, Mrs Maguire, I hear you've been in the wars.'

Nathaniel moved to Mattie's side. She looked drawn and tired.

'I'll leave you now, Mrs Maguire,' he said, wanting to do anything but.

Queenie's frail frame was seized by a lung-tearing, wet cough. Doctor Corbett uncorked a bottle from his bag and carefully poured some syrup into one of his small silver cups.

'Thank you again for your help,' Mattie said, drawing him towards the door leading into the hall.

'While you were gone, your mother-in-law kept muttering about the Fatman. Do you know who she was talking about?'

'Mr Stebbins. I'm afraid Queenie took against him from the first. I don't know why—'

Doctor Corbett called her over.

Nathaniel looked over at the old woman who, now that the medication had quickly taken effect, sat once again with her eyes closed, her sunken chest rising and falling in a laboured manner.

Amos shifted on his seat to restore the circulation to his nether regions as the Reverend Walter Obadiah Cropper, the founder of The God's True Word Society, gathered momentum for the roaring climax of his two-hour lecture.

Despite the tortuous seat, Amos felt better than he had done since discovering Queenie Maguire spying on him. In fact the whole episode had concluded far better than he could ever have imagined. An answer to prayer if ever there was one!

When Queenie wasn't sitting in her usual pew on the following Sunday, he asked Cecily to send a friendly note to enquire after her health. When she'd reported that the old woman had been found in the river mud and wasn't expected to live, Amos had spent a full hour on his knees in the study thanking God for his timely intervention. Queenie would soon pass into a better place, and with her the threat to his carefully laid plans. In truth, he thought it a blessing really, with all she'd suffered over the past three years.

'This, my brothers and sisters,' Reverend Cropper's voice shouted thought Amos's thoughts, 'is the two-edged sword with which we will bring the lost souls of the world back to the true path of God. And if any in this room shirk from the task that God has called you to, be prepared for the sulphur pits of Hell!'

There was a deathly silence and then the audience, packed into the London Domestic Mission rose to their feet and applauded deafeningly, some shouting 'amen' and 'hallelujah'. Amos stood slowly and clapped briefly before weaving his way towards the back of the room where tea was being served.

The trestle tables at the back of the cavernous chapel were staffed by half a dozen middle-aged women wearing black clothes and cheerless expressions. One of the women poured him a cup of stewed looking tea from a large pot and handed it to him.

'Thank you.'

'Praise only God, brother,' she replied, 'lest flattery turns a mortal's head.'

Amos gave her a tight smile and moved away. He took a sip and shuddered. No sugar and, sure enough, stewed. After such a marathon of hell and damnation what he really needed was a brandy and a little jollity at Madame La Verne's, which is exactly what he'd planned for the rest of the evening.

'Powerful stuff wouldn't you say, sir,' a voice from behind him said.

Amos turned to find himself being addressed by a finely-boned young man with fair curls around his beardless cheeks and a narrow moustache. His jacket, though shabby was of some quality and his voice betrayed a refined education.

'I believe the Reverend is known for his passion for the salvation.'

'So I understand, Mr ...?'

'Stebbins.'

'What, *the* Mr Stebbins? Of Grey Friars wharf?'

Amos puffed out his chest. 'Indeed, I am,' he replied, starting to warm to the fellow.

'Why, yes, you're the talk of the City.' The young man drew him aside. 'Are the rumours true about George Hudson and a new railway?'

'That is a very private matter,' Amos said under his breath.

The youthful man looked sheepish. 'I confess I've only just come down from Oxford and am not yet accustomed to London ways.'

'The first thing to learn is to keep such matters under your hat.' He glanced around at the dozen or so other business men drinking tea. 'Especially when an unguarded word could lose business.'

The young man pressed a well-manicured ink-stained index finger to his lips. 'I understand. Be assured you can count on my absolute discretion. The truth of the matter is that my father wants me to make my mark and fortune in the City but I am at a loss as to know where to start. So I see it as providential that I should meet you here in God's house.'

'Well, just so,' Amos straightened his diamond cravat pin. 'I suppose such a display of business acumen was bound to leak out.'

The young man looked about him. 'I say, is there a chance I might able to put a bob or two on the venture?'

'Well, I don't—'

'I could probably get my godfather, the Earl of Danbury interested.'

Earl of Danbury! One of the most influential ministers in the cabinet was this whippersnapper's godfather. Providential meeting indeed.

There had been speculation in the press recently about a peerage for George Hudson, so why not for Amos Stebbins too?

'If I could have the name of your bankers I could ensure my funds are with them in good time. Would two hundred pounds secure a sizeable stake?' the youth asked.

'Indeed it would,' he said, thinking that such a timely and hefty deposit so soon after Mr Dunn's would help to steady the wavering chief clerk. 'It's the City & County. But make sure you only deposit it with Mr Fallon.'

The young man grasped his hand in an extraordinarily firm grip for one so slight. He glanced at the clock behind the tea table.

'Oh, is that the time? I must go,' he said gathering up his hat and gloves. 'I'll wish you a good night.'

'And a good night to you, sir.'

One of the wise but ill-favoured virgins making the tea came past with a tray. Amos turned and put his half drunk cup of tea on it. When he turned back the chap had already manoeuvred his way through the gathering.

Damn!

'Hey there! Sir! You didn't give me your name,' he called, as the doors swung closed behind the young man.

Chapter Seventeen

Kate put her hand on the wall and lifted her head slowly, praying it wouldn't start spinning again. The cool early morning air swirled around her, moving her skirts and cooling her brow. Somewhere a few streets down, a dog barked as the knocker-upper tapped on windows with his long pole. The chickens in the coop sat plump and motionless on their roosts while the first streaks of morning light blurred the edges of the pale moon sitting above the garden fence.

The ground beneath her feet swayed sideways again. She pitched forward and vomited into the small flowerbed beside the rain barrel. She heaved herself up and drew a slow breath through her nose. *Perhaps if I make myself a cuppa I'd feel better*, she thought. The tea had helped yesterday and the day before, but unfortunately no amount of tea would set her right.

Kate fixed her eyes on the back door and took another deep breath before starting towards the house. If she didn't get herself sorted and off to work in the next fifteen minutes she'd be late. Placing her hand just below her breastbone, she willed the contents of her stomach to stay where they were.

Quietly she turned the handle and re-entered the kitchen to find Mattie in her dressing gown, standing beside the cot where her mother-in-law still lay. Queenie hadn't recovered, and even with a dose of laudanum inside her had become so distressed that she refused to be coaxed into her own bed. She'd been sleeping in the cot ever since, eating nothing and only sipping water when Mattie held the cup to her lips.

Kate put her own worries aside. 'How's Queenie?'

'Quiet.'

Guilt cut through Kate. As if poor Mattie didn't have enough to vex her, having to tend to Queenie night and day, now she was bringing a pile of trouble to her door.

'Sorry I woke you,' she said. 'I crept down as quietly as I could.'

'It wasn't the stairs that woke me. It was you heaving your guts up below my window; how far gone are you?'

A denial sprang to Kate's lips but died there. It had been eight weeks since she'd had her monthly, she'd been sick each morning for the last few days and her breasts were tender. There was no doubt about her condition.

'About three months,' she replied, straightening up.

'I suppose its Freddie's.'

Kate nodded. 'But we're in love.'

Mattie rolled her eyes heavenwards. 'For goodness sake, Kate, how could you be so stupid?'

Kate bristled. 'Freddie loves me!'

Mattie gave a harsh laugh. 'Oh, is that what he's told you?'

'He *does*,' Kate shouted clenching her fist tightly. 'And we're getting married.'

'When would that be then?' Mattie asked.

Kate's gaze wavered a little. 'I don't rightly know, but once Freddie knows about the baby I'm sure he'll arrange it straight away. He *does* want to marry me.'

Her sister's eyebrows rose mockingly. 'If that's the case, why have you been sneaking out with him without telling me?'

'Because I knew you'd be like this,' Kate replied stubbornly. 'Freddie wanted us to get to know each other a bit better before he spoke to Patrick. Freddie said he wanted to do things properly —'

'Oh, yes, I can see that,' Mattie cut in. 'Sweet talking an innocent young girl and getting her in trouble is a very proper way to behave.'

Kate jabbed her finger at Mattie. 'You're a fine one to talk. Young Brian was tucked well up your skirt when you walked down the aisle.'

'It's not the same and you know it, Kate Nolan. For a start my Brian wasn't slipping through the back door of every lonely widow on his rounds – nor did he have the Black Eagle Gang as his drinking pals.'

'Freddie said you'd be against us,' Kate said, wiping a tear from her cheek. 'I know all about Bridy Kepple and that slut Sally from the dairy. But Freddie loves *me* and he'll be faithful once we're married.'

'Faithful!' Mattie replied. 'What about the redhead in Prescott Street then? Has he promised to be *faithful* to her too?' Her face grew softer. 'Honestly, Kate, if Freddie had to avoid every woman he's having bit of jiggy-jig with in the area, Mumble would just circle the yard each day.'

'You've never liked him,' Kate shouted. 'And I've seen the way you're always on his back in the yard.'

'I'm always on at him because he's lazy and unreliable, but you're too blind to see.' Sadness replaced anger on Mattie's face. 'Kate. Freddie's just fed you a load of old blarney and you've swallowed it hook, line and sinker.'

'It's not true!' Kate shouted as tears streamed down her face.

Mattie reached out to her. 'Oh, Kate, me darling,' she crooned softly. 'Come, come, nothing's so bad it can't be sorted.'

'There's nothing to sort,' Kate said, stepped back to avoid her sister's embrace. 'Freddie loves me and once he knows I'm carrying his child I'll be Mrs Ellis before the month is out. Just you wait and see.'

Kate brushed past her sister and walked to the hall door. She grasped the handle then turned. 'And when we're married we'll be *very*, *very* happy.'

Mattie put down the quill and rubbed her temples but the pain across her forehead didn't budge. She wasn't surprised. Kate had told Freddie of her condition two days ago and he hadn't been seen since. So now not only did she have a sister with red eyes and throwing up in the yard each morning, she also had another cart without a driver. On top of it all, Patrick had brought his father-in-law, Doctor Munroe, over to see Queenie yesterday but Mattie knew there was nothing he could do. As she sponged down her mother in-law's frail body and cleared the soiled newspapers from under her she wondered how long it would go on for.

Josie had sent Annie over to help look after Brian, which gave Mattie a chance to do the bills, but Annie was only a child and Mattie still had to order the yard and care for Queenie as well as clean the house and do all the cooking. She sighed, then picked up the pen again, intent on making out the next end-of-month bill. A fat drip of ink dripped from the nib and splodged across the sheet of paper. Mattie covered her face with her hands. The office door opened.

'Mrs Maguire?' Jack's voice asked softly. He saw her tear-stained face. 'Is it Queenie?'

Mattie shook her head.

'Then what?' he asked, pulling up a chair beside her.

'Oh, Ja — Mr Archer,' she said, blushing that she'd almost blurted out his name. 'It's—' The sob rising in her chest blocked her words.

'Now, now,' he said, taking her hand.

It would break his heart when she told him about Kate but she had to tell him before he heard it on the street corner.

'It's Kate.'

'What about Kate?'

'She's … she's … tears spilled over. 'Oh, Mr Archer, she's …'

His lips drew into two hard lines. 'Freddie?'

Mattie nodded. 'Kate told him on Tuesday and he's not been near nor by since,' she said, almost unable to look into his furious eyes. 'Patrick has searched every bar in the area but no one knows wh … wh … where he is,' Mattie sobbed. 'I promised Kate I'd try to keep it quiet, but unless we can find him and get the banns posted, word will get out and Kate will be the talk of Knockfergus.'

A picture of Freddie's sly face sprang into Mattie's mind. What sort of life would Kate have with such a philandering ducker and diver? Short of housekeeping money each week, heavy with child each year and doubtless being given a black eye from time to time after the pubs shut. *Sweet Mary Mother of God!* Mattie covered her face with her hands again, and sobbing once more. Jack sat quietly beside her for a moment then the chair scraped the floor as he rose to his feet. She looked up.

They stared at each other for a moment then he flipped his cap back on. 'If you'll excuse me, Mrs Maguire,' he said. 'I have some business to attend to.'

With a mounting sense of desolation Mattie watched him go.

The last rays of daylight forced their way through the dirty windows and illuminated the bustling crowd of market porters and street traders downing their end-of-day pints. Freddie leant on the bar of the Blue Coat Boy and stared gloomily into his half empty glass. The low-ceilinged pub house stood on the north side of Dorset Street just off Whitechapel High Street in the area known as Old Nichol, which was practically a country unto itself – one where wise strangers didn't venture alone.

Freddie threw the last mouthful of beer back and slid his tankard across the counter.

'Pour me another, sweetheart,' he said to the young woman behind the bar, who had flame-red hair and an eye-catching cleavage.

While she swayed off to one of the pumps, Freddie put his hand in his pocket and fished out what remained of his money.

Two shillings and thruppence. Was that all?

He put two ha'pennies on the stained counter. He hadn't eaten yet and still had his bed to pay for so he'd better make this pint last longer than the last three. As he raised his replenished drink to his lips, a heavy hand slapped him on the back. Freddie turned to find Ollie Mac beside him.

Although a good four inches shorter and a stone or two lighter than Freddie, what Ollie Mac lacked in stature he made up for with his cunning mind and unpredictable temper. Tonight, as always, he wore his snazzy brown-and-green chequered suit with a tall crown billy-cock hat perched on his head. Mad Teddy and Stefan Magsen stood behind him like a couple of aggressive bookends.

'Good evening, Mr Mac,' Freddie said, making sure he paid the man who ruled the south end of Spitalfield Rookery the proper respect.

Ollie gave Freddie a good-natured grin. 'Mr Mac be buggered. I'm Ollie to me mates.' He flicked his head and the two men behind him moved out of earshot. 'Oi! Gilly! Forget the beer and give my friend Freddie a brandy,' he said, flipping a half crown at the barmaid. 'Get me one, too, and have one yourself.' He turned to Freddie. 'You still hiding from Nolan, old cock?'

Freddie nodded. 'You'd think after a week he'd 'ave lost some of his bloody steam.'

'Naw, not that bugger. He's like a terrier after a rat. Once 'e gets a scent he won't stray from the track.' An amused expression stole into his flint-like eyes. 'And you can't odds it, can you? After all, you did get his little sister in the family way.'

The brandy arrived and Ollie poured two generous measures. Freddie knocked his back in one.

'Bloody women!' he said, remembering Kate's blotched, tear-stained face. 'I tell you, Mr Mac, I'm done with 'em,' he said, watching the barmaid's neckline as she bent forward to retrieve something from the floor. 'First I had her sister leading me on and then she, Miss Blue-eyed Kate, lets herself get caught.'

'Why didn't you bung her a shilling to see Ma Hobbs?'

'I did, but she just started blubbing again and kept going on about how she thought I loved her and stuff.'

Ollie nudged him in the ribs and refilled his glass. 'So you gave her that old line, did you, you crafty bugger?'

A smile crept across Freddie's lips. 'Well, any man would, for the first bite of the cherry, but the silly girl took it as Gospel and got it into her head that I'd marry her.' He straightened his tie again and tilted his head at a cocky angle. 'Now, I ask you? Do I look like the marrying kind?'

'You? Naw! After all, it wouldn't be fair on all the other gals, would it?'

They laughed, and Freddie caught sight of himself in the etched glass of the mirror behind the bar. He ran his hands through his oiled hair, pleased with his reflection. 'Too true. But I still have to shake that poxy mick, Nolan, off my tail.' Freddie finished off his second drink and banged the glass on the bar. 'I tell you, Mr Mac it ain't fecking fair.'

Ollie splashed brandy in his glass again. 'A bloody liberty, I calls it.'

Freddie jabbed a finger at him. 'You're right,' He lost his balance and staggered a few steps backwards to right himself. 'And after I've worked like a slave for his sister since her old man died. Does she or her poxy brother appreciate it?'

'It ain't in a bogtrotters' nature to be grateful.'

'Too true,' Freddie replied. 'And now Nolan's after my blood and his sister's like a cat in heat after that bastard Archer. And after all I've done for her. And to top it all I've lost me bloody job.'

'They're all a pack of tinkers in Knockfergus and Nolan and his tribe are the worst of them. But,' Olly clasped Freddie around his shoulder, 'you don't want their stinking coalman's job, do you?'

Freddie shook his head and the floor shifted under his feet.

'Someone with a bit of savvy about them like you could make a good living at half the effort.' Ollie lowered his voice. 'As it happens, I might be able to help you out in that regard, old chum. I have a bit of something that needs relocating, on the hush hush, and I'm looking for someone who can handle a wagon.'

'What sort of thing?'

Ollie's matey expression turned chilly. 'That's for me to know. But what d'yer reckon? Are you in?'

Through the brandy haze Freddie studied Ollie's hard features. There was no doubt that whatever needed relocating was from its rightful owner to the Black Eagles Gang's underworld fence and it would be dangerous. And what if he was caught? He would face a long prison sentence and possibly even transportation. But what could he do? He couldn't go back to Mattie's yard, he was sick of sleeping in the dosshouse, and in a day or two he'd be completely skint.

He caught sight of Teddy and Stefan chatting to a couple of luscious trollops in the far corner. Beside the dishevelled working men in the bar they looked like a couple of swells in their double breasted suits and brushed soft-crown hats.

Freddie threw back his drink. 'I'm in. Just tell me where and when?'

The wiry Scotsman squeezed his shoulders. 'That's the spirit.' He let Freddie go and poured them both another large brandy and raised his glass. 'Feck all the bog-trotting micks.'

Freddie chinked his glass with Ollie's 'Feck 'em all.'

They emptied their glasses and Freddie's head swam again.

'You're one of the boys now.' Ollie pressed a coin into Freddie's hand. 'If things go as they should there will be more where this came from. Meet me here tomorrow and we'll talk again. Remember, you're one of us. If you're in a fix come and see me. Meantime, enjoy the brandy.'

'Thank you, Mr Mac.'

Ollie slapped him on the shoulder, 'Call me Ollie!' He turned, and the crowd parted like the red sea before Moses as he bowled to the front door.

Freddie watched him go then opened his hand. A guinea!

He emptied the last of the drink into his glass and threw it back. He looked at himself again in the mirror and as he ran his fingers down his crumpled lapels he imagined himself dressed in a new suit and hat.

Freddie boy, you're on the up and up.

Ollie was right. He was too good to lump coal around all day for the pittance Mattie Maguire gave him. And as for Kate, well she'd just have to manage for herself like hundreds of other women.

Freddie pulled out the last handful of coins from his pocket and slammed them on the counter. 'Gilly!' He waved the empty bottle at her. 'Get me another. I'll be back in a jiff.'

He pushed his way to the rear of the pub and out to the alley at the back. From the far end of the narrow walkthrough a solitary street lamp glowed so faintly that it barely reached him. Freddie propped himself against the wall and relieved his aching bladder.

He adjusted his trousers and started back to the pub but before he'd gone two steps something hit the back of his head.

Black spots popped at the corner of his vision, his head swam, then his knees buckled under him. Just before he hit the floor, someone caught him and turned him upside down. The last thing he was aware of was the sound of hob-nailed boots walking away on the cobbles and the tingle of coal dust in his nose.

Patrick slipped the coins into the brown-paper envelope and sealed it down. He stacked it with the other three at the back of his desk then ticked off the amount in the ledger in front of him.

He'd been at the mooring since five and it was probably nigh on eleven o'clock now. Josie had gone to bed some hours ago, and though his aching muscles and exhausted brain longed to join her, it was Saturday tomorrow and he had to get the wages ready for his crew. On a normal week he would have completed the task before now, but since Mattie had brought Kate red-eyed and crying to their house a week ago, his sister's predicament and the man who had caused it had taken priority over everything else.

He was furious when Mattie told him what had happened. It wasn't so much that Kate was with child, as nearly every other bride hereabouts got in the same situation, but that she'd set her sights on such a wastrel as Freddie Ellis. What was it Josie called him? Flash Freddie. That was about right. As much as he didn't relish Freddie as a brother-in-law, Kate *had* chosen him, and for his sister's sake he'd been prepared to make the best of it. But when they told him that instead of standing up to his responsibilities like a man, Freddie had skipped off, he'd locked himself in his office for an hour to let his rage work itself out.

An image of Kate's tearstained face flashed into Patrick's mind and his hands tightened into fists. He had thought it would be an easy matter to find the bastard who thought he could ruin a Nolan girl and then leave her in the lurch, but Freddie had gone to ground somewhere and Kate was already getting sly looks and sneering remarks from the street corner gossips. Patrick forced himself to concentrate on his late-night task. He'd just picked up the pile of coins to count into the next envelope when someone hammered on the front door.

He stood and slipped his boat knife into the back of his belt. Then he picked up the table lamp and walked into the hallway.

'Who is it?' he shouted through the door, as he grabbed the foot-long ship's pin from the hall table.

'Jack Archer,' came the muffled reply.

What the ...?

Patrick put down the weapon and opened the door to find his sister's coalman standing on the whitened step with a man slumped over his right shoulder.

'I'm sorry to disturb you, Mr Nolan,' he said. 'But I understand you want to have a word with Freddie Ellis. I happened to bump into him earlier in the evening.' He turned slightly so Patrick could see Freddie's unconscious face.

'You had better bring him in.'

'Patrick! Who is it?' Josie shouted from upstairs.

'It's nothing. You go back to bed,' Patrick replied, ushering Jack through into the front-room door.

Jack shrugged Freddie off his shoulder and sent him tumbling to the floor like a rag doll. Freddie didn't murmur and lay with his fair hair flopped over his unshaven face.

'Where did you find the bastard?' Patrick asked, resisting the urge to drag Freddie to his feet and then knock him down again.

'In the Blue Coat Boy.'

'You went there alone?' he said, unable to keep the amazement from his voice.

Archer looked steadily at him. 'Aye.'

Patrick raised his eyebrows. The Blue Coat Boy was more a sanctuary for criminals than a public house, and the area surrounding it was a battleground for rival gangs. Not a night passed without some poor bugger being discovered with his throat cut and penniless in the gutter. How did a yokel like Archer manage to get in, nab Freddie and get out without ending up on the wrong end of someone's blade? Patrick doubted he would have been able to do such a thing himself, at least not without a couple of strong men along side.

'I hope you'll forgive me interfering in your family's business,' Archer said, straightening the front of his jacket. 'But I thought you'd rather have me deliver him than I waste more time by fetching you.'

Patrick's gaze returned to the man sprawled across his carpet. 'Perhaps it was as well I didn't find him or he might look a lot less pretty than he does now.' He hunkered down and slapped Freddie lightly on the cheek. Freddie's head rolled to one side but there was no flicker to show he felt the blow. 'He's out cold.'

Archer gave a hard laugh. 'The blow knocked him out but the drink's keeping him that way. By the smell of him I'd say he'd had a skinful before I met him in the alley.'

Patrick stood up and gathered a length of rope from the corner. He lashed Freddie's legs together, then he and Archer rolled him over to tie his hands behind his back. They left him curled on one side.

'That should keep him until morning,' Patrick said as they stood up and looked down at Freddie, who was trussed up like something in a butcher's window. 'He'll have a hell of a surprise when he comes round.'

'He deserves a whole lot more than a surprise,' Archer replied harshly.

Patrick nudged Freddie with the toe of his boot. 'And when he sobers up that's just what he'll get.'

Jack repositioned his hat and said, 'Well, I'll leave you to your business.' Patrick led him back into the hall and opened it, but as Jack stepped out into the night he turned. 'Goodnight, Mr Nolan,' he said, as if he'd stopped by for a social call. 'And please give my apologies to your wife for disturbing her at such a late hour.'

Although Patrick still wasn't convinced by Archer's story and his so-called sister, he offered his hand. 'Thank you, Mr Archer. I owe you.'

Chapter Eighteen

As Mr Garrett worked his way through the funeral liturgy, Mattie stared at the rough-hewn pine coffin beside the open grave, under a leaden sky that summed up much of her sadness. Queenie had finally given up her struggle three days ago, whispering her son's name with her last breath. Although Mattie was thankful that her dear mother-in-law was now at rest, it left an aching space in her own heart.

As Queenie's only surviving relative, Freddie was his aunt's chief mourner and as such stood beside the minister. Behind him were half a dozen wizened old women from the church who had know Queenie in happier days. When Mattie was a child, it wasn't considered right for women to attend funerals, but as local men couldn't afford to lose a day's money, that convention had long since been ignored. The only other person paying his respects was Mr Stebbins, who stood hat in hand and with a sorrowful expression on his face.

Mattie was grateful to all of them for coming but the only person whose presence would have given her some comfort was Jack's. He couldn't come, of course. Apart from anything else, someone had to run the yard.

'For as much as it hath pleased ... ' the sexton and his assistant stepped forward and grasped the straps running under the coffin. They braced to take the strain then let the rope slip slowly through their hands. A lump caught in Mattie's throat as she watched Queenie being lowered to her final resting place. ' ... commit her body to the ground ... ' There was a dull thump as the coffin reached the bottom. 'Earth to earth, ashes to ashes.' Freddie scooped up a handful of dirt and threw it into the grave. It pitter-pattered on the lid and a tear rolled slowly down Mattie's cheek. Mr Garrett concluded the passage, everyone repeated the Amen, and the vicar closed his prayer book. He shook Freddie's hand, then came over and mumbled something to her about Queenie being in a better place and some urgent appointment then sped back towards the vicarage. The other mourners followed suit and then drifted away. Freddie replaced his hat and came over.

'It was a good service, wasn't it? And I was pleased to see so many of

Queenie's old friends were able to come,' Mattie said, in a pleasant tone.

'I'd better get back to the yard,' he replied, looking coldly at her.

'No rush. I'm sure Jack can ...'

Freddie gave her a venomous look, turned his back on her and stomped off.

Mr Stebbins put his hat on and strolled over. He took Mattie's hand 'Allow me once again, Mrs Maguire, to give you my heartfelt condolences at the loss of dear Queenie.'

'You're very kind.'

'Did she suffer much at the end?'

Mattie shook her head. 'At first her coughing fair tore at your soul but the laudanum settled her. In the end she just drifted off quietly in her sleep.'

Mattie glanced at two men shovelling earth onto her mother-in-law's coffin. 'I just wish I knew why she ended up in the river.'

'It's a mystery to be sure. But she was very ... er ... muddled sometimes,' he replied.

'Well yes, she was, but only as far as her son was concerned. Jack said—'

'Jack?'

'Jack Archer. The driver who replaced Eli.'

'Oh!'

'He thinks something must have upset Queenie to make her run off like that,' Mattie continued.

'Really.' Mr Stebbins's eyebrows rose. 'Any idea what?'

Mattie shook her head. 'By the time we got her back to the house she was barely alive. The poor darling had broken her arm and at least half a dozen ribs. The doctor said he was surprised she survived the fall.'

'So she said nothing at all about what happened?' he asked, studying her face intently.

'Not a thing.'

Mr Stebbins straightened up and flipped his top hat on his head, setting it at a jaunty angle. 'Well, it's between dear Mrs Maguire and the Almighty now,' he said, pulling his gloves on tighter. 'I'll have to wish you a good day I'm afraid, Mrs Maguire. I have several meetings to attend. Business, you know.'

'Of course,' Mattie replied. 'Good day.'

'And to you.' He picked his way around the men working on the other side of the open grave. As the sexton and his mate shovelled earth onto Queenie's coffin, Amos looked across at her.

'You'll forgive me, I hope, for bringing up the subject on such a sad day, but my associate's offer for Maguire's still stands. And now Queenie's gone you might be wise to reconsider it.' He tapped the brim of his hat and sauntered off, swinging his cane.

Mattie's hands clenched into tight fists as she watching Mr Stebbins march across the damp churchyard. No, she would not forgive him for bringing up the subject and no, she would not consider his offer again. Not today, not tomorrow, nor any day.

Nathaniel took the stairs two at a time to Smyth-Hilton's office. Since their initial meeting the reporter had proved to be not only completely trustworthy but also a veritable terrier at sniffing out information. He'd swiftly verified the duplicate documents and had visited the parish council offices to see the records of land and businesses that had changed hands recently.

Nathaniel had arranged to meet James Smyth-Hilton next Thursday at the Green Dragon, three doors down from the Temperance Society's offices in Fleet Street, but was surprised to find a letter waiting for him at Wardell's when he'd dropped in on his rounds. Although Nathaniel had been careful not to give Smyth-Hilton more information than was strictly necessary at their first meeting, it had soon become clear that he could be trusted completely. So Nathaniel had told James to send a letter to the general store in Commercial Road if he needed to get hold of him. There was a change of plan.

James looked up. 'You got my note then.'

'Have you've heard something?'

'I've done better than that. I've quizzed him.'

'What! How?'

'I took a table behind Stebbins at one of The God's True Word Society lectures in Shoreditch. He was most forthcoming about his plans.'

'*He admitted* trying to cheat Mrs Maguire out of her coal yard!' Nathaniel said, looking at James with increased respect.

'Not in so many words, but I mentioned George Hudson and he didn't blink an eye, so it's clear the rumours are true about the Railway King's involvement.'

Smyth-Hilton rose and went to his bookshelf where he picked up a bottle of brandy and waved it at Nathaniel, who nodded, then asked, 'But how does that take us forward?'

'Now we know what he's up to and that he's linked with George Hudson, I'm planning a trip north to talk to my colleague on *The Yorkshireman* – they're after *Hudson's* irregular business practices.

If the Railway King crumbles, he'll take others with him, including Stebbins, and if he is declared bankrupt the City and County will be obliged to open his accounts to the courts to ensure he isn't concealing any capital. Then we'll really have him. All the deeds to the properties will be open for scrutiny, as will his company's books,' he said triumphantly.

'So ... we are dependent on the downfall of George Hudson to catch Stebbins.'

'At present, yes.'

Nathaniel swirled the brandy around in his glass slowly. 'I'd rather see him brought to book for what *he's* done, not as a casualty of someone else's wrongdoing.'

James swallowed the last of his drink. 'Of course, there is a way of doing that now.'

'How?'

'If Stebbins got his hands on the deeds to the Maguire Yard and then floated his company we could buy a dozen shares. Then at the first shareholders' meeting, we would demand to see his accounts. I'm sure that would throw up some—'

'I'll not put my interests before Mrs Maguire's, or let him hurt her.'

James's pale eyes searched Nathaniel's face for a moment. 'Does she know you're in love with her?'

Nathaniel shook his head, surprised at the journalist's perception. 'Are you sure?'

He wasn't. Each word he spoke and his every action towards Mattie was laden with affection. She would have to be blind not to see it. Nathaniel raked his hands through his hair. 'It's no matter, because as things stand I can offer her nothing.'

James nodded and then pursed his lips. 'There's something else. I've heard whispers that Stebbins is partial to *very* young female company – if you get my drift.'

'Good God!' Nathaniel's replied, remembering Lily sitting on Stebbins's lap when Marjorie brought her to the office.

James sat forward and his eyes twinkled. 'Well then, perhaps that's all the more reason for bringing Stebbins down sooner rather than later ...'

The journalist trailed off as Nathaniel's eyes bore into him.

'Very well. I'll say no more about Mrs Maguire.'

'Good. If the rumours are true about his tastes then I promise you I'll get you the evidence but, know this, I will never allow anyone to do *anything* that might harm Mattie Maguire.'

Chapter Nineteen

Mattie carefully poured the willow mixture into a spoon and offered it to Brian. She'd mixed a heaped teaspoon of sugar into the bitter-tasting liquid but that didn't mean he wouldn't spit it out. He pressed his lips firmly together and looked up at her for a moment before finally opening his mouth.

'There's a good boy,' she said, as he gulped it down.

Mattie settled him into the crook of her arm and rested her head on the back of the chair. Her eyes drifted to the pile of washing she hadn't managed to get done, then to the range that needed a good scrubbing with sand to get the grease off.

With Queenie gone and Kate married, the chores were mounting up. Brian shifted and cried out. Mattie kissed his head again, and caressed her cheek against his soft hair. She must have drifted off to sleep because she started awake as the door opened.

Jack stood in the doorway looking down at her with an unreadable expression on his face. As it was Saturday night and there was no work tomorrow, he'd been to the Spitalfield Baths and was wearing his Sunday best. He'd also had his hair cut and beard trimmed. He dropped his bundle of work clothes on the chair, removed his jacket and hunkered down next to Mattie.

'How's the lad?' he asked, looking closely at the child's sleeping face. 'Did you take him to the apothecary?'

Mattie nodded. 'He told me Brian had been tearing around too much and overheated his brain, but young Billy Potter was as right as ninepence on Monday last week and buried on Friday, bless his soul. He started with a sore throat and fever, too, so I took Brian round to Doctor Munroe. He knows what he's talking about.'

'What did he say?'

Mattie pressed her lips on her son's forehead briefly. 'He said Brian's tonsils were inflamed and gave me some of his own medicine to keep the fever down. Bless Doctor Munroe; he refused my offer to pay.'

The weather had been hot since mid May so the crop of summer fever was early this year and there were a number of children already struck down in the surrounding streets. Thankfully, most had recovered.

Nathaniel moved a stray lock of hair out of Brian's eyes. 'He doesn't look so flushed.'

'He's not. He's had a coddled egg for tea and I've been giving him orange juice as Doctor Munroe advised. I'm sure he'll be running around the yard again tomorrow,' she said sending a silent prayer heavenward that it might be so. 'I had better get him up to bed.' Mattie shifted forward in her chair.

'Let me.' Jack scooped Brian effortlessly off her lap.

Mattie followed him to the top of the stairs and together they settled Brian in his bed, stationing his soldiers alongside.

Mattie reached down and smoothed her hand over the patchwork bedcover. 'I can understand why Queenie went peculiar because if anything happened to Brian I ... I ...'

Jack closed his hand over hers and the warmth from it flowed up her arm. 'I know,' he said softly. His jaw tightened and he swallowed hard. 'A child can be so swiftly taken.'

Mattie felt the pain in his voice and suddenly she understood why there was a trace of sadness in his eyes when he looked at her son.

She slipped her hand out and rested it on his arm. 'Have you lost a child?'

'Children,' he replied. 'They caught a fever and died within days of each other. Lily was six and Rose just three. My wife followed them to the grave a week later.'

The raw pain in Jack's voice cut through Mattie's own heart. She glanced down at her sleeping son and couldn't imagine how she would draw another breath if death took him from her.

'I'm so sorry,' Mattie replied, knowing all words to be wholly inadequate. 'Was it while you were working abroad?'

He nodded. 'I didn't know of their deaths until over a year later. When I heard, I didn't think my heart could possibly continue to beat. I blamed myself and then God and then ...' his eyes darted onto her for a moment then he looked back at Brian. 'I begged God to take me too.'

'I know. I know what it's like. In the weeks after my husband died I wanted to follow him to the grave. Then my lovely boy arrived and I started to smile again.' She looked back at Jack. 'But to lose your children as well ...'

'Each morning I would wake and drag myself through yet another empty day. The breath still blew in and out of my body, my hair still grew – somehow I survived. At first I hated myself for enjoying the sunshine or laughing. I couldn't understand how I could take pleasure in anything without them. Eventually, I realised that the best way to remember my two girls would be to live for them.' His eyes changed subtly as they ran over Mattie. 'And Marjorie, too.'

'I'm sure that in time you will find someone who will love you as much as you loved your wife.'

The warmth returned to his eyes. 'I pray so.'

'I am grieved by the way things turned out with Kate, Mr Archer,' Mattie said feeling her cheeks grow warm.

He shrugged. 'I'm sure you are, but now Freddie will have to put aside his wild ways and live up to his responsibility. I wish them well.'

Mattie cleared her throat. 'You show a great deal of fine feeling considering how disappointed you must be.'

'Disappointed?' He looked puzzled.

Mattie's cheeks felt as if they were on fire. 'I mean, I'd need the wisdom of the saints to fathom the girl's reason for choosing Freddie over you. Surely she can see you're ten times the man he will ever be.'

'Me? What made you think I have feelings for your sister?'

'Well, it seemed obvious from the way you were always offering her a lift on your cart,' she replied, trying to stop jealousy from sounding in her voice. 'And I've seen you go over and butt in when she was talking to Freddie on more than one occasion. She's a pretty girl. Why wouldn't you be interested in her?'

'I offered Kate a lift to keep her out of Freddie's way, because I know how much it upset you to see her with him.'

'Oh!'

Nathaniel's eyes changed again and a shiver of something very pleasant ran up Mattie's spine. 'Your sister may be a very pretty girl but she isn't you, Mattie.'

He had said too much. But with her standing so close there was no going back and, in truth, he didn't want to. It was wrong, of course, for so many reasons. He tried to tell himself that if he really did love her he would leave now. But his need to take Mattie in his arms overcame all his good sense and reason.

His hand slid around her waist and he gathered her to him. His eyes ran slowly over her face, taking in every beloved feature, then he pressed his lips onto hers gently.

'I'm in love with *you*, Mattie.'

She melted into him and slid her hands around his neck.

'And I love you, Jack,' she said breathlessly then gripped his hair, pulled his head down and kissed him again. Her hands worked their way underneath his collar. As her fingers slid over the skin at the back of his neck, Nathaniel longed to feel them caress the rest of his body.

His mind urged him to hold back, to think of the consequences. But with Mattie's breasts pressed against his chest and her hips against his, his body wasn't listening. He kissed her harder.

Mattie broke free again. 'Oh, sweet Mary,' she all but sobbed. 'It fair turned me green thinking you loved Ka—'

He stopped her words with his mouth and kissed her again deeply. 'It was always you,' he said.

His lips left hers and made their way across her cheek towards her ear then down her neck. Mattie tilted her head as her nails scratched through the rough fabric of his shirt. He nudged aside the neckline of her gown and planted kisses along her collarbone.

'Make love to me, Jack.'

'Mam! Mam!' Brian screamed.

'Oh, no,' she said, as she twisted in his arms, clamping her hands around his face and kissing him before tending to her son.

'Aroon, there, honey,' she whispered, bending over the bed.

Nathaniel stepped back and raked his hands through his hair.

'I'll leave you to settle Brian,' he said, stepping away from her. He left the room and crashed down the stairs to his room on the ground floor. He strode to the window and threw it open. He unbuttoned his shirt to let the evening air cool his body and stood motionless. He leaned out the window and took in a deep breath as he tried to still the chaotic mix of emotions whirling inside him.

Thank goodness Brian had interrupted before he was beyond thinking. He would have to master his desires, explain everything, ask her to marry him and then leave in the morning to find lodgings elsewhere. She would understand. She *must* understand.

The handle to his door clicked. Mattie came in with a lamp in her hand. Her eyes flickered onto his open shirt then back to his face.

'Is Brian all right?' he asked, hearing the tightness in his voice.

She nodded. 'He was just shouting in his sleep.'

Setting the lamp on the table, she crossed the room and stopped an arm's reach in front of him.

'I love you,' she said and standing on tiptoes pressed her lips onto his and reached for the shirt buttons he'd yet to undo. Nathaniel savoured the light touch of her fingers but managed to pull himself away.

'Mattie, stop. Stop. I have something to tell you,' he said, knowing his hopes and dreams for a life with her crashed to the ground as he spoke the words.

'I'm wanted by the police.'

'What?'

'Embezzlement,' he replied, flatly. 'Taking funds from the feed merchant I worked for in Romford. And I haven't been working abroad, I was sent there by Judge Tindal at Chelmsford Assizes. To Botany Bay in fact. And my real name's Nathaniel Tate, not Jack Archer. It's my middle and mother's maiden name. And I hail from Romford not Hastings,' he said, all in one breath.

'What?' Mattie shook her head and looked up at him as if she never seen him before. She took a step back.

'There's a poster outside the police station with my description on it.'

Mattie's jaw dropped and she stared wide-eyed at him for a moment then and shook her head. 'I'm sorry. I don't think I heard you right. Your name's Nathaniel ...'

'Tate.'

'And you've not been working abroad, you were a ...'

'Prisoner.'

'And you were transported for stealing.'

'To Botany bay.'

Mattie's brows drew together. 'And you're an escaped criminal.'

'That's right.'

'And you've been working as my head coalman for the last four months!' Mattie said, looking at him in horror.

'But I'm innocent!' Nathaniel replied, as the blood pounded in his ears.

'Of course you are,' Mattie said.

Nathaniel racked his finger through his hair. 'No, I truly am. You have to believe me.'

After a moment's pause, Mattie smiled softly.

'I do, because I wouldn't love you otherwise. But who *did* take the money?'

'The chief clerk,' Nathaniel replied, as a weight lifted from his shoulders.

'But how is it that you were convicted?'

'It was my word against the evidence he'd fabricated. He was a respectable pillar of the community while I was nothing but a scholarship boy.'

The hard lines around Nathaniel's mouth softened a little as he remembered his sister Emma combing his hair at least half-a-dozen times before she'd let him walk the three miles to Fairhead's double-fronted shop on his first day.

'My family have worked the land for generations and at first I felt like a pig in a parlour when I joined Fairhead's – they're Romford's main animal feed merchant. It just seemed odd to be sitting at a desk writing orders in the ledger and taking in money, instead of being out in all weathers at the back of a plough. But the senior clerk was friendly and kind and before long I felt at ease with my step up in life. He even spoke up for me when I began to court Marjorie. Her father owned a large farm and had plans for her to marry the squire's son. My friend persuaded Marjorie's father that I had good prospects, and after I married, he encouraged me to take on more responsibility. I'd been there four years when just, after Lily was born, he told me Mr Fairhead had opened a new branch in Chelmsford, where he would be the manager. I was to step into his shoes as chief clerk in Romford.' He gave a hard laugh. 'I remember how proud my father and sister Emma were when I told them. It was all going so well until one day just before Christmas '44. Mr Fairhead went to take the winter quarter money to the bank and found the safe empty.'

Outrage flashed across Mattie face. 'But didn't you tell the judge all this?'

'I did, but the court didn't believe me.' Nathaniel sighed. 'And when the court's officer found twenty pounds buried in my back garden the trial was a foregone conclusion. I was sentenced to seven years transportation. The man I trusted as I would have a brother, who was best man at my wedding and my children's godfather, who I gave my friendship to, in return destroyed my good name and my family. My father died of a ruptured heart a week after the trial.'

Mattie crossed the space between them and gripped his upper arms. 'Who is he?' she demanded. 'Tell me the name of this god-forsaken heathen so I can curse him myself.'

'Amos Stebbins.'

'*The* Mr Stebbins who lives in Mile End Road?'

He nodded. 'The same.'

Mattie legs felt suddenly very shaky. She reached for the chair beside Nathaniel's desk and sat down. 'But he's been so kind and helpful,' she said struggling to conceive of Mr Stebbins, with his paunch and fluffy side whiskers, as the scheming villain Nathaniel described. 'Only last week he told me he was putting Brian's name forward for a place at St Katherine's school.'

'And I'm sure he told you he was only trying to help when he offered to look over your books.'

'And a right jumble he made of them,' Mattie replied. 'It took me over a week to set them right.'

A cynical smile spread over Nathaniel's face. 'That's because the real reason he wanted to look over the accounts was to make sure he got the deeds to Maguire & Son's at the lowest possible price.'

'What are you talking about?'

'Stebbins plans to set up a railway company and your yard is in the way.' He told her everything from his meeting with the sexton in Romford to Smyth-Hilton's visit to York.

'So you see, Stebbins plans to get his hands on the deeds, then sell the land he's acquired at rock-bottom prices back to the Wapping & Stratford railway at a vastly inflated price.'

Mattie nodded slowly. 'I understand that, but how did you know about the railway?'

Nathaniel took her hand gently in his, then told her about Queenie. When he finished Mattie rose to her feet and paced back and forth, pressing the palm of her hand against her forehead to hold his story in her mind. An image of Amos chucking Brian under the chin flashed in to her mind. White hot fury tore through her. How many nights had she stared at the ceiling trying to fathom how to make ends meet and all the while Mr Stebbins was scheming to take her livelihood. Memories of his insistence that selling the yard was the only option open to her 'for the lad's sake' swirled in her head. And God only knew what he'd done to Queenie.

She spun around. 'I'll murder him, so I will,' she shouted, shaking a fist in the general direction of Mile End Road. 'The lying swine!' She bounced on the balls of her feet. 'Let's see if his wife still looks down her nose at me for visiting the Virginia Street Mission when it gets around the streets that her old man's a lying trickster.' She laughed mirthlessly. 'I'd like to see him stand up and read the bit about caring for widows and orphans from the Good Book, so I would. I'd tell the whole congregation how he treats widows and orphans.'

'Now there, Mattie, we can't show our hand yet,' he said trying to gather her to him.

Mattie pushed him away.

'And what about *you*?' she asked, tears springing into her eyes. 'You say you love me with one breath then tell me you've lied to me in the next?'

Nathaniel dropped his arms to his side. 'I'm sorry I had to deceive you, Mattie, but I *do* love you and I swear that's the truth of it.'

For several moments anger and hurt tangled together in Mattie's heart and then a calm cloak of assurance, the like of which she had never felt before, enveloped her. She ran her eyes over Nathaniel's anxious face and any remaining doubt evaporated. He did love her and that was all she needed.

She crossed the space between them and Nathaniel's arms closed around her. His kiss this time was hard and needy. Mattie responded, pressing her body tightly against him. She gripped him tighter as one of his hands made its way to the back of her head; the other grasped her bottom and anchored her to him.

Finally, Nathaniel's lips left hers.

'Mattie Maguire, will you marry me? '

'Yes, yes,' she laughed. Nathaniel lifted her off her feet and hugged her. 'We can't, of course, until I get my pardon but once I have it, I'll come back—'

'Back? Back from where?'

'I can't say. It's just for a while.'

Mattie gripped his upper arms. 'But why?'

'Because if I'm found here you'll now be arrested as an accomplice.'

'But . . .' She paused and thought of Brian tucked up in his bed, his thumb stuck in his mouth and his fair hair tumbling over his forehead. Guilt nudged at her.

Nathaniel hooked his finger under her chin and lifted her face. 'It won't be for long, Mattie, I promise.' He kissed her lips again lightly. 'Who knows, perhaps tomorrow I'll have that vital piece of evidence I need to clear my name. And when I do, I'll make the vicar read the banns all in one day so we can marry the next. And then I'll put a smile on that beautiful face of yours.'

Mattie's gaze left his face and travelled down to the dip at the bottom of his throat and then onto his bare chest. She unbuttoned the last two buttons of his shirt and then reached in and wound her arms around him, drawing him closer. His arms tightened around her as his body tensed.

'Oh, sweetheart,' he said, his voice crackling.

A mischievous expression spread across Mattie's face. 'Nathaniel, you don't have to go just yet, do you?'

Nathaniel opened his eyes and looked down at the woman nestling beside him. Mattie's glossy ebony hair cascaded over her shoulders and down to her hips in a luxurious stream. The ribbon that gathered the neckline of her chemise had unravelled, allowing the garment to slip off her shoulder. It was the only thing she still wore. Her eyes were closed and her hand rested lightly on his chest. He, too, had shed his clothes and they mingled with Mattie's, abandoned on the floor.

The lamp on the table cast a warm light over them and Nathaniel wondered if Mattie would be bashful when she woke to find him appreciating every curve and dip of her body. A satisfied smile softened his features. No, she wouldn't. She had matched his passion with an exuberance that surprised and delighted him. So much so that they had made love twice within as many hours. Mattie sighed and shifted closer to him.

God she was beautiful. He'd been lost to Mattie the moment she'd slid her arms around him and kissed his chest, but he worried that his lack of restraint might well have consequences.

Perhaps just twice will be all right. Mattie's hand stroked lightly across his chest, down his stomach and his groin tightened. *Well, even three probably would do no harm.*

Mattie opened her eyes and ran her finger lightly over his jaw, cheek and forehead.

She twisted around and studied the crudely drawn heart-shaped tattoo on his upper arm. Inside the heart were the letters R, L and M.

'Rose, Lily and Marjorie?' He nodded and she kissed the place. 'Sweet Mary, love and guard them.'

She shifted back onto her elbow. 'You don't *have* to go, Nathaniel,' she said, twirling her finger through a curl of hair. 'You've been here for ages and no one has yet linked you with the poster outside Wapping nick. Why should they now?'

Nathaniel closed his hand over hers. 'Maybe, but someone might still and I can't – won't – put you in such jeopardy.'

'Nathaniel, most folks around here can't even read what it says and those who could wouldn't know what embezzling was anyhow. Even if they did,' she continued before he could interrupt her, 'the fact some judge had found you guilty of it would be enough to cause them to think you harshly treated. The law has no pity for people in these streets, what with magistrates allowing landlords to evict as they will, and the police arresting cripples for selling bootlaces on street corners.'

That was true enough. Most households he delivered to wouldn't have survived if it weren't for the under-the-counter or fly-pitch costers who sold them goods at cheaper rates.

'Twenty pounds reward is a lot of money,' he said.

'Not if your friends cut you dead and your landlady turns you out for being a nabber's nark,' she answered. 'Tell me the last time you saw a peeler wander down this way.'

'I can't rightly say.'

'That's because you'll only see a bobby in Knockfergus if there's a murder or something equally horrible, and even then they'll only come by in threes or fours.' A heavy lock of Mattie's hair slipped over her shoulder and feathered over his chest and stomach. Nathaniel willed his eyes to remain on her face. He remembered the letter he'd collected from Smyth-Hilton that morning. It had indicated that they might be only a week or two away from having all they needed to expose Stebbins. Could he ...?

'But if they did come and find me?' he asked, with a great deal more resolve in his voice then he felt.

Placing her hands on his chest, Mattie leant forward. 'Why, I'd just be telling them that you told me your name was Jack Archer.'

'I wouldn't ask you to lie for me,' he said, knowing she would.

She shrugged and her chemise slipped a little further. 'And how would they prove otherwise?'

Nathaniel's gazed drifted down and the urge to roll her under him again swept over him. Somehow he managed to hold it in check. He sat up and took hold of her hands. Her closeness was making it almost impossible for him to think straight without her fingers adding to the distraction.

'Mattie, if there was another way I would take it, but there isn't.' Dangerous though it was to his resolve, he drew her to him. 'I don't *want* to leave but I must.'

Mattie slipped her hands around his neck. 'It's Tuesday now. Didn't you say Smyth whatsisname is back next Monday?'

'Yes, on the morning train.'

'Why don't you stay until you've spoken to him? After all, if you just disappear overnight people would want to know why.'

Mattie was right. If he didn't roll around the streets on the back of number one cart tomorrow it would be the talk of the neighbourhood by dinner time.

'I'll stay until I see Smyth-Hilton,' he said, as his arm slipped around her again.

Mattie moulded herself into him, her breasts pressing against his chest and her thighs brushing against his. Desire flared through him and Nathaniel let it have its way. After all, it was only six days until Monday.

Chapter Twenty

Mattie took the wooden peg from her mouth and wedged it over the last corner of her chemise on the washing line stretched across the kitchen. She glanced out of the window into the small back garden and noticed the wind shaking the empty runner-bean cane. Although the summer had been a scorcher, now, two weeks into September, there was a decidedly autumnal nip to the air.

Nathaniel's cart, pulled by the sixteen hands dapple grey called Peggy he bought to replace Flossy, rumbled through the gates and he jumped down from the front of the rig. Images of them entwined together stole into her mind and made her cheeks flush.

He had brought Josie and helped her down, then did the same for young Rob who he placed beside his mother. Although Josie wore her loose-fitting jacket, her growing waistline was clearly visible. She was probably only a few weeks away from her confinement. Mattie moved the kettle back onto the heat and had just set the cups and saucers on the table when Josie walked in. Mattie hugged her.

'You look well,' Mattie said.

Josie put her hand to the small of her back. 'I'd be grand if it weren't for this backache.' She tilted her head and regarded Mattie. 'You look a little flushed.'

'I'm fine,' Mattie replied, taking a deep breath and rolling her shoulders. She stretched out her hands. 'Now, you rest your feet.'

Rob dashed around his mother's skirts and joined his cousin on the rug mat. The two boys set about organising the toy soldiers into opposing armies. Mattie went to the range to make the tea, managing – with some effort – to keep her eyes from straying to the door. Nathaniel would come in before he set off on the afternoon round. He didn't need to, but she knew he would.

'Not long now,' she said.

'I can't wait,' Josie replied, smoothing her hand over her stomach. 'I see the new horse is shaping up well.'

Mattie nodded. 'Jack says she's a bit spirited, but she's only five and should settle into the routine in time,' she said, still finding it strange to think of Nathaniel by his real name and not Jack.

'So we'll be seeing Brian trot her around the street in a few years time,' Josie replied. 'I saw Eli over by the stable. Is he all right?'

'He's as right as ninepence as long as he doesn't need to use his left arm. Also, with him in the yard I don't have to keep running out every time a nipper rings the bell for a bucket of coal.'

'You've been busy, too,' Josie said, pointing to the line of washing. 'My gran used to call this weather the washerwoman's answer to prayers.'

Mattie rolled her eyes. 'Not if she lived in a coal yard. If I tried to hang this lot on the outside line they would be black before I'd pegged the last one up. See what the wind's already blown in,' she said, wiping her finger through the fine layer of dust on the windowsill. 'I only dusted it yesterday and look at it now.'

'You've a lot on your plate now that Kate's gone. How is she?'

'She's fine. The morning sickness has passed and she's just about starting to show. I've upped Freddie's wages to two pounds a week, and I'm lighting a candle each Sunday at mass in the hope that Kate sees enough of the money to put food on the table.'

'Mmm ... And what about Freddie?'

'Same as ever. Arrives for work late and slopes off as soon as he can. Gives me a look that would lay me in my grave if I ask him to do anything. He and Bessy Buckle are still the gossip on every corner, *and* there's whisper of him being drinking pals with Ollie Mac.'

'No!' Josie's jaw dropped. 'Even he's not fool enough to take up with the Black Eagle gang, surely.'

'It seems he is.'

Josie's shook her head. 'Oh, dear. Poor you.'

'Poor Kate! She's married to him,' Mattie replied. 'She came by two days ago and spent an hour telling me how happy she was and that Freddie was looking forward to being a father. I would have been glad to hear it, too, if it wasn't for the fresh bruise on her cheek.'

'Perhaps I should mention it to Patrick,' Josie said, putting her empty cup down.

'Don't. It will only make more trouble for Kate. And what can he do? A man has the right to order his household. Even the police won't step between a man and his wife.'

The door opened and Nathaniel sauntered in.

'I'm off on the afternoon round now, Mrs Maguire.'

She smiled up at him. 'Are you?'

'I am.' His expression changed subtly for a second then he looked over her head. 'Billy's delivering an evening order to Salmon Lane,

Mrs Nolan, so I've asked him to take you home. I hope that's all right with you.'

Mattie studied the notch at the base of his throat, revealed between the unbuttoned collar of his shirt.

'That will be fine, thank you,' Josie said, from behind Mattie.

Nathaniel's gaze returned to Mattie. 'I'll be back late. At about five.'

'Good. Because there's something I need you to go through with me in the office,' she said, trying to keep the tremor of passion from sounding in her voice.

'Of course, Mrs Maguire. Anything I can do to help.'

He left the kitchen.

Josie looked amused. 'So, how long have you and Jack Archer been carrying on, then?'

Mattie's cheeks burst into flames. 'I don't know what you're talking—'

'Come on, Mattie,' Josie chuckled. 'You could hardly tear your eyes from him and by the look in *his* eye! Well ... I'd blush to my roots to say.' She cupped her chin on her hands. 'How long?'

Mattie stretched her arms above her head and spread her fingers. 'Two days,' she replied breathlessly. She hugged herself as the thrill of the past forty-eight hours washed over her. 'Two wonderful days that I never thought to see the like of again.'

Josie laughed. 'No wonder you look so relaxed. So when's the wedding?'

Mattie made a play of pouring herself another cup of tea. 'We haven't decided yet.'

Josie caught Mattie's hand across the table and squeezed it. 'You know, you're as dear to me as my sisters and I'm fair bursting with happiness for you. But don't leave it too long or you might be having to hold your flowers to hide your waistline from the parson.'

'You know full well it took me a full six months before I fell with Brian so I think you can put your mind at ease on that score. For a little while at least.'

Kate pressed her forehead to the window pane and gazed down the street. The light was almost gone and the last few stragglers from the docks were trudging their way home but there was still no sign of Freddie.

With a sigh, she turned back into the front room of number ten, Salter Street. If she said it herself, and she shouldn't, she'd made a fair job of turning the drab ten-by-twelve-foot room into a snug home. The bright flowery curtains she'd bought for thruppence in Rosemary Street market had washed up a treat and the rag rug she'd made added a splash of colour to the room, although she'd had to scrub the floor with carbolic and vinegar before she could set it down.

Wedged in the corner was the cast-iron bed from her room at Maguire's. She almost cried when Mattie had given it to her because, without her sister's generosity, the new straw mattress would be on the floor.

The boiling water spat out from the spout and hissed on the hot metal of the grate that sat over the fire. Kate wrapped her apron around her hand and moved it off the heat. She lifted the lid from the saucepan and stirred the thick oxtail stew, which was more turnip and carrot than tail-bone. She began to set their small, wobbly table and bent down to jam the thin block of wood back in place to steady it. As she stood she put her hand in the small of her back to ease the strain. She and Mattie had worked out that the baby would arrive sometime before Christmas so she was well over halfway through her pregnancy.

Kate checked again to make sure everything was just so then returned to the window.

Where was he? she wondered, as she watched the lamp lighters at work.

The lid on the pot rattled and Kate dashed over to stop the stew from spilling over. The front door banged shut. She pinched her cheeks to bring a bit of colour to them. She turned as Freddie came in.

'Hello,' she said, giving him her widest smile.

Although his gaze didn't waver, the smoky smell drifting across from him betrayed the fact that he'd already stopped in at the Admiral. Kate wondered how much of the four pence he'd had in his pocket that morning was still there.

Freddie gave her a sharp look 'Is supper ready?'

'Of course, it's been ready for—' Kate bit back her words. After an afternoon washing in the back yard she didn't feel up to bearing the brunt of his ill humour. She ladled a large helping of stew into one of the bowls and handed it to him. 'It's oxtail.'

He grunted, picked up his spoon and started. Kate picked up her supper and sat down opposite him. She ran her hand over her workaday clothes and a little hand or foot nudged her palm.

'Mam says I'm having a boy.'

'I told you I don't want you going to your brother's house.'

'Mam was at Mattie's this afternoon,' she replied. He didn't like her visiting Mattie either but as she supplied their coal for free, he suffered it.

Freddie grunted. 'There ain't a lot of meat in this. How's a man supposed to do a full day's labour on workhouse gruel?'

Kate continued with her own supper.

'Where's me tea?' Freddie asked, pushing his empty bowl away.

'It's coming.'

Kate collected their dishes and put them in the enamel bowl ready to take to the pump in the back yard then started making the tea.

The chair by the fire squeaked as Freddie settled himself in it. 'And it better not be no second-hand tea leaves you're chucking in that pot. With what I give you each week I should be eating like a king. I don't know what you do with it all.'

Kate swung around and slammed the tea caddy on the table. 'You could eat like a king, Freddie Ellis, if you gave me what you spend down the pub each night.'

For a brief instant Freddie's face registered complete surprise. Kate held her breath.

Anger contorted Freddie's face and he leapt from the chair. 'What I do with my money's my own business.'

'Yours and the landlord's,' said Kate as he loomed over her.

'You want to watch yourself, girl.'

'And you want to give me more if you want to be eating scrag-end and drinking fresher tea. There'll be another mouth to feed soon,' she replied, wondering how she'd ever thought him handsome.

'And whose fault is that? You should have been more careful or gone to the old mother in Hobbs Lane.'

Kate's hands closed over her stomach. 'I couldn't do such a wicked thing.'

'But you didn't think twice about getting that fecking brother of yours to beat seven types of shite out of me to marry you. Did you?'

'Fre—'

Light exploded in Kate's head as Freddie's hand smacked her across the face. She staggered back against the table, gripping the edge to save herself from falling.

'Don't you Freddie me,' he yelled, as he hit her again.

Black spots popped in front of Kate's vision but she willed her legs to hold firm and not buckle. Freddie grabbed the back of her hair.

'Trick me, that's what you did,' he spat out, shaking her until her teeth rattled. 'I wouldn't be surprised if that brat you're carrying wasn't mine.'

Kate forced the swirling blackness in her mind away. 'You know you were the first,' she replied, trying to ignore the pain from her twisted hair.

'Yeh, but who was the second and third?' His lips curled back in a snarl. 'A girl who'd give it away like you do would open her legs to any fella.' He threw her from him and she fell heavily against the chair.

'That's not true,' Kate said, backing away from him. 'I love you, Freddie.'

He threw the chair aside and came towards her. 'You fecking caught me, you mean.' His fist smashed against her cheek.

Kate reeled, staggered a couple of steps then sank to the ground. He loomed over her with his fist clenched and a hateful expression contorting his face. 'Caught me with that brat tucked up your skirts.' He raised his fist again.

'Please, Freddie, don't,' Kate screamed, drawing her knees up and hugging her stomach.

Freddie's boot lashed out and caught her thigh. Agonising pain shot up her leg. The baby stirred and Kate tucked herself in further, praying silently for the precious life inside her.

'That'll learn you to give me lip when I get home, you tinker slut.' He kicked her again then snatched his coat from the nail and opened the door. 'I'm off to find myself some company that pleases me and while I'm gone you might want to chew on this. It was your sister I was after marrying. Not you.'

Amos spotted a large swirl of dog dirt too late to avoid stepping in the centre of it and slipping – to the delight of a couple of barefooted urchins sitting on the kerb, who sniggered behind their hands. He lifted his foot to inspect the sole of his boot then scraped it on the kerb.

His humours had already been curdled at breakfast when he received a letter he could well have done without from Fallon, who pressed him to announce the railway. And it was all that paddy woman's fault. If Mattie Maguire had done as she ought and sold him the deeds weeks ago, he wouldn't be forced now to dig deep in his pockets and offer her three times the amount he'd planned.

He'd judged that the Maguire drivers would be on their rounds, giving him the chance to speak to Mattie alone. He crossed the road and strolled towards the opened gates with Maguire & Son's painted in an arch over them. As he came within sight of the yard, a long-haired mongrel, who'd been mooching around in the gutter, lifted its head and trotted over, barking and sniffing around Amos' shoes.

'Get away.' Amos flourished his cane again.

The dog growled and then trotted into the coal yard.

Two shrill whistles sounded. Amos looked up and an invisible hand closed around his throat, cutting off the air. All at once his legs turned to jelly and threatened to give way beneath him as his gaze fixed on the man he'd never thought to see again this side of eternity. Nathaniel Tate!

It can't be! It's not possible his reason told his disbelieving mind. Amos staggered against the wall behind him and groped for a hand-hold to keep himself from falling. He closed his eyes and tried to steady the chaotic thoughts crashing around in his head. He gulped in a lungful of breath and tried to steady his galloping pulse. Praying his eyes were deceiving him but dreading they weren't, Amos forced his lids open, and now truly believed his heart would stop at the next beat.

It was no dream. No illusion. No figment of his imagination. It *was* Nathaniel Tate standing in Maguire's coal yard.

If he sees me I'm dead.

Amos pressed himself into the wall behind him. Sweat streamed down his spine. He had the sudden urge to empty his bladder.

Horror-struck, he watched Nathaniel jump on the cart and take up the reins. The dog leapt on the back and the horse started forward. Amos's heart thumped against his rib cage and, just as the cart turned into the street, Mattie came through the gates carrying Brian on her hip. Nathaniel pulled on the reins and stopped the cart. With a smile, Mattie stretched up and handed him a parcel before he urged the horse on again.

Amos tried to collect his thoughts. She would look his way at any moment so he *had* to compose himself. He took a deep breath and waited, but Mattie just stared down the street for a moment before walking back into the yard.

Amos pitched forward and vomited into the gutter, sending his top hat tumbling across the cobbles. He wiped his mouth with his handkerchief, picked up his hat and forced his legs to move. Staggering down the street like a drunk, he stumbled back onto the main thoroughfare, calming himself with a long pull from his silver hipflask. He turned towards Wapping police station.

How in God's name was Tate not only still at liberty but working as Mattie Maguire's coalman?

The butcher came out and took his position by the blood-stained block. He lifted a stiff carcass of mutton from the artistic display of dead animals above him and threw it on the block, then prised the chopper out of the wood. With one swing he thumped it through the meat. There was a crack as it split the bone.

Amos swallowed. *My God, that was a narrow escape. If Tate had caught sight of me I'd be as dead as that mutton now.*

But surely if Tate's intention was to kill him he'd already be dead. It couldn't just be a coincidence that Tate was working at Maguire's. He remembered how he'd spotted Tate outside Maguire's a few months ago.

Suppose Nathaniel had followed him there and returned later. What if Tate knew about the railway and was out to scupper his plans.

Well, damn you to Hell, Tate. You farm boy! You'll be back in chains before the sun goes down.

Amos turned into Wapping High Street and marched the hundred or so yards to the front of the police station. He paused to study Nathaniel's wanted poster on the notice board. The black ink had faded in the sun and the edges of the poster were becoming tatty. One corner of the paper had been pasted over by a reward for information about stolen cargo.

Now that his pulse was returning to something akin to normal, Amos turned the matter over in his mind. The police might want Nathaniel but *he* wanted Maguire's yard. What if . . .?

Superintendent Jackson stepped out of the front door followed by Inspector Oakes. Amos had been to see Jackson at Arbour Square police station three times to complain about his officers' lack of zeal. Irritation showed momentarily in the Chief Superintendent's face.

'Mr Stebbins,' he said, crushing Amos's hand as he greeted him. 'What brings you down these parts?'

'This and that.' He glanced at the poster. 'There's no news of Tate yet?'

'I'm afraid not. And frankly, Mr Stebbins, it's been over three months since we had report of him and you thought you'd spotted him in the street. Even if he was here I'd put money on it that he's slipped on to a ship and is half-way around the world by now.'

'Perhaps you're right, Superintendent, but what if someone was sheltering him?'

'Well, then he'd have company on his journey back to Australia.'

Somehow Amos managed to suppress his joy.

Mr Jackson pulled down the front of his jacket. 'Now if you would excuse us, sir, we are a little pressed for time.'

'Your pardon, sirs, I am keeping you from your duty. Good day to you.' Amos touched his cane to the brim of his hat and marched past them, grinning to himself. Perhaps he wouldn't have to pay the market rate for the Maguire yard after all.

Chapter Twenty-One

Freddie sat cradling a brandy in the corner of the saloon bar of the Hoop and Grapes, trying to look as if he drank in such a swell establishment every day of the week. Instead of the usual grey-distempered walls, and oil lamps discolouring the ceilings above, the Hoop was wallpapered and had new gas fittings sprouting from either side of the fireplace. Polished and swept floorboards squeaked underfoot instead of beaten earth and sawdust.

The landlord, a stout, tidy man with slick hair and a waxed moustache made a show of wiping the bar. He glanced over and Freddie raised his glass.

Good stuff he thought, as the mellow liquid slipped down his throat, but then it fecking ought to be at sixpence a shot.

Luckily Amos Stebbins, sitting opposite, was paying.

'New suit?' Stebbins asked, looking Freddie over.

Freddie flicked imaginary specks from his lapel. 'Straight off Moses Brothers quality rail.'

Amos raised his eyebrows in admiration.

Freddie felt pleased with himself. Alongside the clerks and city types in their grey suits and colourless cravats, he cut quite a dash in his pea-green-and-brown-check suit and low crown hat. His yellow cravat added a touch of sophistication. Now that Mattie had started to pay him his worth – at last – he had decided to treat himself. The new clobber cost most of his first week's increased wages.

The barmaid sauntered over with another bottle of brandy.

'There you go, gentlemen,' she said, fingering a blonde curl around her ear.

'Put it on my account,' Amos said, without glancing at her.

She bobbed a curtsy and, keeping her eyes on Freddie, slowly made her way back to the bar.

'She's a pretty piece.'

'I'm afraid I can't look at another woman without thinking of Mrs Stebbins's many perfections,' Amos replied.

Freddie looked at him incredulously before taking a mouthful of brandy. Amos's wife might have tits the size of a baby's head but she had a belly and arse to match; however, it would do him no good to be caught mocking the well-fed, tightly laced Mrs Stebbins.

He raised his glass. 'Cheers.'

Amos did the same then drew his chair closer. 'Thank you for coming, Freddie, I . . . I don't know who else to turn to.' He quickly looked over his shoulder. 'It's your sister-in-law and that new driver. What's his name? Jack . . . ?'

'Archer,' Freddie replied flatly. Although he hadn't seen who'd jumped him and left him senseless on Nolan's doorstep, Freddie would lay his last penny on it being fecking Archer. 'What about him?'

'Well . . . .now that I'm about to tell you my suspicions they seem utterly ridiculous to me. Perhaps my good lady wife and I are so fond of Mrs Maguire and her little lad that I have let my imagination run away with me.'

'If it's about Mattie Maguire opening her legs for him, that's old news.'

Astonishment flashed across Amos' face. 'My goodness.'

Freddie grinned. 'Don't say you hadn't heard.'

'No, I hadn't and I'm shocked. Truly shocked.' He looked beseechingly up at Freddie. 'What sort of man can he be to take advantage of poor Mrs Maguire in such a way?'

The smouldering anger at what he saw as Mattie's cruel treatment of him flared up in Freddie again. If he hadn't been such a gentleman and instead been more forceful, perhaps he would have been able to afford a smart suit years ago.

'Course *I* knew he was a wrong 'un from the first, Mr Stebbins.'

'Perhaps my concerns about the wanted poster outside Wapping police office aren't so unfounded,' Mr Stebbins replied.

Freddie's chair banged on the floor as he sat forward. 'What poster?'

Amos glanced around again then leant across the table conspiratorially. 'There's a poster on the police office railings offering a reward of twenty pounds for information leading to the capture of an escaped felon by the name of Nathaniel Tate. But now you've told me Mattie's new coalman is called Jack Archer, I can't see how it could be him.'

'He could be using a false name.'

Mr Stebbins eyes opened wide. 'You're a sharp one, Freddie. I'd never have thought of that. Does he have a heart-shaped tattoo on his right arm?'

'Archer has such a mark. I've seen it when he's been sluicing himself off at the back of the stables,' said Freddie, smoothing his hair back and thinking how he might impress Ollie Mac with twenty pounds in his back pocket.

'Dear Lord, no!' Amos let out a groan and several heads turned in their direction. 'Do you think Mrs Maguire knows? About Archer being this Tate fellow, I mean.'

Freddie shifted uneasily. 'Well, I don't know tha—'

'Because if she did then she would as likely be arrested, and what would happen to the little lad.'

Freddie shrugged.

'I'm sure a family member, such as yourself and your wife would be ideal candidates to become Brian's guardian, as you're both related to the child. Of course, you would have to run the yard, too. The court would give you power of attorney so you could order the business until he came of age.'

Freddie could have jumped on the table and yelled hooray. With Mattie gone he'd have what he was after all along; Maguire's yard. That would teach Mattie a lesson for overlooking him in favour of this Tate fellow. Let her think on that while she's locked in a cell or on the high seas travelling to the other side of the world.

With some difficulty Freddie suppressed a smile. 'It's a rum business and no mistake,' he said, trying to match Amos's solemnity. 'My poor cousin would turn in his grave if he knew how his widow was carrying on. Me ma's family never liked her, fecking Pope-loving mick that she is.'

He eyed the man opposite him warily. Had he gone too far? Stebbins was a God-botherer himself, after all. They tended to stick together.

Amos sighed. 'I ought to chastise you for your lack of charity, Freddie, but how can I condemn you for proper family feeling.'

Freddie relaxed. 'Family feeling as you say, Mr S. Brian and me were more like brothers than cousins and it makes me blood boil to see his little lad being brought up by the likes of her.'

'Well, I've certainly done my best to help where I can. I've even . . .' he looked away. 'No, perhaps I shouldn't mention the offer for the yard.'

'Offer?'

Amos stroked his carefully trimmed whiskers with his index finger. 'I have an associate, several in fact, who are looking to invest in local business. They are particularly interested in Maguire & Son's,' Amos told him. 'They are all fair and honest businessmen like myself and willing to offer a better-than-market price.'

'Are they?'

An oiled strand of hair fell over Amos's right eye. He smoothed it back. 'Indeed. I would have thought she would have jumped at seventy guineas.'

The image of what seventy shiny guineas might look like stacked in piles alongside the reward money for Tate's capture flashed into Freddie's mind.

'But no, she refused outright.' Amos poured Freddie another drink. 'And now of course if Archer *is* Tate then poor Mrs Maguire won't be in a position to accept the offer – not if she's imprisoned for sheltering an escaped convict.'

Freddie gulped down his newly-replenished drink in one mouthful.

'That would be a shame. For young Brian, that is.' He swallowed. 'I don't suppose your business acquaintances would mind waiting a little while longer for the yard, would they?'

Nathaniel stood back and inspected his repair. Peggy had managed to loosen a plank from the side of her stall so he'd bought a new pine plank from the timber merchant and half a pound of nails from the ironmonger and spent the last hour nailing it back into place

He'd met Smyth-Hilton again on Monday and, as the journalist recounted the result of his trip to York, Nathaniel's spirits rose. Amos wasn't the only one being scrutinised for dubious business practices. After a coup by his own shareholders, the Railway King himself was engaged in an acrimonious fight to save his business and political life. In Smyth-Hilton's view, Hudson was very likely to withdraw his support from the Wapping & Stratford railway and this might prove to be the final straw to bankrupt Amos. This alone wouldn't immediately shed light on Stebbins's part in Nathaniel's false conviction, but once Amos was unveiled as a crook and a rogue, his duplicity would be uncovered and Nathaniel would be exonerated by the evidence he'd accumulated.

He'd wrestled mightily with his conscience for the first few days about staying at Maguire's, but things settled back to normal and, although it grated against every honourable bone in his body, he had to admit Mattie was probably right about the small risk of discovery. No one had yet connected him with the wanted poster and it had been almost five months. Why should they now? With Amos's downfall almost within touching distance and the woman he loved in his arms each night, Nathaniel gave himself up to the pleasures of the moment and prayed that before too long he'd be in a position to marry Mattie.

How could he leave her? She had become his very reason for being. He'd loved Marjorie, but never like this. Marjorie had been the sweet love of his youth but Mattie Maguire was the love of his life.

Mattie's throaty laugh drifted across the space and Nathaniel threw aside the hammer.

'Mrs Maguire. Would you like to come and see the repair?'

'You've finished!' She came into the stable.

Nathaniel's arm shot around her waist and he pulled her out of sight. 'I'll never be finished with you, woman,' he said, enjoying the sensation of her curvaceous body against him.

Her hands flew up to his chest as if to shove him away but her eyes sparkled. 'Nathaniel!'

He pressed her into the sweet-smelling hay.

'I thought you wanted to show me something,' she said, smoothing her hand up his chest and setting his pulse racing again.

He began to unbutton her blouse.

'Honestly, we can't – it's broad daylight.'

'Morning, noon or night is all the same to me, Mattie Maguire,' he answered.

She ran her hands up around his neck. 'I have to go in. Annie needs to get home before dark.'

He pressed his lips to hers gently. 'I'll follow.'

'Don't be too long.' Mattie slipped out of his embrace and had just reached the stable door when three well-built police officers marched through the gates. She stepped back into the shadows dragging Nathaniel with her, just in time.

'I'll go, Mattie.'

'No, you won't,' she whispered, gripping the front of his shirt and pushing him behind her. 'If they're after you I'll tell them you're not here and you can slip away after they've gone.'

'But Mattie—'

'You said yourself the only way you'll ever be able to clear your name is to pursue your investigation into Stebbins's business.'

'Yes, but—'

'Well, tell me, how are you going to do that if you're bound in shackles and on a slow boat back to Australia?'

'Oh my God, Mattie. Be careful, sweetheart,' he said, trying to ignore the deep sense of foreboding settling in the pit of his stomach.

Mattie kissed him. 'Don't fret yourself. I've been dealing with the local coppers since I was a nipper.'

Maguire's yard didn't hold much truck with the local peelers. Occasionally a constable would drop by asking if any of the delivery men had seen a local jack-the-lad they were after and, for the most part, Mattie could truthfully answer no. If she couldn't she kept schtum.

The leading officer marched over, his studded boots scrunching over the coal chips, and halted within an arm's reach. The other two officers followed and stood ramrod straight just behind him, their eyes darting around the yard.

'Mrs Maguire?'

'How can I help you, officer?'

'I'm Sergeant Makepeace from Wapping Police Office and these are Constables Milton and Waverly,' he nodded behind him. 'We're making some inquiries about one of your drivers.'

'Which one?' Mattie managed to force out.

'Jack Archer. Is he here?' Makepeace asked, watching her closely.

Get a grip on yourself, Mattie Maguire,' she told herself. 'No! Not at the moment,' she replied in what could have passed for her normal voice. 'He . . . he stowed his cart an hour ago and went off somewhere. Why?'

Makepeace rested his left hand lightly on the hilt of his cutlass. 'I have good reason to believe that the man you know as Jack Archer is in fact Nathaniel Tate, a convicted embezzler who . . .'

Somehow, Mattie managed to feign shock as she listened to the sergeant recount the story, pretty much as Nathaniel had done himself.

' . . . we understand he's been working here for five months and for the last two of those he has lodged with you,' Makepeace concluded.

Mattie swallowed and just managed to maintain her calm manner as her mouth lost all moisture.

Makepeace nodded to the constables behind him. 'You don't mind if we take a look do you?' he asked as his men marched off to search the yard.

'Er . . . no,' Mattie replied, her heart thundering in her chest. 'But I've already told you he's not here.'

The officers looked behind the carts and kicked the pile of brown sacks waiting to be filled for tomorrow's rounds. They were just about to return to where she and the sergeant stood when Buster trotted in from his evening sniff around the streets. He stopped and cocked his head and barked at the newcomers. If Buster went to the stable they would find Nathaniel immediately.

'Buster!' The dog's ears pricked up. 'Go see Brian,' Mattie told him.

His tail whipped through the air as he scampered towards the garden gate. He scratched at it a couple of times, then nosed it open and disappeared. Mattie's heart slowed a fraction until she spotted one of the constables at the stable door.

'Don't you go unsettling my horses, constable,' she shouted, praying Nathaniel would hear.

The officer drew his cutlass and continued forward. Mattie held her breath expecting to see him reappear at any moment with the tip of his blade in the small of Nathaniel's back. After what seemed like forever he reappeared and shook his head.

'Right, let's take a look in here,' Makepeace said striding towards the house. Gathering her skirts, Mattie dashed after him.

Annie was reading at the table and her jaw dropped when the three men crowded into the kitchen, scraping their hats on the low ceiling as they tried to stand upright.

'It's alright, Annie,' Mattie said, pushing between them.

'Brian was yawning so I put him to bed for you, Auntie Mattie,' Annie said, her eyes like two enormous saucers.

'You can head off home now and tell your mam I'll be around as usual,' Mattie said, smiling reassuringly.

Annie gathered her school books and as she walked past Makepeace his hairy hand clamped over her shoulder. 'Have you seen Jack Archer?'

'No. I ain't,' she replied.

He stared down at her for a long moment then relinquished his grip. 'Off you go now, young lady, and don't talk to strangers.'

Annie shot out of the door.

Makepeace strode towards the hall door. 'Tate's room's through here, isn't it?' He marched into the hall closely followed by the two constables and Mattie.

As the officers searched through Nathaniel's room, Mattie dashed upstairs and stationed herself by Brian's open door. He was asleep with Buster lying at the foot of the bed.

Having finished downstairs the officers, led by their sergeant, clumped upstairs and started crashing through the bedrooms.

'There's only my son up here,' Mattie said, as Makepeace peered over her shoulder into Brian's room. Buster growled and he stood back.

'Anything?' asked Makepeace as his officers reappeared.

'No, Sergeant.'

Makepeace turned and marched them downstairs and Mattie followed. As Mattie reached the last step the sergeant rounded on her.

'When are you expecting him back?'

She shrugged. 'He has a key to the front door so he comes and goes as he pleases. I'm usually in bed when he returns.'

'You mean he don't *rouse* you when he gets in?' Waverley asked.

Milton snorted, and the sergeant's moustache curled up at the edges.

'How dare you?' Mattie demanded. 'I am a respectable widow, I'll have you know.'

Makepeace loomed over her. 'Respectable widow are you, Mrs Maguire? My informant—'

Informant?

'—tells me that Nathaniel Tate does a great deal more than deliver coal for you, a *whole lot more* and that you've been sheltering him from Her Majesty's justice.'

'That is a lie,' Mattie replied calmly, wondering how many Hail Marys Father Mahoney would demand for such a mortal sin.

Makepeace chewed his abundant moustache. 'You know the penalty for harbouring a fugitive from the law, don't you, Mrs Maguire?'

She nodded.

Makepeace stared back at her for a long moment and fear tightened Mattie's stomach.

'Waverly! Make yourself comfortable in the front parlour there and keep an eye on the door.' He turned to Mattie. 'You don't mind, do you?'

'Of course not,' she replied, hoping only she could hear the panic in her voice

'You come with me,' the sergeant commanded the remaining constable as he strode through the kitchen door and into the yard.

As much as she needed to hold him close just one last precious time before he had to leave, Mattie prayed that Nathaniel had taken the opportunity to slip away while the house was searched.

When the two officers reached the front gate the sergeant turned and touched the rim of his top hat.

'Does this gate only open from the inside?'

Mattie nodded.

'Then bolt it after me and I'll put a man to watch the front door.' A devious smile spread across his florid face. 'And when Tate returns tonight we'll have him.'

As Nathaniel heard the sound of metal scraping on metal, he scrambled out of the hay and touched his right cheek. It felt sticky. Another inch to the left and the officer's blade cutting through the fodder would have pricked his eye out. He pulled the spiky stalks from his hair and clothes and peered around the open stable door. The street lamp at the corner of Cannon Street Road glowed and in its dim light he saw Mattie secure the top bolt across the double gates. He cursed himself for not leaving weeks ago but it served no purpose to dwell on his foolishness.

She entered the cool darkness of the stable and Nathaniel stepped out from behind the hay hopper. A watery light filtered through the gaps in the walls and bathed Mattie in a silvery sheen. Love and guilt mingled together in Nathaniel's mind as he gazed at her.

'Mattie, I'm sorry—'

'Ssss,' she whispered and then she noticed his face. 'What happened?' She touched his cheek and set it smarting again.

'It's nothing. I have to go before they come back.'

Mattie pushed him into the shadows. 'You have to stay until it's safe for you to leave without them finding out you've been here all along.' She glanced into the yard. 'One of the peelers is sitting in my front room and he'll wonder what's keeping me. Stay here until I've dealt with him.'

Chapter Twenty-Two

Waverly was still making himself at home in the unused parlour when Mattie returned. She struck a Lucifer and lit two lamps taking one of them with her to check on Brian. He was still asleep in his usual position – on his back with one arm outstretched and the other across his chest. Holding the light high she gazed down on her sleeping son. *If anything should happen to him!*

When she went back downstairs she found Constable Waverly had dragged an old upholstered chair near to the door and had settled himself. Comfortably, he sat slouched in the chair with his arms along the high armrests and his knees struck up at a sharp angle in front. He'd snuffed out his bulls-eye lamp and had set it on the floor but still had his collar buttoned under the rolls of his chin. His cutlass rested across his lap and a muffled, whistling snore betrayed his lack of vigilance. Mattie popped her head around the corner.

'Is everything alright, officer?'

Waverly jumped, and blinked rapidly. He gave her a severe look. 'You should be careful, Missus. It can be very dangerous to startle a member of Her Majesty's constabulary,' he said, struggling to sit upright within the softly padded chair. 'We are trained to respond in an instant.'

'I'm sorry, Constable, it's just that I wondered if you would like a hot cup of cocoa.'

'That's very kind of you, Missus, but I'm not allowed to take refreshments while on duty,' he replied in a regretful tone.

Mattie winked. 'I won't tell Sergeant Makepeace if you don't.' Indecision ran back and forth across his face. 'There's a slice of cake too.'

'Well, a man has to keep body and soul together,' he said, patting the shiny belt straining around his considerable girth.

'You set yourself at ease, and I'll be but a moment.' Mattie shot back to the kitchen, pulled the kettle onto the heat and collected her largest mug and then the tin of cocoa. She poured a splash of milk into the saucepan and while it heated she spooned the powered cocoa and heap of sugar into the mug. Catching the milk as it rose in the pan, she poured it into the cup, stirred it vigorously and then topped it up with boiling water. She held the cup for a second and sniffed the rich, sweet milky aroma of the drink then reached for Queenie's bottle of laudanum on the windowsill.

Nathaniel put one eye to a crack in the stable wall. The moon was high and bathed the yard, the wagons and the house in a jaundiced light. The fog from the river had swirled up and sat in wispy patches, obscuring the carts one moment then floating over the coal heaps like clouds around a mountain. Behind him the rhythmic crunch of the horses working their way through their suppers and the scurrying of mice were the only disturbance in the night. He pressed his forehead to the wooden plank and manoeuvred himself so he could see the back door to the house. Still nothing. Nathaniel forced himself to remain calm and focused. His freedom and, more importantly, Mattie's safety, depended on him keeping a clear head.

As he paced back and forth across the straw-covered floor he wondered why, after all this time, had the police suddenly come looking for him in Maguire's yard? The answer was simple; because someone had told them where he was. Nathaniel had a pretty good idea who that someone might be.

St George's clock chimed the half hour.

Three hours! For the love of God, where was she.

Had more police arrived? Were they trying to extract information from her? Perhaps he *should* just give himself up. But then what?

Finally, he heard Mattie's delicate tip-toe outside. Nathaniel hid himself again in case she had the police with her.

'Nathaniel?' Mattie whispered.

He stepped out from behind the byre and enfolded her in his arms. 'Thank God.'

'I would have been back sooner,' she said, checking the cut on his cheek again, 'but I had to make sure the officer was asleep before I could.'

'Asleep? What if he hears something and stirs,' Nathaniel asked. 'Mattie, it's too risky. Go back in the house and I'll take my chances. If they catch me I'll tell them you didn't know I was hiding.'

'He won't wake.'

'But, Mattie—'

'I added a little of Queenie's laudanum to his chocolate.'

'You drugged him?' She nodded. 'For mercy's sake, how much did you give him?'

'Just a drop. He's grand and snoring away fit to wake the dead.' She shoved his kit bag at him. 'Now come on. I've packed a couple of your shirts and your jacket and trousers. There's two shillings tucked in the pocket—'

'I can't take your money.'

She brushed his objections away with her hand. 'It must be almost five now so you can slip out the gates and mingle with the men on their way to the sugar refinery. Nobody will take any notice of you in the fog. And, Nathaniel, there's something else ... Makepeace let slip that he had an informer.'

'It must be Stebbins. It can't be anyone else'

Mattie urged him towards the door but he pulled her close. 'You must go.'

He lowered his lips to hers and seared the feel of her into his mind. After tonight, there was no telling how long it would be until he could hold her again. He stepped back and held her chin lightly between his thumb and forefinger and studied her face, to remember every little detail. 'Let's go.'

Upstairs in the house, Brian turned and reached for Buster but found his spot empty. He sat up and rubbed his eyes, then scrambled off the bed and jigged on the bare floorboards as his bladder stirred. He pulled his china gazunder from under the bed and when he was done, looked out of the window. The first pink streaks were only just cutting through the cloudy sky so he knew it wasn't time to get up. He went to his door.

'Buster!' he whispered as loudly as he dared.

Nothing stirred. Picking up one of his soldiers to protect him from any monsters lurking in the shadows, Brian trotted along the landing. He poked his head around Mammy's door and he studied the empty bed draped with its unruffled patchwork counterpane. Brian's small hand clutched his wooden toy tighter. *Where was everyone?*

A loud snore echoed up the stairwell – Jack must be here.

Since Jack had moved into the front room the feel of the house had changed. It was as if a cosy towel, like the one Mammy warmed on the front of the range for his weekly bath, was wrapped around them all.

At the bottom of the stairs he noticed that the door to the room opposite Jack's was open. He tiptoed down the stairs and peered around the door frame then clamped his hand over his mouth to hold in a rush of giggles. Wedged in the old chair was the largest policeman he had ever seen. His arms dangled to the floor and his head had fallen back, leaving his mouth gaping as wide as one of the painted heads you threw a ball into at the Bow Fair. The officer's top hat lay upturned on the floor behind him, and as he dragged in each breath the edges of his moustache followed briefly before being blown upward again. Mammy's best mug lay tipped on its side next to the chair.

Brian bit his bottom lip. Everyone knew that you had to answer nicely when a policeman spoke to you and not use bad words like feck or shite. But Brian wasn't sure what you were supposed to do with a sleeping one so he turned towards the kitchen, where Buster was curled up tightly in front of the hearth.

'Where's Mammy?' he asked the dog.

Buster gave a little whine and then trotted out of the kitchen. Brian collected his boots from beside the fire, slipped them on and clopped out of the kitchen after his dog.

Mattie gathered up her skirts and, crouching low, scurried across the open space from the stable to the wagons with Nathaniel close behind. Although it was impossible to walk silently across the jagged fragments of coal, thankfully the fog had practically obscured the main gates on the other side of the yard and muffled the sound.

It only took a moment for her to unlock the bolts but it felt as if time had suddenly slowed.

Nathaniel turned to her. 'I love you, Mattie Maguire, and as God is my witness, I won't rest until we are wed.'

'I know,' she whispered and untangled herself from his embrace.

Suddenly, the garden gate creaked. Surely Waverley hadn't woken up! But what if he had? She felt Nathaniel tense and step in front of her. Mattie grabbed his arm and stared into the fog wide-eyed with terror.

'Mammy,' shouted Brian, clomping towards them with Buster close behind.

Mattie met him half way across the yard, scooped him up and held him close to her. 'Shhhh. You'll wake everyone,' she whispered to him, praying he wouldn't shout again.

'The policeman?' he asked, pointing at the house.

'Yes, the policeman. We mustn't wake him.'

Brian nodded and put his finger on his lips. Mattie settled him on her hip then turned to Nathaniel. He had his hand on Buster's collar and the dog's tail swiped back and forth across the ground and his tongue lolled out on one side as he panted.

'Bolt the gate as soon as I've gone and don't open it again. No matter what,' Nathaniel told her.

'Is Jack going?' Brian asked.

She and Nathaniel exchanged an apprehensive look. Mattie jigged her son on her hip.

'Just for a little while,' she replied, making a happy face at him.

Brian's brow drew together. 'When are you coming home?'

'The very moment I can.' Nathaniel ruffled Brian's hair. 'And I'll take you to see the tiger when I do.'

Brian yawned and laid his head on Mattie shoulder. Nathaniel embraced them and pressed his lips briefly onto Mattie's forehead then slipped out of the gate, which Mattie closed. She waited and listened. No shouts, no police rattles. Nothing other than the clomp of studded boots as the workers passed along the pavement outside.

The tears that she'd held back threatened to overwhelm her as a sob suddenly welled up.

'Don't cry, Mammy,' Brian said, rubbing her cheek with his chubby hand.

Mattie hugged him to her, and kissed his cool cheek before starting towards the back gate. 'I had better get you tucked up in bed, young man, before you take a chill.'

Back in the house she tiptoed past Waverley and carried Brian up to his room

'Jack going to take me to see the tiger at Jamrach's?' he asked in a sleep-slurred voice.

'I know.'

Brian yawned again, and as she sat there listening to his rhythmic breathing Mattie crossed herself and prayed to the Virgin that the Bengal tiger would be the only thing her son remembered in the morning.

Chapter Twenty-Three

Mattie lifted the tea pot and looked across at Sergeant Makepeace and Constable Waverley sitting at her kitchen table. 'Sugar, gentlemen?'

'Two, if you please,' they replied in unison.

Despite the headache cutting across the back of her eyes, Mattie fixed a smile to her face and dolloped in four heaped teaspoons of sugar from her precious supply.

'Good God, Waverly, what's the matter with you? Sit up, man!' Makepeace barked.

The constable snapped up and blinked hard. His gaze wavered as he focused on his senior officer. 'I'm sorry, sir, I've been awake all night.' He shook himself vigorously and took a loud slurp of his tea.

Brian pointed at Waverly. 'You snore.' He shouted gleefully and becan mimicking the noise and dripping the porridge from his spoon.

Makepeace's eyes narrowed.

'I've got a bit of a tickle,' Waverley said, punching his chest. 'It's the damp.' He illustrated his point by coughing dramatically.

'Eat your breakfast, Brian,' Mattie said, repositioning the spoon in her son's hand.

Through the kitchen window she could see Billy and Pete with their heads together as they loaded up the carts. Their eyes had almost fallen out of their heads when they'd arrived an hour before to find the police on the premises looking for Nathaniel. No doubt it would be the talk on every street corner by midday. Unsurprisingly, Freddie hadn't yet arrived, but he would no doubt be crowing all day once he heard the news.

Where had Nathaniel gone? Mattie wondered as a lump formed in her throat. *And when would he be back.*

She turned her attention back to her uninvited guests. 'I'm sorry you've had such a fruitless night.'

Makepeace's moustache twitched back and forth. 'Yes! Well! Has Tate stayed out all night before?'

Mattie shrugged. 'As I said yesterday, he comes and goes as he pleases. As long as he's on number one cart by six-thirty each morning

I don't pry,' she replied, in as disinterested a voice as she could muster. 'This is the first time he's not turned up.'

'Do you think someone warned him?' Waverley asked.

'I shouldn't wonder at it,' the sergeant said looking, pointedly at her.

Although her breath fluttered in her chest, Mattie returned his gaze with a cool stare. She stood up.

'Now, Sergeant, although I'm much obliged to you and your fine officers for keeping us safe this past night, if you've no further business with me, I have a coal yard to run.' She folded her arms.

'Jack going to take me to see the tiger,' Brian's small voice piped up.

Mattie held her breath.

Makepeace squatted and smiled at Brian in a friendly manner quite at odds with his infuriated eyes. 'Is that so?'

'Yes. Yellow eyes and normouse teeth.' He barred his teeth and roared.

Mattie picked her son up and sat him on her hip. 'Now Brian, the policeman's got to—'

'Have you seen, Jack, son?' Makepeace asked sweetly.

Icy cold washed over Mattie.

Brian nodded. 'Number one cart.'

A hysterical laugh threatened to burst from Mattie but she forced it down and fashioned her face into a picture of serenity. She set Brian on the floor. 'Get your boots on and once I've seen the wagons away we'll go to market.'

Brian toddled off to find his boots then sat on the mat to put them on. With a heavy sigh, the sergeant picked up his hat. 'Thank you for the tea, Mrs Maguire, and you'll inform us immediately should Tate turn up.'

'Of course,' Mattie replied, feeling a weight float off her shoulders with every passing second.

Brian stood up and clomped across the kitchen and stopped in front of the sergeant. He craned his neck back and looked up. 'Jack said he's going to take me to see the tiger.'

Makepeace hunkered down until his ruddy face was level with the boy's. 'Did he, son?' Brian nodded. 'When was that then?'

'Last night when Mammy opened the gates for him.' Brian covered his mouth with his hands and giggled.

Mattie stopped breathing but she forced herself not to react. She ruffled her son's hair playfully. 'Children! You wonder what they'll come out with next, don't you?'

'Indeed,' Makepeace replied still looking at Brian. 'And what else did Mammy do when she opened the gate?'

Brian covered his mouth with his hands and giggled. 'She kissed Jack.'

Mattie's heart thumped uncomfortably in her chest. She stared helplessly at the two police officers.

Makepeace straightened up and a smug look spread across his face. 'Mrs Maguire, I am arresting you for sheltering—'

'No!' Mattie snatched Brian up. He struggled in her embrace but she pressed her face against his and hugged him.

'You are not obliged to say anything,' continued Makepeace, 'but what you do say will be taken down and used in evidence against you. *Do* you have anything to say?'

'My son. What about my son?'

Makepeace's mouth formed into a hard line under his moustache. 'You should have thought of that before you gave shelter to a felon, shouldn't you? Waverly!'

Waverly grabbed her and led her to the door. Mattie repositioned Brian's weight on her hip. He twisted in her arms and wound his arms tightly around her neck and buried his face in her shoulder.

'I don't like the policemen, Mammy, make them go,' he mumbled into her hair.

Pete and Billy stopped mid-motion and their jaws dropped as Mattie appeared through the garden gate flanked by two burly policemen. As the officer marched her across the yard, Mattie noticed a small crowd was already gathering outside the gates. As they stepped into the street, Milly, the butcher's wife from across the road, ran over.

'Why you taking 'em?' she asked, planting herself in their path.

'Stand aside, missus,' Makepeace told her. 'Or I'll have to arrest you, too, for obstru—'

'Arrest!' Milly shouted. 'What you arresting Mrs Maguire for?'

'Never you mind,' the sergeant replied.

Brian started crying and Mattie tried to pull herself from the officers' grasp but they held her firmly.

'Don't think you can make a run for it,' Makepeace said, as the mob jostled them.

'For pity's sake, I'm not trying to make a run for it,' Mattie said angrily. 'I'm just trying to give my son to someone.'

'Here you are, Duck,' Milly said, trying to pull Brian from her. 'I'll take him to your brother's.'

'Mammy, Mammy,' he shrieked, clinging to her so tightly she could hardly breathe.

'It's all right, Brian,' Mattie said, feeling tears starting to form in her own eyes. 'You go with Milly and she'll take you to Auntie Josie until Mammy gets back.'

She prised him off her and held him so Milly could take him.

'No, Mammy, no,' Brian sobbed, his small fingers clutching on.

Mattie untangled his hands gently. 'Come on Brian,' Mattie said, with a tremor in her voice. 'Be a good boy and go with Auntie Milly.'

The butcher's wife hooked her hands under his arms and lifted him away.

'There there, Mammy won't be long,' Milly soothed. 'Shall we go and see your Uncle Patrick?' She turned away and walked towards her shop.

Brian twisted in her arms. 'Don't go, Mammy,' he screamed, reaching out for Mattie.

'Mammy'll be back soon, sweetheart,' Mattie called after him.

'Cuff her, Waverly.' Makepeace ordered.

The constable stepped in front of her, obscuring her view, and snapped the inflexible iron handcuffs around her wrists. Mattie peered around him to see Brian for a brief second more but he'd already disappeared inside the butcher's shop with Milly. Her shoulders slumped and she tried not to think about how long it would be before she saw him again.

Mattie woke with a start. By the look of the light streaking through the elongated grill situated at the top of the far wall it was probably just after dawn. She shivered and hugged her shawl around her, but after almost twenty hours locked in the women's cell of Wapping police station the wool was as damp as everything else she wore.

The sound of footsteps approaching echoed outside and Mattie fixed her eyes on the stark metal door. Keys jangled and a lock clicked. She heard voices in the corridor and then the faint retreat of the noise. She stared at the shuttered peephole and she thought of Brian. Her chin started to wobble and she lowered her head onto her knees. How much longer was she going to be left here?

When they'd led her down a long green-and-cream tiled corridor into the wood-panelled charge room, she had been told she was being held for questioning. She'd then been led away to be strip-searched by the matron, a middle-aged woman with a face like a sucked lemon and hands like sandpaper. After it had been established that her corsets were only stiffened with whalebone and there were no blades in her shoes, she was locked in a cell.

The women's holding room at Wapping sat just above the level of the riverbanks. Grey wall tiles glistened with trickling condensation and the odd patch of black mould. A chipped basin served as a toilet. She had the small dank residence to herself until just after midnight when two young women dressed in tatty satin gowns and rouged lips joined her. They'd been arrested for fighting over a soliciting pitch in Betts Street. Neither one of them could have been more than twenty, but by the shadows under their eyes and the hard lines around their mouths they'd probably been working the streets for half their lives. They now slept huddled together in the corner with their lacklustre hair fallen over their dirty, bloodied faces.

Another woman soon followed and now lay spread-eagled in the centre of the cell mumbling and drooling. It had taken four policemen to get her through the door and after running through every known expletive she'd crashed backwards to the floor reeking of gin.

Tears stung Mattie's eyes again as she relived the sight and sound of Brian screaming 'Mammy, Mammy' as Milly carried him away. How *could* she have let this happen? Why hadn't she listened to Nathaniel's good sense and let him go? *Come on, Mattie Maguire*, she told herself firmly, *Pull yourself together*. She damped down the fear that was interfering with her thoughts. Patrick would surely have been told what had happened by now and after he'd run through seven shades of incoherent rage he would have gone to the yard and taken over and Brian would be with Josie.

But for how long?

She couldn't tell the police anything because she had no idea where Nathaniel was or who he was with. But what about knowingly hiding a felon? She didn't know much about the law but she didn't think anyone could be convicted of a crime on the say-so of a three-year old. Besides, as they hadn't actually caught Nathaniel they couldn't prove he was the man they were after. What if they asked her straight out if she knew Nathaniel was wanted? The denial had tripped easily off her tongue in her own kitchen but could she put her hand on the Good Book and repeat the lie?

A door opened some way away and footsteps echoed down the corridor. A key jangled in the lock and a streak of light cut through the dim interior of the cell. Fresh air rushed in. The doorframe was blocked by a large policeman whom Mattie hadn't seen before. Stamping into the middle of the cell, he narrowed his eyes and fixed his gaze on the woman sprawled on the floor.

'Constable Burton, get Dirty Meg sobered up and send her back to her old man,' he barked.

The door creaked again and a younger officer stepped in and threw a bucket of water over Dirty Meg, splashing Mattie and the two prostitutes in the process. Meg let out an almighty snore and sprung upright like a jack-in-the-box, her hands flailing wildly in front of her.

'Bejesus, what the feck are you buggers playing at?' she screamed. She wobbled to her feet, sidestepping one way and then the other. 'A soul could be sent to eternity from waking like that.'

Constable Burton took her arm. 'Give your old man our regards, Meg,' he said affably as he escorted her out of the door.

The sergeant jabbed a finger at Mattie. 'You. Come with me.'

She stood and smoothed her skirt down. A cry like a cat caught under a cart wheel started in the corner of the cell.

'Oi, Diga! Wot about me and Clara?' one of the trollops whined as she clambered to her feet.

The sergeant's bushy eyebrows drew together into a knot over his nose. 'It's Sergeant Bell to you, Mary. And you ain't going nowhere because you and her have an appointment with the magistrate.'

The girls let out an ear-piercing yell then slumped together on the bench, their arms around each other as they sobbed out the injustice of it all.

Sergeant Bell led Mattie back to the charge room. He opened a leather-bound register atop a tall desk, flipped over a couple of pages and beckoned her over. 'Make your mark here,' he said, pointing at a clear line on the page.

Mattie signed her name.

Bell snapped the book shut. 'Follow me.'

Mattie did, through another heavy door into the front reception area. Hysteria bubbled up in her chest – on the other side of the waiting area, with dark circles around his eyes and a day's worth of stubble on his chin, stood Patrick.

Chapter Twenty-Four

St George's church bells were calling the faithful to worship by the time Mattie and Patrick crossed the Highway. Several of her neighbours looked their way and nodded as they passed. Mattie acknowledged them with a smile but Patrick just marched on in silence.

They stopped in front of the yard and Patrick thumped on the gate. 'Eli came by when he heard you'd been arrested.' His eyes flickered over her briefly. 'He's been guarding the place and tending the horses.'

'That was good of him,' Mattie replied.

'Yes, wasn't it?'

The bolts shot back and the gate opened.

'Welcome back, missus,' Eli said, as a toothless smile cut across his weatherbeaten face.

Through the stable door she could see Poppy and Samson's tails swishing back and forth as they stood in their stalls. All five carts were stored alongside each other and the piles of coal glinted in the weak November sunlight. Her bottom lip started to tremble and she caught it with her teeth.

'Thank you, Eli,' she said, hearing her voice falter.

The old man touched the peak of his battered cap. 'Say nothing of it. And don't you fret about the orders or nothing. I'll be back in the morning.' He turned to go. 'Oh, by the by. Freddie's in the office.' He nodded towards the stairs at the side of the house.

'Is he now!' Patrick said.

Mattie turned to Patrick. 'What's Freddie doing in the office?'

'Shall we go and find out?'

He turned and marched across the cobblestones towards the stairs. Grasping her skirts in her hand, Mattie trotted up the stairs behind Patrick, who took them two at a time. She reached the top step just as he opened the door to find Freddie rocking back in the chair with his feet up on the desk. To one side was an open money bag spilling out a dozen or so coins that he had arranged in three neat stacks. His jaw dropped open as they entered and the front legs of the chair crashed onto the floor as he sprang to his feet.

'Mattie!' he exclaimed, darting a wary look at Patrick. 'So the police didn't charge you th—'

'You bastard!' Patrick crossed the room in two steps and punched Freddie square on the jaw. He fell against the desk, shoving it backwards and knocking over the chair behind it. The coins scattered onto the floor falling between the cracks and rolling in all directions. Blood poured from Freddie's nose.

'Feck you, Nolan,' he bellowed, as he threw himself at Patrick.

Patrick jerked his head and Freddie punched into thin air. Patrick's fist found its mark again and Freddie crumpled against the shelves, taking them to the floor with him.

Patrick drew his fist back again but Mattie caught his arm. 'Don't, Pat! Stop! You'll kill him.'

'It's no more than he deserves,' Patrick replied, trying to throw her off. 'He's ruined Kate and now he's trying to drag you down as well.'

Mattie held on.

Freddie groaned and shook his head. From out of his one good eye he peered up at them. 'I just was checking the money. Take a look for yourself if you don't believe me.'

Patrick pulled his arm from Mattie's grip. 'I'm not talking about the poxy money, I'm talking about you grassing my sister to the police.'

Mattie's jaw dropped open. '*You* told them Nathaniel was here?'

Freddie scrambled to his feet and spat out a piece of tooth. He jabbed his finger at them, as his face contorted with outrage. 'That's a lie. You just tell me who carried such a tale and I'll set them right, don't you worry!' He blinked rapidly.

'I'm sure Superintendent Jackson will be pleased to see you anytime,' retorted Patrick. Shock registered on Freddie's battered face. 'You forgot that I helped him put an end to the Tugman gang, didn't you, Freddie?'

'Archer's a bloody felon. I mean, it were my duty to turn him in.'

Patrick shifted his feet and Freddie flinched. 'And was it your duty to tell the police that my sister was his "bit of jiggy" and that she was knowingly sheltering him?'

Patrick drew back his arm to thump Freddie again.

Mattie stepped between them. 'Who told you who Nathaniel was?'

'I can't say as how I remember. Some fella in a pub,' Freddie replied, his gaze shifting from her face to the floor and back again. He dusted down his blood splattered shirt and gently touched his nose, which was now sitting at an odd angle between his red and swollen eyes. 'Just some bloke. I don't know who.'

Mattie balled her hands into tight fists. 'By the saints, Freddie Ellis, if I were a man I'd beat you into a pile of offal where you stand for what I've been through. You're a sorry poor excuse for a man and no mistake.' Mattie's lip curled up. 'What with your sluts, your drinking and your work-shy ways. But you've crossed the line this time and I'm giving you your walking papers.'

Freddie stared at her for a moment and a mottled flush coloured his face.

'What!' He stepped closer and the smell of beer and sweat wafted over her. 'You can't do—'

'For our Kate's sake I'll let you have ten bob from the table to see you through until you get work.' Her eyes narrowed. 'Now get out!'

Freddie's complexion darkened and he didn't move. Mattie's gaze didn't waver.

'You heard my sister,' Patrick said from behind her.

Freddie ground out a collection of guttural sounds, snatched two crowns from the desk and stomped to the door.

'Feck you both, you pair of cussed Irish tinkers. I said nothing but the truth,' he yelled from the doorway. 'You,' he jabbed a dirty finger at Mattie, 'and Archer have been rolling around under the blankets for months and whatever you told the police, you *knew* the law was after him.'

Patrick started forward but Freddie was already running down the stairs.

'Good riddance,' Mattie said, beginning to pick up the coins. 'It's a good thing you knew Jackson or else I'd still be under lock and key.'

'Is it true?'

Mattie squared her shoulders. 'Patrick, we love each other and we are to be married as soon as he can clear his name.'

'Did you know he was wanted?'

'Not at first,' Mattie replied holding her brother's implacable stare. 'But he told me everything, up front. He wanted to leave, to keep me safe, but I persuaded him to stay.'

They stared at each other for a long moment. 'How could you?' he asked, his tired eyes searching her face.

'How could I what, Patrick?' Mattie asked softly. 'Lie to the police? Shelter a wanted man? Or fall in love again?'

'How could you forget Brian. He's only been dead three years.'

'You're wrong. Brian's been dead for three *long* years. Three exhausting years of birthing and raising a child, running the yard, keeping Queenie from harm and going to bed alone. I never believed there would be another man for me, not after Brian.' An image of Nathaniel smiling down at her floated into her mind and her chin trembled again. 'But I do love Nathaniel. And I *know* he is innocent.'

'That's what they all say,' Patrick replied.

Mattie fixed her brother with an inflexible stare. 'You've always looked out for me, Patrick. You walloped that boy from Greenbank when he pushed me in the puddle and took a strapping from the school master when it was me who wrote that he was a Nancy boy on the class blackboard.' Her lower lips started trembling again but this time Mattie couldn't stop it. 'I love you something fierce but I love Nathaniel, too. And, as dear as you are to me, Pat, if you can't stand with me on this then ... then ...'

Her voice caught in her throat as the floor seemed to shift under her feet.

Patrick crossed the space between them and wrapped his arms around her. 'There there, Matt. It's alright,' he said kissing her forehead. 'You've been through enough without me rowing at you.' He held her until the shivering subsided. He squeezed her shoulders. 'Let's get back to ours. Josie has a hot dinner for you and I know there's a young man who's waiting to see you.'

Mattie nodded gratefully and Patrick kissed her forehead. 'You can tell me all about it and,' – he fixed her with a fierce stare – 'I mean *all* about it.'

With his collar tucked up around his ears and his cap pulled low and, keeping as far as he could in the shadows, Nathaniel made his way past St James's church towards the river.

It was dusk, and the men who made their living on the water were lashing in sails and securing boats in the fading light before making their way home. Those without a supper awaiting them stood outside pubs and gin shops with tankards in their hands, while some of the local prostitutes weaved between them.

As he turned into Narrow Street the tangy smell of the river mingled with the sour stench from the local brewery. The tall masts of the barges anchored in the basin swayed in the evening fog and the low boom of their hulls nudging into each other added to the eerie scene. Nathaniel tucked himself out of sight in a doorway and waited.

Two policemen appeared out of the swirling haze walking at the regulation three miles per hour and with bulls-eye lamps in their hands. Nathaniel pressed himself against the wooden door and held his breath.

When Boyce brought the news that Mattie had been arrested, Nathaniel tore out of the Duck, intent on giving himself up to free her. He'd been half way to Bishopsgate police station before Boyce's two heavies dragged him back. Boyce had argued, and tipped spirit down him for three hours before Nathaniel had been carried senseless to his bed.

In the cold light of day and through a splitting headache, Nathaniel conceded that even if he'd turned himself in it would have only proved Mattie's guilt. When he'd told Boyce that he was going to slip down to the river again, 'a brainless, yokel idiot' was one of the milder invectives Boyce had yelled at him. Given that a pair of Her Majesty's finest were now plodding by within a few feet of him, Nathaniel thought perhaps Boyce had a point. But despite the danger, Nathaniel had to leave the safety of Spitalfields rookery and explain himself. His honour – and hers – demanded it.

As the steady footsteps of the beat constables faded, Nathaniel spotted the tall figure he was waiting for making his way along the quay. As Patrick Nolan neared, Nathaniel stepped into the mellow light of the street lamp.

Patrick's face contorted with fury. 'You bastard.'

'I have to talk to you about Mattie,' Nathaniel replied.

Patrick sprung forward. 'Don't you dare mention my sister's name after the way you've treated her, you filthy, lying convict.' He shoved him but Nathaniel stood his ground.

'There isn't a name under God's sky that you could call me that I haven't called myself for leaving Mattie as I did, but surely you can see that I had no choice? If I'd been caught in her yard then there would have been nothing you or anyone else could have done to save her from prison.'

'That may be, but it wasn't you who had to listen to Brian crying for his mother all night, was it? And it wasn't you who had to spend the night in a stinking cell, cold and afraid. No, when the peelers came calling you just showed a clean pair of heels.' He jabbed his finger at Nathaniel. 'I knew there was something dodgy about you from the start. And I almost believed the cock-and-bull story about you being framed for stealing from your employer by your friend. Until Mattie named Amos Stebbins as the man behind it all. You overreached yourself there, chum.' He laughed. 'Amos Stebbins! If you'd named the Archbishop of Canterbury I could have swallowed it, but *Amos Stebbins* burying moneybags in your back garden, visiting brothels and fiddling Mattie out of the yard? Never.'

Nathaniel stepped forward until they were almost nose to nose. 'Are you sure?

'If I saw it with my own eyes I'd still have trouble believing Amos Stebbins would do such things.'

'Well, why don't you try?' Nathaniel drew out a sheet of paper from his pocket. 'You owe me, and now I'm calling in that debt.' He held it in front of Patrick's face. 'This is the address of a discreet establishment that the saintly Amos Stebbins visits at least twice a week. And when you see with your own eyes his true character, perhaps then you'll consider helping me stop him destroying everything Mattie holds dear.'

Chapter Twenty-Five

Swinging his cane in an effort to look unconcerned, Amos turned into the yard and inspected the premises. The mountain of coal at the far end was proof that the Maguire yard had doubled its wholesale order to keep up with demand.

'I'll be but a moment,' a voice shouted from the stable.

Amos flicked the specks of coal dust already settling on his coat then looked up as Eli shuffled out.

'Oh, it's you, sir,' Eli said, wiping his hands on the front of his trousers. 'I thought it were a nipper after a bucket of coal.'

'Is Mrs Maguire in?' Amos asked. 'I thought I would drop by to see how she's bearing up.'

'She's gone to market, sir, But she shouldn't be too long. Why don't you go and rest your plates of meat in the kitchen until she comes back?'

Amos pulled out his hunter and flipped open the case. 'Very well,' he said snapping it shut.

Avoiding a pile of horse muck in the middle of the yard, he marched through the back gate and into the house. As he pushed open the kitchen door a young girl of about eight or nine looked up from the floor where she was playing with Brian.

Her pale green dress was partly covered by a white apron and, even though she was playing on the floor with Brian's toy soldiers, she seemed to have a maturity and self possession about her unusual in one so young. She was dark, too. Not just her hair but her deep olive skin that reminded him of the young girl from Ceylon who'd charmed him at Madame's.

'Hello, young man,' he said to Brian as he closed the door.

Brian scrambled to his feet and presented him with a brick, then went back to his other toys.

Amos smiled at the young girl. 'I don't think I know you,' he said, taking off his hat and gloves.

She stood up and straightened her skirt. 'I'm Annie Nolan,' she told him, flicking her heavy braids over her shoulder. They bounced against her hips.

'You must be Patrick's girl,' Amos said, pulling out a chair from the table nearest to her.

She nodded. 'I'm staying with my Aunt Mattie for a while to help.'

'I'm sure she's very grateful for that,' he replied, in a smooth tone. 'You must be about my stepdaughter Ruth's age.'

'I'm ten next month,' Annie replied proudly, standing tall.

Amos's eyes travelled over her and he settled himself more comfortably in the chair. 'I'll tell you what, Annie, while we wait for your aunt why don't we get to know each other better?'

As the last of the drays rolled westward to the city, Mattie reached the yard. She waved at Pete and Billy unharnessing the horses and made her way across the yard towards the garden.

'Only me, Annie,' she shouted as she opened the door. 'I'm sorry, I—'

Mattie froze as her gaze rested on Amos Stebbins sitting at the kitchen table with Annie beside him. Annie had her school primer open on the table and had drawn her chair alongside Amos's so he could see her work. His knees touched Annie's in a seemingly casual way whilst his hand rested lightly on her bare arm.

With a monumental effort, Mattie only just stopped herself from running across and snatching her niece away from him. 'Mr Stebbins, what an unexpected pleasure. Have you been waiting long?'

'Only five minutes or so.' He beamed at the little girl beside him. 'And five very enjoyable minutes they were, too.'

Mattie mentally crossed herself and said a prayer of thanks to the Virgin that he hadn't been with Annie any longer.

Annie jumped off her chair. 'Shall I get Brian ready for bed, Auntie Mattie?'

Mattie nodded and Annie took Brian's hand and led him upstairs. As the latch clicked shut, Amos rose to his feet. 'My poor, poor, Mrs Maguire.' He crossed the kitchen floor and grasped her hands. 'What you must have suffered.'

Ignoring his moist palms and her creeping feeling of disgust, Mattie allowed him to give her hands a squeeze.

'Would you like a cup of tea?' she asked just about able to maintain her pleasant expression as she removed her hands from his grip.

He nodded. 'I understand. You must maintain your dignity, your pride,' he said, as she moved the kettle on to the fire and collected the cups. 'Of course. How else could you hold your head up after such humiliation. Parading you through the streets in handcuffs like one of the Bett Street doxies or an Old Nichol thief.' He shook his head ponderously, then his eyes and mouth narrowed a fraction. 'And you had no idea that this ... this ...' his face screwed into a puckered ball. 'What was his name?'

'Nathaniel *Tate*,' Mattie replied, taking the kettle from the stove and wishing she could swipe it across Amos's deceitful face.

'Ah, yes, Tate.' He frowned. 'I want you to know that I don't believe one word of the rumours flying around about you betraying your husband's memory with such a rogue and villain. Not one word.'

Mattie went to the larder and, with her back to Stebbins, closed her eyes and counted slowly to ten in her head.

'Thank you, Mr Stebbins,' she replied, returning to the table and pouring the tea. She handed him a cup.

Amos sipped his tea. 'And you had no idea at all? About Tate, I mean.'

Mattie looked at him with wide-eyed innocence. 'How could I? He did his job, took his pay and I didn't pry.'

Amos studied her face intensely. 'So you don't have any idea where he is now.'

'None whatsoever.'

That was the truth.

Her eyes ran over Stebbins's expensive suit, polished shoes and the chain and fob looped across his silk waistcoat. The words liar and cheat sprang into her mind as she looked into his well-fed face. She thought of Nathaniel's wife and children buried together in a country graveyard and then of Queenie's broken body lying in the stinking mud of the Thames. The cup and saucer in her hand rattled and she slammed it down as tears of fury shimmered on her lower lids.

Amos mouth dropped open. 'My dear Mrs Mag—'

'I'm sorry ... it's ... it's been a very trying time,' she forced out.

Amos reached across. 'Here, here,' He patted her hand. 'May I, as an old friend, offer you some advice?' Not trusting herself to speak, Mattie nodded. 'No one more than I admires the way you've struggled on with Maguire & Son's but surely this unfortunate business with Tate shows you just how vulnerable you are to charlatans and fraudsters. Why don't you think about my colleague's offer for the yard again? Mm?'

Mattie took a firm grip of her temper. Any unguarded reaction would alert Amos to the fact that she knew all about his despicable game. She made a show of extracting her handkerchief from her sleeve and dabbed her eyes. 'I need time to think,' she said, trying to look fragile rather than furious.

Amos patted her hand again. 'Of course.' Footsteps ran across the floor above their head and Amos looked up and smiled. 'But remember, Mrs Maguire, you have to think about what's best for Brian, too.' He stood up and shrugged on his coat. 'I'll leave you now but if there is anything I can do ...'

'You're too kind,' Mattie replied, rising to her feet.

Amos opened the door and touched the brim of his hat. 'Good day to you, Mrs Maguire.'

Mattie stared at the closed door for a moment then picked up the cup and saucer she had served his tea in. It was part of her prized tea set that her mother had given her as a wedding present and which Mattie kept for best. She studied the pink and blue flowers around the rim where Amos had placed his lips, the delicate handle that he'd gripped between his stubby fingers and the flute-edged saucer he'd cradled in his palm. Then hurled them into the fire.

As Amos turned off Whitechapel High Street and into the White Swan Yard, a drunk stumbled into him. Wrinkling his nose at the over powering smell of cheap spirits, Amos shoved him away. The man fell against the wall opposite then slid down on to the dirt road with his legs splayed out in front of him. Amos stepped over him and continued towards the far end of the narrow alley.

White Swan Alley was really just a passageway between the houses that fronted onto the High Street. The dwellings clustered behind the busy thoroughfare were no more than a collection of ramshackle wooden fleapits that housed pungent trades such as fur puckers, rag dealers and night-soil men. Somewhere along the way, one of the narrow dilapidated structures had been turned into an ale house and christened the Bird in Hand.

Suppressing his godly repugnance at such an establishment, Amos pushed the door open. It took his eyes a while to adjust to the almost non-existent light from the tallow candles on the walls. A couple of men slouching on the bar glanced his way but swiftly returned to their drinks. Peering through the thick tobacco smoke, Amos spotted Tucker and Dutton wedged into a booth at the far end of the tightly packed bar. He pushed his way through and slid into the seat. The barmaid, wearing little more than her underwear and a tatty skirt, swanned over.

Tucker ordered another two ales but Amos waved her away.

'Nice place to meet,' he said, drawing his hip flask from inside his jacket.

Dicky grinned. 'Well we could have dropped by after Church but we thought it might send the old spinsters into a flutter if we strolled in.'

Tucker took out a half-smoked cigar from his top pocket and lit it. 'Everyone in here is deaf, dumb and blind. They don't see no one or nuffink,' he said, shaking out the match. 'Now what can we do for you, Mr Stebbins?'

'It's Maguire's.'

'I guessed as much,' Tucker said, as the barmaid left the tankards and returned to the board set on two barrels that served as a counter.

Dicky chuckled. 'You ain't had much luck there, have you Mr Stebbins.'

'No I bloody haven't.' Amos took a mouthful of brandy.

'It's the talk of the streets how her rounds-man turned out to be an escaped felon,' Tucker said. 'I tell you, we almost crapped ourselves laughing when we 'eard. Didn't we Dicky?'

Amos's lips curled. 'Well I'm the one laughing now,' he replied. 'And now Tate's under lock and key where he belongs there's no one left to protect Mattie Maguire.' He glanced around and then leant forward. 'Now listen, Tucker. I don't care how you do it or what it costs but I want Mattie Maguire out of that yard. And quick.'

Mattie bent over the bed and took the infant from Josie. Thomas, her newest nephew, burped contentedly and a small dribble of milk trickled down his tiny chin. Mattie closed her eyes and rested her cheek on his warm downy forehead before laying him in the crib.

Josie's bedroom was warmed by the glowing fire in the hearth and the thick long drapes. Traditionally, in the last few weeks before a baby was due the mother spent a great deal of time sprucing up the house and preparing the baby's layette. Even the very poorest women tried to have something new for the baby, and most church and mission visiting societies regularly donated bundles of lying-in clothes. Of course, these often ended up in the pawnshop but at least then the mother had a shilling or so to pay the midwife. Thanks to the success of Patrick's barge, the *Smiling Girl*, Josie had shillings to spare.

'He's a grand boy and no mistake,' she said, tucking the soft, finely knitted blanket around the baby.

Josie yawned. 'He is, too, and was bursting to get into the world so fast Patrick barely had time to get the towels and water.'

'So I heard when he dropped in this morning to tell us the news,' Mattie replied, smoothing her fingers over the baby's fine hair.

She'd been checking over the wagons just before seven when Patrick had pushed open the gate. She'd given him breakfast while he told her of Thomas's sudden arrival in the small hours. After clearing his plate, he'd left to start his day's work, whistling a merry tune.

Josie patted the cover. 'Come and sit beside me.'

Mattie did. She tilted her head and gazed down at the sleeping baby. 'Who do you think he looks like?'

'A bit like Mickey I think,' Josie replied. 'Have you seen Kate?'

The lump formed in Mattie's throat. 'She popped around on Monday last and I've told her that, whatever Freddie says, she's to call me the moment her time is on her.'

'But she's got a month or two to go yet, hasn't she?'

'Oh, yes,' Mattie replied, in what she hoped was a light tone. 'But you never know.'

There were no new marks on Kate's face the last few times she'd seen her, but she didn't trust Freddie to keep his hands to himself and Kate was carrying low.

'And how is Thomas's mammy?'

Josie yawned again. 'I feel I could sleep for a week. I'm going to keep him on the breast longer,' she whispered. 'It might keep the next one at bay for a bit.'

Mattie raised an eyebrow. 'Yes, sometimes babies arrive quicker than you think.'

Josie squeezed her hand. 'Is there no news about Nathaniel?'

'Not yet.'

Mattie had sent a letter to Smyth-Hilton, who'd replied, but only to tell her that although he and Nathaniel had accumulated enough evidence to have Amos Stebbins thrown out of the Chamber of Commerce and St George's vestry there was not yet enough to force him to open his books. She'd shown the letter to Patrick but he hadn't changed his mind.

'Annie tells me you've been under the weather.' Josie studied Mattie closely. 'You've not got a touch of chest ague, have you? '

'I'm fine – just a little unsettled.'

Thomas grizzled and Josie bent forward to soothe him. 'Well, you look grand enough to me. In fact, I'd say you've put on a little ...' Her eyes flew open. 'You're not ...?'

Mattie nodded. 'I've missed two monthlies and I've not been able to face breakfast for a week. I was the same with Brian. It must have happened in the first couple of days of us being together, and there was me telling you not to worry.' She gripped Josie's hands. 'Don't tell Patrick. Not yet, not until I've heard something from—'

'Of course not!' Josie took her hand and squeezed it. 'I pray that you'll be able to tell Nathaniel before Patrick finds out.'

'Sweet Mother, hear my prayer,' Mattie replied, trying to imagine Nathaniel's joy. 'And, if it pleases the Virgin, he'll be a free man when I do.'

'May it be so.' Josie and Mattie crossed themselves.

'But Mattie, what will you do in the meantime?'

What *would* she do? Mattie had been asking herself the same thing for weeks. She had two carts sitting in the yard idle most days, hay prices had rocketed, and Morris's were trying to renegotiate her wholesale price. And even though it was the busiest time of the year, Maguire's was losing two or three customers a week, so the savings she'd managed to accumulate were dwindling rapidly. Plus, as soon as her waistline grew she would be the talk of Knockfergus. Again!

Mattie looked squarely at Josie. 'Anything and everything to keep my children safe.'

A heavy drip from the overhang above splashed on Patrick's ear. He cursed and shifted sideways. He had been standing in the shadows outside the address that Tate had given him for almost two hours and was chilled to the bone.

But what choice did he have? And not just because he was indebted to the bastard Tate for dropping Freddie on his doorstep but because he couldn't bear to see Mattie so miserable. Hadn't she been through enough in the last few years? And as much as he would like to be tucked up in bed he would stand here every night until he could prove to Mattie that Tate was nothing more than a crook preying on her loneliness.

Patrick stamped his feet and pulled his hip flask from his pocket. He'd just taken a sip when a cab stopped at the end of the street. The driver stowed his whip and put the brake on. Patrick waited. It must be almost midnight now and there had already been a steady stream of cabs picking up men with their collars up and hats down.

I've got to be at the mooring at six so another three cabs and then I'm off, Patrick thought, as another mouthful of brandy warmed his bones.

A blade of light cut across the dark street as the door of number thirty-seven opened. Patrick peered into the darkness at the stout figure standing in the doorway. A very young woman appeared beside him dressed in a short chemise and corset, her white stockings tied up just above her knee. She stretched up and planted a kiss on the man's cheek then disappeared back inside.

The man stepped out on to the top step. He still had his hat in his hand and Patrick could clearly see his features in the light cast by the overhead door lamp.

Patrick choked.

No! It can't be. Patrick looked away and then back thinking his eyes must be playing tricks on him. But they weren't.

Standing in the doorway of Madame La Verne's was Amos Stebbins.

Chapter Twenty-Six

Nathaniel stared helplessly into his pint. Despite the hubbub of the Duck's bar, an image of Mattie lying curled beside him in the silence of the early morning danced in his mind. It had been three weeks since he'd kissed her goodbye and, although Boyce had welcomed him like the prodigal son, being thrown back into the society of thieves, pimps and prostitutes showed Nathaniel just how close he'd come to losing his soul before Mattie had rescued it.

He had long since given up judging a man or woman by absolute standards. After all, what father would not steal a loaf to feed a starving child or a mother sell her body to keep her babies from the workhouse? But having emerged from the penal colony, he was reluctant to return to it. The God-fearing Nathaniel Tate who'd disappeared *en route* to Botany Bay had re-emerged as the driver on Maguire's number one wagon.

The curtain that covered the back passage drew aside and Boyce appeared. He spotted Nathaniel and sauntered across. 'Cor, luv us,' he said, throwing himself onto the bench beside Nathaniel. 'If your face was any longer you'd have bloody splinters in your chin.' Nathaniel managed a wan smile and Boyce nudged him sharply in the ribs. 'Let's have another.'

He grabbed the bottle and tried to top up Nathaniel's glass but he put his hand over the top.

'Look,' Boyce said slapping him on the back affectionately. 'I know as 'ow you're pining for your little missus but ...'

Boyce's voice trailed off as his focus shifted to the door. Nathaniel followed his gaze. The trollops and drinkers in the bar had stopped mid-motion, staring at Patrick Nolan framed in the doorway. Nathaniel rose to feet as Patrick crossed the space between them.

'Have you the police behind you?' Nathaniel asked.

Patrick shook his head. 'Around here a man sorts out his own business.'

Nathaniel's stance relaxed a notch and Boyce pushed between them.

'I thought I recognised you, Nolan,' he said glaring at Patrick. 'You ain't fecking in Irish town now, you know. This is *my* gaff and 'e's my mate.' He thumbed at Nathaniel. 'So if you've got a quarrel with him, you've got a quarrel with me.'

Boyce's two heavies put down their pints and stood ready to move at their bosses signal.

'It's all right, Boyce,' Nathaniel said, holding Patrick's gaze over his friend's head. 'It's a family matter.'

Boyce stood his ground. 'Maybe, but if you want 'im dealt with just give me the wink and he's cat's meat.' He spat on the floor at Patrick's feet and left them.

'Nice friends you have,' Patrick said. 'I suppose you met him on your travels.'

'I'd have Boyce as a friend before a hundred others,' Nathaniel replied. 'Now you've found me and you haven't got the police outside, what's it to be?'

'I'm sorry for the loss of your family, Tate,' he said. 'And I saw Amos Stebbins coming out of the brothel.'

Nathaniel let out a long breath. 'So now do you believe my story?'

'God help me, I do,' Patrick replied, sliding into an empty booth. The quiet hum of the bar resumed, although many in the room still cast wary glances in their direction.

'How's Mattie?' Nathaniel asked, desperate for news.

'Bone weary most days. With two drivers down she's run off her feet. I've sent my Annie to help and my wife's trying to persuade her to let the front room to a young widow she knows.'

The barmaid brought two pints of cellar-cool beer.

Patrick took the nearest one and sipped the froth off the top. 'So now what?'

'I love Mattie, Patrick, and intend to marry her as soon as I am able.' He let his head fall back and looked up at the ceiling. 'I curse myself for putting her through all of this. I should have done as I intended and left as soon as she knew the truth.'

A hint of a smile touched Patrick's eyes. 'Mattie tells me she persuaded you to stay.'

'Its not her fault. I should have stuck to my guns.'

'Aye, you should have. But as my sister can argue the back *and* the front legs off a donkey, I can understand why you were turned from your purpose.'

A wry smile settled on Nathaniel's face and Patrick gave a short laugh. They sat back in their seats more comfortably.

'I promise you, Patrick, I won't go back to the yard until I've nailed Stebbins.'

'You can't. It's too dangerous. I got her out this time because Superintendent Jackson owes me, but I couldn't save her if she was found with you.' Patrick took another draft of beer then wiped his mouth. 'I've been to see your newspaper chum.'

'You've seen Smyth-Hilton?'

'Just before I came here.'

'And?'

'And nothing.'

Nathaniel blinked with disbelief. 'But hasn't Stebbins floated the company yet?'

Patrick shook his head. 'According to Smyth-Hilton, Stebbins's credit was so stretched that to stay solvent he was at the point of offering Mattie the full market price for Maguire's. That was before he spotted you in Mattie's yard and decided to get rid of you both. Of course, it didn't work out as he'd planned. But now with you and Freddie gone, Mattie's losing customers. I figure Stebbins thinks he can still scoop up Maguire's for a snip if he holds back for a few more months.'

A few more months! Three weeks apart from Mattie seemed like forever, let alone a few months

'Damn, damn, damn,' Nathaniel shouted, slamming his fist onto the table. 'We almost had him. Has he been to see Mattie yet?'

'Last week. He urged her to consider his offer again. He also tried to wheedle out of her what she knew about you but she gave nothing away.'

Nathaniel raked his hands through his hair. 'God, I shouldn't have put her in such a danger.'

'Knowing my sister's temper, I'd say Stebbins was the one in danger not her.'

Nathaniel's smiled briefly. 'Perhaps. But surely there must be something we can do to make him act sooner.'

'Your friend Smyth-Hilton says he could print his piece about Stebbins now but this wouldn't overturn your conviction.'

'I know, I know.' Nathaniel ran his fingers through his hair again. 'Perhaps I should try to slip along to see Smyth-Hilton myself.'

Patrick shook his head. 'You'll be nabbed as soon as you poke your nose out of here. I'm afraid you'll have to stay here until your journalist friend digs up enough evidence. You're safe enough here in the north end of the rookery.'

Nathaniel gulped down a mouthful of beer.

What if Amos never floated the company and sold off the land? Or when they investigated his accounts they couldn't trace the missing money from Romford? He couldn't spend the rest of his life in the Duck. How under God's heaven would he ever be able to marry Mattie?

From his hiding place in the butcher's doorway Freddie watched Nathaniel and Patrick as they emerged from the side of the Duck and Drake. They shook hands heartily before Patrick walked off towards Bishopsgate. Nathaniel turned down the side alley. Freddie took the last drag on his rolled up cigarette and flicked it in a high arch into the gutter.

'It's 'im. Let's go,' he said to the two men standing behind him.

Mad Teddy and Stefan Magsen were two of Ollie Mac's best men. Teddy, the younger of the two, was in his mid-twenties, just a year or two younger than Freddie. Scrawny, with sharp weaselly features and mousy brown hair, Teddy was never turned out in anything less than dapper. Even now, although they were supposed to be avoiding the notice of the peelers, he wore a green-and-yellow jacket so garish it could have guided ships into harbour, with a Billycock hat at such an acute angle it was in constant danger of sliding off the side of his head. His handle of 'Mad' came not from his readiness with a knife but because every now and then he would fall to the floor, his teeth clenched and limbs rigid for a few moments, after which he was murderously aggressive.

Stefan Magsen was a different kettle of fish. In his late thirties and built like an alley shite house, his broad bovine features and almost white blond hair made him popular with the trollops along the highway. If rumours were to be believed, he'd killed half a dozen men with one blow of his massive fists. He didn't need 'mad', 'crazy' or 'bull' as a prefix – one look in his ice-blue eyes told you all you needed to know.

'He's heading for the back,' Freddie said, as they left their hiding place and crossed the highway.

'Don't worry, we'll catch him,' Stefan told him.

Too bloody right, thought Freddie. This time he'd get the bastard good and proper.

He crossed the road followed by Stefan and Teddy. As he stopped at the corner and peered down the side of the pub the two men behind him flattened themselves against the wall. The whole alleyway was pitch black and for a moment he thought Nathaniel had given them the slip; then he spotted a flicker of movement ahead. He turned and jabbed his finger at Stefan and made a circling movement. The blond giant nodded and, with a speed at odds with his bulk, retraced his steps to the other end of the alley. Freddie removed the cosh he'd hidden down the back of his trousers and beckoned to Teddy. Together they entered the alleyway.

The light from the street lamps immediately disappeared, leaving Freddie blind until his eyes adjusted. Something scrambled beside him then brushed against his leg. A rat! Sliding along the rough brickwork, Freddie tip-toed towards where he'd seen the movement. He reached a back door and pushed it gently to see if Nathaniel could be hiding behind it but it was locked. They had just reached the mid-point between the two streets when Teddy grunted, pitched forward and thumped into his back.

Freddie spun around. 'What the—'

'You looking for me, Freddie?' Nathaniel asked, in a low voice.

Where was Stefan, Freddie thought, frantically trying to back away. His heel jammed against Teddy's body and he only just kept himself upright. Nathaniel's hand shot out and gripped him around the throat. Freddie flayed out with his fists, but they punched into thin air. Something with the density of a hammer smashed into his face. He heard a crack and yelped as pain shot along the base of his lower teeth on the right side of his face.

'Got a new friend have you?' Nathaniel, asked as he dragged Freddie over Teddy's inert body. 'Given up getting the police to do your dirty work, eh?'

Nathaniel caught his collar, necktie and throat in one mighty grasp and dragged Freddie forward. He wrenched Freddie off his feet and slammed him into the wall behind him. Small starbursts popped at the edge of his vision and his ears began to ring. Nathaniel thumped him against the wall again, forcing the air from Freddie's lungs, then let him go, sending him crumpling to the squelchy floor.

'If you want to keep your pretty face, Freddie, don't cross me—!'

Suddenly, Nathaniel staggered sideways. He shook his head and turned, jerked backwards, then crashed into the mud.

Freddie stared up at Stefan's huge body silhouetted in the narrow alley.

'Where the feck have you been?' he gasped, with a stab of pain in his jaw at every word. He spat out a tooth. 'The bugger nearly did for me.'

Stefan looked down at Nathaniel's inert body. 'I can't remember the last time I had to hit a bloke twice.'

'Never mind that. Giss a hand getting him up,' Freddie said, staggering to his feet.

Stefan grabbed Nathaniel and hoisted him over Freddie's left shoulder. He staggered under the weight then found his footing. Nathaniel was a lot heavier than a hundredweight of coal.

'Hey, what about him?' Stefan asked, kicking the sole of Teddy's boot.

'You sort him out and I'll deal with this bugger.'

'Why don't you just drop him in the river. Its high tide and he'll be fishmeat at Southend before dawn,' Stefan said, as he dragged Teddy to his feet.

Freddie moved his jaw sideways and an almighty pain shot up to his ear. He drew in a sharp breath and recognised the dank, cloying smell of the river not half a mile away. He imagined the splash as Nathaniel hit the surface. He'd probably float a bit before his clothes and boots filled with water and dragged him below the surface. The grey river would bubble and swirl as Nathaniel's unconscious body disappeared. With the cold closing around him, Nathaniel might even rouse enough to feel the water filling his nose and mouth. Freddie allowed himself the pleasure of contemplating Nathaniel's terror but replied, 'I ain't no murderer.'

Stefan shrugged. 'See you at the Blue Boy,' he said, wedging his shoulder under Teddy's arm to drag him away. Freddie repositioned Nathaniel over his shoulder and started down the street towards Wapping police station.

Stefan was right of course, it would have been a whole lot easier just to chuck Nathaniel's carcass in the drink but the twenty-pound reward was for capturing Tate, not killing him.

Mattie rolled on to her back with a sigh and stared up at the bedroom ceiling. She had heard St George's church clock strike two o'clock a while ago and she felt sure she would still be awake when it struck three. In truth, she probably hadn't slept for more than three hours a night since Patrick brought her the news two nights ago that Nathaniel had been dumped unconscious on the steps of Wapping police station. And why would she sleep? She was almost five months pregnant and her child's father was under lock and key in Pentonville Prison. It was a foregone conclusion that when he came up before the judge at the Bailey in three weeks he'd be sent back to Australia to complete his original sentence, with added time for escaping.

Mercifully, and despite the shock of the last few days, her baby hadn't budged and only yesterday Mattie had felt the first few flutters of movement. But that wasn't the only thing keeping sleep at bay. With Nathaniel gone they were now down to only two carts and they were losing trade to other coal merchants. Whereas a few weeks ago she was able to pay her creditors promptly, she could already see from the accounts that their income would fall well short of their outgoings by the end of the month. In short, Maguire's would be forced out of business in a matter of weeks. There was one slim and very risky chance she could turn everything around but that too keep her mind churning over.

Mattie sat up and plumped the pillow again then rested back and shut her eyes. Below the window the steady footsteps of the officer on patrol plodded by and she heard Buster pad past her door. He started whining and scurrying back and forth, then he came into her room and nuzzled her hand.

'All right, Buster,' she said, swinging her legs out of bed.

Buster danced around impatiently as she shrugged on her dressing gown, then he dashed out and thundered down the stairs, his paws barely touching the boards.

Mattie turned up the oil lamp beside her bed and, holding it aloft, went down stairs. She found Buster in the kitchen furiously scratching at the back door and barking anxiously. Mattie unbolted the door and the dog shot out, but instead of cocking his leg, he galloped through the garden and into the yard. Mattie left the lamp on the table, slipped on her boots, picked up the poker from the hearth and followed him out.

In the yard the night air was damp and Mattie shivered. It had rained earlier and felt as if it would again before dawn. Buster was over by the fence adjoining the stable, jumping and clawing at it, barking wildly.

'Buster!'

He ignored her and continued to snap and snarl.

Then she heard it.

A low whisper followed by the clink of metal on metal. Then flames burst up on the other side of the fence.

'Fire! Fire!' screamed Mattie, hitting the poker against the iron hoop that served as the yard bell so hard it reverberated up her arm. The ringing sound broke the silence and echoed around the yard.

Throwing the poker aside she ran back into the house, snatched Brian from his bed, and dashed back through the house across the yard and swung the double yard door wide.

Mercifully, windows of the shops and houses opposite were already being thrown open overhead. Men with buckets in their hands were emerging from their doorways and running to the pump at the far end of the street.

Zilla, from across the road, her night scarf still tied around her head, ran over. 'I'll tuck him in with my Charlie,' she said, stretching her arm to take the dazed child.

Mattie handed him over then ran back into the yard and across to the stable.

Ignoring her stinging eyes, Mattie groped her way along to where the four horses stood, eyes white with terror.

With the heat and smoke burning her lungs with each breath Mattie dashed along to the stall where Mumble was tied at the end nearest the fire. Squeezing between the horse and partition, she pulled the looped rope to release the frantic beast, who careered out of the smouldering building. Mattie ducked into Poppy's stall and did the same, then crossed to the other side to set Samson and Peggy loose. She ran out after them just in time to see them race through the yard gates and clatter off down the street. Buster tore after them but turned towards the main road, yapping and growling.

Mattie followed him around to the side where the fire had started. She almost wept with joy when she saw the line of men already passing buckets from the street pump to the fire. The beat officer was there too, swirling his klaxon for assistance. Part of the fence had burnt away at the base and the wood above was already smouldering. Billowing smoke fanned by the breeze from the river filled the air. Although the fire hadn't reached the stable yet, the flames were already licking the edge and it wouldn't be long before the whole thing went up.

Mattie put her hand out to steady herself on a street lamp. Clinging to the cold metal and breathing heavily to draw air into her lungs, she stared helplessly as the flames travelled towards the stable. Suddenly utter weariness engulfed her. For three long years, through grief, childbirth, heartache and bitter disappointment, she had struggled to keep Maguire's afloat and now, in a matter of minutes, everything she had worked for was being destroyed. She closed her eyes and let her head fall back onto the hard metal of the post.

She should scream and cry or rail against her fate but she just didn't have the energy. Perhaps if she just sank to the floor God would have pity and take her, Nathaniel, Brian and the child inside straight to heaven now, then all this pain and struggle would be washed away in eternal bliss.

She brushed a tear from her cheek and another from her nose, then something wet splodged on her forehead. Then a wet drop fell on her lip. Mattie opened her eyes and looked up. Laughter, part hysteria but mainly relief, escaped her lips as the clouds opened.

She held out her arms as large raindrops fell on her face. She smiled up at the dark heavens, relishing the feel of the water dripping on her eyelashes and skin. Others in the street looked up and joined in the merriment as the sudden downpour drenched them.

Neighbours from nearby streets now came running, splashing through the newly formed puddles. The buckets passed back and forth along the human line more swiftly, but with rain now bouncing off the pavement around them the fire was already abating. Although the timbers of the fence would need replacing, stable, house and yard had all been saved.

Someone from Cable Street arrived with Mattie's four cart horses trotting behind him and the owner of the wood yard offered to stable them for the night. Mattie thanked the men, many still in their long johns and vests, who were shaking the rain from their hair and congratulating each other on a job well done. Something nudged Mattie's hand. She looked down to find Buster sitting beside her, with his tongue lolling out to one side, and looking very pleased with himself.

'There you are, you rascal,' she said, tickling behind his sodden ear.

'Is that your dog?' Mattie looked up to see two policemen marching towards her with rain dripping off their hats and gripping onto a heavy set man in handcuffs between them.

'Yes it is,' Mattie replied, gathering her saturated dressing gown around her.

'Well then. I'd say he deserves a couple of sausages for supper tomorrow – he's earned them, catching the bugger who fired your fence,' the officer replied, lifting the miscreant's hand with his truncheon so Mattie could see the soot. 'I'll come around in the morning to take a full statement.' He grabbed the prisoner again. 'Right, Chummy. It's off to the station with you to answer a few questions.'

Mattie glanced at the charred fence then, heedless of the wet pavement, knelt down beside the dog. 'I'd say you certainly saved Maguire's this time, boy.' She scratched behind his ear again. 'Now it's my turn to save Nathaniel.'

Chapter Twenty-Seven

Mattie sat dry-eyed as Smyth-Hilton ran through the details of the evidence he and Nathaniel had collected. She was dry-eyed because she truly believed she had no more tears to shed.

She took a sip of water and Smyth-Hilton nodded at Patrick sitting beside her.

'So you see, Mrs Maguire, although I have enough dirt on Stebbins to publish without fear of being sued, I haven't got the vital piece of the puzzle that would prove Tate's innocence. Without that, the best lawyer in the land couldn't stop him being sent back to Botany Bay.'

'I see.'

Patrick's chair creaked as he shifted forward. 'Surely the evidence you already have from others who've have been swindled is enough. Couldn't you use this to push for an enquiry into Stebbins's businesses? And what about the rogue who fired my sister's yard?'

'Much of what we have is hearsay. Morris won't testify, neither will the feed merchant who was offered a bribe by Stebbins to send mouldy fodder to the yard. They all want to keep their reputations, and admitting you've been cheating your customers is not the way to do that. And as to the fire, the man the police have charged refuses to say who he's working for even though it could get him a lighter sentence.'

'I'm not surprised,' Patrick replied, with a heavy sigh. 'If he did, his family's life wouldn't be worth living.'

'What about the person who turned Tate in?' Smyth Hilton asked. 'Perhaps he had some dealings with Stebbins and we could persuade him to testify. You say you know who it was?'

Patrick and Mattie exchanged a look.

'I will be dealing with him,' Patrick said, formally.

Smyth-Hilton raised an eyebrow. 'Well, no matter. It wouldn't really help Nathaniel, anyway. I'm afraid that unless Stebbins floats the Wapping & Stratford railway, we only have enough information to embarrass him in the Chamber of Commerce.'

'What about the business with the brothel?' Patrick asked.

Mattie hadn't told him about finding his Annie alone with Amos because Smyth-Hilton couldn't very well expose Mr Stebbins for the perverted crook he truly was if Patrick had already tied ship's weights to his ankles and thrown him in the river.

'Ah!' The editor's youthful face lit up. 'There we have better news. An old friend of mine – someone I met at Cambridge – is a member of the Criminal Investigation Department based in Scotland Yard.'

Mattie's and Patrick's eyebrows shot up in surprise. Although the papers were full of Lord this and Sir that praising the constabulary for their invaluable public service, most didn't think it a fitting profession for their sons to pursue.

Smyth-Hilton grinned. 'He was my roommate's valet actually and as sharp a fellow you could meet. Inspector Cross has been putting a case together.'

'That's good news, isn't it,' Patrick said, encouragingly.

Mattie stood, crossed to the window and looked out at the leaden winter sky.

She had hired a couple of men to load the wagons each day while she and Eli hitched the afternoon horses so all Pete and Billy had to do was deliver, but it wasn't enough. There was only enough in the safe for this week's wholesale bill. If she couldn't buy fodder for the horses she was finished. But that wasn't the reason she'd made the most difficult decision of her life.

Mattie turned to face her brother and the journalist. 'Yes, it's good news, but it won't stop Nathaniel being sent back to Australia.' Mattie fixed her brother and Smyth-Hilton with an unwavering stare. 'But I know something that just might.'

Mattie took several deep breaths to steady her racing heart as she walked through Grey Friars warehouse towards Amos Stebbins's office. The clerk opened the door and ushered her in. Mr Stebbins looked up and smiled warmly at her.

'Mrs Maguire,' he said rising to his feet. 'What an unexpected pleasure.'

Mattie offered him her hand and as his thick fingers closed around her hand she was thankful she hadn't yet removed her gloves. Although her morning sickness had all but gone, being so close to Amos was making her stomach churn.

'Get Mary to make Mrs Maguire a cup of tea, will you?' Mr Stebbins instructed the clerk.

'Yes, sir.' The clerk left.

'You look very well,' he said, gesturing her towards a chair. 'Have you recovered from the ordeal of having a wanted criminal under your roof?'

Mattie nodded. 'I can't tell you how relieved I am to know he's been recaptured. The nights I've lain in my bed shivering with fear he'd come back ...'

'I'm not surprised. You poor, poor soul. And what's this I've heard about a fire at the yard?' he asked in his best church voice.

Mattie gave a tight-lipped nod. 'I know it's all ...'

'Please sit down, dear lady,' he said, pulling out the chair for her.

'May I confide in you – as a friend?' Mattie asked as he resumed his seat on the other side of the desk.

'Of course you may.'

'This whole business with Nathaniel Tate ...' As she said his name her voice faltered, but she forced herself to continue, 'has made me realise how foolish I've been, trying to struggle on alone with the yard.' She drew her handkerchief from her sleeve. 'I can see now that running Maguire's is just too much for me.' She glanced up to see his reaction. 'So I thought as you've been such a good friend since my poor husband passed on, I'd come to talk about the offer for the yard you mentioned before.'

Triumph lit Amos's eyes briefly. 'Well now, I'm afraid things have changed since we last spoke. My associate has already found another business that suits his purpose so unfortunately that offer is no longer on the table.'

'Oh dear,' she said, twisting her handkerchief between her fingers.

Amos stood up and came around the desk. He pulled over another chair and sat beside her, taking her hands. Mattie studied his fleshy jowls, his wiry whiskers, noted his moist loose lips and the callous cast of his pale blue eyes. She suppressed a shudder.

'My dear, Mrs Maguire.' He patted her hands and contorted his face into a picture of abject misery. 'I don't like to see you like this. Not after all you've been through. And that little lad.'

'Couldn't *you* buy my yard, Mr Stebbins?' Mattie said, giving him a wide-eyed innocent look.

Amos scratched his chin thoughtfully. 'Well, I don't know. It's a depressed market and with two carts idle and your orders slipping away ...' He sucked on his teeth and shook his head slowly. 'I could give you four hundred pounds for Maguire's and' – he put his hand on his chest and looked heavenward – 'I will trust the Lord to honour my losses.'

Mattie bit her lip and pretended to consider. 'I was hoping to start a little school in Bow by the river. Nothing fancy you understand, just in the front parlour, but I would need fifty pounds to buy the lease on a suitable house and, as it is Brian's father's and grandfather's business, I'm aiming to put at least five hundred pounds by for his future . . . five-seventy-five?'

Mattie held her breath. Perhaps she had gone too far. Or maybe he would refuse and let Maguire's sink further before renewing his offer. He had to agree now or all would be lost! Her heart lodged in her throat.

Amos chewed the inside of his mouth and studied her closely. After what seemed like an eternity a smile crept over his face. 'Very well. But only for your little lad's sake, five hundred and seventy-five.' He stood up and offered her his hand. 'Deal?'

With an unsettling mix of triumph and indecision coiling together in the pit of her stomach, Mattie studied his outstretched hand. An image of Nathaniel smiling down at her formed itself in her mind. She rose to her feet and grasped his hand. 'Thank you, Mr Stebbins. I always knew you to be a true friend.'

Mattie stretched out and picked up the pen from the ebony stand and dipped it in the crystal inkwell. Across the desk sat Ebenezer Glasson.

'Just make your mark,' he said. 'That will suffice.'

'My sister can sign her name,' Patrick's voice rumbled from beside her.

The solicitor raised a grizzled brow but didn't comment further.

From the moment she announced her intention to sell Maguire's to force Amos's hand, her brother had waged an unrelenting campaign to dissuade her from what he described as ludicrous folly. But, despite starting awake some nights with her heart pounding as fears and doubts screamed in her mind, Mattie had doggedly resisted him. All urged caution. In the end, Patrick had thrown his hands up and insisted on coming with her to Mr Stebbins's solicitor. She was profoundly grateful.

'I am just checking to make sure that you've included a rental clause,' Mattie replied.

Mr Glasson jabbed an ink-stained finger at the paragraph half way down the page. 'It states quite clearly that you are to rent the yard for the stipulated quarterly sum until Mr Stebbins sells the property.' His long features moved into what Mattie took to be a smile. 'Now, if there are no further questions, perhaps we can conclude our business?'

Mattie tapped her pen back in the inkwell. Patrick's hand closed lightly around her arm and she looked up at him.

'You don't have to sign it, Mattie.'

Her hand froze mid-air as she studied her brother's worried face.

It was an enormous risk, and not just for her. Eli, Pete and Billy depended on Maguire's and if her plan failed they would suffer too. But if she didn't force Stebbins's hand now then it might be too late. Too late for Nathaniel, too late for them. Under her newly slackened corset a small hand or foot kicked outwards. Mattie tightened her grip on the pen and scratched her name across the bottom of the contract.

From the moment a bucket of iced water brought him back to consciousness in Wapping police station Nathaniel had never been completely warm. He'd spent his first night in the cell in his soaked clothes.

The Thames magistrate sent him on to the Old Bailey without raising his eyes from the charge sheet, and Nathaniel knew that he would be dealt with in the same perfunctory manner when he stood in number one court. The only question was how soon he would be sent back to Australia. His quest to expose Amos Stebbins and clear his own name was over. In a few short weeks, possibly sooner, he would once again be shackled below decks on a transport ship. It would be twelve years at least before he was a free man but even then, because of his double conviction, he would never qualify for an absolute pardon – the only way he could legally return to England.

The last time he would ever see Mattie would be across the court room when he was re-sentenced in a few weeks. And she *would* be there. He knew that. And that would have to serve him a lifetime.

The door flew open and Bice, the senior warden of the wing, stood in the doorway, his polished buttons twinkling in the gaslight in the corridor. Nathaniel snapped to attention and looked at a point just above the officer's right shoulder. The warden's moustache twitched. 'All right, four seven three, make haste! Make haste!' He tapped his baton against his leg.

Nathaniel joined the column of men trudging their way along the second-floor landing towards the washhouse. The drumming of a hundred pairs of studded boots echoed up to the vaulted roof. Pentonville Prison was only half-a-dozen years old but was already bursting at its grey stony seams. Pickpockets, thieves, swindlers and murderers rubbed shoulders with those who had fallen foul of the law for their political persuasion. The regime was designed so that each inmate was kept separate from his fellow prisoners, which was no mean feat given that the jail housed over five hundred men.

As always, the only warmth in the washroom at the end of the wing was the exhalation of the men scrubbing themselves with coal-tar soap. Putting his bowl on the stone bench in the centre of the room Nathaniel stripped off his shirt and started cleaning himself with the allotted pint of cold water. The morning ablutions were carried out in absolute silence, but as Nathaniel rubbed the corner of his flannel around his mouth to clean his teeth he caught the eye of a skinny man who rubbed his left ear. Nathaniel's heartbeat quickened. Although forbidden to speak, the prisoners had other methods of communication. A rubbed left ear meant 'be ready for a message'.

Nathaniel scratched his right ear in response. The man looked away and continued washing.

Nathaniel returned to his cell and began the daily chore of scrubbing the bare stone floor, his mind racing all the while.

The bell sounded just as Nathaniel polished the last water stain from his tin wear and placed it beside his precisely rolled bed linen on the wooden bench in his cell. He stepped out to the landing and, as it was Sunday, he marched to the chapel.

Although the Sunday service was supposed to be a communal act of worship, whoever designed the prison decided that their will, not God's, should prevail. Therefore, in line with the prison's silent regime, each prisoner was allocated a coffin-like booth in which to bow his head to his maker.

Nathaniel shuffled in and took his seat and, as the booth door closed behind him, he stared towards the high pulpit that rose above their heads at the front. The minister swept in like a great black crow with his vestments billowing out behind him. The wardens took their posts along the sides of the pews and the congregation rose to its feet as the organist blasted out the chord to the first hymn. Nathaniel sang out along with the five hundred other men.

'And can it be that I should gain . . .'

It was an old hymn that had been a favourite with the vicar of St Edward's in Romford and Nathaniel knew it well. The man in the booth to his left leant forward slightly and boomed out the first verse. Nathaniel also leant forward and pressed his shoulders hard against the wooden partition.

'Died he for me-e-e, who caused his pain,' sang the congregation.

'Message from Boy ... oyce, la la la,' sang the man to Nathaniel's left.

'For me-e-e who him to dea-eath pursuuuued,' belted out the men around them while the 'messenger' sang, ''e says hold on, you old bugger da da da da,'

The singers went up an octave. 'Amazing Love!'

'Your woman has ...'

Male voices strained higher. 'How ca-a-n it be?'

'Sold her-er yard ...'

'That thou-ou, my God, shouldst die-i-i-e for me,' London's finest criminal elements sang.

'So you-oo, old chum, ca-a-an, can soon be free,' rumbled the voice beside him.

The men in the chapel launched into the second verse as Nathaniel fought to steady himself. Mattie had sold the yard? He shook his head as if to dislodge the fearful idea that she would gamble everything she had, just to set him free, but the thought grew louder and louder until it rang in his ears.

As those around him sang the third verse of Wesley's rousing hymn, images of Mattie and Brian homeless and destitute threatened to overwhelm him.

The congregation gathered their voices together for the final refrain and Nathaniel fixed his eyes on the crucifix nailed to the wall behind the preacher. As those around him sang, 'And claim the crown, through Christ my own.' Nathaniel filled his lungs and roared, 'God, help her!'

Chapter Twenty-Eight

The flunky at the front of the City & County jumped forward as Amos stepped from the cab and looked at the grey clouds gathering above. It had rained off and on since Christmas, six weeks ago. But even the dull February weather couldn't dampen his spirits because today was the day when God would pour out his blessings on all his good works. Today he and Fallow would set the date for the flotation of the Wapping & Stratford Railway Company.

He adjusted his silk top hat, which he'd only just collected from Lock's in St James's, along with several new suits and shirts from Weeks & Rollington in Savile Row. Now that all the worry and uncertainty of the past few months was gone, he felt he deserved to kit himself out as befitted the chairman of a railway company. He'd have to wait a month or two, though, before really splashing out with the profits from selling his properties to the company. He had his eye on a grand terraced house at the back of Cavendish Square: near enough to the City to keep an eye on his business interests, but also cheek by jowl with the top drawer of society, of which he would soon be a member.

But he wasn't a selfish man, and Cecily, too, should profit from his astute business acumen. She was a good wife but would be out of place in the fashionable salons to which he would soon be invited. In view of this, he'd instructed his solicitors to make a few enquiries about a small seafront house in Eastbourne or Weymouth with a long lease for her and Ruth. A long stay at the seaside would settle Cecily's nerves and the bracing sea air would put a bit of colour back in Ruth's cheeks and stop her carrying tales to her mother ...

Amos visualised himself sitting – with a fat cigar in his mouth – on a sofa next to the Prime Minister, discussing trade and commerce in Lady Derby's drawing room.

'Good morning, Mr Stebbins,' the doorman said, bowing low as Amos started up the steps.

Amos flipped him a half-crown. 'It is indeed.'

Sauntering through the open door, he surveyed the room with a deep-seated sense of wellbeing. This was where he rightly belonged, where wealth and power sat side by side.

Deacon the clerk spotted him, slid out from behind his desk and shuffled over.

'Mr Stebbins,' he said. 'How well you look.'

Amos handed his hat, gloves and cane to one servant while another slipped his coat from his shoulders.

'Is Mr Fallon in?' he asked, hoping that the light caught his diamond cravat pin.

The clerk curved to one side, deferentially. 'Of course. If you would follow me, sir.'

Fallon jumped up from his chair as he entered. 'Mr Stebbins!' He gave Amos a hearty handshake.

'I think it's time we set a date,' Amos replied, accepting a very generous brandy from the chief banker of the City & County.

'Capital!' Fallon's pale eyes lit up with excitement.

'I suggest the fifth of next month. It's just a little over four weeks away.'

A flash of anxiety shot across Fallon's thin face. 'It's a little tight. We would have to have a prospectus circulated. The end of April might be more in keeping with current practice.'

Amos's jaw clenched. He'd already pledged thousands against the sale of his properties to the company. 'But surely the sooner we set our intentions the better,' he replied, with just a slight quaver of anxiety in his tone.

Fallon's thin lips pressed together. 'I'm not sure—'

'I heard talk of someone trying to gather investors for an extension to the Fenchurch Street-to-Tilbury line.'

Fallon's expression changed from uncertainty to alarm.

Amos rested his forearm on the table. 'I see you take my point.'

'Indeed. If they float their railway proposals first, they'll take our investors and our trade.'

'And you'll have to explain to your board why the City & County let such an opportunity slip away.'

'Well ... it's usual but if you have an assurance from Mr Hudson of his investment ...'

Amos studied the shiny tips of his new toes. 'Of course,' he replied, guessing that the letter from the Railway King was probably in the post. He looked back at Fallon. 'And of course you're committed to taking a sizeable number of shares on the bank's behalf?'

Fallon's nose twitched. 'In conjunction with Mr Hudson's investment.'

Amos smiled coolly.

'I suppose if we set a whisper in the City it will generate some interest,' said Fallon at last.

Amos threw the last of his brandy down his throat and struggled to his feet. 'Splendid!' he grasped the banker's hand. 'I'll leave you to sort out the details. Good day to you, sir.' He ambled to the door. 'It's men like us, with God's good grace, who will steer Her Majesty's realm into a new age of prosperity.'

As Mattie stacked the last plate on the wooden draining board, the calendar from the New Year's edition of *The Mother's Friend* pinned on the wall over the sink caught her eyes. She stared at the red circle around 12 April. Today. Her heart did a double step then went into a gallop. A prickle of terror fluttered in her stomach, urging her back to the privy, although she had been not twenty minutes before.

Mattie rubbed her hands on her apron and forced herself to still the panic welling up in her again. She grabbed the kettle and dragged it back on the heat. A nice cup of tea would calm her jitters, that's for sure. As she waited for the water to boil, she settled herself in Queenie's old chair and, as Brian was playing contentedly on the hearth, she put her feet up on the footstool.

After tossing and turning from the moment she'd laid her head on the pillow, she'd finally given up and gone downstairs just as the knocker-upper made his first rounds at four. By four-thirty she was already washed, dressed, and on her knees scrubbing the floor. That kept her mind occupied until six when her delivery men turned up. Thankfully, the morning chores had kept her from fretting over the inaugural meeting of the Wapping & Stratford Railway Company.

According to Smyth-Hilton, investors had flooded in to take a stake in the new venture, and Mattie, Patrick and the editor had become shareholders, taking five shares apiece for the princely sum of twenty pounds in total. Mattie had used money from the sale of the yard and Patrick dipped into some of his precious savings from the United Mutual.

As her man of business, Patrick had offered to act on her behalf at the meeting but Mattie had said no. It had been Stebbins's brutal and shameless dishonesty and lies that had brought Nathaniel low and Mattie was determined to be the one to trigger his fall and repay him in kind. She was sure she would raise a few eyebrows; women could own property, shares and businesses, but it was almost unheard of for them to attend a board meeting.

She must have drifted off to sleep because she was jolted awake by the latch on the back door clicking open. Buster jumped up and cocked his head, looking expectantly at the door. It opened, and Kate waddled in with her hand in the small of her back. 'Cor, my bones are giving me jip, today,' she said, pulling the straight-back chair out from the table and easing herself down.

Mattie noticed that Kate's lump sat lower than it had been a few days ago. 'Is it just your back?' she asked, thinking the baby was overdue.

Kate nodded.

Mattie pressed her lips together firmly to stop her thoughts becoming words, and set about making a fresh pot of tea. Freddie and his sudden wealth had been the talk of the streets. After it had got about that Nathaniel had been dumped on the steps of Wapping police station only a day or two before, Flash Freddie had strolled down Cable Street in a new suit and billycock-hat. People quickly put two and two together. Of course, poor Kate never saw any of the money, so she was forced to continue her work at the bakery until a week ago when her ankles started to swell.

Mattie stirred two heaped teaspoons of sugar into her sister's mug. 'That'll keep your strength up and, by the look of it, you'll be needing it soon enough.'

Kate ran her hands over her stomach then took a slurp of tea. 'You're getting a size too,' she retorted, glancing at Mattie's expanding waistline. 'Are you nervous about tonight?'

Mattie's heart gave a hefty thump. 'I'm terrified!'

Kate reached across the table and squeezed Mattie's hand. 'You'll have Pat beside you. And you've got that fine new bonnet. Surely that should give you the courage of the saints.'

Mattie did have a new straw-chip bonnet with emerald ruched ribbon around the crown, and satin ties. It matched the russet-and-sage tartan gown and jacket she'd pulled off the quality second-hand rail in the Wentworth Street warehouse. It had cost two pounds but was worth it; there wasn't a mark on the cuffs or elbows of the jacket and the lace trim around the skirt of the gown was intact. But even so . . .

She put her cup down. 'Even if I had the crown of England on my head, I doubt it would stop me quivering when I stand up and say my piece. But I'll have to – *everything* depends on it.'

'I'm sure you'll sway the meeting, Mat.' A teasing smile Mattie hadn't seen for a long while, lit her sister's face. 'After all, you always could argue the back leg off a donkey. What time's Patrick collecting you?'

'The meeting starts at seven but I have to be there from the start. We're leaving here at six o'clock and meeting Smyth-Hilton at the corner of Bishopsgate at quarter to.'

Kate stretched again, winced and rubbed her stomach.

'Are you sure you're alright?'

Kate's fair brows pulled together. 'It's just me bones creaking,' she replied, letting out a long breath. 'Can I have a splash more milk?' she asked, pouring the last drop from the jug.

Mattie took it from her. 'I'll fetch you some,' she said, rising to her feet and making her way across the room. She opened the pantry door and picked up the quart pot of milk. 'Do you want me to save your legs and fetch you a bit of fish on Friday when I —'

'Mattie!'

Mattie's head snapped around. Her eyes fixed on Kate's shaken face and then travelled down to the pool of water around her feet.

From his vantage point on the dais, Amos surveyed the thirty or so men sitting in neat rows in front of him in the function room above the Albion Tavern. Gas lamps illuminated the fashionably papered walls and re-plastered coving and architraves.

'Thank you, gentlemen, for agreeing to Mr Fallon as the financial director of the company,' he said smoothly, indicating the man in a suit so pale and grey that it almost matched his complexion.

Although he was loath to share his good fortune with anyone, Amos thought it wise to include Fallon in his scheme. You never knew when you might need a favour. The banker had taken full advantage and purchased half-a-dozen dilapidated properties along the route, only to sell them back to the company at a substantial profit in the same way that Amos had.

Amos took hold of his lapels and puffed out his chest. 'Well, gentlemen, that concludes our business for the evening. It only leaves me to commend you on your astute business sense in buying shares in what will soon prove to be the most profitable of companies.' There was an appreciative murmur from his audience. 'So, if there is nothing else to raise, perhaps this would be a good moment to lay the whole project before the Almighty—'

The door at the far end of the room was flung open and Mattie

Maguire, her brother Patrick, and a young man who looked vaguely familiar, stepped into the room. Oddly, Mattie's gown, jacket and bonnet wouldn't have looked out of place in Cecily's wardrobe. Her brother, too, could have been mistaken for a commodity trader in his well-fitting suit and modest necktie. All eyes turned towards the bottom end of the table as the three latecomers took their seats.

What on earth are they doing here, the bone-headed Irish? Amos thought, trying to remember where he'd seen their young companion before. *Can't they read the bloody notice on the door?*

'I think there is some mistake. This is the Wapping & Stratford Railway Company shareholders' meeting,' Amos said, not bothering to keep the irritation from his tone.

Mattie folded her hands in front of her. 'Yes, I know. We were unavoidably delayed.'

'Let me repeat, Mrs Maguire,' Amos said, in a tone he used when speaking at St George's Sunday school. 'It is a *private* meeting. For *shareholders.*'

Mattie drew a share certificate out of her crocheted handbag and spread it on the table. 'I am a shareholder.'

Patrick delved into his inside pocket and withdrew a folded sheet of paper. 'So am I,'

'Me too,' added the young man whom Amos was still trying to identify.

He hadn't bothered to look at the list of shareholders before the meeting began. It didn't actually matter who they were as long as they voted as he instructed, but finding that Mattie, Patrick and this slight young man beside them owned shares in his company made him feel uneasy.

These Nolans are jumped up micks all right. That's what's wrong with this country – people not knowing their place.

'Very well,' he replied, as they took their seats. He drew a deep breath. 'As there were no further question perhaps we can *now* bow our heads—'

'Mr Chairman.' Mattie rose to her feet and thirty-two pairs of eyes stared along the table at her. 'I have a question.'

A shiver of apprehension crept up Mattie's spine. Could she do it? Could she really persuade the stony-faced men sitting around the table that Amos had lined his pockets with company money? She swallowed and took a deep breath.

'I would like to ask a question about the properties bought on behalf of the company.'

A rush of blood coloured Amos's face for a moment, then an indulgent expression spread across it. 'Although I am pleased to see you've invested your windfall rather than squander it as some would, Mrs Maguire, perhaps it would be wiser to observe the proceedings for a while before seeking to participate.'

The men sitting around the table in tailored suits, gold watch chains strung across their portly midriffs and diamonds twinkling in their cravats, nodded in agreement.

'Women in the boardroom?' someone muttered.

'Whatever next,' another added. 'Perhaps the vote.'

This brought forth a general titter of laughter. The knot that had twisted Mattie's innards from the moment she'd walked into the room, tightened. Forgetting the men looking down the table – and their noses – at her, Mattie fixed her eyes on Amos.

'I would like to know how much you sold my coal yard to the Wapping & Stratford for?' she asked in a clear voice.

'I can't recall.' he snapped.

'Why don't you look at your accounts?' Smyth-Hilton offered smoothly. 'Mr Smyth-Hilton, editor of the *Working Man's Defender.*' He inclined his head ever so slightly.

A bead of sweat sprang up on Amos's brow.

A well-stuffed man turned to Mattie. 'Madam, we have come here to set up this company in proper order and I, for one, would be grateful if we could do that without interference from one who clearly has no understanding of such matters.' He gave Patrick a caustic look. 'I call upon you, sir, to take your wife home.'

Patrick drew himself upright. 'This share certificate,' he jabbed the elongated paper on the table with his index finger, 'means that my *sister* is entitled to be here as much as any of you.'

A rumble of discontent ran around the table and someone muttered, 'Who let the tinkers in?' Which brought forth several more snorts. Patrick's mouth hardened.

A bald-headed shareholder curled his top lip into a sneer. 'You might have bought yourself a couple of shares but that doesn't mean that you and your sister have the right to sit alongside or question your betters. I do not know *who* you are, nor wish to, but *what* you are is abundantly clear.'

Mattie grabbed her brother's arm to keep him in his seat. 'And I know what *you* are, sir. A patsy,' she told the bald-headed shareholder. 'And just in case you're not familiar with the term, it's Irish for a fool, a dupe, someone who's been diddled. In fact, you're all patsies here, because you've all been hoodwinked. By him!' Mattie pointed at Amos.

Pandemonium broke out as the men in the room shouted their outrage.

'Gentlemen, gentlemen,' Amos said as held his hand up for silence. 'Mrs Maguire, how *you* can accuse *me* of dishonesty when, out of regard for your fatherless child, I paid well over the current price for your own yard, not a month back.'

'That you did, but I'm still wanting to know how much you sold it to the railway for.'

'Well, I don't see that this is a question for this—'

'And how much did you sell all the other properties you owned along the route of the railway for?' Mattie continued. She turned to the other shareholders. 'I don't suppose that Mr Stebbins told you that he owned nearly all of the land along the route, which the company has now bought? Well, that's to say it was owned by him and Mr Fallon there' – she moved her finger onto the ashen man sitting beside Amos – 'who you wise and sober businessmen have just voted in as the company treasurer. I have evidence that Mr Stebbins has been buying up properties along the route on the quiet, with the intention of selling them to the Wapping & Stratford at a vastly inflated price with *your* money.'

Smyth-Hilton held a hefty file aloft, and there was a moment of total silence before several of the shareholders jumped to their feet.

'Stebbins?' asked a slim, distinguished looking man.

Amos stretched his neck out of his collar. 'I sold a couple of plots of land—'

'How many?' demanded another.

Amos drew out his handkerchief and mopped his glistening forehead. 'One or two ... a few. I can't remember exactly.' He spread his hands. 'And I ask you, gentlemen, does it matter who owned them?'

'It bloody does if you've used our money to pad your pocket,' a bald-headed investor yelled. 'And, now that you've paid yourself, are there sufficient funds in the company's account to engage the engineers we need?'

Amos licked his lips. 'I'm sure the City & County will be able to loan the company the funds it—'

'Loan!' bellowed another investor, who shook his silver-topped cane at Amos. 'Over fifty thousand was raised in the share issue. Perhaps you ought to answer this good lady's question, Stebbins. Just how much did you pay for the properties along the route!'

Panic, fear and fury mingled on Amos's face.

'Fallon owned the Hawkins timber yard in Limehouse and the row of houses in Fieldgate Street.'

The company's newly elected treasurer leapt to his feet. 'Only because you offered them to me.' He prodded Amos's chest just at the point below his carnation in his lapel. 'It's you who owned the lion's share of the sites.'

The room exploded. Men who, until a few moments before, had looked down at the latecomers with an air of superiority now raged and shouted as if they were a bunch of costermongers in the Garrick's penny pit.

Patrick stood up and smashed his fist on the table twice. The noise ceased abruptly and the men in the room turned back towards Mattie. She caught Patrick's eyes and he winked.

Mattie cleared her throat. 'I would like to put forward a motion of no confidence in the chairman, Mr Amos Stebbins, and further propose that the shareholders appoint an independent auditor to investigate fully the financial dealings of Mr Stebbins. And Mr Fallon.'

There was a moment of silence. Then two dozen voices shouted that they would second the motion.

Chapter Twenty-Nine

Mattie leant back as the besuited waiter placed a bowl containing a small island of plum pudding in a sea of creamy custard in front of her.

'Thank you,' she said.

The waiter placed the same dish in front of Patrick, Smyth-Hilton and Josie and retired to his place by the kitchen door. The men picked up their spoons and scooped them into their desserts without breaking their conversation. Smyth-Hilton wore a charcoal frockcoat while Patrick was dressed in the suit he kept for best. The party of four received a series of admiring, and curious glances as they walked through the restaurant into the private room where they now sat.

Josie turned towards Mattie, her eyes sparkling under the lace trim of her new bonnet. 'Isn't this exciting?' she said, as the sweet steam from the pudding drifted up between them.

'Yes,' Mattie replied, thinking terrifying might be a better word to describe having lunch at Crosby Hall, one of Bishopsgate's most fashionable restaurants. She'd barely tasted the braised lamb with dumpling as she couldn't stop her eyes roaming around the plush surroundings. The interior of the small dining room they sat in had half-panelled walls adorned with landscape paintings. The gas lamps had cut crystal shades and the table was set with the finest china and the shiniest silverware Mattie had ever seen.

A week after their coup at the shareholders meeting, Smyth-Hilton suggested that they dine out to celebrate their victory. Mattie had thought it a splendid idea, thinking he meant at the Hoop and Grapes, or perhaps the Pie Bull, but when the cab stopped outside the double-fronted Crosby Hall her heart had missed a beat. As Smyth-Hilton led her in on his arm, followed by Patrick and Josie, Mattie felt that everyone in the room knew that her gown and jacket were second hand.

'How's Kate?' Josie asked, popping a spoonful of pudding in her mouth.

'Grand,' Mattie replied. 'Although I barely had time to boil the kettle before young Ella started to squeeze her way into the world.'

'Well, let's hope that now he has a family to keep, Freddie will start to shape up,' Josie said.

'Yes, let's hope.'

Kate's marriage was a sad state of affairs to be sure, but there was nothing she nor anyone else could do about it. Kate was married now for better or for worse and all Mattie could do was pray for her sister.

Smyth-Hilton raised his glass. 'I propose a toast to Mrs Maguire, whose bravery in the face of the enemy is an example to us all.'

'To Mattie,' Josie and Patrick said in unison, raising their glasses, too.

Mattie felt her cheeks grow warm. 'I only asked the questions. You did all the work trawling through the land registry to prove that Mr Stebbins really did own the properties.'

'But what a question, eh? It led to the total collapse of the Wapping & Stratford, a run on the City & County, Fallon's resignation, and the discovery of enough irregularities and dubious payments in Stebbins's ledger to keep the accountants working until Christmas.' Smyth-Hilton placed his well-manicured hand on the three-day-old copy of *The Times*. 'And then this.'

A satisfied smile spread across Mattie's face. 'I hear he's already been asked to resign from St George's Vestry.'

'And that he's been booed at in the streets when he walked to his office the other day,' Josie added.

'Well, he hasn't got an office any more. Not now the bank's foreclosed on his mortgage. And the traders who are owed hundreds by him have applied to the court for payment, so I wouldn't be surprised if he were declared bankrupt by the end of the month.'

'A good job, too,' Josie said.

Patrick grinned at her.

A solid lump of unhappiness settled on Mattie's chest. 'Is there any word from the auditors about the stolen money?'

Smyth-Hilton shook his head. 'It's early days,' he replied sympathetically.

Mattie put down her wine glass untouched. 'Then I can't celebrate,' she said, her lower lip threatening to tremble. 'Not until Nathaniel is free.'

'You'll have to be patient, Mattie,' Patrick said, reaching across to pat her hand. 'These things take time.'

'But Nathaniel hasn't *got* time.'

Tears pinched at the inside of her eyes but she blinked them away, determined not to make a scene with everybody looking on. They had turned up for Nathaniel's appearance at the Old Bailey only to be told that the list had been brought forward and the court had heard his case the day before. Mattie was distraught that she hadn't caught a last glimpse of Nathaniel before he was sent back to Botany Bay, but tried to console herself with the thought that it was better this way. It was now abundantly clear that she was with child, and at least he wouldn't be sent back knowing he would never see his child.

Josie slipped her arm around her. 'And at least Nathaniel knows that you've shown the world Amos's true nature. Isn't that what he came back for?'

Mattie gave a little nod.

Patrick had finally got permission to visit Nathaniel and had recounted the events of the shareholders' meeting. Nathaniel had said he could face being sent back to Botany Bay now that he knew Mattie's financial future would be secure. That was all well and good, but Mattie didn't want to have a future without Nathaniel beside her.

'And we've not finished with our friend and his secrets yet.' Smyth-Hilton tapped the side of his nose. 'Just keep your eye on the next edition of the *Working Man's Defender.*'

'I've spoken to the solicitors dealing with the Wapping & Stratford,' Patrick said. 'They are keen to realise as much money as possible for Stebbins's creditors, and I took the liberty of putting in an offer of three hundred and twenty-five pounds for your yard. It looks as if they will accept it.' He grinned. 'Not bad, eh?'

Mattie forced a smile and wondered how she was going to tell him that, if they couldn't free Nathaniel in time, she was considering using every penny she had to follow him to Australia.

Mattie pushed open Wardell's door and set the bell attached to it jingling. Samuel Wardell, who was showing a customer a variety of Parisian jugs, acknowledged her arrival with a professional smile.

Wardell's had stood on the corner of Hessle Street for as long as Mattie could remember. From every hook and beam hung metal hoops for cart wheels and baskets of all shapes and designs. The counter too was stacked high with jars of glue for the women who made matchboxes at home for the local factories.

Carefully sidestepping the rat traps on the floor, Mattie took her place at the back of the queue. Her heart sunk as recognised

Dot Milligan and Bridget Keane standing in front of her. Dot nudged Bridget and a look of undisguised glee lit their faces. Mattie held her shopping basket in front of her, hoping that this would shield her waistline from too much scrutiny.

'Oh, Mattie, my dear!' Bridget cried, as she squeezed herself between Mattie and a barrel of pickling vinegar. 'Why I was only talking about you the other day.' Her small hazel eyes searched Mattie's face and then the rest of her. 'How have you been keeping?'

'Very well,' Mattie replied, as Dot elbowed her way forward to join them.

'You look it, don't she, Dot?' Bridget said, her pale eyes lingering just a little too long on Mattie's middle.

'That she does,' Dot replied, as her eyes followed her friend's.

Dot drew closer. 'What about all this business with Mr Stebbins? Railways and land and kiddy knocking shops! Fair curdles your innards.' Her eyes narrowed. 'But, you'd know all about that seeing how it was you who brought 'im down.'

Mattie felt her cheeks grow warm. 'I wouldn't say that.'

Dot gave her a chummy smile. 'Come on, Mattie, tell us how you knew about the railway and all.'

'I just asked some questions about who owned the land, that's all,' she said, knowing they would have read as much in the paper.

'I read that Nathaniel Tate—'

'*Your* coalman,' Betty cut in as her eyes drifted again onto Mattie's stomach.

'—is to be sent back to Australia for a fourteen-year stretch,' finished Dot.

The barrels alongside Mattie seemed to press nearer for a moment. *Please God, let them find the money*, Mattie prayed, as she had done almost every waking moment. Smyth-Hilton kept telling her that they would find the money but it had been almost ten weeks since the auditors were called in and each day that passed was a day nearer to the date of Nathaniel's transportation.

The queue moved forward again and the door to the Wardell's living area opened. Jane, Samuel's wife appeared, still tying her apron.

'Oh, Mrs Maguire!' she cried, waving a large envelope at her. 'I was just going to send the boy around to tell you this arrived an hour ago.'

Bridget and Dot stood aside as Jane passed the letter between them. Mattie took it and looked at the smooth manila paper with well-ordered writing on the front and a red wax seal on the back.

Mattie's heart thumped in her chest as she flipped it over and broke the seal. She scanned down the page and one phrase leapt off the page: '... have located the missing £2000 from Amos Stebbins's holding in Romford ...'

Mattie shoved Smyth-Hilton's letter in the front of her coat. 'I ... I have to get home,' she said, dashing towards the door.

Mattie twisted the handkerchief in her hands and fixed her eyes on the wooden doors of Pentonville prison. She, Patrick and Smyth-Hilton stood amongst a small crowd of women and children also waiting for the gates to open.

She tucked her collar up higher to keep out the early morning chill. 'Do you think we'll have to wait much longer?'

Patrick smiled down at her. 'Just a few moments longer, I'm sure, and then you'll be able to see him, Mattie.' He winked. 'Just in time, too.'

It was mid April now, so she couldn't have more than a month or so before the baby was born. And now, Mary be blessed, Nathaniel would be with her when her time arrived to welcome their child. As if sensing her excitement, the baby turned over; she smoothed her hand over her stomach then fixed her eyes on the stark prison doors. She could hardly believe that after all these months of fear and uncertainty Nathaniel would soon, very soon, be a free man again. A smile lifted the corner of her lips as she pictured Nathaniel's surprise when he saw her.

The prison clock chimed six, bolts were scraped back and one of the doors opened. The crowd surged forward to greet those who had paid their debt to society as the prison gate closed behind them.

Patrick grasped Mattie's elbow and guided her towards the door. He banged the metal hatch in the door with his fist. Keys jangled on the other side, then it opened.

Inside stood the receiving officer, a man with a magnificent moustache and an enormous bunch of keys slung on a chain from his belt.

'The prison isn't open for enquires until ten o'clock,' he said, pushing the metal doors closed again.

Patrick put his hand on it to halt its progress. 'We've come to see the officer in charge on a very urgent matter.'

'What?'

Smyth-Hilton squeezed himself between them. 'This warrant,' he replied, holding up the sealed magistrate's order, 'for the release of Nathaniel Tate.'

'Well, he ain't going anywhere is he, so you can come back at ten o'clock,' the officer replied without even glancing at the paper.

Mattie ducked under Patrick's arm and gripped the bars. 'Please. Can't you just fetch the officer in charge?'

The prison warden looked her over. 'I'm sorry, Missus, I—'

'What's the problem here, Trent?' a deep voice boomed from inside the guardroom.

The officer snapped to attention and saluted. 'Some people with a magistrate's permit, Mr Callow, sir.'

The reception officer stepped aside and a tough individual with a jagged scar down his left cheek, granite eyes and three brass pips on his shoulders, took his place.

'Good morning, sir,' Mattie said, smiling up at him through the grille. 'I'm sorry to trouble you so early in the day but we have a court order for the immediate release of Nathaniel Tate,' she said, as Smyth-Hilton flourished the folded paper again.

Mr Callow's brows drew together. 'Tate! Tate!' He pulled down a ledger from the shelf above. He laid it across his forearm and opened it. He ran his finger down the line of names. 'Fredrick Tarling, Albert Tatar, Nathaniel Tate—'

'That's him! Nathaniel Tate!' Mattie seized the warrant from the journalist's hand. 'We have his release papers. Here!' She opened it and held it up to he could see it.

The officer glanced at it then back at Mattie. 'Well, that all seems in order but you're too late.'

'Too late?' Mattie replied, as the floor under her feet seemed to tip sideways.

Callow tapped the page. 'Tate was sent to the *Randolph* two days ago. It sailed this morning from Brunswick dock.'

Mattie staggered back and Patrick put out his hand to steady her.

'But we have a court order for his release,' Smyth-Hilton said.

'Well, you'll have to take it to Australia then, won't you?' The senior officer replied. 'Because he's gone.' He slammed the register shut with a thud. 'Now, if you'll excuse me I have a prison to run.' He closed the grille.

Mattie, Patrick and Smyth-Hilton stood staring at each other in disbelief for a moment, then Patrick grabbed her hand.

'Come on!' he said, hurrying her across the road.

'Where are we going, Patrick?' Mattie asked, panting to keep up with him.

'I'll tell you on the way,' Patrick replied.

Nathaniel raised his head and drew in a deep breath as the pungent stench of the Thames mud filled his nostrils. Above his head, the sailors on the *Randolph* rolled the last few barrels across the deck above him. He and the other nine prisoners of number four mess sat squashed together on the narrow benches, their heads down and shoulders slumped, behind the iron bars of the cage. He'd recognised a couple of them from Pentonville but the others were from Millbank and Cold Bath Fields. No doubt by the time they reached their destination a hundred days from now, they would be much better acquainted. On either side of them were the ten men of numbers three and five mess.

The cell was just over two-arms-stretch wide and a little deeper with crude benches nailed around the edges. There was barely enough room for them all to sit, but during the day they would be taken out five at a time for their ablutions and exercise. Those who remained would take advantage of the extra space, be it ever so briefly. At night, they were allocated hammocks which they would string across.

Nathaniel had managed to secure himself the most tucked away hammock position so that he didn't have men clambering over him on their way to the slop bucket during the night. In many ways the provision on the transportation ships had improved since he had last travelled on one. Previously, the captain held sway; now a surgeon superintendent was in charge. There was also a parson on the ship to give spiritual succour and run reading classes.

When he was marched aboard at Woolwich two days before and into the prison deck, the acrid residue of human excrement sent his guts churning. Horrific memories flooded back: of being locked away in the bowels of the ship for days on end and of the sheer terror of being chained to a post during a hurricane.

In some ways it was as well that he was chained to the men before and behind him or he might have jumped into the swirling waters of the Thames. But that was the coward's way out, and now the initial urge had passed he knew that when they set sail the routines of the journey would do the thinking for him. Smyth-Hilton had been most apologetic at his last visit when he told him that the auditors hadn't unearthed the money from Stebbins's Romford business. But it had always been a slim chance that it would be found and he was just thankful that Patrick had been able to buy back Maguire's from the bank. He could better face the long, lonely years ahead knowing that Mattie and Brian were safe. He was resolved to fix his mind on her each day, be it under the hot sun of the patched bush or in the cool of evening by a billabong. That way she would always be with him. He would mark the passing years and picture her prosperous and well.

He let his head fall back on the metal bars of the cell. He hadn't failed in his quest entirely, after all he *had* shown the world Stebbins's true nature. But he had failed utterly in the part of his plan that touched his core; he would never now clear his name or marry Mattie.

The muffled sound of the boarding ladder rolling down the side rumbled through the wooden ship. The dozen or so prisoners from Maidstone prison would soon be on board and then the next stop would be Kingston, Jamaica or Bridgetown, Barbados before they sailed south to battle through the storms of the Cape and into the Pacific.

Nathaniel stretched his right leg to ease the cramp in his calf. They wouldn't be allowed on the top deck to wash or exercise until they were at sea, which made the atmosphere in the tightly packed cell oppressive. The spring weather didn't help as it brought out the flies and midges in the nearby marshland.

A light cut through the gloom as the hatch above them opened. Everyone craned their necks to get a glimpse of the newcomers but instead of a line of sorry-looking prisoners, the ship's surgeon squeezed himself through the opening and clattered down the narrow stairs. The prison officers snapped to attention.

Mr Goldney drew a handkerchief from his sleeve and covered his nose and mouth. Nathaniel rolled his eyes. If the surgeon thought this was bad wait until they'd been at sea a fortnight.

'Which is number four?' he mumbled through the fabric covering the bottom half of his face.

A pock-marked senior officer saluted sharply and motioned to Nathaniel's cell. 'Over here, sir.'

'Prisoner Tate?' he asked.

Nathaniel stood up. 'Sir.'

Goldney nodded his head sharply to the warden, who produced an enormous bunch of keys. The other officer picked up their rifles and came over.

'All of you except Tate stand back,' the senior officer ordered, as the men behind him cocked their weapons and aimed it into the cell.

The men fettered to Nathaniel shuffled back as best they could and when the officer came in he unlocked Nathaniel's ankle chains.

'Follow me,' Mr Goldney commanded.

As Nathaniel walked between the cells his mind raced through the various reasons a captain might call a prisoner out. Punishment. But for what? A special task perhaps? He was one of the few prisoners who could read and write but he doubted the ship's master needed him on that score. He followed the surgeon up the narrow ladder to the crew deck and then on to the top deck. Instantly, the wind whipped though his hair and the salty smell of the sea filled his nostrils. He took a deep breath and blinked as the sunlight dazzled him.

For a moment his brain couldn't make sense of what his eyes were seeing. Mattie? It couldn't be! His mind was playing a cruel trick on him. He shook his head and looked back again. Time seemed to stop. He stared across the battened-down canvas on the cargo hold at the woman he loved. The wind tugged at her chip bonnet and she had a hand on the crown of it to stop it from flying away. She was dressed in the dark green gown and jacket he liked her in and she was smiling up at the captain. Behind her stood Patrick, Smyth-Hilton and a river police officer. He registered their presence but had eyes only for Mattie. Then he saw her swollen stomach.

'Mattie?'

Her head whipped around and her eyes, her lovely eyes fixed on him.

'Nathaniel!'

She sidestepped a coil of rope and waddled along the deck towards him. She threw herself in his arms. She buried her face in his chest and clung to him. Nathaniel put aside all the questions of why and how she was here. He kissed her forehead and ran his finger through her hair. The faintest smell of violets drifted up to him.

She tilted up her face as tears shimmered on her bottom lashes. 'They found the money.'

'Thank God.'

She wound her arms around him, fitting snugly under his arm and into his hips as she always did. Well, not quite. He released her and, keeping one arm around her, rested his hand on her stomach. He felt a faint movement press against his palm. Love, pride and utter joy swept over him forming a lump in his throat.

'How soon?'

'About a month or so.'

Patrick stomped down the deck and joined them. He and Nathaniel shook hands.

'Thank you,' he said, seeing the top mast of Patrick's boat, the *Smiling Girl*, poking up over the side rail.

'Thank St Nicholas for a strong easterly and a swift current or you'd have passed Shoeburyness by now and we'd never have caught you in open sea.'

'But we did,' Mattie said, as Smyth-Hilton joined them.

'We'd better get those banns read soon,' Nathaniel said, grinning.

'That might have to wait a week or two as you're not free just yet. Your transportation has been deferred,' Patrick said. 'You're now in the custody of the police.' He nodded at the river police officers standing with the captain.

'I'll be pushing for your hearing as soon as possible,' Smyth-Hilton said, looking a little green around the gills. 'With the evidence the auditors uncovered, it should be an open-and-shut case. I think you'll be able to make an honest woman of Mrs Maguire but with only a week or two to spare.'

Chapter Thirty

The vicar of St George's extolled the virtues of marriage as Mattie stood beside Nathaniel, her hand resting in his. The sweet smell of the first crop of spring flowers drifted over them as they exchanged their vows. Although it was only the legal part of their marriage, with a nuptial mass planned for next week, the whole family was there. So many people had crowded in that the vicar had opened the door to the main part of the church because they wouldn't all fit in the porch.

True to his word, Smyth-Hilton badgered the courts, and Nathaniel's case was heard within two weeks of his transfer to the river police. The evidence had been so overwhelming that it took less time to find him innocent than it had to have him re-sentenced not two months before.

Nathaniel's sister Emma and her husband Jacob had arrived from Romford on the train the day before the hearing. She and Mattie had wept in each others arms in the public gallery when the judge pronounced Nathaniel innocent. He was released instantly, with his reputation restored.

Mattie and Emma had become fast friends from the moment they'd met. With Mattie growing larger by the day and Brian's boundless energy enough for two boys, having Nathaniel's sister around the house had been very welcome. Delicious buns and country pies appeared on the table for tea each day, once Emma had got the hang of the range in the kitchen. Her husband Jacob had made himself useful by taking over the care of the horses. Brian loved his new relatives and happily sat on Auntie Emma's lap – and thank goodness too, because Mattie's lap had disappeared. Emma and Jacob were set to stay with them until after the baby was born, but Mattie knew Nathaniel was hoping to persuade them to stay permanently. Jacob was getting on and if he could no longer work then he and Emma would be forced to seek relief from the parish. Nathaniel was adamant that his sister wouldn't end up in the workhouse.

Emma and Jacob now stood in their best clothes alongside Sarah, who was holding Brian so he could see everything. Kate and her baby, Ella, stood with Patrick, Josie and their children. Behind the immediate family were Pete, his wife and children, Billy and his intended, and old Eli and his daughter. Behind them stood Nathaniel's old friend Boyce, wearing an oddly sentimental expression.

Mattie glanced up at Nathaniel, standing tall and upright beside her. His hair had grown out from the prison crop and he'd been to the Italian barbers opposite the Crown and Anchor to have a proper beard trim. He'd also been to Moses & Sons to buy a new grey suit and top hat. With his white shirt-collar framing his firm jaw and the added swirl of colour from his necktie, Mattie marvelled at how one man could be so handsome.

He turned and smiled down at her and a thrill of pleasure ran through her. Just when she thought she couldn't be any happier, Nathaniel slipped the narrow silver ring that had been his mother's wedding band over her finger.

There had been times over the last few months when she'd almost given up hope that this day would ever come.

'You look beautiful,' Nathaniel said quietly as they waited for the vicar to write their marriage lines.

She and Josie had spent the last few weeks unpicking her original pink-striped wedding dress and reworking it to fit. It looked well enough but even with a new bonnet and Josie's very large lace shawl draped around her, Mattie still felt like the elephant in Jamrach's back yard.

'I look like a merchantman in full sail,' she replied.

Nathaniel's eyes danced with amusement. 'You look perfect.'

The vicar handed her the folded certificate. 'There you are, Mrs Tate.'

Mrs Tate! Joy burst through Mattie and set the baby inside her off on somersaults. At last, she was Nathaniel's wife.

He offered her his arm and they turned to face their families. Sarah wiped a tear from her eyes as did Josie and Emma from theirs. Leaving the cool of the church behind they emerged into the May sunlight. Their families gathered around to throw handfuls of rice. Mattie let go of Nathaniel's arm as the men shook his hand and slapped him on the back with their congratulations. Annie and Mickey herded the younger children on to the grass as the adults mingled and talked.

Josie slipped her arm in Mattie's and drew her aside. 'I am so happy for you,' she said hugging her friend again.

Sarah hobbled over to join them. 'You look such a blessed bride, and with such a fine looking fella, too,' she said, glancing at Nathaniel laughing and joking with Emma and Jacob. Her lined face crinkled into a smile and her old eyes twinkled. 'I'm thinking there *must* be a touch of Irish blood in his family somewhere.'

The women laughed.

'And here's my other darling girl,' Sarah continued as Kate came over to join them. She took baby Ella in her arms and kissed her forehead.

'All blessing on you, Mattie,' Kate said, embracing her.

Mattie hugged her, wishing fervently that Kate was married to someone who would love her as much as she was loved by Nathaniel. Despite having the responsibility of a wife and child, Freddie had carried on as before. There were worrying rumours that he was now in thick with the Black Eagle Gang; however, now that she had Ella, Kate demanded he give her the housekeeping she was due. She even threatened to go to the Blue Boy with Ella in her arms on payday so all his flash drinking pals would see how he treated his own flesh an blood. Freddie backed down and grudgingly gave her five shillings a week.

Her mother ran a concerned eye over Mattie. 'You should get the weight off your feet, my girl.'

'In a while – I swear this baby's playing hopscotch.'

'You've dropped since the other day.'

'I know,' Mattie replied. She'd had the sensation of the baby's head deep in her pelvis for two or three days, and since then there had been one or two contractions each day.

'I'd say you got that ring on your finger just in time.'

Mattie smiled, knowing her mother was right.

She shifted her weight and her ankles felt tight. Perhaps she *had* stood for too long. Breakfast was waiting for them at the yard so maybe they should think about making their way back. As she looked across at Nathaniel out of the corner of her eye she caught sight of someone hovering behind the Raines family memorial in the corner of the churchyard.

An image of Amos flashed into her mind and a prickle of unease started between her shoulder blades. Although the gossip about Cecily's flight to her cousin's shot around the street in a matter of hours after the report in the *Working Man's Defender* was published, no one had seen Amos. He was a ruined man, shunned by everyone. The general consensus was that he'd got no more than he deserved and a lot less than he should have for his cavorting at Madame La

Verne's. Some said he'd gone abroad and others that he'd thrown himself in the river. No one really knew.

Mattie took a step to the right to see if there *was* someone behind a square stone monument.

'Mammy! Mammy!'

She turned to see Nathaniel striding towards her with Brian on his shoulders.

'Here she is,' Nathaniel said, as he lifted Brian down.

Brian stretched his arms up to her then saw Nathaniel's eyes on him. 'Remember what we talked about, son.'

Brian gave him a solemn nod and took her hand. 'Pa said I'm a big boy now and big boys don't have to be carried. And Pa's going to take me to see the Queen's soldiers in the Tower. Aren't you, Pa?'

'I am,' Nathaniel replied. He smiled at Mattie. 'He's getting used to calling me Pa.'

'It sounds just right to me,' Mattie said, as happiness almost stopped her speaking.

'Let's go home.'

She nodded, knowing that from this day forth only death would ever part them again.

Something nipped behind Amos's ear as he darted behind the square base of Raines monument in St George's churchyard. He flicked whatever it was away without taking his eyes from the bride and groom – the two people responsible for his present misery. He snagged his foot on brambles and shook it free. He caught sight of his frayed trouser bottoms and scuffed shoes and tried to remember when he had last taken them off. Probably the night before the bailiffs evicted him from his house. He gnawed the side of his nail then spat on the grass.

Look at him in his new suit and top hat, he thought savagely. *Still trying to ape your betters, are you, Tate?* His eyes moved on to the heavily pregnant woman at his side. *And her too! The trollop! It's a disgrace. The vicar should never have allowed her to waddle into the church with her belly full of a convict's bastard.*

But he's not a convict now is he? A sarcastic little voice at the back of Amos's head reminded him.

No, he damn well wasn't. He was the poor but honest working man wrongly imprisoned but 'freed by the love of a good woman', as the report of his court hearing in *The Times* put it. He was the champion who'd unearthed supposed wrongdoing in a company, saving the shareholders from losing their money. He was the 'hero' who'd uncovered Madame's establishment.

A dull, rhythmic throbbing started over Amos's right temple.

Make the most of your wedded bliss, Tate, he thought, *because the next time you go into St George's church, Mattie will be walking behind your coffin.*

Chapter Thirty-One

Nathaniel had been up since before dawn to see out the four delivery carts and consult with the farrier who'd come to check the horses. After bolting down his dinner at noon, he'd caught the omnibus to Cheapside then walked to the offices of Blair & Caldwell, attorneys at law, in Upper Thames Street. The result of his hour-long meeting with Mr Caldwell now sat in his breast pocket.

Although he was bone weary, he put aside workaday worries and contemplated his new family awaiting his return. When he pushed open the door to the kitchen the warmth from the hearth dispersed the swirling fog clinging to him. He was welcomed by the homely smell of fresh bread and roast meat.

His sister, ruddy-faced and bare-armed, was shelling peas while Brian played on the rug. He noticed them in passing but his eyes fixed on the woman who really made the house a home: his Mattie.

Thankfully, Emma had taken on the heavy chores and Millie took Brian to play with her girls most afternoons so Mattie could have an hour or two with her feet up. His gaze settled on her stomach and a thrill of anticipation ran through him.

She had already cleaned the bedroom and washed Brian's layette in preparation for the new baby's arrival. Nathaniel could hardly wait to hold their child who, according to all the Nolan women, would arrive any day now.

Buster scampered around his legs and Mattie's eyes danced with joy as she looked at him. If he lived to be a hundred, he would never lose the thrill of having her lovely green eyes rest on him that way.

'Evening, Nat,' Emma said. 'I'll make you a brew.'

'That would be grand, sis,' he replied, rubbing his hands together.

'Pa! Pa!' Brian shouted as he leapt to his feet, scattering his carefully stacked bricks.

'Hi there, young man,' Nathaniel laughed, as the boy caught him around the legs. He scooped him up. 'Have you been good for your mother today?'

Brian nodded. Nathaniel kissed him on the cheek then set him back on his feet. Brian trotted over to Buster and they started their evening game of tag at the far end of the kitchen.

Mattie rose from the chair and came towards him. 'Well?' she asked, a look of barely concealed impatience on her face.

He went to her and slipped his arm around what was left of her waist. 'How is Mrs Tate?' he asked, giving her a little squeeze.

'Grand, grand,' she replied, 'But what about the—'

'And the little one?' Nathaniel cut in.

'Still dancing a jig,' she answered. 'Nathaniel, will you tell me—'

'How long now, do you think?' he asked, answering her exasperated expression with a guileless one.

'For the love of Mary, will you tell me if we have the house or not?' she all but shouted at him.

'House?' he replied, giving her a puzzled look.

Mattie grabbed his lapels. 'Nathaniel Tate, I'm giving you fair warning that you risk life and limb if you don't stop shilly shallying about and *tell me*!'

Nathaniel released her and stood back.

'Well, now, I have here ...' he drew out a folded piece of paper from the inside of his overcoat, 'the signed and sealed lease—'

'Nathaniel!' Mattie threw her arms around his neck, almost choking off his breath.

'Of number seventeen Repton Street,' he continued as she bounced on her toes and hugged him. 'Co-co-complete, will you let me have some air, woman?'

Mattie's arms loosened a little.

'Complete with parlour, a kitchen including a full range, pumped water, three good upstairs rooms, gas fittings downstairs, an outside privy—'

Mattie interrupted by kissing his chin.

'—and not five minutes' walk from your mother and brother's house,' he concluded as she kissed him again. He unwound her arms from his neck. 'Now stop jumping about before you give our poor baby a headache,' he said, trying to look severe but unable to keep the grin from his face.

Mattie's fingers caressed his cheek. 'Thank you.'

'It's my pleasure, Mrs Tate.'

His hand slid down to her hip and pressed her into him and Mattie gave him a private glance from beneath her long lashes which set his pulse racing. They *were* still newlyweds, after all.

She untangled herself from his arms and turned to her son. 'Did you hear that, Brian? We're moving into a house right by your gran and Auntie Josie.'

'Are Auntie Emma and Uncle Jacob coming too?'

'Of course,' Nathaniel replied, as he took Mattie's hand and kissed it. They would lose the use of a downstairs room but it meant the whole family would be together. 'And so is Buster and all your soldiers.'

'Yippee!' Brian shouted and started chasing Buster around the kitchen. Mattie turned back to Nathaniel. 'How soon?'

'Whenever you'd like after the twentieth. The sooner the better perhaps,' he said, indicating her stomach. 'I'll speak to Patrick when I see him in the Town tomorrow.'

It wouldn't take much to load up one of the carts with their furniture. Thanks to Patrick buying back Maguire's at two hundred and fifty less than Amos had paid for it, they could afford not only a new house but some new furniture and china, too, including several new cast iron beds. It also meant they would almost be within shouting distance of Sarah when the baby came. She'd delivered Brian and all of Josie's children and was as good as any midwife.

Mattie hugged him again then a look of dismay spread across her face. 'What sort of wife am I, nagging the ears off you when you've not even had time to take off your coat?' She slipped her hand under his lapels and started to pull it off. Nathaniel's hands closed over hers.

'I'm just going to run next week's order round to Morris's before they close,' he said. 'I would have gone straight there but I wanted to tell you about the house first.' He picked up his hat. Buster sprang to his feet ready to follow but Nathaniel signalled for him to stay. 'I'll be no more than half an hour and then I can lock up for the night.' He planted a swift kiss on her lips. 'Sure, won't I be back before you miss me,' he said, in what he considered to be a pretty decent Irish accent.

Mattie turned to the stove but Emma jumped in before she reached it. 'Now, you just set your rump down on that chair, my love, and let me see to that,' she said, tasting the stew then adding a pinch of salt from the jar.

'Are you sure?' Mattie asked, feeling the ache in her back. 'You've been chasing Brian around all day as it is.'

'And it is my pleasure to do so,' she said.

'I'll feed Buster then,' Mattie said.

Turning to fetch a half-pound of horse flesh from the scullery, Mattie's eyes fell on the order book on the dresser.

'Nathaniel's forgotten this,' she said picking it and her shawl up in one movement. 'I'll just run after him.'

'Take the dog with you,' Emma said, 'He'll dash after Nat and save you dancing that baby about.'

Mattie clicked her fingers. Buster's floppy ears stood up and he came to sit by her, ready to move when she did. She quickly shrugged on her coat. It might be spring, but once the heat went out of the day the fog from the river could chill you to the bone.

She reached up to wrap her shawl around her head and the niggle in her back tweaked again. She let out a quiet gasp so Emma wouldn't hear. The dog tilted his head, looked at her and gave a little whine. Mattie stroked his head.

'I won't be a moment,' she said, as she and Buster went through the door.

'And keep an eye out for my Jacob. He said he was only having a swift half with Eli and that was an hour ago!'

The fog in the yard was so thick she could barely see the double gates so, tugging her shawl around her, Mattie walked as swiftly as she could, with Buster staying close to her heels. Nathaniel had trained the dog well, but today he seemed more attentive than usual.

Mattie lifted the latch, pushed the gate open and stepped out into the street. She could hear the hollow echo of barges knocking together as they floated in their moorings and she peered down the road towards Limehouse. The one street lamp cast a mustardy haze through the swirling mist and even though Nathaniel was probably only at the end of the street she couldn't see him through the murkiness. Her shoulders slumped as she thought about his wasted journey. She could have sent Buster after him but although he was a clever dog, he was young, and if distracted by an interesting smell or a scurrying rat he could dart off and lose himself.

She was about to step back into the yard when Buster's ears strained forward and he started to growl. Mattie followed his gaze.

Mr Stebbins!

She could hardly believe it, but there was no mistaking his rotund figure half hidden in the shadows three doors down on the other side of the road. It had been over a month since the warrant for his arrest was issued but he had yet to be apprehended. Mattie had begun to believe the rumour that he'd left the area so seeing him not twenty yards from her sent fear coursing through her veins.

She gripped the rough wood of the gate to steady herself and watched as Amos Stebbins slipped silently out of his hiding place and disappeared into the fog. The cramp in her back tightened again sharply and the dog beside her whimpered and fussed around her skirts.

Sweet Mother of God! Please don't let it be the baby. Not now, not yet.

As if in answer to her prayer, the tightening in her back faded. She knew she really shouldn't be out in the street alone. The sensible thing to do would be to get help but there was only Emma in the house. By the time they fetched Jacob and raised the alarm Stebbins would have caught up with Nathaniel.

Mattie snapped her fingers to get Buster's attention. 'Go, fetch Nathaniel.' He hesitated and she urged him on again. 'Good Boy.' The dog circled around her a couple of times, darted off but doubled back. She couldn't blame him for not leaving her as Nathaniel had trained him to guard her and Brian.

'Good boy,' she said, stroking behind his ear.

There was nothing for it. She would have to go herself and pray that she met the beat constable along the way. At the very least she could raise the alarm once she got to the coal depot. A picture of her first husband Brian, his face bloodless and still as he lay in his coffin, flashed into Mattie's mind. *Sweet Mary, please don't let it happen again.*

She took a deep breath and walked as far as she could before resting against one of the high dock walls. She peered desperately into the gloom for the bright light of a police officer's bulls-eye lamp.

Jesus, Mary and Joseph, she thought, holding her hand on her stomach. *Isn't the truth of it that you can never get sight of the buggers when they could be of service!*

A band of pain shot around her middle and she doubled over and tried to breathe through it. She bit her lip and Buster's wet nose snuffled at her hand. *Come on, Mattie*, she told herself, *you have to keep going*. Gathering all her willpower together she straightened up and rested her back her on the wall again, praying the contractions would fade soon.

'Can I be of assistance?'

She nearly jumped out of her skin as she found herself looking into the youthful face of a policeman.

'Blessed Mercy. Amos Stebbins is heading for the Morris Coal depot after my husband,' she said, grabbing his arm and dragging him along with her. 'He's a wanted man. There'll be murder if we don't stop him.'

The officer dragged his rattle from under his cape and swung it. The clackity-clack echoed around the street and when they arrived at Morris's a few minutes later, four other officers joined them. The small access door was half open and Buster scampered through it followed by the officers and then Mattie. The dog stood rigid for a moment then dashed away barking for all he was worth, disappearing into the darkness of the yard.

'Over here,' one of the officers called.

Mattie's heart nearly leapt out of her mouth as the police lamp flashed onto a body slumped at the foot of the scales. Another of the officers joined the first and crouched beside him.

'It's the watchman,' he called back. 'He's hurt but alive.'

Stopping in front of Morris's office door Nathaniel shoved his hand in his breast pocket.

Damn!

He'd knew he was too late to catch the yard manager but the watchman had let him in and loaned him a spare lamp so he could leave the book in the message box. Stupidly, he'd forgotten that he'd left their order book on the dresser before going to sign the lease on the house. What a wasted journey. If he'd done as Mattie suggested he'd now be warming himself by the fire with a hot cup of tea in his hands.

The sound of boots crushing fragments of coal sounded behind him. Nathaniel turned and swung his lamp at what he thought was the watchman

'I've left my—'

But it was Amos Stebbins who stood in the beam of light pointing a gun at him.

'Good evening, Tate,' he laughed, aiming the barrel at Nathaniel's chest. 'How's married life?'

Nathaniel didn't answer or even blink. At this distance, if Stebbins's finger slipped on the trigger the shot would tear through his chest and he'd be dead before he hit the ground.

'Is dear Mrs Tate well?' Amos continued in a conversational tone. 'When I saw her on your arm outside the church last week she looked blooming. Is baby Tate due soon?' His expression changed from convivial to vicious. 'What a tragedy that, yet again, poor Mattie will lose her new husband just like the first. Before he sees his child born.'

No! screamed a voice in Nathaniel's head but he forced himself to remain calm. 'It's over, Stebbins, and killing me will just make things worse for you.'

'Worse!' Amos bellowed. 'How could it be worse? Look at me!' Nathaniel's eyes flickered over Amos's unshaven face and tatty clothes. 'And it's your fault, you poxy bastard.' His face screwed up into a ball of loathing. 'Why couldn't you have been bitten by a snake or caught some horrible disease while you were in Australia instead of coming back to destroy everything I've worked for.'

Fury rose up in Nathaniel as he thought of his trial at Chelmsford, three blistering years in the barracks at Botany Bay, his family's grave and, lastly, Mattie, almost swindled into the workhouse; however, despite his sensible mind screaming at him not to rile a man aiming with a gun at you, Nathaniel took a step forward.

'But you didn't work for it, did you? You lied, cheated and robbed others to line your own pockets,' Nathaniel spat out. 'And the reason I came back was because *you* destroyed *my* family. You, Amos Stebbins, are reaping the harvest you sowed seven years ago. If you want to lay the blame of your downfall at anyone's feet, it should be your own.' He reached out an open hand. 'You have wronged me and many others,' he said, in a calm, almost soothing voice. 'And now you have to be a man and face up to the consequences. There's no avoiding it. At present you are only looking at a prison sentence but if you pull that trigger it will be the rope.'

A vacant look spread over Amos' face. With his hand outstretched and his heart thumping in his chest, Nathaniel took another step forward.

'Give me the gun, Amos.'

Amos raised the pistol. 'Give my regards to Marjorie.'

A shot cracked though the air and the baby inside Mattie jumped. A picture of Brian's open coffin sitting on the table in the front parlour burst into Mattie's mind, but instead of Brian lying in his best suit with his hands folded across his chest, it was Nathaniel.

'No!' she screamed.

Ignoring the band of pain gripping her stomach again, she stumbled into the yard. The sharp tarry smell of a thousand tonnes of coal filled her nostrils and she choked on the fine dust that never quite settled.

She stared into the two-acre yard with its mountains of coal rising all around them. She screwed up her eyes to see something, anything, in the dense blackness, but the fog and now the jagged nuggets of coal absorbed what little light there was, making the yard's interior blacker than the street.

Two other beat officers ran in and joined their colleagues and six beams of light frantically criss-crossed one and other. Mattie's eyes darted back and forth as her panicked heart nearly burst through her chest. One beam landed on a ghostly movement and the other beams rapidly honed in on two men scrambling over the coal piles.

'Blessed be sweet Mary,' she sobbed, as she recognised Nathaniel's tall figure silhouetted. A few yards in front of him, Amos Stebbins stumbled and lurched towards the peak but something seemed to be dragging him back. Buster barked and Mattie realised that the dog, too, was on Amos' heels.

Another belt of pain tightened around Mattie's middle and she felt water spurt down the inside of her thigh. With some difficulty she held onto her rising fear. Even if it were the baby were coming, she'd taken six hours to birth Brian and surely must have a few hours yet to go ... The contraction eased and she looked back at Nathaniel, still scaling after Amos with Buster hanging on with all his might. Nathaniel surged forward but the coal shifted under him and he slid down, flaying his arms to keep upright. Amos saw his advantage and renewed his push to the top.

The police ran forward.

'Come down,' one of them shouted, his voice echoing around the black chasm.

Amos redoubled his efforts but Nathaniel found his footing and closed the gap to just over an arm's reach. Amos stumbled and Nathaniel threw himself onto him, dragging him down into the razor-sharp coal. The police were now climbing up the mound towards the two men. A low rumble began to shake the ground and large coal chucks started cascading down the heaps.

'Stop!' screamed Mattie.

The rumble grew louder and two of the policemen fell sideways while their fellow officers struggled to stay upright. A sound like a thousand fingers clawing at a blackboard tore across the open space as the crest of the coal pile that Nathaniel and Amos were fighting on suddenly dipped. An ear-filling roar drowned out Mattie's scream as a hundred tonnes of coal avalanched downwards.

The officers jumped off in time as did Buster, but Mattie stared in stark horror as the coal surrounded, then engulfed, Nathaniel and Amos.

'Nathaniel!' she screamed, stumbling onto the dislodged coal.

The police officers pulled her off. 'Get back, madam. We'll never find him under that lot,' he spluttered unable to take in a full breath due to the billow of coal dust pluming up around them.

'We *have* to,' Mattie shouted, breaking free to tear at the coal.

The police exchanged glances, then one of them caught her again while the others started digging as if their own lives depended on it.

Another contraction tore through her body and she put her hands on her hardened stomach. Dear God! *Would she deliver Nathaniel's baby in the midst of Morris's coal yard as they dragged his lifeless body to the surface?* Buster darted over to her and ran around her skirts. She seized his collar.

'Buster!' she commanded. 'Where's Nathaniel?'

Buster circled around her and then clambered over the coal with his nose close to the jagged edges. He worked his way back and forth and then shot off to the left. Stopping halfway up he began barking and scratching at the surface.

'Over here!' bellowed an officer.

Grit scratched Nathaniel's eyes as he tried to open them. He could see nothing. It was as if he were blind. He tried to cough but couldn't expand his chest because of the weight of the coal pressing down on him. He strained to shift himself upwards but failed. He was buried alive.

Frantically, he tried again to kick and claw his way out but the coal settled closer around him. Sweat sprang out on his forehead and between his shoulder blades and ran down the length of his spine in an icy stream. Suddenly the air was gone and his lungs were burning desperate for breath. Gritting his teeth until his jaw cracked, Nathaniel focused on Mattie, heavy with his child. Forcing himself to think methodically, he moved his fingers and checked that he could feel the rough coal on the tips of each one. *Good.* He tensed the muscle in his legs and arms. Pain screamed all over his body and he'd probably be the colour of a over-ripe plum from head to foot tomorrow, but nothing to indicate a broken bone anywhere. *Better. Now to get myself out of here!*

He gripped a lump of coal near to his right hand and tried again to shift it aside. It clattered through the gaps between the nuggets. He grasped another and did the same. Yanking his left leg up a fraction he managed to push himself forward. The coal around him shifted slightly and he managed to slide to the right. Stretching his hand again he grasped at the coal but his fingers closed around a hand.

Stebbins.

Nathaniel crushed it but the well-manicured fingers remained flaccid. Stretching his arm until his shoulder ached, Nathaniel searched the wrist for a pulse but there was nothing.

He let go.

Pictures of Marjorie, Lily and Rose rolled across his mind, followed by Judge Tindel's hard-bitten face, then the prisoners' deck of the *Comet*, and the barracks in Botany Bay, the vicar's letter ... and then his passage back to England to take revenge on the man who had caused it all. The man who now lay dead an arm's reach away. Amos Stebbins!

It was over.

In the darkness, he saw Mattie's beautiful face and laughing eyes. Yes, the life that Amos Stebbins had forced him to live for the past seven years was over, but his new life with Mattie and their child had only just begun. When he got out of this choking hell, he vowed to live it to the full.

The coal shifted around him and panic threatened to rise up and overwhelm him again. *Hold steady, man. Hold Steady!* Nathaniel told himself. *You thought you were dead when the gun went off but Buster leapt at Stebbins to save you. Get a bloody grip now!*

Buster! Nathaniel forced spit into his mouth, took as good a breath as he could manage and let out a shrill whistle.

Mattie cradled her rock-hard stomach with her hands as the officers grunted and cursed, struggling to heave Nathaniel to the surface. For a brief moment second Mattie thought the worst had happened – again – then Nathaniel moved, and found his footing on the uneven surface. Joy and relief swept through her.

He was alive!

A spasm of coughing overtook him, then he straightened up and tried again to open his eyes. Two unnaturally white slivers set off his blackened face. He closed them, coughed again then stumbled with his hands outstretched, towards her.

Mattie rushed towards him and took his face between her hands. 'When I heard the shot—' She broke down, crying uncontrollably.

'Shhh,' he said, holding her to him.

Nathaniel whistled to Buster, who dashed over, his tail wagging his hind quarters as he ran.

'It was this fellow saved me,' he said, his mouth cutting a gleaming crescent across his black face as he fussed over the dog. Buster fussed around their legs letting out little yelps.

One of the policemen had found a broad spade and was digging deep into the coal. She shuddered and buried her head into Nathaniel's chest, giving silent thanks that it wasn't him the officers were still searching for. The officers slowly pulled Amos's body to the surface. They hoisted him up and his head fell to one side. When they reached the bottom they lowered him to the floor and set his head square. Amos's face was hardly recognisable. The coal had flattened his nose and both eyes were abnormally puffy, with a trickle of blood slowly leaking from the corner of the right one. His jaw sat at an awkward angle, his mouth gaped showing a splash of pink.

Nathaniel stepped in front and blocked her view. 'Don't look, Mattie,' he said, gathering her to him. 'It's over. Let's go home.'

'Yes, let—'

A contraction gripped her with such intensity that she cried out and doubled over. 'Mattie!' Nathaniel cried.

Her knees buckled. Time seemed to slow as Nathaniel's strong arms caught her and scooped her up. Her head fell into the crook of his neck and stayed there as he bellowed orders she couldn't quite understand until the blackness swallowed her.

Chapter Thirty-Two

Nathaniel shook the water from his hands, picked up the towel from the draining board beside him and dried the back of his neck. He turned and collected the clean shirt Emma had fetched for him before she disappeared upstairs to tend to Mattie.

'You look a right mess,' Patrick said.

'I know,' he said, running his hands tentatively over his face and feeling the criss-cross of fine cuts that covered his cheeks, forehead and chin. 'The carbolic stung like buggery and I doubt I'll be able to shave for a week. And my eye . . .' He tried to stretch his left eye open a little but it remained closed. 'But it could have been worse,' he said, briefly thinking of Stebbins lying on a cold slab in the morgue.

'You'll mend,' Patrick replied, offering him a mug of beer. 'Get that down you.'

Nathaniel thirstily drank half then put the mug on the table. He glanced up at the ceiling and thought of Mattie in the room above; he wished he could be there with her.

He'd practically ripped the door off Morris's office to provide a makeshift stretcher for her and although he hurt in places he never knew he had, he and three of the policemen carried her the half mile back to Maguire's. The fourth officer ran to Patrick's house to summon Sarah, leaving the remaining policeman to tend to the night watchman.

By the time her mother and Patrick arrived in their commandeered hansom, Mattie was battling through wave after wave of contractions with very little space in between. Sarah had quizzed Mattie and pronounced confidently that everything was as it should be. The men were then promptly shooed away.

While Patrick fetched the beer, Nathaniel had taken three buckets of water from the yard pump and stripped off behind the stable to wash himself down. Having cleaned the worst of it off, he came into the house and washed himself again with soap and a brush to get the dust from his ears and nails. That was an hour ago, in fact, the longest hour he'd ever lived through.

'So Buster brought Stebbins down,' Patrick patted the dog standing sentry by the hall door, his ears alert to each sound from the floor above.

'Thank God. He pounced on Stebbins just before he pulled the trigger,' Nathaniel said.

Patrick whistled through his teeth. 'Close!'

'Very,' Nathaniel replied, thinking of the tear in the shoulder of his coat where the bullet scored through.

There was a flurry of activity upstairs. Footsteps scurried across the floorboards.

What if the shock of the last few hours had brought on the baby before it was ready and the child came feet first or was wedged across. Women could struggle for days to birth awkward infants and then died of childbed fever. What if . . . what if . . . .

'Nathaniel!'

He looked back at his brother-in-law.

'Will you calm yourself, man?' Patrick said.

'Mattie ran all the way to the yard, thought I'd been shot and she saw me buried alive. If that weren't enough to bring on the babe, she saw Stebbins, who looked like a piece of beaten meat when they dragged him out.' Guilt and fear gripped at his vitals. 'I should have taken her away sooner.'

Something that could have been a cry sounded above. Buster sprang to his feet and whined at the hall door. Nathaniel tucked his shirt in, dashed across the room and strode to the bottom of the stairs with Buster and Patrick at his heels. Both men and the dog stood motionless in the passageway.

Suddenly a baby's cry cut through the silence. Nathaniel grasped the balustrade and mounted the stairs two at a time.

'There you go, me darling, here's your new girly,' Sarah said, as she handed Mattie her new daughter wrapped in a clean towel.

The baby yawned and hiccupped, and love and gratitude welled up in Mattie.

'Oh, Mattie, she's so beautiful,' Emma said, placing a pillow behind her.

'You have the truth of it there,' Sarah replied. 'God love her and the saints preserve her.' She crossed herself three times, then bent forward and pressed her lips on Mattie's forehead. 'Well done,' she said, softly. 'Now you and the wee'un get yourself acquainted. Me and Emma'll set things right so I can call Nathaniel.'

'Call him now,' Mattie said, knowing that he would have been pacing the floor below ever since her mother shoved him out the door.

'As soon as you've been sponged clean and have a new sheet under you,' her mother replied, giving her the do-as-your-mam-says look.

'Call him now please, Mam,' Mattie pleaded.

'As soon as—'

But the door burst open and Nathaniel crashed into the room. There wasn't more than an inch of his face that wasn't etched with thin, bloody cuts. His top lip and right cheek had a deeper cut and his left eye was all but closed by a blood blister. But to Mattie's mind, as he stood with love and relief blazing forth from him, he'd never looked so good.

He stood motionless for a heartbeat, then crossed the room and sat on the bed beside her. 'Are you alright?'

'Yes, I'm fine. A bit weary perhaps after pushing this young lady into the world.' She tilted their daughter so he could see her better. 'But I'm grand.'

Nathaniel's gaze moved to their sleeping daughter. He reached out a finger, moved the towel aside and gazed down at the baby in Mattie's arms.

Sarah came over and stood at the other side of the bed. 'We've not cleared away yet,' she said, her face a picture of disapproval.

Nathaniel smiled up at his mother-in-law. 'I'm sorry, Mrs Nolan, but I heard the cry and I just couldn't wait.'

'Well, why wouldn't you?' Sarah looked at Mattie and winked. 'Your father never came nearer than the pub around the corner when I had you but I suppose we'll just have to get used to these new ways won't we, Emma?'

'Indeed we will, it be the modern age, Sarah, and we 'ave to adapt to it,' Emma replied, smoothing a lock of Nathaniel's hair from his forehead as she must have done a hundred time when he was a boy.

Nathaniel slid his little finger into his daughter's hand. Her tiny little fingers closed around his and tears sprang into his eyes.

'She's beautiful,' he said, studying the sleeping baby. 'And all that black hair.'

'Just like yours,' Mattie said, looking up into his face. 'I think she has your eyes, too.'

'Has she?'

Mattie laughed and Nathaniel gathered her and their daughter into his embrace. He lowered his lips on hers and gave her a gentle kiss.

'I love you,' he whispered.

'And I you,' she replied. 'I thought we might call her Elizabeth, after your mother.'

'Yes, I'd like that.' He stretched out his hands. 'Let me hold her.'

Mattie carefully placed her along his forearm with one of his large hands cupping her head and the other holding her tiny bottom. He raised her up. 'Hello, Beth, he whispered, 'I'm your pa.'

Beth gave him a hiccup and her parents laughed.

'Thank you,' he said, in a voice heavy with emotion.

Sarah bustled over. 'Right, make yourself useful, son, by taking your young 'un to have a look out of the window so we can tend to her mam,' she said, her eyes twinkling as she regarded the new family.

Nathaniel grinned, stood up and took Beth to the chair in the corner, keeping his back to the three women in the room. Sarah and Emma made short work of washing Mattie and slipping a fresh nightgown on her. As her mother helped her back to bed, Beth cried out.

'She needs her mam,' Sarah said, putting the bolster and pillows behind Mattie.

Nathaniel handed the baby to Mattie then sat back on the bed beside her. Sarah lowered the wick of the lamp and a warm hazy light filled the room.

'We'll be downstairs if you need us,' said Sarah. She and Emma gathered up the pail of dirty linen, along with all the bowls and jugs, and crept out of the room, closing the door behind them.

Mattie unbuttoned her nightdress and offered the baby her breast. After a little bit of fussing she latched on, her little jaws working up and down. Nathaniel took off his boots, swung his legs onto the bed and propped himself beside her. Mattie rested against his chest and his arm closed around her. With Beth nursing at her breast and Nathaniel embracing her, peace and contentment stole over her.

Bliss, perfect bliss, she thought. Of course, she wasn't so foolish to think that misfortune or ill luck would not pass their way again, perhaps even tomorrow. But if it did, then she and Nathaniel would face and conquer it together.

Acknowledgements

As with my first two books, *No Cure for Love* and *A Glimpse at Happiness*, I have used numerous sources to get the period setting and feel of *Perhaps Tomorrow* and would like to mention a few books and authors, to whom I am particularly indebted.

As before, I have drawn on Henry Mayhew's contemporary accounts of the poor in *London Labour and the London Poor* (edited by Neuburg, Penguin, 1985). His painstaking reporting of the worries, concerns and language of the people he interviewed and scenes he witnessed was invaluable. Millicent Rose's out of print *The East End of London* (The Cresset Press, 1951) gives an account of East London before the slum clearances in the late 50s and early 60s as well as a tantalising glimpse into tight-knit communities clustered around the London docks. I again want to give credit to Ellen Ross for her study of the trials and tribulation of mothers living and raising children in squalor and poverty in Victorian London in *Love and Toil: Motherhood in Outcast London 1870–1918* (Oxford University Press, 1993). In addition, for Nathaniel's time in Botany Bay I used Robert's Hughes well-researched *The Fatal Shore* (Vintage, 1986) as my main guide. To plot the railways and station of the time I used Charles Klapper's *London's Lost Railways* (Routledge & Kegan Paul, 1976). I am grateful to Robert Beaumont's *The Railway King* (Headline Review, 2002) for helping me make sense of Amos Stebbins's financial machinations and to the Railway & Coal website http://myweb.tiscali.co.uk/gansg/8-yards/y-coal.htm for invaluable information on coal merchants, wagons and coal grades.

I again used several photographic books of old East London that helped me visualise the streets that Nathaniel would have delivered coal to. These include *East London Neighbourhoods* by Brian Girling (Tempus, 2005), *Dockland Life* by Chris Ellmers and Alex Werner (Mainstream Publishing, 1991) and *London's East End* by Jane Cox (Weidenfeld & Nicolson, 1994) Lastly, I would like to mention Lee Jackson's brilliant website The Victorian Dictionary: http://www.victorianlondon.org/ and Liza Picard's *Victorian London*

(Orion Books, 2005), packed with little details of Victorian London life.

I would also like to take the opportunity to thank a few people – my husband Kelvin, my three daughters, Janet, Fiona and Amy, and my best friend Dee – for their support. My fellow authors Elizabeth Hawksley and Jenny Haddon who, through our bi-weekly critique meetings, encourage me on when the muddle in the middle seems almost irresolvable. My lovely agent Laura Longrigg, whose incisive editorial mind helped me sharpen Amos Stebbins. Finally, but importantly, a big thank you to the editorial team at Orion, especially Sara O'Keeffe and Natalie Braine, for once again turning my 400+ pages of typed print into a beautiful book.